I0654085

J.C. REEDBURG

The Price Of Silence

A No Tears For Black Girls Story - 1 of 1

DATZHOTT
BOOKS

First published by Datzhott Books 2025

Copyright © 2025 by J.C. Reedburg

All rights reserved. No part of this publication may be reproduced, stored or transmitted in any form or by any means, electronic, mechanical, photocopying, recording, scanning, or otherwise without written permission from the publisher. It is illegal to copy this book, post it to a website, or distribute it by any other means without permission.

This novel is entirely a work of fiction. The names, characters and incidents portrayed in it are the work of the author's imagination. Any resemblance to actual persons, living or dead, events or localities is entirely coincidental.

J.C. Reedburg asserts the moral right to be identified as the author of this work.

J.C. Reedburg has no responsibility for the persistence or accuracy of URLs for external or third-party Internet Websites referred to in this publication and does not guarantee that any content on such Websites is, or will remain, accurate or appropriate.

Designations used by companies to distinguish their products are often claimed as trademarks. All brand names and product names used in this book and on its cover are trade names, service marks, trademarks and registered trademarks of their respective owners. The publishers and the book are not associated with any product or vendor mentioned in this book. None of the companies referenced within the book have endorsed the book.

First edition

ISBN: 978-1-7365535-3-4

This book was professionally typeset on Reedsy.
Find out more at reedsy.com

To my mother,
the strongest person I know—
thank you for teaching me resilience,
and for always encouraging me to keep writing.

"Silence has its own language; some women speak it fluently."

—J.C. Reedburg

Contents

Preface

The stories woven into **The Price of Silence** emerged from years of conversations I've had while creating and producing the *No Tears For Black Girls* podcast. Though this novel is a work of fiction, its narratives echo the real experiences of women who have paid dearly for their silence—and sometimes even more for breaking it.

Queen's Crown Salon may not exist on any Atlanta street corner, but spaces like it do—sanctuaries where women gather to share truths that often remain unspoken elsewhere. Tasha's defiance, Quanda's steady wisdom, Roxie's dangerous documentation—each character carries fragments of women I've known, interviewed, and mourned. Their struggles against systems designed to ignore them reflect battles fought daily across America, often without witness or record.

Content Warning:

This novel contains depictions of domestic violence, abuse, human trafficking, and systemic injustice, including violence against women and children. Reader discretion is advised.

The pain portrayed here exists beyond these pages. This story honors the real women and communities affected by these issues. I tried to approach these topics with respect, empathy, and accuracy. Violence or trafficking affects if you or someone, resources and support are available. For more information or help, please visit humantraffickinghotline.org or call 1-888-373-7888. Additional crisis hotlines, community organizations, and safety planning tools can be found at https://tinyurl.com/3vrfj8s6.

Sometimes silence speaks louder than your voice ever could—until that silence becomes your tomb. This book honors those learning to speak again, and stands alongside those still searching for their voice.

To hear the real stories that inspired this novel and join our growing community of advocates, visit https://tinyurl.com/4hb5wthv.

J.C. Reedburg

Los Angeles, California

Acknowledgments

To the survivors who shared their stories, the communities who protect their own, and the listeners who refuse to let these voices be silenced – this work exists because of you.

For Our Latest Music Releases

Search & Follow: "No Tears For Black Girls Soundtrack" on all streaming platforms.

The No Tears For Black Girls universe extends beyond these pages into sound. Stream the official soundtrack featuring artists whose music pulses through this story universe.

AVAILABLE NOW

https://tinyurl.com/zhkw7ss8

NO TEARS FOR
BLACK GIRLS
SOUNDTRACK
VOLUME 1

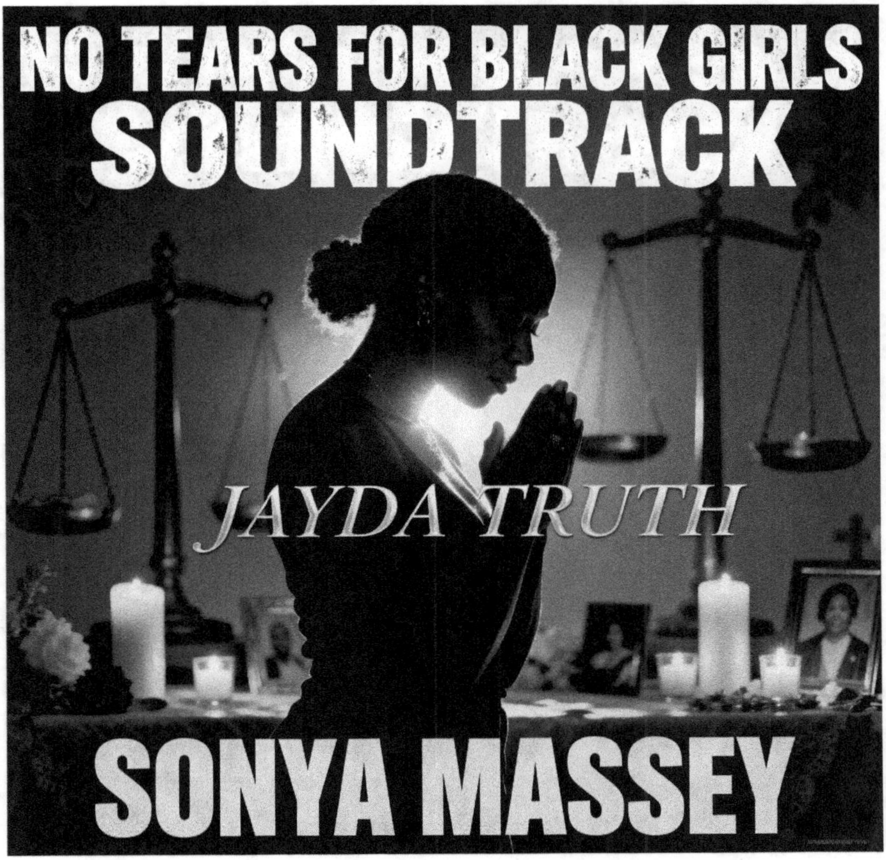
NO TEARS FOR BLACK GIRLS
SOUNDTRACK
JAYDA TRUTH
SONYA MASSEY

Through The 'No Tears For Black Girls' Podcast

150+ Episodes Available – New Episodes Weekly – Because Your Story Matters.

Stream Now on Spotify And All Podcast Platforms.

Get exclusive content at

NoTearsForBlackGirls.com

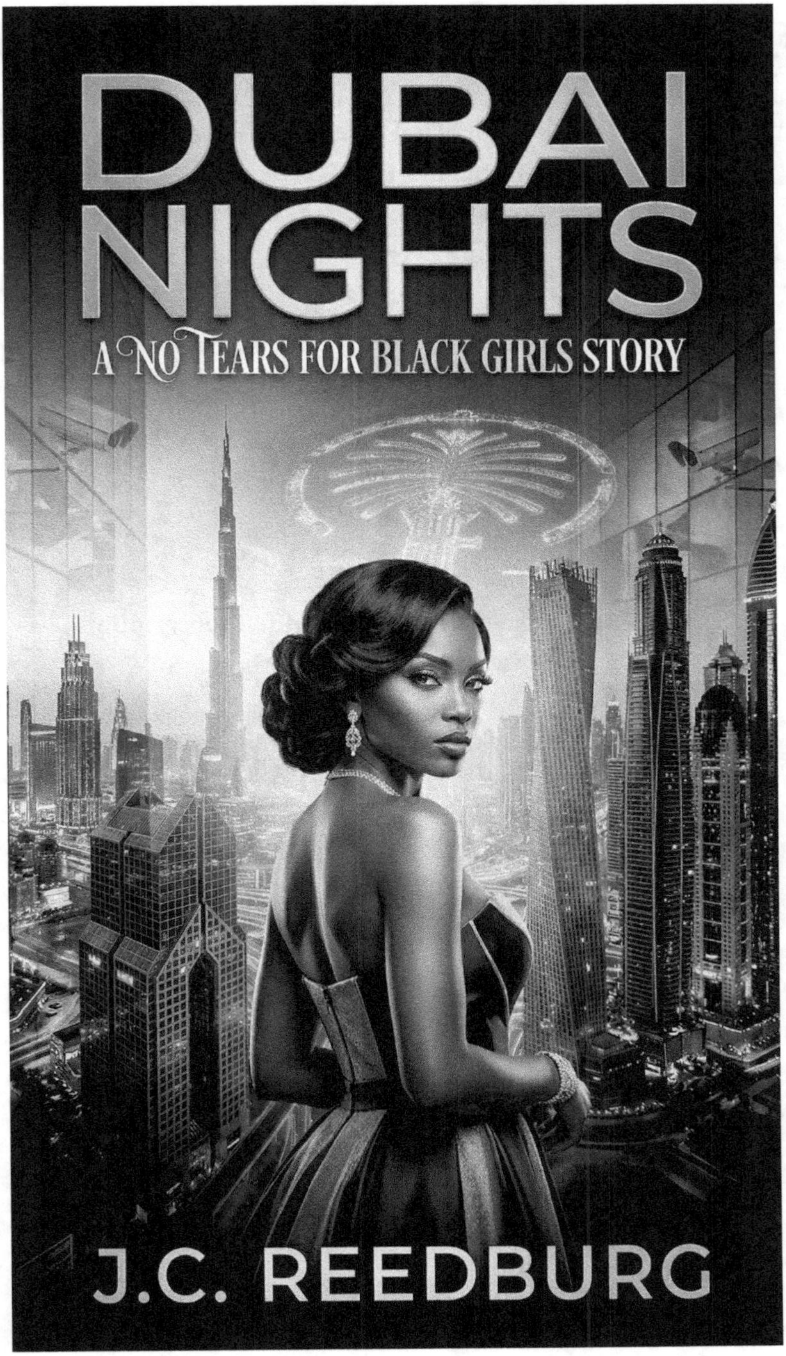
DUBAI NIGHTS
A NO TEARS FOR BLACK GIRLS STORY
J.C. REEDBURG

DISCOVER THE NO TEARS FOR BLACK GIRLS SERIES

https://tr.ee/sTmU6vT4YF

Search “No Tears For Black Girls” on Amazon to find all books in the series.

SERIES READING ORDER:

- *The Price of Silence* ⭑ **You are here**
- *The Girl Who Knew Too Much*
- *God’s Hands*
- *No Tears For Black Girls: Prison Pimp’d*
- *Roofied*
- *Angel Face*
- *Dead Mic*
- *Dubai Nights*

Read FREE with your Kindle Unlimited subscription

All titles available in paperback

Prologue

ECHOES OF SILENCE

"Every knot in the braid tells a story—some whispered, some screamed, all of them true."

PART I: THE COLLECTION

Roxie | Atlanta, Night

The atmosphere off Metropolitan Parkway tasted like cigarette butts and motor oil. The distant rumble of MARTA trains punctuated the night like a metronome, steel wheels grinding against steel tracks. Streetlights carved the darkness into slices of amber and shadow, each pool of light on its own its own little stage. Night had settled thick over Atlanta's south side, bringing with it the usual players—hustlers, night shift workers, and the occasional patrol car creeping through with high beams cutting harsh angles.

The girl worked the strip with the same military precision every week—never early, never late, always in the sweet spot between the first round of Johns and the late-night dopeheads. Tonight, the humidity hung wet and heavy, pressing sweat under collars and patience thin.

Roxie approached, hips swaying beneath a skirt too thin for the evening chill. She dropped an envelope through his window, heavier than the last. Detective Lance Rivers sat in his unmarked Crown Vic, engine idling, face half-lit by the dashboard's blue glow. His badge hung from the rearview, catching light when he shifted.

"All there?" His voice was gravel wrapped in silk—professional, almost bored, but with something underneath that raised the hairs on her arms.

"Always is." Roxie leaned into the window frame, one hand braced against the door. Her nails—long, pink, ridiculous—tapped a quiet rhythm against the metal. "Business been good this week."

Rivers didn't count the money. He never did. Just tucked the envelope into his jacket with the same fluid motion he might use to holster his weapon. "Keep it that way." His eyes never left the street ahead, like she was just another transaction, another note in his ledger.

"You need anything else tonight?" she asked, the practiced smile never wavering.

Rivers checked his watch—department issue, too expensive for his salary. "Nah. Next week, same time." He reached for the gearshift, a dismissal.

Roxie nodded, stepping back from the car. Her hand brushed under the passenger seat, fingers pressing something small beneath it—a tiny recording device no bigger than a button. The click of her heels faded as the first streetlights hummed to life.

The Crown Vic pulled away, tires whispering against asphalt. Rivers never looked back, never saw how Roxie's posture changed once the taillights disappeared around the corner.

Around the block, she ducked into a narrow alley, pulled a burner phone from her bra, and sent a quick text: "Rivers collected again. Same route. Adding to file H." She slipped the phone away, straightened her shoulders, and resumed her streetwalker's sway—one woman playing many parts.

Three blocks south, she passed the vacant lot where Keisha Powell was last seen alive. Four blocks east, the bus stop where Tamika Wilson waited for a ride that never came. Roxie knew all their names, had mapped their last known locations, had watched as their cases grew cold and their families grew bitter.

The city kept its own kind of silence, a heavy, knowing silence that settled over certain neighborhoods like fog. But Roxie had learned to listen differently—for the spaces between official statements, for the names no one mentioned anymore, for the stories that got buried alongside young women in unmarked graves.

Tonight's envelope was one more piece of evidence. One more link in a chain that stretched back years, connecting missing girls to badge numbers, connecting silence to power. She'd been building the case for months now, piece by careful piece.

The system isn't broken—it's working exactly as designed.

She vanished into the historic district's shadows, where the streets narrowed and the houses stood shoulder to shoulder, each one hiding its own secrets. Tomorrow, she'd follow another lead. Tonight, she'd transcribe another recording, add another entry to the files hidden in a storage unit across town.

Patterns speak their own language; only those who learn to listen can hear what they're saying.

In her wake, Atlanta's lights flickered on, one by one, illuminating everything except the truth.

PART II: THE PATTERN

College Dorm, 2:11 a.m.

2:11 a.m. and Arman's dorm room thrummed with the blue glow of four monitors. He hadn't bothered with the lamp for hours, hadn't bothered with sleep for days. The only things multiplying in here were data and the empty Red Bull cans breeding in the corner, one can teetering on a Domino's box crusted with cheese residue. The room stank of synthetic sweetness from Monster and the burnt circuitry of an overheating Lenovo.

He hunched over his main screen, eyes narrowed, finger flicking over the battered mouse. The screen mapped Atlanta's Southside, but not the streets or schools or Waffle Houses. Arman's Atlanta bled color-coded violence: tiny blue circles for police brutality complaints, pink for missing women, yellow for formal incident reports, all stacked and timestamped into a convulsing digital beehive. Sometimes the colors overlapped, making little plum bruises that clotted around particular blocks, certain stations.

He zoomed. Clicked deeper. The neighborhoods flattened into crisp geometry. The dots pulsed to show recency, the most recent ones throbbing like open wounds. Arman toggled between datasets, his other hand skimming a notepad already covered in columns of numbers and checkmarks. The numbers scrolled by so fast, he stopped seeing numbers and just felt the logic behind them—ratios, spikes, sudden silences.

He grunted. The data wasn't telling a story; it was screaming one, only nobody else wanted to hear it.

He'd started the night with a single question—how many Black women vanished in Atlanta in the past five years, and how many cops had records of domestic violence in the same window? Now he had a multi-tabbed browser apocalypse, every window screaming for attention, none giving closure.

Arman toggled on the "Officer Domestic" layer. New blue dots speckled the map like cigarette burns. He clicked one—badge number, complaint, summary, disposition. Most read "Unfounded" or "No Further Action." He clicked another. And another. They piled up, unremarkable in their unremarkability, but the numbers said otherwise. Complaints flooded in, many names recurring.

He glanced at the big wall clock—half the numbers gone, its ticking only a memory, battery dead since October. He knew he should shower, call his grandma, maybe eat something not wrapped in foil, but the map had him. It always had him, the way Atlanta always had his mother and grandmother and every version of him that could've been if he hadn't lucked into this full ride.

He dug deeper. He set the overlays to a 72-hour window, then a rolling average, then a time-lapse. The colors stuttered, danced, then clotted again—this time around a cluster in East Point, a triangle of dots that refused to dissipate.

"Why you gotta be so loud?" he muttered, clicking into the overlap. Three pink dots, one blue, one yellow. He cross-checked with the missing persons log, eyes darting between the screens. Same date, different years. The same four-block stretch is always patrolled within days of a particular officer's shift. The same four-block stretch is always patrolled within days of a particular officer's shift. He ran a Python script to match the badge numbers across complaints. It spit out four names. One name appeared in every overlap.

He whispered it under his breath, let it burn in his mouth like old news. **Lance Rivers.**

College Dorm, Pre-dawn

He scrolled the data back five years, ten, toggling off then on the different complaint overlays. The dots didn't change; the name kept coming back. **Rivers.** Not the worst cop in Atlanta, not even the most famous, but his blue dot haunted the same streets as the pink ones. Arman took a deep breath, made himself read the actual complaint forms. The language was always the same, just like the city. The victim refused to follow-up; the subject was uncooperative; and no credible threat was determined.

He opened a Word doc, started a new timeline, even though the last one was finished. Maybe this would be the one. He copied the names, the locations, the badge numbers. Sweat prickled under his shirt, in the valley of his back. He let it run down his spine, ignored it. He would shower afterward.

He snatched another can, discovered it empty, then flung it in the trash. The metallic sound registered; he'd gotten used to living inside a fortress of beeps and clicks and filtered light. Some nights he missed the chaos of his mother's salon, the gossipy noise, the endless parade of women getting their hair straightened, twisted, and washed. All the drama there was legitimate—out in the open, never hiding behind a badge and a weapon.

Arman massaged his forehead, trying to coax the numbers into a narrative. There had to be a link, but the dots refused to line up with anything as easy as motive. He clicked through the old news coverage, scrolling past mug shots, protest photos, grainy screenshots from security cameras. The women's faces dissolved into statistics. The cops' faces stayed the same, full of tired confidence and local-boy charm.

The cursor blinked in the timeline. He started typing again, fast, raw, as if the words alone could catch up to the violence that always seemed five steps ahead of the world. The hours bled together. The map pulsed, mocking him, never sleeping.

Outside, the campus was silent. Somewhere down the hall, someone laughed—drunk, not awake enough to know what haunted the city three thousand miles away. Arman didn't care. He tuned it out, let the silence build, let it push him deeper into the digital arteries of his city.

He gave the map one last zoom, set the timer for the next data pull. The clusters glowed steady, refusing to be forgotten. He stared until the colors blurred, until the map was nothing but a bruise against the darkness.

When the script finished its run, Arman stared at the name at the top of the output. **Rivers, L. Badge #48516.**

He leaned back, eyes gritty, shoulders aching, and let out a low, bitter laugh. The ghosts never changed; they just wore different uniforms.

Tomorrow he'd dig up more, make calls, maybe even talk to someone who remembered the first name, the first badge. But tonight, he saved the file, shut down the monitors one by one, and let the room finally go dark.

College Dorm, Sunrise

Sunrise inched through the window, gray and mean, when Arman rebooted his laptop. He didn't bother with breakfast. Just wiped last night's sweat from his forehead, tugged on a clean shirt, and dived right back in.

He'd logged into the police database scraper when the script hiccupped—a new alert pinged, not on the schedule, urgent as a fire alarm. The email header read: **"MISSING: Bradley, Mya N."**

His stomach clenched. He scanned the summary: last seen Tuesday, a complaint against Officer Lance Rivers filed the previous Sunday, a location less than a mile from the last data cluster he'd been analyzing. He sat upright, threatening to knock over his mug.

For a second, his brain refused the connection. **Mya Bradley?** It was a common enough name. He clicked through, opened the full report. Date of birth, address, last known employer. The words danced on the screen—he had to read them twice before the shock set in.

He scrolled down to the attached photo. Mya, grinning in front of a graduation banner, arms thrown around two friends he didn't recognize. She was older now, maybe nineteen or twenty, but he knew that face: same apple cheeks, same sharp chin, same crooked dimple in the left cheek. The dimple delivered the punch.

For a second, Arman just stared. He remembered her from a hundred summers ago: their mothers setting up folding chairs in a patchy backyard; the kids running wild and sugar-crazed, Mya was always the fastest, the loudest, the first to try a dare. She used to ride her bike down the block, cut the corner sharp and throw a wheelie, just to impress him. She was always laughing, always talking. He hadn't thought about her in years. Now a database sent him a JPEG of her frozen smile, treating her like a mere file to process.

He forced himself to keep reading. The timeline was brutal in its precision: Sunday, Mya files a complaint with Internal Affairs. Monday, she's scheduled for a follow-up interview—she doesn't show. Tuesday, reported missing by her roommate. Wednesday, nobody's looking except a shell script running on a college campus three thousand miles away.

His hands shook. He wiped his palms on his jeans, trying to slow his breathing. He dug up the original IA complaint. Rivers's name glared from the top. Mya had accused him of harassment—unwanted calls, stops outside her apartment, intimidation. The complaint sat in the system for less than forty-eight hours before she vanished.

He clicked deeper, pulling up every report with Mya's name. A string of traffic stops, mostly warnings, all from the same officer. Even the way the forms were written—it sounded like Rivers, the clipped professionalism, the way every encounter ended with **"Subject released. No further action."** Arman's jaw locked. **No further action was code for "We don't care."**

He cross-checked with the data clusters from last night. The overlap was exact. Mya had lived inside the triangle of bruises on the map. Her missing persons report was the latest dot, already threatening to fade into the background radiation of the city.

He opened a fresh doc, pasted on every scrap he could find. Case number, timestamps, badge number. He wrote out her name, then circled it, hard, like a charm against the helplessness building in his chest.

The algorithm confirmed what his gut already knew. **This wasn't random. This was a pattern, and Mya was in the next entry.**

College Dorm, Late Morning

Arman couldn't sit. He paced the tiny room, anger boiling in his veins. How many times had he told himself this work was academic, just a project for grad school, a way to prove his worth to professors who'd never seen Atlanta except from a passing Uber? It always comprised more than data. Not when the ghosts looked like people, he used to know. Not when the violence had a face and a story and a goddamn dimple.

He squeezed his eyes shut, but the photo stuck behind his eyelids. He couldn't shake the feeling that Mya was waiting for him to do something, anything, instead of just running scripts and stacking up evidence for some invisible audience.

Arman sat back down. He double-checked the timestamps, the addresses. He fired off an email to the campus contact for missing persons, flagged it as urgent. Then he called the number in the report, even though he knew nobody would pick up.

He left a message anyway. Voice steady, no hint of the dread flooding his head. "This is Arman Dowans. I'm following up on the Bradley case. I have information. Please call me back." He hung up, then soon regretted not saying more, not clarifying that this wasn't just another missing girl.

He stared at the screen, the blinking cursor. For a while, he couldn't move. His hands poised above the keys; a new theory, a new hope, died unspoken. The algorithm had stripped it all down to a simple, ugly truth.

He didn't want to admit it, but he already knew how this story ended.

For a minute, Arman just stared at the screen, watching Mya's dimple freeze in time. Everything else went silent. The battered hum of the dorm fridge, the street noise outside, even his own shallow breaths—it all collapsed into the photo's white margins. Her smile had always lit up a crowd, even when the crowd was just a mess of kids with sticky hands and dirty knees, fighting over the last slice of watermelon.

He dragged himself up from the chair, every joint stiff and unwilling. He crossed to the desk drawer where he kept the things he couldn't throw away but couldn't look at, either. Old report cards. Letters from his mother. A handful of Polaroids that had yellowed along the edges.

He pawed through them until he found the one he wanted. The memory felt unreal, like it belonged to someone else, but there it was: two children side by side, both squinting in the Atlanta sun, Arman with a juice mustache and Mya's braids sticking out in all directions. His arm curled around her shoulder, like he could keep her safe just by holding tight enough.

Memory, Childhood

The backyard that day was chaos. Somebody's cousin was grilling cheap hot dogs, the smoke thick and acrid. A Bluetooth speaker kept skipping between OutKast and Drake, never long enough on one song for anybody to finish a verse. Women lounged under a makeshift tent, gossiping and sipping at Solo cups. The kids formed their own gang, roaming from trampoline to garden hose to the forbidden patch of alley behind the garage.

It was hot enough to melt the ice before it hit your tongue. Mya had on her favorite pink T-shirt, the one with the cartoon unicorn, and she never took her eyes off the grownups' table. She kept daring Arman to sneak over and grab a cookie, even though the last time he tried he'd been sent away with a slap to the wrist and a threat to tell his grandma. He went anyway, because she told him to.

They got caught, of course. But even when Mya was marched back across the grass, clutching the stolen cookie and grinning like a bandit, she never looked scared. She leaned against Arman, licking crumbs from her fingers, and said, **"Told you we'd get away with it."**

He blinked, and the memory broke into a sharp, ugly present. He set the photo on the desk, right next to the laptop. The girl in the picture looked nothing like the woman in the database, but he saw it now—the same eyes, same mischief, same refusal to be ignored.

He pressed his thumb against the plastic, willing the moment to last. But the heat of his body did nothing except smudge the glass.

He sat back down, pulled the photo closer, stared at it until his vision blurred. The smell of charcoal and sunscreen lingered in his nose, even though he knew that was impossible. He tried to remember when he'd last seen Mya in real life. It had been about at least seven years or more. Their parents stopped getting together after middle school, after the grownups found new reasons to stop talking. He wondered if Mya had ever left the city, or if she'd just carved out her own place in it and dared anyone to move her.

He opened the database again, this time pulling up every incident with Rivers's badge in the notes. He read each line twice, sometimes three times, looking for something he'd missed. It all felt mechanical, empty, until he remembered the voice from that summer—the laugh that refused to back down, the dare to get in trouble together.

He checked the email again. Still no response from missing persons. He hit refresh three times, as if that could will a reply into being.

He picked up the photo, looked at the tiny, fierce girl with juice on her chin and dust on her legs, then looked at her in the graduation cap, smiling defiantly into an indifferent camera.

"I'm not letting this happen again," he said, voice dry and flat. Not like a vow—more like a threat.

He started a new timeline. This one wasn't just for the data. This one was for her.

He reached for his phone. The movement should've been automatic, but his hand trembled like the silence just before a summer storm. The first unlock failed; he wiped his thumb on his jeans and tried again. It buzzed, painting his face in blue and white.

He scrolled to his mother's name and typed: **Mom, it's happening again. And this time it's someone I know.**

His thumb hovered. He could hear her voice—tired, always wary, never surprised by what Atlanta could do to its own children. He almost deleted the text, started over, but in the end he just pressed send and set the phone face down.

He didn't wait for a reply. He buried himself in the work, dragging open every file on Lance Rivers, every scrap of PDF and bodycam transcript and complaint summary. The timeline on his wall, built over months of sleepless obsession, looked different in the morning haze. Before, it had been a project, something to explain away as research. Now, it was a monument to every girl like Mya who'd slipped out of the system and into the silence.

He pinned Mya's photo above the map. She didn't belong with the other mug shots and news clippings and case numbers, but maybe that was the point. She wasn't a number. She was the daredevil kid who ate cookies with him and laughed when she should've cried.

He double-checked Rivers's shifts—old police union PDFs, public records scraped from the dark corners of the internet. He charted every address, every stop, every time Rivers filed a report or "checked on a suspicious person." The pattern was ugly, but it was real: he'd never been over five miles from any of the missing girls, and half the time he was off duty. It was like the badge gave him a license, and the city made damn sure nobody noticed.

Arman ran another script, this one searching for patterns in Rivers's off-duty hours. He pulled up satellite photos of the neighborhoods, traced the routes from Mya's last known location to every place Rivers had clocked in or out. He built an animation, watched as the blue and pink dots converged and spiraled across the city, always ending in the same tight circles.

He drank water, but it tasted like metal. He didn't bother with food. It was noon before he realized he hadn't moved from the chair, hadn't stretched, hadn't let go of the pen he'd clutched all night.

The phone buzzed again. This time, it was his mother.

You okay?

He stared at the text, then wrote back: **Not really. Will call later.**

She replied: **Love you.**

He didn't know how to answer. Instead, he turned back to the screens, rage settling into a cold, clear rhythm. For the first time, the work wasn't just about making sense of chaos. It was about stopping it. About making sure nobody else's childhood got erased by a line in a database.

He printed out the map, lines and circles annotated in angry red. He stapled it over the old timeline, right where Mya's photo looked back at him. She dared him to do something. He would not let her down.

He opened his email and began drafting a message to the only investigative journalist who'd ever answered his cold calls. He attached the map, the PDFs, and a note: **"You need to see this."** He stared at the cursor, then added, **"Before they make her disappear for good."**

He hit send. Then, he watched the screens pulse; each new data point was another heartbeat, another reminder that the city still needed him.

PART III: THE SANCTUARY

Quanda | Queen's Crown Salon, Night

By the time she finished the fourth letter, Quanda's hand ached and the fluorescent lights above the mirrors cast shadows that sharpened every wrinkle on her reflection. Queen's Crown Salon stood dead silent, except for the tick of her dollar-store wall clock and the faint hum of traffic three stories below. The after-hours darkness thickened the pink walls and turned the row of waiting chairs into an audience of ghosts, everyone watching her.

Quanda capped her pen and flexed her fingers. The hand lotion she kept near the register couldn't touch the ache that crept into her knuckles anymore. It was nothing compared to the bruises the women wrote about from inside; she could handle this. She smoothed the envelope against the desk, admiring the neatness of her own cursive, then tucked the stack into her worn-out Target purse.

The salon still reeked of this morning's flat iron smoke and the cheap almond oil her cousin insisted on selling as "all-natural." She liked the way it clung to her, the way it coated her clothes and hair and even her breath, so she tasted it when she exhaled. Sometimes she wondered if it was how mothers smelled after birth—something scorched and bitter layered over the sweetness, warning you the real work had only just begun.

She leaned back in her rolling chair and closed her eyes. She could almost hear the laughter and the shade-throwing and the spatter of gossip that filled these walls every day. **People paid for the wash and set, but they came for the safety, for the way secrets bounced off the mirrors and landed soft in the cape at their throat.** Quanda had built this place from nothing, put her son through four years of private school with a single-woman's hustle and a talent for hearing what people really meant. She did not scare easy.

The phone vibrated on the counter, rattling against the jar of combs she still hadn't disinfected. Quanda peeked at the screen, thinking it'd be another robocall from the county or maybe her mother, Quanda, on a late-night prayer bender. But the name stopped her cold.

Arman. She opened the message with her thumb.

Mom, it's happening again. And this time it's someone I know.

She set the phone down, face-up. Her heart pounded slow and heavy, like she'd just stepped off a tilt-a-whirl. She kept her hands still, refused to let the tremor show.

She looked up at the empty chairs, then at her own pale reflection, then at the envelope she'd just sealed. Quanda unclenched her jaw, picked up the letter, and put it aside. She reached into the bottom drawer under the reception counter, the one with the busted lock, and pulled out a thin red folder marked **MISSING WOMEN—ATLANTA.**

It had started as a shoebox, then a plastic grocery bag, before she'd graduated to the folder. She didn't like to look at it much, not during daylight when the other stylists could see, but tonight she pulled the whole thing out and dumped the contents onto the counter: creased newspaper clippings, blurry photos, some printed from Google, some torn straight from the AJC crime section.

She thumbed through the pile, sorting the faces. Most were strangers, some only a first name and a yearbook headshot. A few, she'd known: regulars who never made their next appointment, cousins-of-a-cousin who got a baby picture in the obituary and nothing else.

She slowed down at a fresh clipping. This one wasn't old news; it was last week, still crisp and uncreased. **MYA BRADLEY,** the headline screamed, but the photo showed a girl who looked barely older than Arman's old playmates. Mya's eyes were too bright, like she'd caught the camera off guard, and her smile looked forced, the kind you wear when you don't know the rules.

Quanda set the photo aside. She wiped her hand on her skirt, then picked up her phone and reread Arman's message. The ache in her chest threatened to crack her open.

She looked for more on Mya. There, behind two other faces, was a half-page article with a caption so careless it hurt: **"Local Woman Disappears After Filing Complaint."** They always called them "woman," no matter how young.

Quanda flattened the articles on the counter, lining up the faces with a precision that bordered on obsession. The wall behind her reflected it all back, multiplying every missing girl into infinity. She pressed her palm to the counter, grounding herself in the cold, hard surface, and tried to gather her thoughts.

The TV in the corner, muted and ignored all evening, flickered with the blue light of a breaking-news banner. She reached for the remote, turned up the volume just enough to hear the familiar lilt of the Channel 5 anchor.

"—last seen Tuesday near the intersection of Lee and White. Family and friends say she'd recently filed a complaint with Internal Affairs. The Atlanta Police Department declined to comment."

A grainy shot of Mya flashed across the screen, then lingered a fraction too long. Quanda stared at it, memorizing the slope of her nose, the set of her chin. There was nothing remarkable about her, except she'd vanished, and no one seemed to care.

She muted the TV again. The silence pressed in, denser than before. She pulled a roll of clear tape from the drawer, tore off a strip, and carefully fixed Mya's photo to the edge of the bulletin board she'd hung behind the counter. The board already bristled with faces—some faded, some fresh, all waiting for somebody to say their name.

Quanda stepped back and surveyed her work. She whispered, barely loud enough for the room to hear: **"You still got people out here. Don't let them take that, baby girl."**

The plastic snap of a new thumbtack broke the stillness. She added two more faces to the board, lining them up in a row, neat as soldiers.

She moved to the chairs, straightening each one by its metal legs, pushing them close to the wall so they wouldn't trip through the morning rush. She circled the salon, collecting stray magazines, wiping down the glass-topped coffee table with a lemon-scented spray that stung her nose. The motions soothed her, a muscle memory older than her son. She reloaded the towels, lined up the shears, checked the inventory of edge control and cheap relaxer.

When every surface gleamed and every chair sat perfect, Quanda turned back to the wall of women. She stood there for a minute, studying the faces. Some had curled at the edges, yellowing with the years; others looked like they'd just stepped out of a high school hallway.

"This is how it starts," she said, so quiet it felt like a secret. "Quiet. One note at a time."

She shut off the lights, locked the door, and walked out into the night, the smell of hair products trailing her all the way down the empty stairs.

1

CROWN ROYALTY

The salon chair had heard more confessions than a church pew.

Quanda | Queen's Crown, Late Morning

Each secret soaked into its vinyl arms, whispered under the mask of blow dryers and laughter. **Queen's Crown Salon hummed with life:** women perched under chrome-domed dryers, phones in hand; fresh white towels stacked like pyramids near the sinks. Community flyers and certificates dotted the purple walls, competing with vibrant hair ads.

Quanda moved through the chaos like a queen on her turf, the stylist's smock hugging her curves, fingernails a flash of yellow and green. She worked on three heads at once, straightening iron in one hand, comb in the other.

"You still holding up over there, baby?" she called over her shoulder, hardly waiting for an answer. **"Girl, this weather is something else. Y'all see that rain this morning?"**

"You know that wasn't rain," said a client with a laugh. **"That was California crying."**

The salon erupted, laughter bouncing off mirrors and walls. A child fiddled with a toy while the juke pumped a slow groove through ceiling speakers. The place smelled of hot combs, sweet conditioner, and fresh gossip.

Quanda checked the time again, chewing her lip while watching the door. The bell jingled, and for a moment her face lit up, but it wasn't who she expected. Instead, an elderly woman with silver-streaked locs wrapped in a vibrant headwrap stepped inside, carrying a small leather bag that smelled of herbs and oils.

"Mama Esther!" several voices called in greeting.

The old woman nodded, her dark eyes scanning the room with the intensity of someone who saw more than just people and chairs. She made her way to Quanda, moving with deliberate grace despite her weathered hands and the cane she leaned on.

"You expecting that boy of yours?" Mama Esther asked, her voice low and smooth like aged bourbon.

"Been expecting him for an hour," Quanda sighed, glancing at the door again.

"He's coming. I feel it."

Mama Esther patted Quanda's arm. **"The spirits never lie about the ones who carry our blood."**

Queen's Crown, Noon

Outside, the West End grew different skins. New construction signs crept up like stretch marks on familiar blocks. But in Queen's Crown, she ran things. Even as she watched the door and checked her watch again, she moved from client to client, hand to hair, laughs to pep talks. Here, at least, things were hers. The door stayed shut.

Quanda flipped on the faucet, water rushing like applause. **"I know this isn't what you want to hear, sugar, but Jerome might be doing you a favor."** She tilted her client back, steam curling up like questions.

"I thought you said he wasn't cheating," the woman said, hope and doubt wrestling in her words.

"And I didn't lie. He's got plenty of time for that later, but right now it's

just cold feet. That man don't know how lucky he is."

As she rinsed the client's hair, Quanda caught her own eye in the mirror, then the door. Still no sign of him. She toweled off the woman's hair, wrapped her in a cloud-soft robe, and directed her to the drying station.

Mama Esther settled into a corner chair, not a client but a fixture, watching the comings and goings with muted attention. She removed a small notebook from her bag, jotting something down with a knowing nod.

"You still reading those fortunes, Mama E?" asked a woman under the dryer.

"Not fortunes," Mama Esther corrected, her eyes never leaving her notebook. **"Patterns. There's a difference between what might be and what's already set in motion."**

Queen's Crown, Early Afternoon

Everywhere Quanda turned, someone wanted more of her time, her hands, her words.

"We need more relaxer over there, boo," she told an assistant, never breaking stride.

The rush never ended, a moving puzzle that only she could keep together. The young man by the register fumbled with the broom between chairs.

"Quanda, you still want me to—"

"Y'all! I can't believe how good these babies look," she interrupted, talking over the kid, her voice sweet as syrup.

Near the windows, another stylist adjusted a woman's headscarf.

"When's Arman getting back?" she asked.

Quanda tucked a loose lock behind her ear. **"Soon,"** she said. **"That boy got a wild idea of what time means."** Her tone sang of both affection and worry.

"You need to put a bell on him," said another voice.

"What that boy needs is protection," Mama Esther murmured, though only Quanda stood close enough to hear. **"Dreams been restless lately. Seen fortune changing hands around you, child."**

Quanda frowned. **"I need no more of your dream-talk right now, Mama E. I need my son to show up."**

Queen's Crown, Mid-Afternoon

Queen's Crown hummed, an orchestra of overlapping sounds. One woman thumbed through her phone, side-eyeing a text. Another yelled over the noise, **"You heard about Jasmine?"**

"No," came a chorus of lies and questions.

"Guess who she's been seeing?"

Inside, Quanda expanded and contracted with each moment, trying to fill spaces as they opened. Her heart fluttered while she waited. The salon moved around her. She controlled everything here—except him. Except time. She scanned the room like a general, but only the door ignored her command. She counted beats between heartbeats, seeing him already here, every time.

The salon chair had heard more confessions than a church pew.

Quanda's watch said too many things, none of them right. She reached for the counter when a heated conversation cut through the salon.

"You think the white girl with dreads got more respect for the culture than me?" The voice cleaved the busy air, left it wounded.

"That's not what I said. All I'm saying is—"

Clients lined up on either side like teams at halftime. Quanda moved to the front, smiling.

"I'm saying at least she ain't ashamed." The older woman's voice flew from the dryer like a blade. Her sweatshirt read: 'Black is Beautiful, Always.' **"But you over there with the chemicals and excuses. I just call it like I see it."**

"You see it like you're still in 1972, Bernice." The younger woman wrapped her words around the room. Her wet hair clung to her head like defiance. **"This is 2023. This is the real world. You think I'm putting my career on the line because you got your fists raised?"**

Some nodded. Some twisted lips into scorn. A waiting child looked up, curious at the grown folks getting loud.

"I'm teaching my girls to be proud of who they are, what grows from their heads, what's in their blood. That's real. What's real about selling out for some white man's job?"

A low murmur—**amen and maybe**—reached from the salon's corners. Quanda checked her watch again, her eye flicking to the door. She moved in like a referee, all sweet smiles and calming words.

Mama Esther watched from her perch, nodding as if confirming something only she could see.

"The hair tells the truth even when the mouth can't," she said to no one in particular, but her voice carried just enough for several women to glance her way.

"What you gonna teach them if you're ashamed of what you see in the mirror?" The young one wasn't backing down. **"That's what I want to know."**

"At least they won't be hungry."

"Damn right." Another woman pushed her headphones back. **"You can't feed your kids with pride."**

"Oh, but you can starve them with it?"

"This what you're teaching?" Bernice turned toward Quanda, eyes hidden under curlers. **"Sisters cutting each other down?"**

Quanda held her ground with authorizing experience. **"Long as they got a weave or some straightener in there somewhere, it's all love,"** she said, words dulling the sharpest edges.

The younger woman gave her that skeptical, one-eyed look. **"So that's where you at?"**

"I'm wherever y'all want me to be," Quanda said with a wink, the door and watch nagging at her again. She kept the balance without choosing sides, a trick mastered over years. **"We got choices up in here."**

One woman snorted. Another twisted her mouth. The dryers hissed, noise and heat taking over.

"So I'm a sell-out? I just need to know. I'm not down enough?" The young woman's tone changed, less fight, more need.

Bernice adjusted her headphones, didn't look up. **"You're just...you,"** she said, quieter than before.

That seemed to satisfy something. A deep breath settled the room's shoulders, tension releasing in a wave.

Queen's Crown, Late Afternoon

Quanda lingered near the windows, pretending interest in passersby. But her eyes stayed trained on the room while her mind remained elsewhere, with him, with time.

The street outside buzzed with its own rhythm. A police cruiser rolled by, and several women in the salon tracked it with wary eyes.

"That's Rodriguez," said a woman near the window. **"At least she decent."**

"For a cop," someone added.

"She not like the others," another woman defended. **"Remember when she helped find Keisha's girl after that party?"**

"Yeah, but did you hear about her partner? That detective—what's her name? Vega? My cousin works dispatch. Says she's obsessed with missing girls' cases. Got a sister that disappeared a few years back, never been the same."

Mama Esther's eyes narrowed at this, her fingers tracing a pattern on her notebook cover.

"Y'all know I got love for this place." The young woman's words were an apology, a confession. **"But I got rent to pay too."**

"It's gonna be alright," Quanda said, smooth as a stylist who knows her work. **"It always is."** With her promise sealing the edges, Queen's Crown stayed safe, even with all its dangers.

Women nodded to each other—*next time, good game, I see you*—as the dryers took over, loud as a second heartbeat, with Quanda's watch keeping pace and the door holding tight to its secret.

Queen's Crown, Early Evening

The bell over the door shivered as Tasha walked in, all shades and shut-down attitude. The cloudy day questioned why the glasses, but no one asked. Not yet. Quanda watched her land under the dryer, watched her pull out a phone with jerky movements. She stayed on her perch until Quanda approached with a conditioning treatment.

"This one's on me," Quanda said, setting the soft cream down with softer words. Tasha nodded, just a fraction, like it hurt. The salon lowered its volume.

Tasha, this quiet was unusual. Like she carried the storm inside this time. Her movements spoke: **don't ask, don't push, don't look too long.** Quanda knew that language. She let her settle in, the sunglasses and all their weight, then returned to her rhythm.

Mama Esther studied Tasha from across the room, her gaze lingering on the woman's hunched shoulders and concealed eyes. She leaned toward Quanda when she passed by.

"That one's carrying more than bruises," she whispered. **"I see patterns in her aura—like broken glass trying to piece itself back together."**

Quanda squeezed the old woman's shoulder. **"Not now, Mama E."**

A woman signaled for water. Quanda nodded to an assistant. The noise crept back up.

"Who was Jasmine seeing?" The question hung unanswered, then repeated.

"No one," Quanda called back. **"And y'all ain't either if you leave here bald."**

The laughter warmed the room, drew eyes away from the unspoken tension curled under Tasha's chair.

Tasha stared at her phone like she expected it to buzz. But it didn't. She lowered her head further, then winced it back up like her neck was full of broken glass. Quanda stayed busy—not too busy to notice, but busy enough to give it time.

She moved from chair to chair, keeping everyone else happy. **"Who needs more hot water?"** she asked, grabbing pitchers before anyone answered. She dropped towels at stations, then floated back to Tasha. The jar of conditioner was special stuff, for emergencies, for silent situations.

"You gonna give me this every time I'm late?" Tasha said. Her voice fell short of its mark.

"It's gonna be one of those weeks, huh?" Quanda kept her words soft. **"Might be more than just one."**

Tasha snorted, a pained sound, like even that broke something inside.

"Remember when this place was nothing but us?" She lifted the glasses, blinked misery into the silence.

The salon stayed quiet, people unsure whether to look or not.

From the corner, Mama Esther watched the exchange, her fingers tracing invisible patterns in the space. She caught Tasha's eye for just a moment before the sunglasses fell back into place. Something passed between them—recognition, perhaps. A shared knowledge of pain.

Quanda gave her time, enough to let the glasses fall back. Enough to be certain. Then she returned to her station, brushing long strokes, longer silences.

She came back with tools in hand, shea butter and gentle fingers. She removed the scarf from Tasha's head with care.

"We gonna do this the right way," she whispered. **"Gonna take care."**

This time Tasha didn't speak. Her look—full of doubt and gratitude—said all she couldn't. Quanda started in, keeping her hands steady as the ground shifted.

They went quiet together, a different bond than what Quanda had with others. This was their history packed into quick breaths and long hesitations. She massaged the conditioner with a light touch, then set a dryer to its gentlest heat.

When she touched Tasha's neck, Tasha winced, but stayed still. Stayed soft, in that fragile way that meant trust. She watched Quanda's hands like they were the most important things in the world. At that moment, they were.

The salon waited, all eyes pretending to be elsewhere. That wait, that hopeful expectation of such a small kindness, held power.

Quanda let the silence tell its story without so much as a comma.

Tasha's jaw set hard, unsteady but willing. And in the gentle way that friends sometimes do, they finished, leaving more unsaid than most could manage with a book's worth of words.

Queen's Crown, Dusk

A young woman in tight jeans and a crop top strolled past the front windows, glancing inside. Her eyes lingered on Tasha for a moment too long. She pulled out her phone, typed something, then continued walking, her face a mask of indifference.

"That's Roxie," someone whispered. **"Girl's been working that corner since she was sixteen."**

"Shame," another voice responded. **"Pretty girl like that."**

The door opened, then closed, the bell over it shaking a little less now.

The door moved again, and this time it was him. Arman walked in, part son, part sunshine, all relief. Quanda dropped everything and moved in like gravity.

"There you are! I thought you got lost." She looked him over with quick hands and quicker eyes. **"You good? Where you been?"** The questions rushed out. Arman tolerated the fixing, the dusting off.

"Mom. I'm good," he said, voice sweet with annoyance and warmth.

Her worry lit up in a smile. The salon knew she was his before she spoke again, saw it in how her face shone. She worked over him like he was a stubborn stain.

"What took you so long?"

"I'm here, aren't I?"

"Barely."

Her fingers checked him like a doctor's tools, seeing possibilities for injury everywhere. Her eyes were x-rays, and he had the healthy bones of the boy she'd raised, the one who let her worry like he was supposed to.

Mama Esther rose from her seat, making her way over with that same deliberate grace.

"Let the boy breathe, Quanda," she said, reaching up to touch Arman's face with weathered fingers. **"He's carrying good fortune today. I can see it around him."**

Arman smiled at the old woman. **"Hello, Mama Esther."**

"You stop at your grandma's?" Quanda asked, ignoring Mama Esther's interruption.

"Yeah," he said. **"She's good. Wanted me to stay longer."**

"She always does," Quanda said, grabbing his chin to catch the light better. She liked what she saw but kept on anyway, not ready to believe what was right before her. **"And your phone?"** She held out her hand.

"I'm telling you," Arman said. **"No one cares if I get straight A's. But as soon as you take my phone—"**

"You still got A's?"

He grinned, the sly, happy kind that made her forget the clock for a whole minute. **"Mom, come on."**

Quanda pinched his cheek, then smoothed his collar a third time. **"This week,"** she said, playful and protective.

His phone buzzed. A low hum she felt like a threat. She snapped it up in one move.

"Oh, so you can answer it?" He shook his head, that knowing way. The way she always went.

The missed call—one friend, some silly nickname.

"You don't trust me." He kept his tone light, not meaning it. **"Thought you were gonna loosen up since I got taller than you."**

"Taller, not smarter."

Their talk was its own language, with no one but them to translate.

Mama Esther watched their exchange with a small smile. **"He'll need your guidance more than ever soon,"** she said to Quanda. **"The numbers been speaking to me. Changes coming for you both."**

Quanda shot her a look that said not now, but something piqued Arman's curiosity.

"What numbers, Mama E?" he asked.

"The kind that change lives," the old woman replied. **"I've been seeing them in my dreams. Wrote them down for your mama last week."**

"Mama Esther thinks I should play the lottery," Quanda explained with an indulgent eye-roll. **"Says her dreams told her the winning numbers."**

"They did," Mama Esther insisted calmly. **"And they will. Mark my words."**

Arman shifted his bag higher, took the phone back with a small sigh, practiced and easy. **"I told you I'd be here."** His voice dipped but kept its warmth. **"You just have to chill."**

Chill was the last thing Quanda could manage. She covered it with more questions, more hands-on mothering. But it was written all over her, that refusal to do what she must.

"So you want me to sign it, huh?" She played it like a joke, though Arman didn't buy it.

"The essays are the real thing," he said. **"That's where they get you."**

"Better start writing, then."

"I've been writing."

They went back and forth, the rhythm like a familiar dance. It held them together, even when Quanda thought the leaving was just too much.

"You wanna look at my list?" Arman opened his bag, ready to prove he wasn't lying about applications. **"See what I've got?"**

"I already know what you've got." She saw promise everywhere, just like she saw danger. **"Stanford,"** she said, trying to sound casual.

"Other places, too. Just in case."

In case, she thought. In case you need another reason to leave. In case you don't get as far away as you can.

Arman watched her like he knew every word crossing her mind. Like he read it before she wrote it.

"This is gonna be good," he said.

He had no clue how much his confidence hurt. How much she loved it. All at once, those feelings folding together like origami birds.

She held him there for another second, one more wishful pause. It was her version of control, though she didn't call it that.

"Yeah," Quanda said, wrapping him up with eyes, with words, with all she had. **"Gonna be good."**

Queen's Crown, Evening

The ring cut through the salon's noise. Quanda grabbed it before the second buzz, faster than most could say hello.

"Yes, this is Shaquanda. Mr. Harrington! Yes, of course." She switched from the music of her day to his tone. A sharper pitch, less laughter. She spoke the language of what men like him wanted to hear.

"That sounds great," she said, but her back went straighter than her words. Arman watched, knowing what this was. **"I'll think it over."** Her voice dropped to the other kind of real. **"Always making you jump through hoops."**

"Let me put my team at ease," the loan officer said. She could picture him with her eyes closed, him and all the Harringtons she'd had to out-talk since day one. **"A place your size—"**

"We've been busy," Quanda cut in, gentle but firm—the right blend of please and push. She couldn't have him thinking they couldn't keep up, but she didn't want him thinking she had too much going on either. This was its own game, and she played with more practice than heart.

"We can't ignore the economy."

"Oh, no," Quanda said. **"Never that."** Her voice stretched out, reached up, met him where he stood, looking down. **"I completely understand."**

She listened to more excuses. They fell like soft rain, wetting her optimism just enough to make it hard to light again.

When she hung up, she muttered to the counter, to the world, to herself. **"Think it over. I'll give him something to think about."**

Arman stood near, waiting like he had more questions, but she beat him to it.

"He's got me wrong," she said, smiled that worried smile—the best kind she had. **"These folks don't know me."**

Arman saw the transformation, like he'd seen it a million times before. Each time was new.

"But they will," he said, finishing her thought, completing her resolve.

Mama Esther shuffled over, her cane tapping a gentle rhythm on the floor.

"Banking men always think they hold the power," she said, her voice low but clear. **"But there are other ways fortune flows. The ancestors been whispering about you, Quanda. Been telling me to watch for signs."**

"Mama E, please," Quanda sighed. **"I don't need spirit talk. I need a business loan."**

"You need both," the old woman replied with muted certainty. **"And you'll have both. The numbers don't lie."**

She placed a folded piece of paper on the counter. On it, she wrote six numbers in a shaky but deliberate hand.

"Your grandmother came to me in a dream three nights running," Mama Esther continued. **"Said her daughter's daughter would need help to break chains. Said these numbers would open doors when human hands wouldn't."**

Quanda hesitated, then tucked the paper into her pocket with a half-embarrassed smile at Arman. **"If you say so, Mama E."**

She set the phone down, picked up a comb—her weapon against whatever Harringtons came next. The salon rose to life around them, women buzzing like freshly cut heads, dryers hissing steam and secrets, her voice the softest heat.

"I don't mind jumping," she said, words light and fierce. **"Long as they know, I'm landing on my feet."**

The words looped through the room, ran rings around the quiet place where Arman stood, and met the loud world where she lived. From her corner perch, Mama Esther watched, her ancient eyes seeing patterns that no one else could—threads of fate beginning to weave together, fortunes about to shift, and chains waiting to be broken.

2

BEHIND THE BADGE'S SHADOW

Power without accountability is just organized crime with a badge.

Roxie | Auburn Avenue, Dusk

Detective Lance Rivers adjusted his rearview mirror and watched the girl approach his Crown Vic. Third Thursday of the month, same routine—Roxie would drop the envelope, he'd count the bills, and another piece of Atlanta's underbelly would stay buried under his protection.

The badge hanging from his mirror caught the streetlight as he shifted, a reminder of the authority that made all of this possible.

Roxie stood near the crumbling mural of John Lewis, her skinny frame draped in too-bright clothes, eyes tracking his car with practiced indifference. When he rolled past, she pressed three fingers to her temple—their signal established long before he made detective.

He circled back to Auburn Avenue, navigating around the historic district's one-ways until he found the spot behind the old Atlanta Daily World building. Nobody came here after six—just another forgotten corner of a neighborhood Atlanta tourism brochures claimed to celebrate.

She slid into his backseat without a word, bringing vanilla perfume and the sour smell of desperation. The car's interior light caught the bruise blooming beneath her right eye, masked with drugstore makeup.

THE PRICE OF SILENCE blooming beneath her right eye, masked with drugstore makeup.

"Protection's due Thursday," Lance said, not bothering to look at her in the rearview. He pocketed the cash-stuffed envelope without counting. They both knew better.

Roxie's laughter rattled like the MARTA tracks overhead. **"You ever want more than money, Detective..."** Her nail traced a line along his jugular, visible in the mirror. A threat disguised as flirtation.

He flicked her hand away. **"Get out."**

She vanished into the historic district's shadows, but not before her fingers pressed something small beneath the passenger seat—a tiny recording device no bigger than a button. The click of her heels faded as the first streetlights hummed to life. Lance checked his watch—still time to make the precinct briefing if he hurried.

Alley Near Auburn, Night

Around the corner, Roxie ducked into a narrow alley, pulled a burner phone from her bra, and sent a quick text: **"Rivers collected again. Same route. Adding to file H."** She slipped the phone away, straightened her shoulders, and resumed her streetwalker's sway—one woman playing many parts.

As she walked, her fingers found the small notebook in her inner pocket, the one where she documented every collection, every threat, every girl who disappeared after crossing Lance's path. **Three years of evidence, all leading to File H—her insurance policy against the day they came for her.**

APD Headquarters, Night

At APD headquarters, the day shift was winding down while night patrol geared up. White officers greeted him with Falcons talk and backslaps as he passed the Peachtree Center mural in the lobby. Their voices carried across the bullpen, easy with privilege and inside jokes.

"Rivers! Heard you pulled overtime in Sweet Auburn again. Finding any sweet spots down there?" Officer Keller winked, his wedding ring catching the fluorescent light.

Lance matched their volume, their swagger. **"Just keeping the streets clean, brother."**

Black officers nodded from their desks beneath the framed photo of Mayor Jackson. Their silence spoke volumes—professional courtesy without warmth. Lance felt their eyes on his back as he moved toward his station, measuring the distance between his badge and his blackness.

Dispatcher Laverne watched him from her station, her desk decorated with competing symbols—Black Lives Matter postcards beside a Thin Blue Line sticker. Atlanta's divided soul in one glance. She handed him a call slip without meeting his eyes.

"Domestic on Bankhead. Again." Her voice was flat, betraying nothing.

Lance took the paper, fingers brushing hers for a second too long. **"Thanks, Laverne. Always looking out."**

"Just doing my job, Detective," she said, pulling her hand back. **"Unlike some."**

As he turned away, he caught sight of Detective Vega hunched over the case files at her desk. Photos of missing women spread before her, one image hidden beneath her hand—a young Latina with her eyes and jawline. Vega looked up, met his gaze with unmistakable suspicion. Something in her expression made him uncomfortable, like she was piecing together a puzzle only she could see.

"Rivers," she acknowledged, her voice cool.

"Vega. Still chasing ghosts?" He nodded toward the missing persons files.

"Every ghost has a story," she replied, covering the photo with her forearm. **"And someone who remembers their name."**

He moved past her desk, feeling her eyes tracking him all the way to the door.

Bowen Homes, Night

The domestic call came from Bankhead's Bowen Homes—a neighborhood fighting gentrification's slow creep. Construction cranes loomed on the horizon, preparing to devour another block. Lance pulled his cruiser to the curb, where children scattered like startled birds.

He approached the sagging porch where a woman clutched two boys near a rusted grill. Behind her, the skyline glimmered—the new Mercedes-Benz Stadium looming over their crumbling project like a spaceship from another world. The contrast made his jaw tighten.

"Ma'am? APD. Someone called about a disturbance?" Lance softened his voice, the way he did for victims. He kneeled at the boys' level, watching their eyes fix on his badge, polished to mirror-shine.

"Everything's fine, officer," the woman said, her words a little too fast. She grasped the children's shoulders. **"Just a misunderstanding with the TV too loud."**

Lance noticed the fist-shaped bruise flowering on her collarbone, visible beneath her thin cotton shirt. **"You sure about that?"** He gestured toward the mark.

She covered it with one hand. **"Walked into the door. Clumsy, that's all."**

The lie hung between them, familiar as an old song. Lance had heard it a thousand times—from his mother, from neighbors, from women who thought they could manage the storm if they just stayed silent enough.

"The boys okay?" he asked, eyeing the smaller one's trembling lip.

"They're fine. Their daddy's working late. Won't be back until morning."

Lance nodded. From his pocket, he slid her a card for the Ebenezer Baptist Church food pantry. **"No sermons required,"** he murmured, watching her flinch at Martin Luther King Jr.'s face embossed in gold.

She took it, tucking it into her waistband. **"Thank you, officer."**

As he walked back to his car, the older boy watched him with eyes too old for his face. Lance looked away first.

Back in his cruiser, he made a call on his personal phone—the same phone he'd use later to call his father after collections. **"It's Rivers. Got another potential for the list. Bowen Homes, single mother, two boys."**

He paused, listening. **"No, I didn't approach yet. Just marking territory. Judge Holloway's charity drive could make contact next week."** Another pause. **"Yeah, they always need the money."**

The pattern was always the same—identify vulnerable women, create dependency, then exploit. **His father had taught him well.**

Tasha | Cascade Heights, Noon

Tasha Rivers counted expired groceries in their Cascade Heights kitchen, smelling jasmine from her hidden garden mixing with fear-sweat. The milk would last three more days if she was careful. The bread could stretch to five. She arranged cans by expiration date—a calendar of survival measured in preservatives and aluminum.

Lance's surveillance cameras watched from every angle—tiny black eyes nestled in smoke detectors, thermostats. Even the Sub-Zero fridge had a lens behind the ice dispenser. She crept beneath their gaze, each gesture measured and mild.

Her phone buzzed. She scanned it, scrolling through banking apps with practiced indifference. The declined card notification from Sweet Auburn Curb Market still burned her eyes. Third time this month he'd emptied their joint account without warning.

She switched to texts, finding nothing but automated reminders and a message from her mother that ended with **"Praying for you both."** No mention of the bruises she'd seen at Sunday dinner. No acknowledgment of the way Lance had gripped her arm at the church steps.

Pastor Wilkins had seen it too, his eyes sliding away when Lance approached. **"God tests those He loves most,"** the pastor had whispered to her after service, squeezing her shoulder before hurrying to greet a well-dressed man who looked vaguely familiar from the courthouse.

Tasha checked the time—three hours until his shift ended. Just enough to risk a trip.

At noon, she walked to West End's African Braiding Market, passing "For Lease" signs on Black-owned shops being replaced by BeltLine boutiques.

The neighborhood was changing faster than people could pack their belongings, history scrubbed clean for cold brew coffee and yoga studios.

The salon bell chimed as she entered. Three women looked up, then away—recognizing her, respecting her privacy. The owner, Fatima, nodded toward the back room without speaking.

In the storage closet, between boxes of Blue Magic hair grease and bundles of synthetic hair, Tasha kneeled at the bottom shelf. Her fingers found the loose floorboard, prying it up to reveal her emergency stash—a prepaid Visa card loaded with tips from private clients. Lance didn't know about this money. **Couldn't track what he couldn't see.**

The GPS tracker on her ankle bracelet hummed against her skin, its green light blinking. Range limited to home, church, and approved shopping. The salon wasn't on the list, but Fatima's back door opened to the alley where the tracker's signal couldn't reach.

"You need anything else, sister?" Fatima asked from the doorway, eyes kind but cautious.

"Just a trim today. Something that won't show."

"I understand." Fatima's hands were gentle on Tasha's shoulders. **"We all do."**

As Fatima worked on her hair, Tasha spotted someone through the window—a thin woman in too-bright clothes, watching the salon with unusual intensity. Their eyes met before the woman turned away, vanishing around the corner.

"You know her?" Tasha asked, nodding toward the now-empty sidewalk.

Fatima glanced up from her scissors. **"That's Roxie. Works Sweet Auburn. Been coming around taking pictures of the neighborhood changes. Says she's documenting the erasure."** She lowered her voice. **"But she watches more than buildings, if you know what I mean."**

"What do you mean?"

"That girl sees everything. Knows who does what to who." Fatima's comb moved rhythmically through Tasha's hair. **"Some say she's collecting stories. Others say she's just hustling. Either way, she's got eyes everywhere."**

Tasha said nothing, but filed the information away—another woman navigating dangerous waters, perhaps finding paths she hadn't considered.

Cascade Heights, Evening

That evening, Lance found her praying at their home altar featuring MLK and a cross from Big Bethel AME. Candles flickered over the polished wood, illuminating scripture passages she'd highlighted in yellow—verses about endurance, about bearing burdens.

"Church again?" he sneered, his shadow falling across the altar's glow. He'd been drinking—she could smell the whiskey seeping through his pores.

"Pastor Wilkins says forgiveness is strength," she whispered, eyes fixed on the flame.

Lance laughed, adjusting his APD-issued body cam to make sure it was off. The red light died under his thumb. **"Then forgive me this."**

The slap echoed through their renovated Craftsman, its historic charm masking modern prisons. Tasha's head snapped sideways, but she didn't cry out. Experience had taught her silence.

"You went to the market today," he said, showing her the banking app on his phone. **"Card declined. You embarrass me like that?"**

"I needed groceries." She kept her voice even. **"You took the money again."**

"My money," he corrected, grip tightening on her wrist until the bones shifted. **"You need to remember that."**

His phone buzzed, interrupting his grip. He checked it with a frown, then stepped away to take the call.

"Holloway," he answered, voice transforming to respectful deference. **"Yes, sir. I understand the timing concerns."** He paced near the kitchen, voice lowered. **"The package is ready for transit tomorrow. No, no connections to us. Clean routes."** He glanced at Tasha, noticing her attention. **"I'll call you back."**

The neighborhood outside their windows was picture-perfect—manicured lawns, restored Victorian homes where Atlanta's Black middle class had carved out stability. **Nobody would believe what happened behind their glossy front door.**

"I'm sorry," she said, the words bitter as ash. **"It won't happen again."**

He released her, satisfied with her surrender. **"Good girl. Now fix me a plate before I lose my patience."**

As she moved toward the kitchen, the GPS tracker chafed against her ankle, reminding her of boundaries she couldn't cross. But her mind raced, piecing together fragments—Holloway, packages, transit. Each scrap of information might someday be a key.

Edgewood & Krog, Late Night

Later that night, Lance cruised past Edgewood's buzzing bars, patrol lights off but badge gleaming on his chest. Weekend crowds spilled from the doorways, a mix of young professionals and locals not yet priced out. Music thumped from competing sound systems—trap beats warring with indie rock as Atlanta's cultures collided.

Near Krog Street Tunnel, where graffiti transformed concrete into canvas, he spotted Roxie again. She was working, head bent toward a man in a business suit, her hand already reaching for his wallet. She looked up as Lance's car slowed, flashing him their signal—three fingers to the temple.

The customer scurried away when he noticed the patrol car. Lance parked behind the old Atlanta Stock Exchange building, its art déco façade crumbling into luxury condos.

Roxie approached, hips swaying beneath a skirt too thin for the evening chill. She dropped an envelope through his window, heavier than the last.

"Business good?" he asked, counting the money. Three hundred more than usual.

"Better when you stay away." She leaned against the car door, voice sharp. **"Your wife came by West End today. Pretty little bird. Easy to pluck."**

Lance's hand shot out, fingers closing around her throat. **"What did you say?"**

"Saw her at Fatima's," Roxie choked out, not struggling against his grip.

"Just saying. She shouldn't be wandering so far from the nest."

He tightened his hold, the Georgia Bureau of Investigation patch visible on his visor as he pulled her closer. **"Mention her again, and I'll revisit that warrant on your brother. He still on parole in Cabbagetown?"**

Roxie's Saint Jude medal—patron of lost causes—bit into his palm as she twisted free. **"You're all the same,"** she spat, backing away. **"Badge just makes it legal."**

She fled past murals of civil rights martyrs, their painted eyes watching her disappear into shadows between streetlights.

Roxie | Abandoned Storefront, Night

In the darkness of an abandoned storefront, Roxie caught her breath, hand at her bruised throat. She retrieved a small camera from her clothing, verifying the encounter had recorded. Every collection, every threat, every moment of violence—all documented for File H.

Slipping into a narrow alley, she opened a rusted door with a key she wore around her ankle, entering a cramped room that served as her true workspace.

Photos, maps, and documents covered the walls—Lance Rivers dominated among them, connected by red string to other officers, to local businesses, and to courthouse staff. A framed journalism degree hung in the corner, obscured by stacks of notebooks filled with meticulous observations. She added today's memory card to a fireproof safe, whispering to herself, **"Another piece of the puzzle."**

File H grew thicker each week—recordings, photos, transaction logs. **Three years of evidence that would either save her life or end it.** But tonight, she'd captured something new: Lance's mention of his wife, the threat about her brother. Personal details that revealed the man behind the badge.

She opened her laptop, began transcribing the night's events. Each word typed was another nail in Lance Rivers' coffin, another step toward justice for all the girls who'd disappeared into his father's network.

APD Headquarters, Dawn

At shift's end, Lance stood before APD headquarters' dual memorials—one for fallen officers, another for Black lives taken by violence. His reflection split between them, distorted in polished granite. The morning sun caught his badge, throwing golden light across both monuments.

Across the street, Officer Rodriguez watched from Slutty Vegan's neon glow, her APD blues swapped for a "Stop Cop City" tee. She'd been Internal Affairs before requesting transfer to Homicide—the cop who asked questions nobody wanted answered.

She wasn't alone. Detective Vega sat beside her, both women sharing a coffee and intense conversation. Vega clutched a small photo in her hand, glancing toward Lance with concealed contempt.

Their eyes met through the morning traffic—her suspicion, his challenge—before the downtown streetcar clanged between them, its bell drowning out whatever might have been said. **Atlanta's contradictions rolled on, metal wheels on ancient tracks, moving forward while staying in place.**

Lance straightened his uniform and headed home, where Tasha would be waiting with breakfast ready and bruises hidden beneath long sleeves, regardless of the weather. As he drove, his phone rang—Judge Holloway's private number lighting up the screen.

"Rivers," he answered, voice shifting to the same deferential tone he'd used earlier.

"The timeline's moved up," Holloway's voice was clipped. **"Your father wants the next shipment moved tonight instead of Thursday."**

Lance's grip tightened on the steering wheel. **"That's risky. We haven't vetted the new route."**

"Not my problem, Rivers. Just make it happen." The line went dead.

Lance stared at the phone, then dialed another number—one he knew by heart. His father answered on the first ring.

"Got Holloway's message," Captain Rivers said without preamble. **"The girls from Metropolitan need to be moved. Use the Cascade safe house**

first, then transit through the airport route."

"Copy that," Lance replied, his voice shifting to the obedient son. **The same pattern, generation after generation—fathers giving orders, sons carrying them out, women disappearing into the machine.**

Lance straightened his uniform and headed home, where Tasha would be waiting with breakfast ready and bruises hidden beneath long sleeves, regardless of the weather. The city rolled past his windows—gentrified blocks next to crumbling projects, wealth and poverty separated by a single street. **Atlanta's contradictions embodied in his badge.**

He thought about Roxie's recording device, still hidden under his seat. **Let her document. Let her try.** His father had taught him well—the system protected its own, and he was deep inside its heart.

But as he pulled into his driveway, he couldn't shake the image of Detective Vega's eyes, the way she'd looked at him like she could see through his skin to the rot beneath. Or the way Roxie had said **"File H"** like it was a weapon she was sharpening.

The game was changing. He could feel it in the air, like the pressure drop before a storm.

Inside, Tasha would be waiting. Always waiting. He checked his reflection in the rearview mirror, straightened his tie, and prepared to play the devoted husband one more time.

The performance never ended. It just changed audiences.

3

INTERLUDE: THE PROMISE

Some wounds don't heal in silence—they echo,
until someone is brave enough to listen.

Arman | Stanford University Dorm, 2:43 AM

Arman Dowans lived in the **smell of burnt circuits, spilled Monster, and dollar-store ramen**. The room glowed radioactive green from his triple-monitor setup. Each screen choked with lines of code, scatterplots, and the raw mugshot faces of Atlanta's missing. The air staled with old gym socks and the perpetual tang of hand sanitizer—he hoarded it, a habit from childhood, back when **germs felt like the world's most solvable enemy**.

His dorm's white cinderblock walls hid under layers of maps, printouts, and notebooks scribbled with the math his professors called "unorthodox." Pizza boxes fossilized on the dresser, stacked like **core samples of neglect**. He'd built a pillow fort for his desk chair, duct-taped to fix the backrest at a perfect typing angle. Next to his mousepad, an army of empty Red Bull cans formed a lopsided ziggurat.

Arman's eyes, always big for his face, now glowed bloodshot, the whites sliced with tired pink. He picked at a scab near his thumb knuckle, working it loose with slow, surgical intent. Sometimes, he'd stop mid-keystroke and stare at his reflection in the turned-off screen—**see if he still looked like himself or if the research had hollowed him out**.

The only thing not covered in digital glow was the Polaroid, taped crooked to his monitor's edge. A backyard somewhere in DeKalb, the paper color fading at the edges. Two kids, both eight, arms around each other, front teeth missing and laughter blurred by the slow shutter. **Mya Bradley's smile took up half her face. Even in the photo, you could see the way she leaned into Arman, claiming him for the team.** There was barbecue sauce on her chin. He couldn't look at it long. He ran his thumb across her side, erasing the dried fingerprint smudge, then putting it back again.

Arman worked in **silence**, fingers tapping rapid fire as he wrangled data from an Atlanta PD leak. Names, badge numbers, incident reports. Some files came raw—misspellings, time stamps off by hours, digital rot. He'd written a script to parse it clean, flag what mattered. He watched the processor spike the lines scroll.

His phone vibrated in the nest of sheets he called a bed. He ignored it. If it was his group project team, they could wait. If it was his mom, he'd call her at dawn, say he'd just pulled a late study session. He'd learned that lie from his mother herself—Quanda always worked doubles, told him she was "at church" when she needed a cry or a drink. The next buzz was a text. He peeled himself off the chair and checked.

— *Group mtg resched 2mrw, 7pm. Pls don't ghost again.*

Under it, a stream of unread notifications: party invites, roommate complaints, a reminder from his academic advisor titled "Urgent: Midterm status." He thumbed them all into the void. **He'd rather drown than tread social water.**

Arman flicked back to his monitors. On the leftmost, a spreadsheet scrolled past, column after column of names: brown and Black girls, 11 to 18, missing dates. He highlighted the rows where the Atlanta PD closed cases in less than a week. On the right, GIS software layered street maps with heat signatures of police calls, every red dot a call about "suspicious activity." The middle monitor cycled through old news stories, his scraper ripping everything with the keyword "runaway." The local news always blamed the kids for vanishing, then forgot them before the first rain washed their flyers off telephone poles.

He tapped a shortcut. Up came a directory of every officer who'd responded to a missing person in his target zip codes, 1998 to the present. There, buried in the middle, the first hit: **Mya Bradley, missing at age 8, last seen playing hopscotch two blocks from her house.** He remembered the smell of that day, the weird metallic taste in the air. His mom got the call, her voice flat and alien as she told him, "Mya's gone." The street filled with searchers by dusk—neighbors, volunteers, police with clipboards and search dogs. Arman's grandma prayed the whole night, beads clicking. He'd helped tape the first batch of flyers, but by week's end the printers had stopped.

She never even made the evening news. Nobody called it an abduction, just a "runaway risk" because Mya's mom had a second job and skipped two PTA meetings. The neighborhood shrugged and moved on. The playground got repainted, then torn down the next year. Arman learned to stop looking, but his body never forgot.

He clicked back to the present. His search tree branched out, mapping every case with the same badge numbers, cross-referencing the responding officers with closed files. More hits than he wanted. He traced the patterns with a Sharpie on the paper map, red lines crossing neighborhoods like veins.

His phone buzzed again. This time, he let it go, but his pulse kept time with the vibration. A thud sounded in the hall, maybe the RA making rounds or someone drunk from Greek Row. Arman almost missed living with a roommate—at least then, there'd be a witness when the insomnia got real bad.

The Red Bull pyramid toppled as he reached for another can. It rolled across the desk and smacked into the Polaroid, flipping it over. For a moment, all he saw was the blank white back of the photo, then he set it upright again. He checked the timestamp in the corner: 2008. He'd written it himself, in a blue gel pen, careful to get the numbers right.

He wiped his hands on his sweats and stretched, joints popping. If he closed his eyes, he saw code. If he opened them, he saw the ghosts of Mya and a hundred other lost kids staring back from the glow. **He promised**

himself he'd crack the pattern, prove it wasn't just bad luck or "urban decay" or whatever the mayor liked to call it. The system was rotten, the cops lazy or worse. If he couldn't bring Mya home, maybe he'd stop the next name from turning into a footnote.

Arman hunched over the keyboard, typing until the sun threatened the horizon. Even then, he didn't stop.

Atlanta Suburbs, Summer 2008 (Flashback)

Back then, the world came in two flavors: wet grass and sidewalk chalk. If Arman woke to sunlight, he knew Mya Bradley was already out in her yard, soaked to the knees and ready for war. They called it "Sprinkler Olympics," but Mya set all the rules and kept score by how many cartwheels she could string together without eating dirt. The record stood at eight, plus a half-turn that always ended with her giggling on the ground, claiming the bonus point for "dramatic landing."

That morning, Quanda let Arman run outside before breakfast—some kind of treat for passing a spelling test, though he forgot the words the second the screen door smacked behind him. The dew snuck through his socks. Mya already had the sprinkler going, sweeping the sky like a fire hose. Her hair, which she hated, haloed out in loose black curls that caught the water and sparkled in the sun. She wore her favorite purple shorts and a plastic tiara left over from a birthday party. The neighbors called her "little royalty," but Arman knew she was a warlord: she'd once knocked out a tooth defending him from the twin boys down the block.

Mya greeted him with their secret handshake: thumb-wrestle, knuckle-snap, double clap. He only got it right half the time, but she never made fun. She handed him a water gun, one she'd fixed herself after the trigger snapped last week. "Try me," she dared, and Arman did. She soaked him back before he could blink. The water stung, but so did her laughter, **bright and sudden as bottle rockets**.

They tore up the yard for hours, trading dares. Mya challenged him to a cartwheel contest—winner picks tomorrow's game. She lined up by the crabapple tree and flipped, arms strong, feet barely wobbling. Arman managed three, maybe four, before the world twisted and he face-planted in the grass. Mya helped him up, brushing the mud off his elbows, then tried to teach him again, slower this time. He followed her lead, focused on her words: **"You gotta plant your hands flat. Pretend you're glue. Don't even look at your feet. Trust yourself."**

He didn't get it right, but he got closer.

At lunch, they slumped on the steps, sharing a box of Goldfish crackers and a sweaty bottle of Gatorade. She showed him her scabbed knee, earned from last week's bike jump. She poked it with a stick and didn't flinch. "It's healing," she said. "You think it'll scar?" He shrugged, then said maybe, but scars meant you survived. She smiled, dimple opening wide. **"Cool," she decided, and that was that.**

Late afternoon, the clouds bunched up and the air got heavy. Mya's mom called her in early. Mya stuck out her tongue at the sky and yelled, "Loser!" before disappearing inside. Arman waited for her to sneak out again, but it started raining hard and his grandma shouted him home. The whole house smelled like bleach and wet carpet. Quanda handed him a towel, eyes on the old TV, and let him drip all the way to his room. He watched the storm from his window, hoping for thunder. He thought about calling Mya, but decided he'd see her tomorrow.

He almost didn't. Next morning, the Bradley house was quiet. The car was still in the driveway, and the yard looked untouched, sprinkler lying on its side. He didn't see Mya at all that day, not even a flash at the window. He tried the secret knock, got nothing back. He didn't worry, not really, until he saw the police car out front at dinner. Quanda told him to come inside and hush. He hid in the hallway, watched his mother talk to a uniformed man with a clipboard, voice low and careful. He heard her say, **"She wouldn't just leave."** Heard her say, **"Her mama works two jobs."** Heard the police say, **"We're doing everything we can."**

After that, there were neighbors, then volunteers. Someone set up a folding table with donuts and coffee, like it was a festival. Grown-ups canvassed the blocks, paired up and handed out flyers. Quanda told Arman that kids couldn't help. He sulked in his room, cutting out every mention of "missing child" from the free newspapers until the stack reached his knees. That first week, he dreamed Mya was running a new Sprinkler Olympics and he could never catch her. She was always across the fence, waving him over, smiling like she'd found a secret. Every time he got close, the world went blurry, and he woke up, shivering and mad.

The flyers spread out, but they never got farther than the bus stop before the rain got them. The missing poster faded, then yellowed, then peeled off in chunks. Mya's mom stopped coming outside. The searchers packed up. The donut table vanished, replaced by someone's trash can. The twins from down the block started calling Arman **"ghost boy,"** and he slugged one in the arm, hard enough to get sent home from school. The principal called it "acting out," but he knew what it really was: **if he didn't keep moving, the hole would swallow him, too.**

He remembered the last time he'd seen her. Mya didn't say goodbye; she just handed him the water gun and told him to keep practicing, as if they'd pick up tomorrow. He kept that water gun for years, hidden in a shoebox in the back of his closet. He only threw it away the day he left for Stanford, but sometimes he still felt the plastic weight in his hand, cold and cheap but real.

If anyone asked, Arman would say Mya's vanishing made him a fighter, or maybe a scientist. Truth was, it just left him pissed off and hungry for answers, the kind grown-ups never provided. He could track any variable and decode any pattern, but the only thing that made sense was that people like him and Mya were always expected to disappear. And no one would ever call it a crime.

He opened his eyes to the dorm ceiling, paint peeling at the corners. The west coast sun already spilled through the blinds, tinting the world orange. His mouth tasted like sleep and metal. Arman blinked a few times, wiped the crust from his lashes, and pulled the Polaroid off the desk. He looked at her dimple, the barbecue sauce stain, the way their arms locked around each other. He thought: **you don't forget a person like that. You just keep running after them, forever.**

He let the picture fall into his lap, then set his feet to the floor and started his day.

Stanford Dorm Room, Late Morning

The morning crawled through Arman's window, burning off the fog of nostalgia with a slab of California light. He cracked his knuckles, cleared the browser cache of last night's binge, and rebooted into what he called **"combat mode."** First: blast from the protein bar. Second: triple-shot instant coffee, microwave still caked with old oatmeal. Third: slap the laptop's spacebar and watch the monitors spring to life.

His desk had migrated from clutter to command post. Maps of DeKalb County and downtown Atlanta tiled the wall, seams reinforced with packing tape. Pushpins marked "victim last seen" in blue, "police response" in red, and "case closed" in black. Strips of yarn, stapled into desperate polygons, sketched the city's arteries. Under the main map, newspaper stories ripped from the AJC—**MISSING TEENAGER, PARENTS FRUSTRATED, POLICE BAFFLED**—each one annotated with Arman's own forensic chicken scratch.

On the desktop, his project folder exploded with data dumps, shapefiles, and scraped court records. He'd designed the algorithm for a machine learning class, but what he'd built was a predatory sieve: feed it a case number, it chewed through every public record, every social media post, every back alley of the web, then spat out the timeline of a disappearance with probability scores. Arman called it the **Harrower**. The name felt right; it hurt to use.

He cross-referenced the old newsprint with the Harrower's outputs, overlaying spikes in missing person calls with police shift changes, traffic cams, even the school lunch calendar (he once found three missing students who all had the same lunch period). He tracked patterns, found clusters nobody else bothered with. All his code pointed one direction: when young Black girls vanished in Atlanta, the cops followed the script. **Blame the parents. Shrug it off. Sift a few blocks, then wait for the problem to solve itself.**

Arman leaned into the monitor, zooming on a cluster from 2014. Five cases in two weeks, all in the same three-mile radius, all stamped "runaway—

closed." He flipped to the timeline taped above his keyboard, traced each point with a thumbtack. If he connected the last four years, the dots lined up with the city bus route. Coincidence? Maybe. But the Harrower flagged a pattern: every disappearance matched the shift of a specific patrol car, 38J.

He muttered, **"Somebody's working overtime."**

His phone vibrated again—email alert. He squinted at the header: "Academic Progress—Immediate Attention Required." The body was pure Stanford, all "wellness check" and "student resources," barely hiding the threat. He closed the tab. The university would survive without him. He'd figured out by now that most people didn't really want answers; **they wanted quiet, and for problems to stay in their lane.**

Arman's knuckles ached. He checked his posture and found himself hunched like a gargoyle over the keyboard. He stretched, rolled his neck, then scrawled another note to himself: **run anomaly test on patrol data**. He wondered if the campus shrink could diagnose "obsessive spreadsheet syndrome." Doubtful.

The left side of the dorm felt haunted. His roommate—last year's, technically—had bailed after two quarters of Arman's "insomniac creep" routine. The empty bed now held stacks of case files and ramen boxes, the sheets never changed. A few old posters lingered on the wall: Kendrick Lamar, a NASA Mars rover, and, inexplicably, a puppy calendar stuck on March. Arman almost missed the noise, the blunt way the other guy would say, **"You working a murder board again, bro?"** At least it made him sound less crazy.

He flipped a page in his notepad, transcribed new outputs from the Harrower. The handwriting had started neat, but by now it was half symbols, half angry slashes. On the latest run, the algorithm caught something: a string of "routine wellness checks" done by the same two-officer team. Both transferred to another precinct after the last disappearance. Arman googled the badge numbers, then hit paydirt: an internal review, buried in a city records dump, had flagged one of the officers—**Lance Rivers**—for "incomplete reporting" in missing youth cases.

He froze, mind racing. **Rivers. The name stuck, like a song hook.** He'd seen it before. He thumbed through last semester's casework, the one where a judge's daughter had gone missing for three days before surfacing at a friend's apartment. Same precinct, same cop. Same story: paperwork lost, no follow-up, the city memory-holed the rest.

Arman felt a weird surge—adrenaline mixed with dread. He clicked through to the police personnel files, which he'd hacked from a city HR portal. There he was: Officer Lance Rivers, service record glowing, a few commendations for "community outreach." Smiling in the headshot, square-jawed and clean-cut. The Harrower didn't care about looks, only patterns, and Rivers's had a stench all its own.

He wrote the name on the map in fat black marker. Underlined it. **"You're my guy," he said aloud, voice hoarse from disuse.**

He felt the cold creeping up his arms. Not fear, exactly, but something heavier. He remembered what his grandma used to say about hunting bad spirits: **don't stare too long, or they look back.** But he couldn't help it. He zoomed in on Rivers's transfer date, backtracked to every case he'd ever touched. Arman's hands shook, just a little, as he built the list.

Phone buzzed again, but he let it ring out. This wasn't about grades anymore.

On a hunch, he reran the Harrower on his own neighborhood, inputting every scrap of data from the year Mya vanished. He held his breath as the lines filled in, a heartbeat at a time. The cop on the call was Rivers, rookie then, but the same badge. The system hadn't changed, just put on a new face every few years.

He clutched the Polaroid, pressing it flat to the desk, and stared at the cluster of pins on the wall. **It didn't matter how hard the rain came down, or how many times they painted over the playground. Some stains stuck forever.**

He typed until his fingers numbed, building the case file nobody else would touch. The work was ugly, and it never ended. But he owed it to Mya, to the angry kid inside him who still believed that **proof was the closest thing to justice**.

The sun arced higher, bleaching the dorm in colorless light. Arman sat in the middle of it, a shadow on the map, piecing together the thing that nobody wanted found.

Stanford Dorm Room, 2:09 AM

The lines between yesterday and tomorrow blurred. Arman's algorithm ran nonstop, processing old police logs with machine-fisted rigor. Code spilled down the screen in neon pulses. Each row of data cut sharper, like bone fragments poking through skin.

He'd gone six hours without blinking at anything but his screens. The air inside the dorm soured with sweat and ozone from the battered fan. He tunneled through city servers, rolling dice with security filters that barely tried to keep him out. The names built up—dozens of girls, none of them Mya, but all of them almost.

He closed his eyes for half a second, fighting the dry burn. Opened them to the algorithm's new run, populated with police dispatch logs. This time, the Harrower spat out something new: a pattern even he hadn't predicted. It flagged the day Mya vanished, then scraped a "welfare check" logged by her mother two days before. The badge number in the margin: 1192. **Lance Rivers. It punched through the list, marked in digital red.**

He checked it again, then again. Same badge, both times. The odds of it being random hovered near zero.

He sat back, chest tight. The memory felt like a cold hand squeezing his ribs.

Arman scrolled to the incident details. Rivers showed up to the Bradley house after a neighbor filed a noise complaint. Official report: "verbal warning, no further action." But the log's timestamp showed Rivers on scene for forty minutes, way over the department average for a call like that. Mya's mother left two messages for the city hotline in the following forty-eight hours. Both calls went unanswered.

Arman's fingers trembled on the keyboard. He pulled up Rivers's personnel file. The face from before, even younger, but the same predatory calm. He tracked the officer's promotions, his transfers, his commendations for "youth outreach." With every line, the bile rose in Arman's throat.

He ran a cross-check on every missing girl in the zip code, 2008 to present. The number of overlaps was sickening. Rivers responded to over half of them, all closed with "no evidence of foul play." Arman underlined the names on his wall, one after another, his marker digging through the paper.

He smashed his fist onto the desk, hard enough to knock over the half-empty Monster. The can bled blue down the side, pooling across his notes and shorting the post-it collage. Arman didn't wipe it up. He just stared at the spreading stain, feeling something crack inside.

He looked at the Polaroid. He didn't speak for a long time. Then, real quiet, he whispered: **"I'm not done. Not yet."**

A new alert pinged. The Harrower had flagged an anomaly—something just added to the city records. Arman clicked in.

The file header: "Captain Rivers, disciplinary review, 2017." He read fast, absorbing the details. The date matched a department shakeup where Lance Rivers got promoted under his own father, Captain Rivers. The review cited "possible conflict of interest" but closed with "insufficient evidence to proceed." The Rivers family ran the whole precinct, cleaning up after itself, burying any trace that would lead to real answers.

Arman felt the anger settle in his bones, slow and permanent. **The pattern wasn't a bug; it was the system working as designed.**

He slid the Polaroid off the desk and slipped it into his wallet. He wiped the blue energy drink from his notes with the sleeve of his hoodie, then started a new list. He wrote the names slow, careful, like a prayer. The machine kept humming, hungry for the next clue.

When he was ready, Arman opened a new project tab and started coding again. **If they thought they could erase Mya, or anyone else, they'd never met someone willing to do the math.**

4

SISTER CIRCLES

Every Black woman needs three things: a good hairdresser, a ride-or-die friend, and a story no one believes.

Salon Ensemble | Queen's Crown, Saturday Morning

Saturday morning at Queen's Crown Salon was its own kind of church. The place pulsed with coffee, nerves, ambition, and gossip. Curling irons hissed like serpents, dryers bellowed over chatter, and every inch vibrated with bodies in motion—arms raised in testimony, voices climbing, stories unspooling like scripture.

The scent of hot oil, relaxer, and coconut conditioner thickened the air. Steam rose from flat irons like incense, blow dryers humming a mechanical heartbeat beneath the conversations.

Women of all ages filled the space: children slumped on benches, sticky fingers on phones; old ladies flipping through dog-eared Jet and Essence magazines; young professionals tapping TikToks with fresh acrylics; and the regulars—the true congregation—holding court beneath the dryers.

The salon chair had heard more confessions than a church pew.

Jonesha Livingston perched beneath the biggest, loudest dryer, dressed head to toe in real Chanel. She wore the interlocking Cs with the confidence of someone who knew the logo meant something different here than in Buckhead. She adjusted her satin headband, scrolled her phone with manicured nails, lips moving as she read. Purple and gold flashed where her foundation thinned. She checked her powder line, reapplied, then set her smile and started talking loud—just in case anybody thought she was shy.

"I told that man, you don't gotta take your work home with you. Nobody asked for overtime in this house," she projected over the mechanical roar. **"But here he go, every night, like he's the only one who pays bills in Atlanta. Like Livingston Developments gonna collapse if he don't answer emails at three in the morning."**

The dryer roared, but her voice cut through like water finding stone.

Two seats down, a college girl with braided cornrows said, **"At least he got a job. My man's entire career is 2K and Uber Eats."** Her braids snapped as she tossed her head back, grinning to see if her joke would land.

Jonesha gave her that look—half pity, half warning—then pointed a French-tipped finger. **"He play games and brings nothing? Girl, trade him in for store credit. Best Buy might give you five dollars and a receipt."**

Laughter rippled down the row. Quanda moved through it like a queen, owning every breath in the room. She set down a jar of coconut oil in front of Jonesha, twisting the cap shut.

"You want edges next time. Don't run your mouth with the cap off. That's how you lose them." She winked, her smile slow but sharp as a honed razor.

Jonesha returned it, but her eyes darted, quick as hummingbird wings, checking the door, the windows, the clock.

Quanda | Queen's Crown, Late Morning

Quanda saw everything: the bruises beneath the Fenty, the flickering glances at the door, the way Jonesha flinched when anyone passed too close. She'd seen this dance before—designer clothes, invisible chains, pride refusing to bend. **Women like Jonesha came in speaking about everything except what mattered most.**

In the corner, Mama Esther sat in her usual chair, fingers working a string of wooden beads, her eyes following Jonesha's nervous movements. The old woman nodded to herself, as if confirming a private thought, then resumed her work.

At the shampoo bowls, Andrea scrolled her phone with one hand, nail bitten to the quick, her foot tapping an anxious rhythm against the tile. The buzz sounded in rapid, angry bursts—text after text demanding responses.

"That your boo?" the shampoo girl asked, barely older than Andrea herself, hands deep in another client's scalp, working conditioner through 4C curls with gentle, circular motions. The texture was coarse but responsive, softening under the warm oil treatment like silk awakening to touch.

Andrea shrugged with one shoulder, feigning casualness. **"Just checking on me. Said he's coming at six."** She sounded annoyed, but the way her thumb returned to the screen, again and again, tapping replies before the bubbles disappeared, told the true story.

"That's cute. Or crazy," the shampoo girl offered, eyebrows raised.

"Probably both," Andrea admitted, a half-smile playing at her lips. **"But he worries. You know how it is with all these girls going missing."**

Quanda caught the exchange in the mirror, her face unreadable but her eyes taking mental notes. She dropped a warm towel around Andrea's neck and whispered, **"Let him wait. Queen's time is different from his time."**

The message was gentle but firm—a lesson Quanda had taught generations of young women who passed through these doors.

Andrea grinned, just for a second, then wiped the expression away like a smudge on glass. The phone buzzed again in her palm. She glanced down, her face tightening at whatever she read.

Queen's Crown, Noon

The noise at the front desk built up. A woman in worn jeans and a neat button-down entered, her APD badge clipped to her belt despite being off duty. The salon quieted for a half-second—the instinctive pause that comes when law enforcement enters any Black space—before the chatter resumed.

"Officer Rodriguez," Quanda called, genuine warmth in her voice. **"I got your deep condition ready. Bee's finishing up at station three."**

Officer Lena Rodriguez nodded, settling into the waiting area, her fingers tracing a small photo she'd pulled from her wallet. The image showed a younger woman with her eyes and jawline, smiling in graduation robes.

Jonesha leaned forward under her dryer. **"That your sister?"** she asked, nodding toward the photo.

Rodriguez hesitated, then tucked the picture away. **"My cousin Elena. Been missing three years now."**

The salon quieted again, this collective hush deeper than the first.

"That's why Detective Vega's always working those missing persons cases, right?" someone asked. **"Wasn't Elena her sister?"**

"Marissa doesn't talk about it much. But yeah. She transferred to Missing Persons right after Elena disappeared," Rodriguez replied, her jaw tightening. She glanced around, then added quietly, **"Three more girls gone missing from South Atlanta in the past month. No coverage, no press conferences, nothing."**

Jonesha shifted under her dryer, her foundation seeming too thin for the bruises underneath. **"Media don't care when it's us,"** she said, voice sharp.

Queen's Crown, Early Afternoon

The TV mounted in the corner switched to a news segment. The anchor, blonde and perfect-toothed, reported on a missing white college student from Emory with the somber urgency of breaking news. Photos of search parties and tearful parents filled the screen.

"Day twelve of the search for Kelsey Wilkins," the anchor intoned. **"The community has rallied around the Wilkins family..."**

"Day twelve," Quanda echoed, reaching for the remote. **"Remember Taysha Jenkins? Girl from Bankhead who disappeared walking home from her shift? Took three weeks for Channel 2 to even mention her name."**

"What about that girl from Cascade?" An older woman under the dryer chimed in. **"Mya something? My niece went to school with her. Said she**

filed some complaint against that officer—the one that got stabbed—right before she went missing."

The salon went quiet for a beat. Quanda's hands stilled on the remote, something flickering across her face—recognition, maybe, or concern. She glanced at Mama Esther, who had stopped working her beads.

"Mya Bradley," someone else supplied. **"Sweet girl. Used to work at the Kroger on Cascade. Her mama still putting up flyers every week."**

"Lord have mercy," Jonesha whispered. **"How many that make now?"**

"Too many," Quanda said, voice hard. She flipped through channels until she found a local news program showing flyers for missing Black women, including one that made her pause—a young woman with a crooked smile and dimples deep enough to hold secrets. Mya Bradley's face filled the screen for just a moment before the segment moved on.

"I put some of those up near the MARTA station," Andrea said, finally setting her phone down. **"Someone tore them down the next day."**

Quanda nodded grimly. **"That's why we keep printing more."** She gestured to a stack of flyers by the register. **"Free wash and set for anyone who takes twenty to put up. I want these faces everywhere."**

Rodriguez watched from her chair, expression unreadable but appreciative. **"Vega would thank you,"** she said simply.

From her corner, Mama Esther shook her head. **"The spirits say some of those girls aren't coming back,"** she murmured. **"But they want their stories told. They want justice."** Her fingers never stopped working the beads, forming patterns only she could read.

Quanda & Arman | Queen's Crown, Early Afternoon

The bell over the door jingled, and Arman stepped in, backpack slung over one shoulder, fresh fade catching the light. A wave of maternal pride crossed Quanda's face before she schooled her features into professional neutrality.

"Look who finally remembered where his mama works," she called, hands planted on her hips.

The room transformed around him—women straightening their clothes, adjusting their hair, smiles flaring brighter. Arman navigated the attention with practiced ease, nodding to the elders, fist-bumping the younger stylists, careful not to disrupt anyone's process.

"Ma," he said, crossing to Quanda and accepting her quick inspection—eyes checking his fade, hands smoothing his collar, gaze scanning for any sign of trouble. **"Had study group, told you I'd be late."**

Andrea perked up at the sound of his voice, but didn't rise from her chair. Her phone, forgotten, buzzed again.

"Stanford applications are due next week," Arman continued, voice low but excitement evident. **"Professor Jennings says my personal statement is strong, but I wanted you to read it."**

Something crossed Quanda's face—pride and pain. **"Stanford,"** she repeated, the word heavy with distance.

He'd been just a toddler when they fled LA, but the stories were family lore—his father's fists, a night that ended with bruises and a duffel bag, Mama Esther's lottery money their ticket out.

The price of silence is always paid by the women who survive.

The salon knew pieces of the story—it explained why Quanda never missed the signs with clients like Jonesha, why she insisted Queen's Crown be more than just a business. **It was a sanctuary she'd built because she'd once needed one herself.**

Arman's hand found hers, a gentle squeeze. **"It's different now, Mom. I'm not going back there to find him. I'm going to build something new."**

She nodded, pride pushing through the memory. **"I know, baby. And you're gonna build it right."**

"That's the point," he said with a gentle smile. **"Best program for what I want."**

"And what exactly is that again?" Jonesha called from under the dryer, invested like an honorary aunt. **"Remind us what's worth leaving all this behind."**

Arman's posture shifted—shoulders squared, voice deepening into what the salon regulars called his "interview voice." **"Urban planning with focus on community preservation. I want to help neighborhoods like ours grow**

without losing what makes them special."

The salon approved with nods and murmurs. Quanda beamed, despite the worry lingering in her eyes.

"He gonna save us from these gentrifiers," she announced, hands back on her son's shoulders. **"Gonna make sure places like Queen's Crown don't get replaced by some overpriced coffee shop."**

Salon Ensemble | Queen's Crown, Early Afternoon

The reminder of the neighborhood's precarious state sobered the room. Two doors down, the longtime Black-owned bookstore had closed last month, replaced by a gourmet dog bakery. Across the street, a juice bar charging twelve dollars a serving had opened where Miss Josephine's soul food cafe had stood for thirty years.

"Speaking of," Quanda continued, voice tightening, **"rent notice came yesterday. Another increase."**

Arman's face clouded. **"How much this time?"**

"Fifteen percent. Third raise in eighteen months." She shook her head, moving back to her station. **"Mr. Harrington at the bank still giving me the runaround on that business loan. Says the 'area demographics are shifting' and they're 'reevaluating investment priorities.'"**

"Meaning they don't want to invest in Black businesses in a neighborhood they're planning to whiten," Rodriguez translated from her seat, her directness a refreshing cut through polite evasions.

Quanda nodded sharply. **"You said it, not me."**

"We should protest," Andrea suggested, finally looking up from her phone. **"My social justice group at Clark has connections—"**

"Protest won't pay the rent," Jonesha interrupted. **"You need someone with connections. My husband knows people at the city planning commission."** Her hand rose unconsciously to her bruised cheek. **"I could talk to him."**

The offer hung in the atmosphere, weighted with what everyone knew but didn't say: any favor from Jonesha's husband would come at her expense, paid in private pain.

"We'll figure it out," Quanda said firmly, squeezing Jonesha's shoulder gently. **"We always do."**

Arman watched the exchange, eyes tracking between the women, absorbing the unspoken. He'd grown up in this salon, learned to read these signals early—which women needed space, which needed a friendly word, which was one bad day away from crisis. **His mother had taught him to see people's pain without commenting on it, to offer respect instead of pity.**

Andrea's phone lit up again. Arman frowned at the string of messages visible on her screen: **where r u and who r u with and answer me.**

"Everything good?" he asked quietly.

"Fine," Andrea replied too quickly. **"Just Jamal being Jamal."**

Arman nodded, but his eyes held a question he didn't voice. Instead, he turned back to his mother. **"I got two hours before work. Want me to look at those books? Maybe we can find some tax breaks or grants you qualify for."**

Quanda smiled, the weight on her shoulders lifting. **"My business major. Always trying to save me."**

"Someone has to," he replied, the joke carrying a current of truth.

Queen's Crown, Late Afternoon

As the afternoon progressed, the salon's rhythm shifted. The Saturday rush brought new clients—women preparing for dates and church and family reunions, each with their own hopes and secrets pressed between their shoulders. Quanda moved between them all, hands steady, eyes sharp, missing nothing.

Rodriguez's turn came. As Bee worked oil through her hair, Rodriguez pulled out her phone, scrolling through what looked like case files. Her brow furrowed at images of street corners, abandoned buildings, and maps marked with red pins.

"Work never stops, huh?" Bee asked, her fingers massaging Rodriguez's scalp with practiced precision. The texture was coarse but willing, responding to the warm oil like it had been waiting all week for this moment. Rodriguez's shoulders, usually rigid with the weight of her badge and gun, melted under Bee's touch.

"These girls deserve someone thinking about them on weekends too," Rodriguez replied, voice low. She paused on a photo of a street corner in Sweet Auburn, where a thin woman in bright clothes stood watching something off-camera. **"You know a girl named Roxie? Works that area by the MARTA station?"**

Quanda, passing by with clean towels, paused. **"Everybody knows Roxie. Been around since she was sixteen."**

"She's been talking to my partner," Rodriguez said carefully. **"Vega thinks she might have information about the missing girls."**

"Roxie sees everything," Jonesha commented. **"My husband's driver says she can tell you who's coming and going from every building on Auburn Avenue, down to the minute."**

"She's also scared of something," Rodriguez continued. **"Or someone. Won't meet at the station, won't give a formal statement."**

Mama Esther spoke up from her corner. **"That girl's collecting stories. Been watching, writing things down for years."** The old woman's eyes were distant, seeing patterns others missed. **"She's waiting for the right time to speak."**

Rodriguez studied Mama Esther with fresh interest. **"How do you know that?"**

"I see her sometimes, at the library. Writing in those little notebooks. Drawing lines between names." Mama Esther's fingers traced invisible connections in the atmosphere. **"She's building something. A web of truth."**

5

WHEN FORTUNE SHIFTS

Luck can be a ladder or a trapdoor.

Quanda | Her Living Room, Night

Shaquanda Dowans never built her living room for comfort, but she claimed it anyway—threadbare couch angled just so for the best TV sightline, plastic slipcovers crinkling like the inside of a bag of chips. There were no fancy lamps, no art on the wall, just a droopy spider plant rescued from her last landlord's trash and a discount air freshener plugged in near the door, huffing out artificial blasts of lavender chemical hope. Quanda lounged in a pink terrycloth robe, feet propped on the sticky faux-wood coffee table, watching Channel 5 through the haze of a half-eaten Lean Cuisine and the tang of nail polish drying on her toes. In her lap, a Powerball ticket, corners curling from where she'd fingered it all week, digits already smudged with sweat and ambition.

A photo of her boy Arman, front and center on the side table, peered at her with his chipmunk cheeks and sly half-grin. His cap and gown posed with the hope they only sell Black families by the photo packet—two years old now, the print already sun-faded where afternoon light streamed through thin curtains. Arman was gone three years and counting, down at Georgia

Tech, chasing a mechanical engineering degree and a basketball walk-on that stayed just out of reach. She paid tuition with a smile, every quarter, and paid for his phone, and paid for the dorm groceries, even when it meant ramen and utility bills stacked like Jenga blocks in her kitchen junk drawer.

But tonight wasn't about Arman. Or maybe it was, because **what was a lottery ticket if not one last Hail Mary for a better future?** Quanda jabbed the remote, kept the volume low—she didn't want to wake the upstairs neighbor's baby, the one who sounded like a smoke alarm every time he shrieked. The Powerball was up to $43 million. She had four dollars left in her checking account, and she'd spent two of them on that rectangle of hope.

Next to the lottery ticket sat a small folded paper, worn at the creases from being opened and refolded dozens of times. Mama Esther had pressed it into her palm three weeks ago, after their Sunday tea ritual. **"These numbers came to me in a dream," the old woman had said, eyes distant but sure. "Your grandmother was there, standing by water. She showed me these numbers, said they were meant for you."** Quanda had played them ever since, half-believing, half-desperate.

Channel 5 cycled through the nightly anchors. Sports. Local body found on MLK Drive. Weather. Commercials. The lottery segment slotted in at 10:28, same as every Wednesday, the hostess with the too-bright lipstick spinning the drum and shooting the balls into the air like a game show for people who never got past the auditions. Quanda's palms grew clammy, the anticipation baking her cheeks, but she never let herself believe—not fully, not after what happened to Dee.

She had played right after Dee's conviction. For the first six months, she told herself it was just for fun, just a thing to distract from the empty side of her bed. After year one, she upgraded to superstition, buying tickets with the same battered Bic every time, signing her name with a Sharpie on the back before she even got home. **Rules existed. Rituals. If she ever forgot one, she'd spend the rest of the night gnawing at her nails, sure she'd thrown the entire universe off-kilter.**

Quanda's numbers were always the same: *3, 12, 22, 29, 42*. The Powerball was *11*—Dee's old football jersey from Booker T. Washington High, before everything went sideways. Or at least, those had been her numbers until Mama Esther's dream message—the same exact numbers, handed to her like an inheritance from beyond.

The balls in the machine bounced like bingo in a church basement dryer. "Here we go, folks!" the hostess sang, her voice honeyed with practiced excitement, and the first number popped out. *Three.*

Quanda sat up straighter, the plastic cover beneath her squeaking in protest.

Twelve. A laugh scraped up her throat, dry and disbelieving.

Twenty-two. Now the edges of her vision tightened, tunneling everything to the crackling TV screen, the rest of the room falling away like shed skin.

Twenty-nine. She said it out loud, then clapped both hands to her mouth, afraid to jinx what was coming next.

Forty-two. Her chest squeezed until it hurt, ribs contracting around a heart too big for its cage. Then, the Powerball rolled and landed at eleven.

She forgot how to breathe. For a second, the entire apartment went soundless—the TV, the fridge, even the neighbor's kid. She checked the ticket, the numbers, then the screen. Checked again. The world snapped back into focus, and her heart thundered in her ears like summer storms over the Westside. Her hands shook so hard the remote slipped to the carpet. The ticket almost tore from her grip. The glow of the television painted her skin in ghostly blue, and all she could do was stare at the impossible miracle in her lap.

She'd done it. Not almost—not three numbers and a pat on the back. She'd hit every single one. All five, and the Powerball. The whole forty-three million.

A giggle burst out, then another, until it was just straight-up laughing and ugly-crying in turns. Her lungs didn't know what to do with all the air. "Oh my God," she wheezed, "oh my God, oh my God," and she needed someone, anyone, to witness this or she might explode from sheer disbelief.

She thumbed her contacts and hit Mama Esther's name before she could chicken out.

On the third ring, the phone picked up. "Quanda, you know it's late, right?"

She heard a spoon clink in a glass and pictured Esther in her own living room over in Collier Heights, silk scarf tight on her head, feet up, sipping something brown and strong from a mug she pretended was for tea.

"Mama," Quanda whispered. "Mama, you up?"

"Not if you calling me at ten-forty-something for your usual drama."

"This ain't drama. You not gonna believe—Mama, I did it. I won. I won big."

The silence on the other end stretched so long Quanda doubted it had ever happened.

"You won what, girl?"

"The lottery. The big one. Forty-three million. I swear, I ain't even playing with you."

Mama Esther's laugh always sounded like gravel in a wind tunnel. She let it rumble a good five seconds before answering. "Child, you lying. They finally broke you at that salon, huh?"

"I swear, Mama. Look, I got the numbers right here. 3, 12, 22, 29, 42, and the Powerball's eleven. All of them. I checked three times."

A hum replaced the laughter, deep and thoughtful, but not surprised. "The numbers I gave you," she mumbled, almost to herself. Then, her voice was firmer: **"Lord, child, you been blessed exactly as intended. Money ain't nothing but opportunity dressed in dollar signs. Question is, what you gonna do with this blessing?"**

"You knew, didn't you?" Quanda whispered, certain. "You knew these numbers would hit."

"I don't know nothing for sure," Mama Esther replied. "I just listen when the ancestors speak. Your grandmother had plans for you, always did. Said some chains need breaking, and you are the one to do it. Now you got the means."

Quanda squeezed the ticket until it bent in the middle. Her mind spun in six different directions: paying off Arman's tuition, a down payment on a real house in Cascade Heights or Collier Heights, hiring two more stylists at the salon, maybe even building that side room for herself, so she could sleep without seeing Dee's ghost in every shadow. She tried to imagine a life without scraping, without rationing tips for groceries or charging rent to her own credit card.

Her voice wobbled. "I don't know, Mama. I think—first, I gotta make sure it's real. Then, maybe I could do something for the girls at the shelter? And get Arman's loan people off my back. Maybe even take a trip, just once."

"That's good, Quanda. That's the real test, right there. **Money don't fix what's broke, it just lets you see yourself clearer. Don't you let it change who you are, hear me? The spirits don't give gifts without purpose."**

Quanda nodded, wiping her cheeks on her sleeve. "I hear you, Mama."

"You call me in the morning, and we'll talk. Get some rest, baby. Tomorrow's gonna be a whole new world."

The line went dead, but Quanda sat with the phone pressed to her ear, letting the moment sink in. On the screen, they cycled the winning numbers again, like fate wanted to make sure she understood. The ticket felt hot in her hand, almost vibrating. She pressed it flat against the coffee table, then pulled out a notepad and copied the numbers, checking her handwriting three times just to be safe.

She let her mind wander to all the places it hadn't dared in years. The image of Arman in a cap and gown, not just staged for Sears but for real, walking across a stage at Georgia Tech. The sound of her own laugh in a car she didn't have to jump every morning. The taste of real crab legs, not the imitation stuff from the freezer aisle. She let herself want these things—truly want them. No apology, no shrinking back.

Then, with the apartment settling around her, Quanda slid off the couch and kneeled on the threadbare carpet, the ticket pinched between her palms like a prayer. She closed her eyes and pressed her forehead to her hands.

"Lord, I know I ain't been perfect. But you see me. You see what I got to deal with. I just wanna do right by Arman. By myself. Maybe by Dee, too. So if this is real—if I'm not just losing it—let me use it for good. And don't let it ruin me. Please. Amen."

The numbers on the ticket blurred, her tears turning the ink to watercolor, but she held on anyway. **It was hers, for better or for worse.**

Tasha | Rivers' Bedroom, Late Night

Tasha Rivers scrolled with the ferocity of a woman who already knew the answer and wanted to see it in ink. Her thumb flicked up and down the length of Lance's phone, blue light glazing her cheekbones, jaw set hard enough to crack. She sat hunched at the edge of their bed, still in her work blouse, collar wilted and deodorant rings mapped under the arms. A tight scarf pulled back her hair, a style that said "I'm done for the day," but her eyes made it clear she was just getting started.

The Rivers designed their bedroom without romance in mind. Everything about it was functional—king mattress jammed up to the window, mismatched nightstands, dresser with drawers that leaned open like broken teeth. There were family photos, sure, but not like other people's. These were all angles: one with Lance in full dress uniform, rigid as a toy soldier; another of Tasha and Shaquanda at their old cosmetology graduation, both smirking over a giant frosted cake. Not a single shot of the two of them together outside of staged events, and Tasha knew what that meant, even if she never said it aloud.

She didn't bother pretending she'd stumbled on Lance's phone by accident. She'd waited until his shower was running, then fished it from his jacket pocket, almost daring him to walk in and catch her. The man locked his screen, confident in his routines and his secrets. Tasha had been married too long to fall for that.

What she wasn't ready for was how easy the truth was to find.

A text chain at the top: "Redbone still on for Friday?" No name, just a number, Atlanta area code. Tasha's stomach coiled like a snake preparing to strike.

She moved to the banking app, which Lance never used unless it was something he didn't want showing up on their joint account. The balance told a story: regular paychecks, then big random cash deposits, always rounded to clean hundreds, always after midnight. Transfers went out to strange names. "Diamond," "Roxie," "BabyG." She recognized "Diamond" as Roxie Williams's street name—the girl who'd vanished from her chair at Queen's

Crown after two appointments, both times walking in with bandages she called "work accidents."

Next, she pulled up Lance's photo gallery. Deep in the deleted folder: screen grabs of cash-app usernames, photos of stacks of bills, even a pixelated shot of a young girl with a cut lip and glitter nail polish. Tasha identified Roxie from the pink hoodie years younger before life had worn her down.

She scrolled, finding a hidden album with dozens of photos—young women, some drugged, posed on motel beds. Another folder contained screenshots of text conversations with someone named "Holloway," discussing "merchandise" and "transit routes." A third folder held financial spreadsheets that made her blood run cold—names, dates, locations, amounts. This wasn't just Lance exploiting a few vulnerable women. This was a planned operation. Systematic.

She felt her pulse pound in her ears like drums at a funeral procession. She wanted to scream or throw the phone or walk out and torch the whole house. Instead, she took photos of everything, working fast, her own phone shutter muted. She made a new folder and dumped the evidence in, naming it something no one would ever open—"DMV Receipts."

Her hand shook. Tasha closed her eyes and counted backward from twenty, an old trick from childhood storms. She tried to remember the first time she'd met Lance at a department picnic at Piedmont Park, him already a rising star, the kind who made everybody in a room gravitate his way. She recalled him cornering her by the grill and telling her that her laugh could scare the devil himself. How he'd slipped his number in her purse and waited two entire weeks to call. She remembered the taste of his sweat and the way he'd pressed his mouth to her wrist when he thought she was sleeping. She remembered, too, the first time he came home with a busted knuckle and a story that didn't add up, the way he'd lied without blinking.

The difference now was evidence. Now it transcended a feeling.

The shower cut off. Pipes in the wall clanged, then a thunk as Lance stepped onto the bath mat. Tasha froze, shoving his phone back on the nightstand, screen-down, where she found it. She checked her own phone—ten new photos, all timestamped, all ready.

She could hear him singing, low and out of tune, as he toweled off in the hall bathroom. "Always Be My Baby" by Mariah, which he claimed to hate but knew every lyric of. Tasha sat on the bed, phone in hand, spine rigid. The air felt thick enough to bite.

She ran through her next moves in her head, lips moving in silent rehearsal. She would start simple. Ask about the banking. Then the girl. Then the texts. Give him a chance to come clean, to trip up, and maybe even to act sorry. Tasha didn't expect him to confess, but she had to hear it from his mouth.

She smoothed her scarf and squared her shoulders. On the way to the kitchen, she passed the open closet—his uniform crisp and waiting, all medals and shiny buttons, the badge glinting under a low-watt bulb. The sight made her want to spit.

Downstairs, the ice maker clattered as Lance made himself a drink. The first words would be hers, but she knew the rest of the night would belong to the truth, and nothing could stop what was coming next.

Lance always poured his whiskey the same way: two inches, no ice, in a chipped glass that had survived more fights than their marriage ever would. He wore a plain white tee, creased from the package, and dark slacks that left lint all over the kitchen chairs. He looked up as Tasha entered, eyebrows arched, mouth curled in the smirk she used to find sexy.

"Evening, babe. Want one?"

Tasha shook her head, arms folded tight under her breasts. She took the far side of the island, the way she would with a suspicious client at the salon, and watched him nurse the drink. He leaned back against the counter, so easy and confident you'd think he'd never hid a thing in his life.

"So what's got you pacing up there?" he said. "Thought you'd be watching your stories by now."

Tasha bit the inside of her cheek until she tasted copper. "Can't sleep."

He sipped, eyes never leaving her. "What's on your mind?"

She played it slow, a hunter tracking through tall grass. "Got a weird call at the salon. Some girl crying, talking about a cop who won't leave her alone. Said she knew me, but wouldn't say her name." She met his gaze head-on.

"Why would a girl call me about you, Lance?"

He let a beat pass before he smiled, white teeth too perfect, the kind you buy with department insurance. The same practiced smile he'd used on Roxie just hours before, collecting his envelope on Metropolitan. "Baby, you know how it is. Girls like to stir shit. Especially when they think they can get a free ride off a cop's wife."

She waited. Silence stretched between them, heavy as wet wool on a summer day.

"You sure that's all it was?" Tasha asked.

Lance set down his glass, the sound sharp in the kitchen's hush. "I work vice, Tash. These girls, they'll say anything. You know that better than anybody." He ran a hand over his jaw, the same move he used in interrogation rooms down at the precinct. "You okay?"

She let the next words slice out, low and hard. "You ever hear of a girl called Diamond? Or Roxie?"

His body stilled. The jaw clenched just enough for her to catch it.

"Why you asking?"

"Because I know her. She used to come to Queen's Crown." Tasha unfolded her arms and braced herself against the countertop. "She's missing, Lance. Haven't seen her in weeks."

He looked away, fussed with the whiskey bottle. "That ain't my business. Last I checked, you run a salon, not a missing person."

She came around the island, getting closer than she'd ever dared when he was on edge. "You can stop lying. I saw the messages, the bank transfers. I know what you're doing."

His head whipped back to her, and the coldness in his eyes made her gut twist like a wrung cloth. The facade crumbled. "The fuck you doing in my phone, Tasha?"

Her heart jackhammered, but she didn't flinch. "You want to hit me? Go ahead. But I'm not scared of you anymore."

He took a step forward. She could smell the whiskey, the faint trace of his aftershave, the sweat that always bloomed on his upper lip when he got mad.

"You got no idea what you're talking about," he said, voice dropping to the dangerous register she knew too well.

"I know enough. I know you're taking money from these girls, and not just as evidence. I know you set up Roxie to get busted, then you kept seeing her after. She told people, Lance. She's not stupid." She pressed on, nerves hardening into steel. "And I know about Holloway. About the 'merchandise.' I know it's not just you—it's organized. How many girls have you trafficked, Lance? How many lives have you destroyed?"

His hand shot out, caught her by the wrist. The squeeze sent pins and needles racing up her arm like fire ants. The same grip he'd used to control so many women on the streets, now turned on his own wife.

"You need to stop this right now."

She tried to twist free. "Let go of me."

He pulled her in, so close she could see the tiny scar above his eyebrow, the one he got in high school and never explained. His fingers dug deeper, pressing bone against bone. "You think I won't do it? After all this time, you really think you matter that much? You know how many women I could replace you with tomorrow?"

Tasha wrenched sideways, but his grip was iron. Her other hand shot out, grabbing for anything, and found the heavy-bottomed whiskey glass. She swung it with everything she had. The glass caught him on the temple, a dull crack, and for a second he just stood there, stunned. Then the blood started, slow at first, then running down his cheek in bright, fiery streaks like summer rain on a windshield.

He let go. Tasha staggered back, chest heaving. Lance covered his head, studying the blood, doubting its reality.

"Bitch," he said. Not even loud, just full of pure hate.

She fumbled for the nearest weapon, hand closing on the butcher block. Her fingers curled around the handle of the chef's knife, the weight of it sending a weird calm through her like a river running clear. Lance saw the blade and took a step forward, daring her.

"Go ahead," he said. "Do it."

She didn't hesitate. She lifted the knife, pointed it dead at his heart. "Back up."

He lunged, not fast enough. The knife caught him in the shoulder, more meat than bone, but it still knocked him sideways. He bellowed, grabbed at the blade, and for a moment, it looked like he'd rip it out and come at her again. Instead, he staggered to the floor, blood painting the tile in wide arcs.

Tasha pressed herself against the pantry, hands trembling, knife still outstretched. Her brain flickered with memories—every time he'd yelled, every time he'd slammed a door or a fist or his badge on the table.

Lance tried to stand, but his legs wouldn't work right. He stared up at her, a strange mix of rage and disbelief, as if he'd never once considered the tables could turn.

"You...you fucking crazy," he said, voice slurring.

"You did this to yourself," Tasha said. "All I ever wanted was the truth."

Somewhere outside, a siren wailed. The sound rose and split, dopplering closer like a banshee. Tasha realized, with a weird clarity, that she must have been screaming the whole time. The neighbors would have heard. Maybe even the entire block.

She let the knife clatter to the floor, then crumpled to her knees beside it. The blood on her hands felt warm and sticky, like the time she'd sliced her palm open on a shampoo bottle and watched it pulse onto a white towel, staining it forever.

Lance tried to crawl, but only managed a few feet before he collapsed, breathing wet and ragged. She didn't move to help him. She just watched, hands shaking, as blue and red lights stuttered through the blinds and footsteps pounded up the walkway.

Tasha closed her eyes. She'd always thought she'd go out with a fight, but she never pictured this—her husband dying at her feet, the entire city about to know what she'd done.

But at least, she thought, **someone had seen her.**

Roxie | Outside Rivers' House, 2:00 a.m.

Roxie Williams hugged the shadow of a busted streetlamp, eyes fixed on the house across Cascade. Her knees ached from crouching behind the city trash bin, but she kept them locked. Muscles tensed for a sprint if shit went sideways. Even at two in the morning, the air was thick with sweetgrass and sprinkler funk, the fake peace of the burbs concealing the smell of old sweat inside her hoodie.

She watched as the first black-and-white rolled to a stop, engine gunned up like a pit bull on a leash. Two uniforms bailed out, weapons drawn, one yelling into the radio while the other charged the Rivers' front door. Cascade Heights always played itself as safe, but every cop in Atlanta knew who lived here. The rest of the neighborhood—regulars, teachers, night nurses—watched from behind curtains, lights winking off in quick succession as the show got real.

Roxie pulled her hood low. She'd been here almost thirty minutes, ever since Lance came home. It wasn't the first time she'd staked out this block, but tonight felt different. The air was electric, like every molecule in the cul-de-sac vibrating with old secrets.

Her fingers touched the small notebook hidden in her inner pocket—filled with dates, times, and detailed notes about Lance's movements for the past eight months. The mini-camera disguised as a button on her jacket had captured tonight's activity. Another piece of evidence for her growing file. Her journalism degree served a purpose; it was the foundation for what might be the biggest story of her career—if she lived long enough to publish it.

She could see into the kitchen from here. Dark, irregular shapes, not quite clear in the porch floodlight, splattered the window. She counted three more squads before the paramedics arrived, creeping, like they already knew nobody in there wanted saving.

Then they brought out Tasha.

She was hunched, hands cuffed behind her back, head down but eyes defiant. Red-black stains ruined her blouse, sticking to it from shoulder to hem. An EMT tried to dab her arm, but Tasha shrugged him off. She limped, but didn't stumble. Roxie watched the whole thing with her mouth tight, a weird hope burning in her chest like the first warm day after winter.

It took another ten minutes before they carried out Lance on a gurney, shirt ripped open, and bandages everywhere. Even half-dead, he looked mean. Blood streaked his face; his hands still curled like he was ready to strangle somebody. They loaded him into the ambulance without fanfare.

Roxie let herself breathe. She ducked lower when a new set of cops arrived, older guys in plainclothes. She recognized one as Detective J, the kind who shook you down for information, not justice. She guessed they were Lance's boys, here to do damage control.

She stayed until the news vans showed up, satellites spinning, reporters spitting soundbites into the empty night. By then, the whole block was awake, neighbors whispering in clusters at the edge of their driveways. She waited for the crowd to thin, then slipped out from behind the trash bin, moving quick but not enough to draw attention.

She circled the block, keeping to the darkest parts. When she hit the next corner, she pulled out her burner phone and thumbed a text to the number saved as "Editor."

shit just went down at lances. rivers woman finally fought back. he's critical. she's in custody.

She snapped a quick pic of the flashing lights for proof, then added:

this could be our way in. the whole network might unravel.

Roxie hesitated, then typed one more message:

tasha a real one. we need to help her.

She slipped the phone away and reached for her second device—the regular one that everyone knew about, with all her street contacts. She sent a simple message to her network: **eyes open, ears up. big fish bleeding tonight.**

Roxie grinned. For the first time in forever, it felt like **somebody had won.** She ghosted down the alley; the night swallowing her up, ready for whatever came next. Three years of documentation, of playing a role, of swallowing her pride and fear—maybe it was finally about to pay off.

Quanda | Her Living Room, Early Morning

The clock on Quanda's microwave blinked 2:04 AM, but she'd lost all sense of time. She paced her living room in pajama pants and a faded Morehouse sweatshirt, clutching the lottery ticket like it was a winning scratcher, not a key to a whole new existence. She had tried calling Arman, but it rolled to voicemail five times, so she left a message that started as a scream and ended in tears. Then she called Mama Esther, who made her promise to sleep before telling anybody else. Quanda lied, said she would, but who could sleep with forty-three million reasons rattling around their head?

She turned the TV back on, volume low. Local news had already cycled the Powerball story twice, but she kept watching, waiting for the confirmation crawl at the bottom of the screen. The anchor wore the same syrupy smile she'd practiced all week: "And tonight, one lucky winner from Atlanta's historic West End will be waking up a multimillionaire." Cut to B-roll of the corner gas station on Ralph David Abernathy, people grinning and holding up tickets, the cashier dabbing her eyes like she'd birthed the winner herself.

Quanda laughed, sharp and lonely. "That's me, y'all. Little ol' me."

She flicked through the channels, restless. Crime report, weather, sports, infomercials selling miracle creams for ten easy payments. Her thoughts wandered to Queen's Crown Salon—her real baby, built from nothing but sweat and reputation. She pictured the blue-walled shop, the row of dryers humming, the sweet funk of setting lotion and gossip. Tasha had come in just yesterday, sat in her chair, and asked for "something that means business." Quanda had delivered a sharp, angled bob that made Tasha look ten years younger. She'd walked out of the shop with a smile, promised to send more friends, maybe even her own cousin.

Quanda wondered if that was what life would be now. More hair, more laughter, a house that didn't sound like a toddler running on the ceiling every night. Maybe even Arman home for an actual meal, instead of microwaved leftovers on Christmas.

The next channel was national news. She paused, watching their slick graphics announce the lottery win again, this time with a digital rendering of her zip code and a confetti explosion. The sight made her shiver. She pressed mute and set the remote down, hands trembling.

That's when she saw the headline: "Officer-Involved Domestic Violence: Shots Fired, Two Injured." Live footage flickered on, all flashing lights and caution tape. The camera zoomed in on the Rivers house, familiar with the Christmas cards Lance used to send every damn year. Uniforms crowded the walkway; yellow tape drooped like tired bunting. The anchor's voice cut back in, grave and unhurried: "Veteran APD officer Lance Rivers is currently hospitalized following an altercation with his wife, who is in custody."

Quanda stared, mouth open. She didn't breathe until they replayed the video, showing Tasha—her Tasha, the only person who knew how to cut layers into 4C hair without making it look choppy—led out in cuffs, blouse streaked with something dark and sticky.

She felt her chest tighten. The ticket slipped from her hand, landing on the carpet next to a crust of old pizza. Quanda leaned forward, eyes wide, frozen.

"Lord, no," she whispered. "Not her."

On the screen, Tasha kept her head up, even as a reporter shoved a mic in her face. Quanda thought about the last thing Tasha had said before leaving the salon: **"Some men, you gotta draw blood to get 'em to listen."** It sounded like a joke. Now, it sounded like a curse.

She watched as the story played out on repeat—slow-mo of Tasha's arrest, scrolling past her own smiling face from earlier in the hour, both women trapped in the same cycle but on different ends of luck. Quanda reached for the ticket, hands shaking harder than before. She pressed it to her chest, eyes locked on the TV.

"This ain't no coincidence," she breathed.

Mama Esther's words echoed in her mind: **"The spirits don't give gifts without purpose."** Tasha's arrest and the lottery win were connected; they had to be. As if the universe had handed Quanda the means just hours before presenting the mission.

The news kept rolling, but Quanda just sat there, pulse racing, fate twisting in her hands like a live wire. In one night, everything had changed—for both of them. **Luck had shown its two faces: the ladder she was climbing, and the trapdoor that had opened beneath Tasha's feet.**

She reached for her phone, pulled up Mama Esther's number again. "Mama," she whispered when the old woman answered, her voice thick with sleep. "You watching the news? It's Tasha. She needs us."

"I been awake," came the reply, sounding not at all surprised. "I told you, child. The ancestors don't give without purpose. Now you know what the money's for."

Quanda nodded, though no one could see her. Her grip tightened on the lottery ticket—no longer just a windfall, but a weapon. A tool. A key to unlock different freedom.

"I know what to do," she said, voice steady. And for the first time that night, she did.

6

SYSTEMS OF INJUSTICE

The system isn't broken—it's working exactly as designed.

Vega & Rodriguez | Rivers Estate, Dawn

The FBI raid on Captain Rivers' compound began at dawn, black SUVs rolling through the gates like a funeral procession for corruption itself. Agent Martinez had waited three years for this moment—three years of building the case that would finally expose the network.

At the gate, two Feds unclip the padlock with a bolt cutter and swing it open on silent hinges. The only warning is the digital chirp of the intercom. Then twenty boots hit the drive in a syncopated rush. Vega walks the line, head low, vest loose, breathing in the mulch and cut azalea that cost more than her car.

Rodriguez falls in behind her, badge in one hand, fist ready in the other. **"This place smells like money laundering,"** she mutters.

Vega grins, teeth flat and hungry. **"Let's see what else it launders."**

By the time the team hits the front door, the Rivers estate security is two steps behind, groping for sidearms that are six months out of date. The first battering ram takes the deadbolt clean off; the door folds like a cardboard box. The inside is all marble and mirrors, a museum of trophies: signed jerseys, a gold-plated shotgun, and, over the stairwell, a hand-painted portrait of Captain Rivers himself, staring down at the chaos with courtroom gravitas.

They blitz the foyer, split left and right, shouting **"Federal warrant!"** over the crash of shattered vases and screaming smoke alarms. Upstairs, a shape moves—a flash of blue silk, old-school opulence. Captain Rivers, minus his badge, but still wearing the smug.

Vega leads the way, feet hitting the stairs two at a time. She's practiced this in dreams: the final sprint, the way a man's face shatters when he realizes he's the one being hunted.

They find him in the master bath, standing over a Jacuzzi that gurgles with pulp and bleach. His hands are pink with effort, paper drifting in clumps around the drain. Even cornered, he's composed, jaw squared, eyes daring her to play cop in his house.

His phone sits on the marble counter, screen still lit with a recent call. The contact name visible for just a second before the screen goes dark: **"Lance - Son."**

"Captain Rivers," Vega says, voice steady as granite.

He wipes his hands on the silk. **"Detective Vega. Didn't expect you to bring so many friends."**

Rodriguez trains her gun on his chest. **"Step away from the tub."**

He lifts both hands, slow and theatrical. **"What's the charge? Early-morning trespass?"**

Vega nods at the stack of folders on the counter—sealed court documents, property transfers, two passports and a burner phone still warm from his palm. **"Trafficking, conspiracy, accessory to homicide, and about eight other felonies you can't flush."**

He shrugs, like it's an academic disagreement. **"You know how many cops it takes to keep this city from falling apart? You want to bring me in, fine. Just know there's nobody better to replace me."**

Vega cuffs him, wrists tight enough to leave marks. **"I'd rather have a vacuum than a parasite,"** she says. Then, low so only he can hear: **"This is for my sister, and for every woman you've trafficked."**

The words hit. For the first time, his eyes flicker—not with fear, but calculation. He's already trying to game the system, to find the weak spot in the net.

Rodriguez reads him his rights, quick and efficient. By the time they haul him out, the neighbors are filming on their phones, trading rumors on the HOA text chain. Rivers walks with his chin up, pajamas barely hiding the tremor in his knees.

Inside, the search team opens the house like a forensic dissection. The den is lined with liquor bottles—rare, never touched. The dining room is a gallery of medals and "thank you" plaques from three governors, six police chiefs, and a Supreme Court justice whose name alone would clear a city block. But the real muscle is in the basement, behind a false wall painted to match the rest of the cinderblock. Vega finds it by accident, tapping her Maglite along the seam. She calls it in, then pries it open with a crowbar.

Inside: three rooms, each colder than the last. The first is a mini-NSA—rack-mounted servers, monitors scrolling lines of code, phones wired to record and scramble calls in four languages. The screens flicker through traffic cams, courthouse entrances, the cell block at Phillips State Prison. Rodriguez grins when she spots the backdoor feed: Rivers had eyes on his own men, probably as insurance.

On one monitor, a call log is still open—dozens of calls to **"Lance - Son"** in the past week alone, each one timestamped right after collections or incidents. The pattern Roxie had documented in File H, now confirmed in digital form.

The second room is pure logistics—whiteboards, color-coded, mapping the transit of girls from city to city, dates and initials and dollar amounts. At the center, a hand-drawn network: Miami, Nashville, Charlotte, Atlanta. A different color for each tier. Every major bust of the last decade, every disappearance, explained in three dry-erase lines.

The last room is locked, three deadbolts in a row. Vega pops them one by one. The air inside is musty, unconditioned, heavy with chemical sweet—formaldehyde or worse. Along the far wall are plastic bins, labeled by year. Inside: hair clips, scarves, old cell phones, even a couple of dolls. Trophies, all. One shelf is reserved for jewelry, each piece bagged and tagged like evidence in a private museum.

Vega sifts through, hands shaking for the first time. She finds a locket, heart-shaped, cheap, with a small paper photo faded to sepia. Her sister, fifteen, smiling like she just heard a joke. Vega's knees go soft; she steadies herself on the shelf.

Rodriguez touches her shoulder. **"You want a minute?"**

Vega shakes her head, snaps a picture of the locket, then seals it in an evidence bag. **"Not yet. We're just getting started."**

Upstairs, in Rivers' study, the lead Fed sits at the desk, grinning at a framed photo he's just swiped from the credenza. He holds it up as Vega enters.

"Look at this. Three generations of Rivers men, standing in front of the old police academy. Looks like a campaign ad."

Vega takes the frame, studies the faces: Captain Rivers in uniform, Lance at nineteen, already suspicious of the camera, and Dejuan, thin as a reed, clutching his father's side with a white-knuckle grip. The legacy is right there in black and white—unbroken, unrepentant.

"Three generations of the same poison," Rodriguez says, studying the photo. **"Father to son to grandson. Each one worse than the last."**

Rodriguez flips through the desk drawers, pulling out file after file. **"He documented everything. My guess, he never thought anyone would come for him."** She pauses at a leather-bound ledger, flipping it open. **"Jesus. Look at this—it's like a family business ledger. Every collection, every payment, going back decades. And here—"** she points to an entry, **"—'Lance collected from R. on Metropolitan. $200. Sent to holding account.' This is from just last week."**

Vega places the photo on the pile, careful not to let it fall. She stands a moment in the middle of the ruined office, breathing in the smell of burned paper and victory.

They drag Rivers through the front hall, past his wife—still in curlers, howling that they'll sue for damages. The media is there now, lights popping like paparazzi, each photo erasing another inch of his myth.

Outside, in the rising heat, the news trucks park side by side, transmitters raised like antennae on an insect. Rodriguez looks at Vega, eyebrows arched.

"You want to say something for the cameras?"

Vega tucks the locket into her vest. **"I'll wait until they ask the real questions."**

But when she walks past Rivers, she can't help herself. She leans in, lips close to his ear.

"This isn't the end. Your whole house is coming down."

He looks at her with a hatred so sharp it could bleed. But he says nothing.

The Fed team loads him into the cruiser. Rodriguez grabs the evidence bag, follows. Vega stands on the porch, sunlight washing the marble steps, and stares down at the locket in her palm.

Some victories are hollow, but some are just the beginning.

Rodriguez | Phillips State Prison, Sunrise

Sunrise at Phillips State Prison hits like a cattle prod. The charged air flickers with overly bright lights, and every step echoes the previous night's screams off the prison walls. Rodriguez has been awake since 2 a.m., palms sweating through two layers of nitrile, waiting for the moment the radio tells her to go.

When it comes, it's just static, then a single word: **"Now."**

She's already in position—near the south yard, where Dejuan holds court. He's surrounded by the usual lieutenants: a big white kid with a neck tattoo, two shrunken old-timers who hang on his every word, and a couple of fresh meat wannabes circling like gnats.

Rodriguez walks the line, nightstick clipped to her belt, head low and eyes scanning for the real danger. Three steps in, she feels it—a shift in the current, a buzz in the way the guards move. Some are with her, real corrections; others wear the stink of payoff and the smug of knowing this whole block is about to break.

She keys her lapel mic. **"Target in the yard. Perimeter ready."**

Over the wall, a drone hums, its lens locking onto the patch of red Dejuan wears like a crown. He's smiling, loose, in command. He's heard about the Rivers raid already—nothing travels faster than bad news to a man who's built his kingdom on other men's misery.

Two guards on the far side of the yard throw nervous glances her way. The taller one, name tag "Monroe," pulls out his phone, thumbs a quick text, then pockets it. Rodriguez files it away; Monroe's been on the take since before she got here, but this is the first time he's sloppy with it.

She steps in front of Dejuan, keeps her posture bored. **"You got business up front,"** she says, nodding toward intake. **"Let's move."**

He shrugs at his crew, like he's doing them a favor. **"Hold my spot,"** he says, and they snicker as if this is the funniest thing on Earth.

Rodriguez walks him toward the admin wing, but before they reach the gate, Monroe slides in behind, blocking the path. **"We got a problem?"** he says, eyes too wide.

Rodriguez sizes him up—he's got twenty pounds and four inches, but she's got the panic of a lifetime. **"Warden needs the prisoner in the interview room, not the hole,"** she says.

Monroe grins, showing the chip in his tooth. **"Not what I heard."**

He moves to grab Dejuan by the elbow, but Rodriguez is faster. She spins Monroe's arm up, snaps the wristlock, and slams him face-first into the chainlink. **"You wanna do this?"** she spits.

Monroe thrashes, but she's got leverage, and with one smooth motion she cuffs his left wrist to the fence. **"Interfering with a federal operation,"** she whispers in his ear. **"Bet you didn't see that one coming, bitch."**

The yard goes quiet. Even Dejuan's crew freeze, unsure if this is part of some bigger play.

Rodriguez drags Dejuan through the gate, up the ramp, and into the sallyport. Two real Feds wait, all business, faces like they're carved from the same stone. **"We'll take him,"** the taller one says, snapping out his own set of cuffs.

Dejuan looks at Rodriguez, trying to read her. **"You got a death wish?"** he asks, voice low.

She smiles, tired and ugly. **"Not anymore."**

They march him down the admin corridor, ignoring the shouts and pounding from the yard. At intake, the warden is waiting—red-faced, lips quivering, the faintest sheen of fear behind his bluster.

"What is the meaning of this?" he demands, looking past Rodriguez to the Feds.

The taller agent hands him a warrant. **"Special investigation, under direct order from the Department of Justice. You are to provide full access to all records and staff."**

The warden's face collapses. **"This is highly irregular."**

"Not as irregular as a corrections captain with a private email to a convicted murderer," the Fed says. He gestures for Rodriguez to follow. **"Let's get started."**

They push Dejuan into the interview cell, bare but for a bolted-down table and two plastic chairs. The Feds flank him, one at each shoulder. Rodriguez stands in the corner, letting him stew.

It takes twenty seconds for the cracks to show. Dejuan starts with bravado: **"You know I got rights. You know none of this sticks. You want to talk, call my lawyer."**

The agent on the left pulls out a stack of affidavits, slides them across the table. **"These are sworn statements from six inmates, two guards, and a paralegal from the women's block. You want to keep running your mouth, or you want to read what they said about you?"**

Dejuan's jaw tics. He flips the first page, then the second, then stops. **"All of them lying. You pay them off?"**

Rodriguez steps forward. **"You ever tell Quanda Dowans the truth?"**

He looks up, slow. **"You got nothing on me."**

She throws a packet of photos on the table—snapshots of every transfer, every visit, even one of him laughing with Rivers at a barbecue, arms wrapped around each other like family.

"You see this?" she says, tapping the photo. **"Your whole world is paper thin. We got proof you used the prison network to run girls from here to halfway houses, then out to the city. Rivers is already talking."**

Dejuan shifts, for the first time really scared. **"You're bluffing. He wouldn't flip."**

The Feds lean in. **"You can testify, or you can get indicted. Either way,**

you're done."

Dejuan's confidence slips, replaced by something raw and animal. **"You think any of this matters? There's always another man waiting in line. Cops, judges, all of them. You're just a pawn."**

Rodriguez leans close, so their faces nearly touch. **"I'd rather be a pawn than a coward."**

He lunges—wild, desperate—but the Feds have him, pinning his arms to the table. **"Fuck you!"** he screams, voice echoing off cinderblock. **"I'll kill you just like I killed her!"**

Rodriguez steps back, lets the moment sit. The cameras catch it all.

When it's over, they drag him to solitary. He tries to spit, but his mouth is dry.

The rest of the takedown happens in layers: the guards who tried to warn Dejuan are lined up in the admin office, questioned one by one. Some fold immediately, trading years for weeks. The smarter ones say nothing, but their phones and burner accounts tell the story. The Feds walk the tier, seizing every document, every hard drive, every thumbprint of Rivers' empire. By lunch, the whole place is in lockdown. Nobody moves unless they say so.

Rodriguez walks the block, watching the other inmates. Some cheer when they see Dejuan's crew get marched away in cuffs. Some look lost. In the women's wing, she hears snatches of rumor—**"He's gone. They're all gone. Maybe it's over."**

A former cellmate of Dejuan's, scrawny and shaking, calls her over to the laundry. **"You want a statement?"** he says. **"I got one."**

Rodriguez follows him to a corner. He whispers, **"He bragged about it, you know? After she visited. Said he 'handled' her when she found out too much."**

Rodriguez makes him repeat it, then writes it down, careful and neat. She thanks him, and he shivers, staring at the ground.

She checks the cell they'd kept for Dejuan, finds it trashed—sheets ripped, floor sticky with orange drink, but in the ceiling vent, a small plastic-wrapped package. She pries it loose. Inside: a flip phone, two batteries, and a thumb drive. The phone is cracked but still works. She scrolls the messages.

All of them are to a single number, tagged **"Pop."** The texts are blunt, no code: **"Quanda is problem," "She's talking to people on the outside," "Handle it tonight."** The last: **"Salon needs cleanup. Rivers knows what to do."**

Rodriguez's blood runs cold. The connection between father and son, grandfather and grandson—all of it documented in these simple, damning texts. Three generations of corruption, each passing the poison to the next like a family heirloom.

Rodriguez brings it to the Feds. **"This nails him,"** she says, but the agent shakes his head. **"He's already nailed. This gives us the rest of the network."**

The warden, who two hours ago ruled this kingdom, now sits in his office, hands shaking, answering every question they throw at him. The Feds copy his laptop, raid his safe, and photograph every log from the last decade. The stack of suspicious deaths—**"natural causes"**—is longer than her arm.

Rodriguez sits in the empty break room, head in her hands, watching the sun crawl across the tile. The adrenaline is gone, and all that's left is the ache.

She's survived another day in a place that should have killed her, but the world outside is still waiting.

Some wars end in gunfire; this one ends in paperwork and ghosts.

Tasha | Courthouse Steps, Morning

The courthouse steps gleamed white in the morning sun, but Tasha saw them for what they really were: **another stage where Black women came to beg for justice from the same people who'd stolen it in the first place.** She paused at the bottom, the city's noise swirling around her—car horns, the distant wail of an ambulance, the low hum of reporters already gathering by the doors. The stone beneath her feet radiated heat, even this early, and she felt it seep through the thin soles of her shoes, grounding her and burning her at the same time.

She could feel eyes on her—some curious, some cold, some just passing by. A pair of officers in pressed uniforms leaned against the railing, arms crossed, watching her with the blank, practiced indifference of men who'd seen too many women like her climb these steps and come back down broken. A group of church ladies in pastel hats whispered prayers, their voices a soft counterpoint to the click of camera shutters. Somewhere, a child laughed, the sound sharp and out of place.

Tasha straightened her shoulders, feeling the weight of every woman who'd ever walked these steps before her. **She wasn't just here for herself. She was here for all of them.** She took a breath, then climbed, each step a small act of defiance, each footfall echoing the promise: **"We are not invisible. We are not done."**

Queen's Crown, Morning

The city wakes up to sirens—police, media, then a second wave of ambulances called in to handle the bystanders who collapse from shock or giddy, vindictive joy. By 7 a.m., every TV, phone, and jumbotron in the metro is screaming the same headline: **"POLICE CORRUPTION RING EXPOSED."** News choppers swarm the Rivers estate like flies, lensing every angle of the takedown. In every beauty parlor and barbershop, the TVs flicker with the mugshots of Captain Rivers and Dejuan, side by side, both looking like they just smelled something rotten.

But at Queen's Crown, the salon is calm, almost reverent. The neon OPEN sign blinks slow and steady. Women line up on the sidewalk, some still in pajamas, arms crossed against the morning chill. They bring donuts and cinnamon coffee, post up on folding chairs, and trade stories about the night before—who saw what, who recognized which badge number, who called their aunties to tell them the good news.

Inside, the air is thick with old smoke and fresh lavender. Tasha stands behind the front desk, baby Crown strapped to her chest, fielding calls and texts and the occasional landline from people who refuse to leave a digital trace. Roxie is camped at the corner table, tapping out messages to her "sources" at the AJC and the local NPR affiliate. Jonesha brings in a tray of pastelitos from the Cuban place three blocks over; Andrea pours mimosas into plastic salon cups and leaves one on every station, like communion.

By 8:30, the first wave of reporters arrives. They're mostly Black women, all of them with notepads or digital recorders, none of them playing polite. The leader—a woman with box braids, gold nose ring, and a smile like a fresh cut—introduces herself as Nia. She asks, without lowering her voice, **"You running a press conference or just letting us fight for questions?"**

Tasha shrugs. **"Ain't nobody here but family. Ask what you want."**

Nia grins, parks herself on the booster seat at the first chair, and flips on her recorder. **"What's it feel like, knowing the whole city is watching you?"**

Tasha looks down at Crown, who's chewing on her hoodie string. **"I don't care if they watch. I care if they remember."** She shifts the baby, then locks eyes with Nia. **"It's not just about them men going to prison. It's about what comes after. Who fills the space."**

The other reporters lean in. One, from a hip-hop podcast, asks about the roots—how deep the Rivers family really went. Another, a blogger from Black Mothers United, wants to know what Tasha will do with the Queen's Crown now that it's free of ghosts.

"We make it into a shelter," Tasha says, without hesitation. **"Not just for women, but for kids, too. I want a space where nobody has to run or hide or act smaller just to survive."**

Jonesha chimes in from the back: **"And we're starting a scholarship fund. For girls who age out the system. No matter what their grades look like."**

Roxie stands, baby on her hip, and addresses the room. **"This place saved my life, twice. First when I had nowhere to go. Then when I realized I didn't have to die to leave the past behind."** She wipes her eyes, then laughs. **"You want a soundbite? That's your soundbite."**

The room bursts into applause. Outside, the crowd doubles, word spreading down the block that something worth hearing is happening inside.

Nia clicks off her recorder and leans in close. **"You know the hashtag is trending? #JusticeForQuanda. Even the mayor had to tweet it."**

Tasha shakes her head, not quite believing. **"She would've hated that,"** she says, voice thick with fondness. **"But she would've loved to see you all in here. Tearing down the old world, making room for a new one."**

The reporters nod, some scribbling, some just letting the moment sit. Then the NPR woman, voice calm but cutting, asks: **"You think it's over? Or just starting?"**

Tasha grins, sharp as a blade. **"The men in charge think you cut the head off and the snake dies. But in our world, you cut the braid and the pattern just grows back, stronger."**

There's a rumble from the crowd as Arman appears in the doorway, dragging his rolling suitcase behind. He's taller, hair longer, skin gone soft from the California sun. The moment he sees Tasha, he lights up, crosses the room in two steps, and hugs her so hard that Crown squeals and grabs his chin.

The room quiets, the story shifting as they watch. Arman whispers, **"I got your messages. I ran the data like you said, and it worked. The Feds called me. I think I'm famous, or maybe just on a watchlist."**

Tasha ruffles his hair. **"Long as you use your powers for good, I don't care which."**

Nia spots him, then addresses the group: **"This is the son? The hacker?"**

Arman shrugs, awkward. **"Just numbers. Tasha's the one who did the real work."**

Tasha shakes her head, pride and grief mixing in her eyes. **"He's my brother now. We do this together."**

Someone turns on the TV—muted, but the captions blaze across the screen: **"Multi-state Trafficking Ring Busted; Atlanta, Miami, Charlotte Linked."** Footage rolls of the Rivers estate, the cells at Phillips, the Queen's Crown sign. The camera pans to Tasha, holding Crown, baby's head resting on her heart.

Roxie raises her phone and snaps a photo. **"You look like a queen,"** she says.

Tasha snorts, then lets the smile take over. **"Not a queen. Just the woman holding the line."**

The crowd grows, the noise rises, but inside, the salon holds its center. A circle of women, and now men, building something that the city can't burn down.

Outside, the hashtag keeps rising.

Inside, the family keeps growing.

Arman | Bus Stop, Dusk

The sun was low, painting the city in bruised gold, when Arman waited for the bus, backpack slung over one shoulder, headphones around his neck. Two guys from his old high school leaned against the shelter, talking too loud, their laughter sharp as broken glass.

"Man, you see that flyer? Another girl missing. Probably just ran off with some dude," one said, shaking his head.

The other snorted. **"Or she's just fast. You know how they are."**

Arman felt the old anger rise, hot and steady. He pulled off his headphones and stepped closer. **"You ever think maybe she didn't run? Maybe something happened and nobody's looking because she's Black and poor?"**

The first guy rolled his eyes. **"Come on, Arman. You always gotta make it deep?"**

Arman's voice was calm, but it carried. **"It is deep. My mom and her friends—they keep track. They know the names. They help the girls who come back, and they remember the ones who don't. You should too."**

The second guy shifted, uncomfortable. **"Whatever, man."**

Arman didn't back down. **"It's not whatever. It's somebody's sister. Somebody's daughter. If you hear something, say something. If you see something, do something. That's what men do."**

The bus pulled up, brakes hissing. Arman got on, leaving the two behind, but as the doors closed, he saw them looking at each other; the joke gone flat.

He sat by the window, heart pounding, and texted his mom:

Told them. Didn't let it slide. Fixing crowns, even out here.

Tasha & Family | Queen's Crown Apartment, Next Morning

Morning drapes the apartment above Queen's Crown in a syrupy gold. The walls are still bare—no art yet, just patches where fresh paint hides what came before. On the pullout sofa, baby Crown wriggles on a blanket, chewing a fist and squawking at the light. He's fat now, all rolls and dimples, every noise he makes answered by one of the four women orbiting him like satellites.

Jonesha arrives first, arms loaded with miniature onesies and sock hats. She lines them up on the counter, color-coded and pressed, each with a tag from her boutique. **"Ain't nobody in Atlanta gonna dress better than you,"** she says, smoothing the fabric with a gentle hand.

Andrea bustles in next, carrying two glass jars of homemade carrot mush and a bottle of formula. She spoons a little onto her finger, lets Crown gum it off, then grins at Tasha. **"Gonna have him eating collards by Christmas,"** she promises. **"Watch."**

Mama Esther brings up the rear, slower but steady, cane tapping the stairwell, beads clacking like a metronome. She sits by the window, pulls a handkerchief from her purse, and starts stringing tiny shells and red thread. **"Protection,"** she mutters, **"old as dirt and twice as strong."**

Tasha watches, heart swollen and tight. She waits for the right moment, then scoops Crown off the blanket and perches him on her lap. His hair is baby-fine, soft as spun sugar, but she sections it with care—first a gentle misting, then a slow, deliberate part down the middle.

"He's not even a year, Tasha," Jonesha says, laughing.

Tasha winks, tongue between her teeth. **"Start 'em young or the world'll do it for you."**

She works his hair into a spiral, fingers sure and steady, then fastens the end with one of Esther's beads. At the very top, she loops the last bit into a tiny, lopsided crown.

"Your name is your destiny," she whispers into his ear. **"You gonna grow up protected and loved, nothing like your daddy or his people."**

Crown giggles, gums her thumb, and flaps his arms like he understands.

Roxie stands in the doorway, silent and shaking. She's a different woman now—sleep-starved, yes, but her shoulders squared and her eyes soft with something like hope. She bites her lip, then cries, but nobody makes it a thing.

Esther finishes the bead-string, ties it into a circle, and rests it on Crown's head like a coronation. **"The world gets to keep trying,"** she says, voice thick, **"but this one belongs to us."**

For a minute, nobody says anything. Then Andrea claps her hands, breaks the spell. **"Enough with the ceremony! We got to eat."**

They pile into the kitchen, passing baby Crown hand to hand, everyone getting a turn. Over bagels and fresh fruit, they talk plans—how to finish the mural in the salon, how to petition the city for daycare funding, how to set up a hotline that the old badge men still lurking in the system won't trace.

"We turn the basement into a safe room," Jonesha suggests. **"Stock it with food, first-aid, maybe even some books for the kids."**

Andrea nods, already listing the shelves in her mind. **"And we need a web page. Make it easy for people to ask for help, so they don't have to walk in scared."**

Tasha listens, every word a balm. She thinks of Quanda, gone but somehow everywhere—her laugh echoing in the faucet's drip, her stubbornness in the way the paint refuses to cover the wall stains. **"She'd love this,"** Tasha says.

Roxie wipes her nose. **"She does. She's here."**

Esther nods, eyes shut. **"She's always been here."**

After breakfast, Tasha sets Crown in a sunbeam on the window ledge, watching the dust motes dance around his head. She sits back and lets herself breathe, the ache in her chest finally, finally quiet.

From outside, the sound of kids on scooters, the old men hollering at the corner, the bells from the church on the next block. The city moving on, loud and messy and alive.

In the salon below, light streams through the fresh glass, catching on every mirror, bouncing until the whole room glows like a lighthouse, guiding those who needed shelter.

And on the top floor, Tasha holds the baby close, promising him everything, and meaning it.

7

PAPER PROMISES

Ink dries faster than tears, but tears leave deeper marks.

Queen's Crown Salon, Late Night | Quanda

The name on the arrest record stopped Quanda cold: Jonesha Johnson, age 19, solicitation. Same Jonesha who'd been in her chair yesterday, bruises hidden under foundation. Same Jonesha who'd whispered about a cop who wouldn't leave her alone.

Quanda's pen hovered over the prison correspondence list. This wasn't coincidence. This was a pattern.

She sat hunched at the front desk, the single lamp making Queen's Crown look like a morgue after hours. Hair clippings ghosted the floor. Every chair flipped and lined like tombstones. The only sounds: the fridge's death rattle and her pen scratching paper like fingernails on concrete.

On the desk: white envelopes, stamps bought on credit, a spreadsheet of every woman locked up in Fulton County for six months. Six months since they took Tasha. Six months of the world pretending nothing happened.

Her phone buzzed. Arman's text lit the screen: "Mom, it's happening again. And this time it's someone I know."

The familiar dread crept up her spine—same feeling she'd had when Tasha first told her about Lance's visits. She typed back: "You okay?"

Three dots appeared, disappeared, appeared again. "Not really. Mya Bradley. She filed a complaint against Rivers last week. Now she's missing."

Quanda's hand trembled. She reached for the bottom drawer—the one with the broken lock. Inside, her manila folder: MISSING WOMEN—ATLANTA. She spread the contents across the desk. Newspaper clippings, social media printouts, photos from families who still came to the salon.

There—Mya Bradley's photo. Twenty-one, crooked smile, dimples deep enough to hold secrets. Last seen leaving Kroger on Cascade. The same girl from the news. The same pattern.

She arranged the photos by neighborhood. The pattern looked like cornrows—each row a different street where a woman had vanished. All connected to police complaints. All closed within forty-eight hours.

Patterns speak their own language; only those who learn to listen can hear what they're saying.

"Dear Tasha," she wrote, then stopped. The mugshot from the news kept flashing—cold-eyed, hollow. Not the Tasha who'd laugh loud enough to rattle dryers.

She started over: "They think silence will save us. But I see the pattern now. Every woman who speaks up disappears. I'm writing to you and every sister behind bars because somebody needs to know the truth before—"

Her pen froze. Before what? Before she became another photo in the folder?

The clock ticked past midnight. Ten letters done, each signed "from your sisters at Queen's Crown." She added her cell number in tiny script. If anybody needed her, they'd know where to find her.

As she sealed the last envelope, her phone buzzed again. Arman: "Found something. Lance had six complaints in three years. All disappeared. Sending files."

Quanda stared at the message, then at the wall of missing women she'd been building. The pattern was clear now. **The silence wasn't protection—it was a trap.**

Print Shop & Queen's Crown Salon, Morning

Next morning, she hit the print shop early. The guy behind the counter loaded her flyer into the machine: "Write to a Prison Sister—Break the Silence."

"This what the world's come to?" he asked.

"World's always been like this," Quanda said. "Now we're done being quiet about it."

By 9:30, Queen's Crown buzzed. Every chair full, air thick with gossip about Tasha's case. But underneath the usual chatter, something new—fear.

"Y'all hear about that girl from Cascade?" An older woman under the dryer spoke up. "Mya something? Filed a complaint against that officer—the one that got stabbed—right before she went missing."

The salon went silent. Quanda's hands stilled on the flyers.

"How many that make now?" someone whispered.

"Too many," Jonesha said, voice hard. "And ain't nobody doing nothing about it."

Quanda pinned a flyer at reception, set the rest by the tip jar. By noon, three clients had taken handfuls. But not everyone approved.

Jonesha cornered her at the sink. "You sure about this? People already talking. Say you're stirring up trouble."

"Trouble's already here," Quanda said. "We just been trained not to see it."

Her phone vibrated. Unknown number. She almost ignored it, then saw the text: "This is Officer Rodriguez. Heard you're asking questions about missing women. We need to talk. Not at the station."

Quanda's pulse quickened. She typed back: "Queen's Crown. After close."

The day crawled. Every time the door chimed, she tensed. By evening, only shadows remained. She was sweeping up when Rodriguez arrived—young, Latina, nervous.

"I shouldn't be here," Rodriguez said.

"But you are."

Rodriguez pulled out a folder. "These are the cases that got buried. The ones Rivers made disappear. Your friend Tasha—she wasn't the first to fight back. Just the first to survive."

Quanda opened the folder. Dozens of photos. Women she recognized, women she'd styled, women whose families still asked if she'd heard anything.

"Why now?" Quanda asked.

Rodriguez's voice was tight, but her eyes were fierce. "Because Mya Bradley was my cousin's daughter. And I'm done watching them disappear."

Enhancement:

Quanda reached out, her hand hovering over the photos. "We can't let them keep doing this. Not to our girls. Not to any of us."

Rodriguez nodded, her jaw set. "We need to move fast. The more we talk, the more they'll try to shut us up."

Quanda felt the weight of every woman in those photos, every story that had ended in silence. "We'll build something they can't ignore," she promised. "We'll make them listen."

Arman | His Room, Night

Arman's room glowed blue from dual monitors. Empty Red Bull cans formed a skyline on his desk. He'd been digging for twelve hours straight, following digital breadcrumbs through APD's system.

The pattern was everywhere once you looked. Every domestic violence complaint against a cop—buried. Every missing woman who'd filed a report—case closed, no investigation. The same supervisor's signature on every cover-up: Captain J. Rivers.

Lance wasn't just dirty. He was part of a system.

Arman's fingers flew across the keyboard, building his case file. Screenshots, metadata, email chains. Evidence they couldn't bury or burn.

His phone rang. Mom.

"You see what I sent?" he asked.

"I see it. Rodriguez is here. She brought more."

"Mom, this is bigger than Lance. It's—"

"I know, baby. That's why we can't stop now."

Through the phone, he heard voices—women gathering, planning. The salon transforming into something else. A war room.

"Mom, be careful."

"Careful got Mya killed. Careful got Tasha locked up. We're done being careful."

The line went dead. Arman stared at his screens, at the mountain of evidence. His college applications lay forgotten. Some fights you couldn't walk away from.

He cracked his knuckles and kept digging. Somebody had to.

Quanda & Rodriguez | Queen's Crown Salon, Midnight

Midnight at Queen's Crown. Quanda stood before her wall of missing women, Rodriguez beside her. The officer had brought more photos, more files, more proof of what they both knew: **the silence was killing them.**

"How many?" Quanda asked.

"That I can prove? Seventeen. That I suspect? Triple that."

Quanda touched each photo—a benediction, a promise. "What do you need from me?"

"Keep writing those letters. Build your network. When we move against them, we need witnesses who aren't afraid to talk."

"And if they come for me?"

Rodriguez met her eyes. "Then we better work fast."

After Rodriguez left, Quanda sat alone in her salon. The chairs watched her like an audience waiting for the show to start. She picked up her pen, pulled out fresh paper.

"Dear Sisters," she began. "The time for silence is over. They think our voices don't matter, that our stories will die with us. They're wrong. Every letter you write, every truth you tell, builds our case. They can lock us up, but they can't lock up the truth."

She wrote until dawn, until her hand cramped and her eyes burned. Fifty letters to fifty women. A network of voices they couldn't silence.

As the sun rose over Atlanta, Quanda looked at her wall of missing women. Soon, she thought. Soon, their stories would shake the entire city awake.

The revolution wouldn't start in the streets. It would start in a beauty salon, one letter at a time.

8

PATTERN RECOGNITION

Patterns speak their own language;
only those who learn to listen can hear what they're saying.

Arman | Queen's Crown Salon
Three Months Before the Night
That Changed Everything, Evening

Arman slipped into Queen's Crown just as the streetlights outside started blinking orange, the last smears of daylight bleeding out behind the skyline. The salon still hummed with life—three chairs occupied, blow dryers running on their last breath, the air thick with coconut oil and lavender. He slipped into the far corner near the window, ducking under the glass beaded curtain to sink into the seat nobody else ever claimed.

He preferred the salon at night, when it transformed from neighborhood gossip central into something more intimate. During the day, you heard toddlers wailing and clients dissecting their men's shortcomings, debating which cousin was selling weed to the teachers at Westview Middle. But after dark, the space belonged to the women who worked it—stylists with their hair wrapped up, shoes kicked off, comparing cash tips while the radio played whatever old-school jam got the most heads bobbing. Laughter thicker than edge control.

His phone buzzed. A text from his mother, timestamped two minutes ago: you coming by after work, babe? He let the message sit unanswered, thumb hovering over the screen, until a familiar voice cut through the blow dryer noise.

"Look who showed up in person. You got good news for us or just here for a line-up?"

Tasha commanded the front station like a general, edges slick and uniform, locs pulled back with a colorful scarf. She wiped her hands on a towel, arching a perfect brow at him. Tasha always seemed prepared to curse you out and then serve you a plate of rice and beans.

"Neither. I got something for you." He gestured at the notebook wedged under his arm—a cheap black Moleskine bursting with sticky notes and half-shredded pages.

She nodded toward the emptying chair beside her. "Don't just stand there, genius."

He sat, eyeing the glass jar of combs on the counter, each one a different color, all swimming in blue disinfectant. He opened the notebook and flipped to the diagram he'd drawn the night before—a braid chart where each diamond shape was labeled with a date, a name, or a question mark.

"I found a pattern," he said.

She shot him a sideways glance. "You say that every week."

"This is different." He pushed the notebook toward her. "Look."

She leaned in, fingers splayed to avoid her fresh manicure. She smelled like clove and peppermint—a combination that always made him want to confess secrets. "It's just hair patterns."

He shook his head. "It's the city. Each diamond represents a day. Each strand is a girl who went missing. See how they overlap? There's always a new knot the week after." He pointed to a dense tangle. "This is where Mya vanished—right after a cluster of other disappearances, but the news never connected them."

He felt foolish explaining it through hair metaphors, but it made sense in his head. His mother always said, Always read the scalp before you touch it.

Every head tells a story. He'd grown up believing it applied to people, too.

Tasha thumbed the page's edge, eyes scanning the tiny numbers he'd penciled in. "So you think they're connected?"

"I know they are." He tried to keep the urgency from his voice. "But it's not just about the girls. It's about where and when they disappear. Every time, it's like someone's testing for weak spots."

Tasha set down her comb, leaning closer. The scar on her chin tightened when she frowned, and right now it was a deep crease. "What kind of weak spots?"

"People who won't be missed by cops. Women without family to raise hell when they go missing. The last three—nobody filed reports for at least five days. By then, the trail's cold."

Silence stretched between them, heavy with unspoken understanding. Tasha finally said, "I don't like how that sounds. Makes me think of..." She didn't finish.

He didn't need her to. Some names carried bad luck if spoken aloud.

Tasha tapped the page with a lacquered fingernail. "Where's your mother right now?"

"She went home," he lied. He couldn't admit that Quanda had barely slept all week, or that she'd started hiding the salon's spare keys in the flour bin at their apartment.

Tasha's lips pressed together. "Show me the map. You got one, right?"

He always did. Slipping a folded city map from his backpack, he spread it across the counter. The transparent overlay he'd created at three AM lay on top, pinned down with the disinfectant jar. Aligning the roads and highways felt like working on a puzzle designed to make you lose.

Each colored dot represented a girl. Every crisscrossing line marked a day, a sighting, a rumor. When he positioned the overlay correctly, the pattern came alive—a lattice of vanishings stitched perfectly into the city's anatomy.

"Jesus," Tasha breathed, her usual sarcasm absent. "You see this cluster by the bus depot?" She traced a knot in the lines. "That's where my cousin got picked up last year. Never saw her again. Cops said she probably ran away."

He nodded grimly. "That's what they always say."

She stood, restless, pacing behind the empty chairs. "You think it's somebody local? Someone who knows how to blend in?"

He considered this carefully. "I think it's someone who knows exactly who nobody will look for." He traced the map, following the overlaps where dots clustered so densely they nearly fused. "This isn't random. It's targeted."

Tasha stopped behind him, arms folded. "So what's the move? You taking this to the police?"

He snorted. "You know how many times I tried? Last time, they told me—" He mimicked a bored desk sergeant's drawl: "'We appreciate your concern, son. Let the professionals handle it.'"

Tasha rolled her eyes, then returned to the notebook. "We need someone who'll actually listen. You got any press contacts? Anyone who owes you a favor?"

He didn't, but he knew who might care—someone with reason to make noise, who wouldn't let it die in a file cabinet. "I'll find someone. Just... can you keep the map here? If anything happens to me, I want you to have it."

Tasha smirked, but her eyes stayed sharp. "You acting like you're about to jump in front of a train."

"Not a train," he mumbled. "Just... something bad. You feel it too, right?"

She hesitated, then nodded slowly. "Yeah. I feel it."

The weight of that admission settled between them.

A faint voice pierced the room's silence. "Excuse me, Miss Tasha? Can you check my part?" A girl, maybe twelve, wearing tiny gold hoops, sat holding a phone, gazing around uncertainly.

Tasha moved to her, hands gentle, and practiced through the girl's hair. "Hold up, baby. Let me get you right." She shot Arman a look over her shoulder: Don't go anywhere.

He sat in the salon's warmth, watching city lights flicker through the blinds. The smell of hot comb and burned sugar clung to everything, even the map. He thought about the girls whose faces populated his charts, how the world grew smaller and colder with each new dot.

His phone buzzed—a news alert from Atlanta PD: "Missing: Bradley, Mya

N." He closed his eyes, letting dread settle in his chest like swallowed ice.

Always read the scalp before you touch it. Every head tells a story. His mother's voice echoed as clearly as if she stood beside him.

When Tasha finished with her client, she returned to the map, eyes fierce. "We need a plan."

He nodded, tracing the overlay's last line with his finger. "We need to move fast. This isn't just history—it's a warning."

Together, they pinned the map to the wall behind the counter, right beneath the board of missing girls' photos. They stood in silence, watching as the network of lines pointed a path straight into the city's dark heart.

Tasha | State Prison, Intake & Dayroom, Present

By orientation's end, Tasha's mouth tasted like metal. Whatever nerves she'd carried from the holding cell, the COs had crushed with barked commands and constant threats of force. Every surface looked designed to cut or bruise—concrete, steel, and layers of paint the color of old scabs. They issued her a uniform two sizes too small, an off-white sports bra, and canvas slip-ons that pinched her toes.

The hair cutting was the worst part. She'd known it was coming, but watching thick coils fall onto the linoleum nearly broke her composure. She didn't speak. Years ago, she'd learned never to offer an opening.

Two guards frog-marched her through the intake corridor, past thick glass panels where older inmates lined up for pill call. The women watched her with flat, exhausted interest. Someone spat on the floor. One guard squeezed her shoulder as they turned the corner—hard enough to send a clear warning.

"Welcome to H-Unit," he said, as if seating her at brunch.

The women's cellblock reeked of sweat, mop water, and industrial bleach. Every echo from the catwalks doubled back until it became a constant drone. Dayroom doors hung open, inmates milling in loose clusters, their uniforms customized in small, defiant ways—rolled sleeves, folded pant legs. One girl had painted her state-issued shoes neon orange.

There was a system to where everyone sat and stood, but Tasha couldn't read it yet. She kept her head down, shoulders squared, replaying processing advice: Don't run your mouth. Don't look scared. Find someone, quick.

A television blared near the back wall. Black women, mostly older, clustered around its low hum—some braiding hair, others just resting their feet. To the left, three Latinas in sharp cornrows controlled the phone table, arms folded, jaws working gum. Near the commissary line, white women huddled over what looked like a chessboard but moved faster, louder—all smack talk and cackling.

Tasha caught a flash of pink: a baby-faced girl with a busted lip and eyes swollen half-shut. She'd stepped into the wrong section of dayroom and got shoved sideways so hard her slippers nearly came off. Nobody flinched. Guards on the balcony above slapped nightsticks against their palms but didn't descend.

She slowed just long enough to register who ran the floor, then kept moving.

At the dayroom's edge, Tasha hesitated. No open tables, no invitations. She'd spent the night in holding with a tweaker who talked to shadows—that woman was gone now, probably in medical. Tasha pivoted, trying to choose a spot that didn't scream alone or fresh meat, but everywhere she looked, someone was already watching.

A woman in state blues with faded tattoos sat by the soda machine, eyes fixed on Tasha. Her salt-and-pepper hair was cropped tight, a jagged scar bisecting her left eyebrow. The woman tipped her chin subtly, like calling a dog to heel. Tasha checked behind her—no one else. She drifted over.

The woman radiated coiled patience. Scars along her knuckles spoke louder than words.

"First day's the worst," she said, voice low and surprisingly gentle. "Sit. I don't bite."

Tasha sat. The chair legs screeched across the concrete like a gunshot.

"Celestine," the woman said.

"Tasha."

Celestine's eyes inventoried everything—the starchy uniform, the shorn hair, the tension in Tasha's hands. "They always go for the scalp first. Makes you easier to identify on cameras."

"Doesn't work," Tasha said, jaw locking. "I got a lumpy head, anyway."

Celestine grinned, gold tooth flashing. "That's the spirit."

The soda machine made a hollow thunk, refusing Celestine's dollar. She pounded it with her fist. "You need the lay of the land, fast. If you want to last."

"I noticed the TV crowd."

"Queen Bee's table. They've been here forever. Don't talk to them unless they talk to you first. Mostly, they just want to watch their stories in peace."

"And the phone, girls?"

Celestine grunted. "Don't touch those phones without backup. You get one call a day—maybe—and if you miss it, that's your ass."

Tasha nodded, already having memorized the clock, counted guards, mapped exits. The girl with the split lip approached the water fountain, glanced their way, then dropped her eyes and shuffled off.

"Chess table?" Tasha asked.

"Aryan Barbie and her crew. They got hustles, but keep your head down and they'll forget you exist."

Celestine reached into her pocket, produced a mini Snickers, and slid it across the table. "You eat breakfast?"

Tasha took it, peeling the wrapper with shaking fingers. Sugar hit her tongue, and she felt almost human again. "You always feed the new ones?"

"Only the ones who don't whine." Celestine studied her as if weighing calculations. "You don't look like you killed nobody. That true?"

"Depends who's asking."

Celestine laughed—sudden and loud, but not unkindly. Heads turned, then looked away. "I like you. You got a brain. Most don't last a week before they're in seg or crying for mama."

"What's the catch?"

Celestine looked across the dayroom. "You'll see."

Tasha followed her gaze. Guards walked along the balcony in lazy figure-eights. Inmates operated in their own tempo, rhythm layered over the constant threat of violence. Noise, stares, ciphers: Each moment felt like an ordeal.

Tasha finished the candy, thinking. Celestine watched without smiling or scowling—just watching.

"Why help me?" Tasha asked.

Celestine tapped her temple. "You remind me of someone. She used to do my hair, back before all this." She rubbed her scalp, nostalgia warring with bitterness. "Anyway, ain't nobody else gonna teach you the rules. They want you to fuck up."

Tasha looked at her hands. "So, what are the rules?"

Celestine leaned in, voice dropping to a whisper. "Don't run errands for nobody, not even guards. Don't owe nothing, not even a cigarette. You see someone coming at you, swing first. But only if you know you can win."

"And if I can't?"

Celestine shrugged. "You get creative."

A scream erupted from the showers—short, sharp, then nothing. Guards moved slowly to respond. The dayroom barely paused.

Tasha wiped the chocolate from her fingers. "What about the COs? They seem lazy."

"They're not lazy. They're waiting. You don't want them to notice you—trust me."

A buzz echoed down the corridor: count time. Celestine stood, motioning for Tasha to follow. They filed into the hallway single file, every woman finding her mark. Count went quickly—names barked, faces checked off.

Back in the cell, Tasha claimed the top bunk. The mattress crunched when she sat; someone had etched "FUCK THIS PLACE" into the vinyl. She closed her eyes, replaying the rules until they nested in her skull like seeds.

Celestine snored almost instantly—deep and uneven. Tasha lay awake, tracking every footfall, cough, distant howl. When she finally slept, it was shallow and fitful, punctured by loss. She dreamed of hair salons with wide windows and laughter, the hum of dryers instead of guards' boots. In sleep, she braided her own hair, strands growing longer with each pass—black, healthy, shining. No matter how many times she wove them, they always fell away, scattering like shadows across concrete.

She woke to darkness and clattering metal trays. Breakfast: runny eggs, bread that could double as packing foam. She ate anyway, grateful for the warmth. Celestine sat across from her, already awake, eyes bloodshot but sharp.

"You want to survive this?" Celestine said softly. "You gotta find a reason."

Tasha looked at her hands, the faint ghost of polish still clinging to her nails. She thought of Quanda, her sister in Palmdale, the women she used to make beautiful one head at a time.

"I got a reason," she said. "I just need to remember it."

Celestine nodded. "Good. Now eat. We got a long day."

Noise filled the room, yet for a moment, Tasha felt safe. She ate slowly, deliberately, watching the world around her, learning it piece by piece. She would survive. She'd done worse.

Tasha & Celestine | Prison Rec Room, "Vocational Enrichment," Later That Week

Tuesday brought "vocational enrichment"—the guards' euphemism for two hours in the rec room with battered tables and broken curling irons from 1998. The prison called it "Personal Grooming Center" but the women called it the Pit—two hours a week to clean up, provided you didn't stab anybody.

Celestine staked out the best table, hustled two plastic chairs together, and snapped her fingers at Tasha. "Let's go. You're up first."

Tasha slid into the seat, hyper-aware of the onlookers. The Black women clustered near the TV area but watched every move. The Latinas sat near the window, pretending to play cards. Even the guards, bored out of their minds, hovered by the door. A woman with tribal tattoos nudged her friend, nodded in Tasha's direction.

Celestine draped a towel over Tasha's shoulders and, with a practiced twist, parted what was left of her hair. "They butchered you," she said, almost tender. "These COs got no respect."

"I used to do my own," Tasha said, voice tight.

"Everybody got a 'used to' in here," Celestine replied, tongue clucking. "But the question is, what you gonna do now?"

She worked methodically, fingertips nimble despite joints gnarled from years of concrete and winter. She wetted the hair with water from a dented spray bottle, combed it through with something that looked suspiciously like a fork from chow. "Don't judge," she said. "We make do."

She sectioned the hair into tiny rows, hands moving with gentle precision. Tasha flinched when the fork's teeth scraped her scalp.

"Beauty's always been pain," Celestine said, not unkind. "You think them girls out there with five-hundred-dollar weaves don't cry when the tracks come out?"

The women in line laughed. Tasha grinned, just a little.

Celestine leaned in, voice dropping. "My grandma used to do mine on Sundays. After church, before the cousins came over. She'd smack my hands away if I squirmed. Said a Black woman's hair is a crown, and if you let it slip, the world'll snatch it right off your head."

"Sounds about right," Tasha murmured.

"She came up in Louisiana," Celestine said, fingers flying. "Wasn't no beauty shops in the parish. If you didn't know how to braid, you either learned or walked around looking crazy."

"She teach you all this?"

Celestine nodded. "And a whole lot more." For a moment, her hands slowed, eyes fixed on the part line. "Used to dream about opening my own shop. Had a name and everything—Heavenly Hands." She let the memory sit there, then resumed, faster. "Now look at me, doing time with a bunch of bitter-ass women who don't tip."

Tasha bit back a laugh. She recognized the rhythm of it—the safe topics, the small confessions, each story a test balloon for trust. "You ever get tired of it? Braiding, I mean."

"Never." Celestine's voice went hard. "It's the only place in here I still feel human."

A woman in the back of the line called out, "Yo, Celly, hook a sister up with that fishbone when you done!"

"Wait your damn turn," Celestine shot back, but there was pride in it.

The braids took shape, tight and close to the scalp, intricate as chain-link. But instead of the familiar cornrow pattern, Celestine created something more complex—geometric shapes that formed a pattern across Tasha's scalp.

"This ain't your regular style," Tasha observed, feeling the unfamiliar pattern.

Celestine's fingers paused. "No, it's not. This here is old. From before." She lowered her voice. "My grandmother taught me these patterns. Said our ancestors used them to map escape routes during slavery. Each pattern meant something—which way north was, where the safe houses were."

Tasha's eyes widened. "For real?"

Celestine nodded. "Messages right on top of your head that only our people could read." Her voice dropped even lower. "In Angola, where I did my first bid, there was a woman who'd been inside thirty years. She knew patterns that could tell entire stories—who to trust, which guards took bribes, which ones were dangerous."

As she worked, Celestine explained each section. "This zigzag means 'danger ahead.' These three connected loops mean 'allies nearby.' The circles with lines through them? That means 'someone's watching.'"

When she finished, she handed Tasha the foggy hand mirror. "Take a look."

Tasha studied her reflection. Her scalp tingled, the tightness almost electric. The rows formed an intricate pattern, both beautiful and purposeful. Something more than vanity or even dignity—it was history, resistance woven into her crown.

"It's beautiful," she whispered, almost surprised.

Celestine grinned. "Told you. Even in here, your crown's your power. And with these patterns, you carrying something they can't take away—our history, our way of speaking without words."

Tasha traced the pattern with her finger, careful not to disturb the fresh parts. "My ex hated braids. Said it made me look 'ghetto.'"

Celestine's face went flat. "Ain't nothing ghetto about knowing who you are. Men like that—they want to control how you look 'cause they scared of what might happen if you remember where you come from."

She gathered up the tools, wiped the chair with a practiced flick. "Tomorrow I'll teach you how to do these yourself. Every woman should know how to speak this language."

Tasha lingered by the wall, fingering her new braids, letting the warmth of it work through her chest. It was the first time she felt somewhat visible since arriving, as if the skin she brought in belonged to her, not the state.

She caught her reflection in the cracked window. For a split second, she saw herself back at Queen's Crown, laughing with clients, hair swinging, hands always moving. She cherished moments when women found beauty in their own reflections. This power was within you, a fleeting gift.

The illusion snapped, replaced by concrete and cinder block, the guards tapping on their phones. But the braids stayed. They were real, tight, and hers—carrying messages from her ancestors that no guard could decode.

Arman | Stanford Dorm Room, Late Night

Arman spread printouts across his dorm room desk, color-coded and annotated with yellow sticky notes. His Stanford roommate had cleared out for spring break, leaving him alone with the data that had consumed his thoughts for months.

His laptop glowed in the dim room, three different analyses running simultaneously. The wall above his desk had transformed into a makeshift investigation board—a map of Atlanta with pins marking missing women cases, police reports, and domestic violence complaints filed against officers.

He reached for the old photo tucked behind his laptop—him and Mya at that backyard barbecue, both grinning with juice-stained mouths. He'd pulled it from his desk drawer after discovering her name in the missing persons database. The dimple in her left cheek was exactly as he remembered. He pinned it to the wall next to the data, a reminder that these weren't just statistics.

He rubbed his eyes, checking the time: 2:17 AM. His mother would kill him if she knew he was still up, putting this ahead of his AI Engineering midterm. But some patterns couldn't wait.

The phone buzzed. Officer Rodriguez.

"Tell me you found something," she said without greeting.

"I think so." Arman swiveled to face his laptop. "I cross-referenced domestic violence complaints with missing persons reports. Every woman who filed a complaint against a cop in the last three years—seventeen of them disappeared within six months."

"Jesus." Rodriguez's voice was tight. "How many were Lance?"

"Six directly. But here's the pattern—they all got closed by the same supervisor. Captain J. Rivers."

"Lance's father."

"Yeah. There's a recurring number in his call log—appears right before each disappearance. Always the same pattern: call comes in, Lance moves to the location, woman vanishes."

"How did you get his phone records?" Rodriguez's tone was careful.

Arman hesitated. "You don't want to know."

A pause, then: "No, I don't. What else?"

"DNA evidence from Lance's home office—hair samples from three missing women, including Mya Bradley. Logged by a rookie officer, then marked 'mishandled' and removed from evidence by order of Captain Rivers."

Rodriguez's breath was audible through the phone. "You need to be careful with this, Arman. These people are dangerous. They've been operating this way for years."

"Is that why you've been investigating them?" Arman asked. "I noticed the case files on your desk when you were at the salon."

Another long pause. "My sister disappeared five years ago. Filed a complaint against an officer for harassment. Case went nowhere. I joined the force to find out what happened to her."

Arman stared at his wall of data. "I think we can help each other."

"This stays between us for now," Rodriguez said. "Captain Rivers has eyes everywhere. I've spent three years building this case. One wrong move, and they'll bury it—and us."

"Send me what you have encrypted. And Arman? Delete everything from your computer after. Use a secure cloud only."

"Already on it," he said, fingers flying across the keyboard.

After they hung up, Arman stared at the map on his wall. Each pin represented a woman—someone's daughter, sister, friend. The patterns were clear to him now: not just data points, but a web of corruption spanning generations.

He thought about Tasha in prison, serving time for defending herself against a monster. A monster with a father who protected him, who seemed to protect an entire network.

Arman took a photo of his wall, encrypted it, and then began taking everything down. By dawn, no trace would remain in his dorm room. But now, he had burned the patterns into his memory—undeniable, unmistakable.

Different patterns, same inescapable truth.

9

CONJUGAL ARRANGEMENTS

When truth finally speaks, it doesn't whisper—it echoes.

Quanda | Phillips State Prison, Morning

Love behind bars grows different—harder, more desperate, more real.

Quanda's hands shook as she signed the visitor log at Phillips State Prison. Three months of letters, phone calls, and sleepless nights had led to this moment—her first conjugal visit with Dejuan.

She paused, pen hovering over the paper, and tried to steady her breath. The waiting room was all hard plastic and fluorescent light, the kind of place that made hope feel like contraband. Around her, other women sat with their own bundles of nerves and longing, clutching clear bags of snacks and family photos, eyes darting to the clock.

Every head tells a story.

Quanda wondered what the guards saw when they looked at her—just another woman in love with a man behind bars, or someone who'd learned to survive on the outside by holding tight to what little she could save.

She thought of Tasha, of Roxie, of all the women who'd written letters to men and women locked away, building bridges out of words and memory. She thought of the price of silence, and how every visit, every touch, was an act of defiance against a system that wanted them to forget.

Vega | Metropolitan Pawnshop, Night

Through binoculars, Detective Vega tracked the woman's measured stroll past the same pawnshop where she'd stood every Thursday since the surveillance began. Something was off about Roxie's movements—too deliberate for a street worker, too aware of sightlines and escape routes. She had the look of someone gathering rather than selling, her eyes constantly scanning, one hand always near the phone in her pocket.

Her burner phone buzzed. The text made her blood run cold: **Captain Rivers meeting with Holloway tonight. Don't approach Roxie until green light.**

But as Vega watched Roxie duck into an all-night diner, instinct overrode protocol. Three years undercover had taught her when to break the rules.

Inside the diner, fluorescent lights cast everyone in a sickly pallor. Roxie didn't look up when Vega approached, just kept writing in an expensive leather notebook—another incongruity in her carefully constructed persona.

"Mind if I join you?" Vega asked, already sliding into the booth.

Roxie's eyes flicked up. "I'm not working tonight, Detective."

"Never said you were. And I never said I was a detective."

"Please." Roxie closed her notebook. "I can spot a cop from three blocks. It's a survival skill."

Vega leaned forward. "Cut the shit. You're gathering evidence. I want to know why."

A long silence stretched between them. Finally, Roxie exhaled.

"You here to arrest me or recruit me?"

"Neither. I want to compare notes."

Roxie laughed, bitter and sharp. "With a cop? No thanks."

"Not just any cop." Vega slid her badge across the table. "Internal Affairs. I'm investigating corruption inside Atlanta PD."

Roxie studied the badge, searching for the lie. "Why should I trust you?"

"Because we're both after the same thing." Vega pulled out her phone, showing Lance Rivers in uniform. "This officer—you know him, right?"

Roxie's jaw tightened. "Yeah, I know him." Old pain flickered in her eyes.

"He's part of something bigger. A network running through the department, the courts, maybe higher." Vega swiped to another photo—Lance with an older man in dress blues. "His father, Captain James Rivers. Retired three years ago, but still pulling strings."

"The Rivers problem," Roxie murmured.

"What?"

"Nothing." But her fingers had gone white around her coffee mug.

After a tense negotiation, Roxie made her decision. She pulled out a press credential. "Roxanne Washington, investigative journalist. I've been undercover for eighteen months investigating trafficking networks connected to the police department."

"Jesus." Vega sat back. "You're a reporter?"

"I'm a survivor first. Worked these streets for real when I was sixteen. Got out, got educated, came back to expose the system that almost killed me."

They agreed to meet the next day at Roxie's storage unit—a risk for both, but necessary.

As they parted outside, neither noticed the black SUV photographing their meeting with a telephoto lens.

Quanda | Queen's Crown Salon, Night

Queen's Crown Salon glowed in the darkness, the only business still open at 9 PM. When the bell jingled, Quanda looked up from her client's silk press. Her smile faltered when she saw Pastor Willoughby, Bible tucked under one arm.

"Pastor. Little late for a haircut."

"Just passing by, Sister Dowans." His eyes scanned the salon, lingering on the bulletin board where Tasha's photo was pinned. "Admirable work with your prison outreach. Though I wonder if some souls are beyond redemption."

"Funny. I don't recall Jesus turning anyone away."

The pastor smiled thinly. "Even Jesus recognized wolves among the sheep."

After her client hurried out, Willoughby revealed his true purpose: "That woman who's been hanging around—Roxie. She's not what she appears to be. She's gathering information. For a newspaper."

The threat in his voice was clear when he added, "Captain Rivers is a pillar of this community. A generous donor to our church. He doesn't deserve to have his family's tragedy exploited."

After he left, Quanda texted Rodriguez: **Pastor Willoughby just stopped by. Asking about Roxie. Something's happening.**

Outside, she watched Willoughby's Lincoln pull away—and behind it, a black SUV with tinted windows, waiting.

Roxie & Vega | Storage Unit, Next Day

The storage unit smelled of dust and determination. Roxie revealed three years of meticulous documentation: hundreds of notebooks, maps with colored pins, surveillance photos.

"This is File H—the Rivers file." She showed Vega dates, times, payment records. "Lance collected from girls on Metropolitan. Regular schedule. But then I noticed a pattern—girls who couldn't pay or tried to report him started disappearing."

She pulled out a map bristling with red pins. "Each marker is a woman who filed a complaint against Lance. All missing within two weeks."

"And the connection to his father?"

Roxie laid out surveillance photos. "Lance always called the same number after collections. Captain James Rivers."

The evidence built—photos of Rivers meeting with Judge Holloway and Pastor Willoughby, then accepting an envelope from Marcus Donovan, the Southeast's biggest trafficking operator.

Vega placed a small recorder on the table. "Last month, Rivers met with

Holloway after Tasha's sentencing. They didn't sweep for bugs."

The recording was damning:

"The Rivers problem is closed," Holloway said.

"For now," Rivers replied. "But that salon woman—Dowans—she's still digging. And there's a journalist sniffing around Metropolitan."

"Handle it. Same way I handled the evidence in my son's case."

Roxie's burner phone buzzed. Her face paled. "Pastor Willoughby just visited Queen's Crown, asking about me. They know."

They loaded evidence quickly, but neither noticed the black SUV parked three rows away, engine idling.

Quanda | Her Apartment, Early Morning

Quanda jerked awake at 3:17 AM, Mama Esther's dream still vivid—cowrie shells forming a river flowing toward a crown, warnings about patterns repeating through generations.

Her phone showed a message from an unknown number: **Stay away from Roxie. Final warning.**

She called Mama Esther, who answered immediately. "The Rivers are rising. Captain Rivers has been controlling things for decades. My own sister went missing in '79 after talking to Officer Rivers."

"Tasha found evidence connecting Lance to missing women," Mama Esther confirmed. "Evidence that led back to his father. That's why she confronted him that night."

Quanda texted Arman: **Secure all your data on missing women cases. NOW.**

Then Rodriguez: **We need to find Roxie. Today. Before they do.**

Outside, a black SUV sat motionless, windows reflecting darkness.

Quanda, Arman, Rodriguez | Safe House, Doraville, Later That Day

The safe house above a Vietnamese restaurant in Doraville became their war room. Evidence spread across tables, phones in airplane mode, windows covered.

"Still no word from Vega?" Quanda asked.

Rodriguez shook her head. "She should have checked in by now."

Arman arrived, shaken. "Someone broke into my dorm room. They took my desktop, but I have everything backed up." He displayed his findings—twenty years of missing women cases, all connected to Captain Rivers. Financial records linking offshore accounts to Judge Holloway, Pastor Willoughby, and the Police Benevolent Association.

"Each dot represents a woman who disappeared after filing a complaint," Rodriguez said, pointing to the map. "Including my sister Elena."

"This is why Tasha killed Lance," Quanda realized. "She found his trophies—jewelry, photos from the missing women."

The sound of an engine drew them to the window. The black SUV had found them.

Heavy footsteps on the stairs. Then a voice: "Detective Vega? It's Captain Rivers. We need to talk."

Rodriguez positioned herself by the door. "Arman, take your mother and the evidence. Fire escape. FBI field office. Ask for Agent Morris."

"I'm not leaving you," Quanda protested.

"This is bigger than any of us. If Rivers gets this evidence, women keep disappearing, and Tasha stays in prison. GO!"

As Quanda and Arman slipped toward the fire escape, they heard Rodriguez's steady voice: "Captain Rivers. Fancy meeting you here."

Outside, clutching evidence that represented decades of silence, Quanda looked at her son. Together, they descended into the Atlanta heat, carrying truth that would echo loud enough to bring down walls.

Behind them, breaking glass. Before them, an uncertain path to justice.

But for the first time since Tasha's arrest, they weren't running from the truth—they were running toward it, and the echoes were already beginning to sound.

The fire escape groaned under their weight, rust flaking off the railings. Three stories down, the alley stretched empty except for overflowing dumpsters and a stray cat that hissed before disappearing into shadows.

"Mom, move!" Arman urged, helping her navigate the last ladder.

They hit the ground running, Quanda's sandals slapping against wet pavement. Behind them, the sound of splintering wood echoed from the apartment—Rodriguez buying them precious seconds.

"This way," Arman pulled her toward the restaurant's delivery entrance. They burst through, startling the kitchen staff who barely looked up from their prep work. The smell of pho and lemongrass followed them out the front door onto Buford Highway.

No black SUV in sight. Yet.

"My car's two blocks over," Quanda gasped, clutching the evidence envelope to her chest.

They moved fast but not running—two Black folks sprinting through Doraville would draw the wrong attention. Every car that passed made Quanda's heart skip. Every siren in the distance could be coming for them.

Her Honda sat where she'd left it, looking beautifully ordinary. Arman pulled out his phone as they dove in.

"No," Quanda said, starting the engine. "They could be tracking—"

"Already thought of that." He produced a second phone from his backpack. "Burner. Paid cash. I've been paranoid since they broke into my dorm."

While Quanda navigated toward downtown, Arman called the FBI field office. "Agent Morris, please. Tell him Detective Vega sent us. It's about the Rivers investigation."

A pause. Then: "He'll meet us in the parking garage. Level 3. Come alone."

The federal building loomed ahead, all concrete and tinted windows. Quanda's hands shook on the steering wheel. "What if this Morris is connected too? What if—"

"Then we go to the media," Arman said firmly. "Roxie's editor at the Sentinel. We make it public before they can stop us."

They circled the garage twice before entering, checking for tails. Level 3 was nearly empty—just a few government vehicles and a man in a gray suit standing beside a sedan.

Agent Morris looked like every FBI agent from every movie—clean-cut, serious, hand resting near his weapon. But his eyes showed genuine concern when they approached.

"Ms. Dowans? I've been expecting you." He glanced at the envelope she carried. "Vega called me an hour ago. Said if anything happened, you'd have what we need."

"Is she okay?" Quanda asked.

Morris's expression darkened. "We lost contact after she left the safe house. But we have teams moving now. Your evidence could be the key to everything."

Quanda hesitated, then handed over the envelope. Twenty years of silence, passed from her hands to his.

Morris opened it carefully, scanning the contents. His eyes widened. "This is... Jesus. This goes all the way up."

"My son has digital copies," Quanda added. "Everything's backed up."

"Smart." Morris looked at them both. "We're going to need you in protective custody until—"

"No," Quanda interrupted. "I have a friend in prison because of these people. I'm not hiding."

"Mom," Arman warned.

But Morris nodded slowly. "I understand. But at least let us put security on you. And we'll need full statements, everything you know."

As they talked, Quanda's phone buzzed. Unknown number. She almost ignored it, then saw the text:

Rodriguez and Roxie safe. Vega in custody—Rivers has her. Move fast.

She showed Morris, who immediately made a call. "We have an officer down. Detective Elena Vega. Send all units to—" He paused, listening. "What do you mean you found her car?"

The blood drained from his face. "Where?"

He hung up, turning to Quanda and Arman. "They found Vega's car in the Chattahoochee. She's missing."

The parking garage suddenly felt like a tomb. Somewhere in the city, their friend was in danger. The evidence in Morris's hands felt heavier—not just papers and photos, but lives hanging in the balance.

"We move now," Morris said, his professional calm cracking. "Rivers doesn't know we have this yet. But once he does..."

He didn't need to finish. They all understood. The Rivers family had made people disappear for decades.

But now, finally, their victims had a voice.

And it was about to echo through every courthouse, every precinct, every corner of Atlanta where silence had reigned too long.

Quanda thought of Tasha in her cell, of Roxie risking everything, of Rodriguez facing down a killer, of Vega somewhere in danger. All these women, refusing to be silenced anymore.

"Let's go," she said, steel in her voice. "Time to make some noise."

As they left the garage, sirens began wailing across the city. The echoes had begun, and there would be no stopping them now.

The truth had found its voice, and it was screaming.

10

TESTIMONY

Some stories can only be told once, but they change everything forever.

Quanda | Courthouse, Morning

The courthouse loomed like a colonial plantation house—all white columns and imposing steps designed to make the small feel smaller. Quanda arrived early, dressed in a navy pantsuit with gold earrings that caught the morning light. She'd spent an hour on her locs, weaving in subtle gold threads that matched her jewelry—armor for a battlefield where appearances could determine survival.

The gallery overflowed. Women from Queen's Crown occupied the first two rows, a unified front in shades of burgundy and gold—the salon's colors. Jonesha sat, sunglasses hiding fresh bruises. Denisha clutched a tissue. Asia kept checking her phone until an officer asked her to put it away.

Across the aisle, a sea of blue uniforms. Officers who had served with Lance filled three rows, their faces hard as concrete, badges gleaming under fluorescent lights. Detective Vega leaned against the wall, watching everything with careful eyes. When she caught Quanda's gaze, she gave an almost imperceptible nod.

Officer Rodriguez slipped into the seat beside Quanda. "You ready for this?"

"As ready as anyone can be," Quanda replied. "How's Tasha holding up?"

"Scared but steady. Her attorney got the prosecution to agree to let her wear civilian clothes instead of prison orange. Small victory."

The bailiff called for order. Judge Holloway entered, his robes pressed and heavy, face a practiced mask of impartiality. He settled into his chair like a man accustomed to deciding fates.

District Attorney Helen Lewis rose, her crimson suit a slash of blood against the wood paneling. "The People are ready to proceed, Your Honor."

Defense Attorney Marcus Coleman stood next. "Defense is ready, Your Honor."

"Bring in the defendant," Judge Holloway ordered.

When Tasha entered, Quanda almost didn't recognize her. Prison had carved away the softness from her face, leaving sharp cheekbones and watchful eyes. Her hair, once her crown, had been cut short and was now styled in simple twists. She wore a modest navy dress that matched Quanda's suit, a silent solidarity.

As she passed the gallery, her eyes caught Quanda's for a moment. Something passed between them—an understanding deeper than words. **Every head tells a story. Every crown carries its scars.**

Tasha | Witness Stand, Late Morning

The prosecutor began with a familiar narrative: Officer Lance Rivers, decorated police officer, murdered by his vengeful wife. DA Lewis painted Lance as a public servant, a community hero.

Quanda watched the jury—eight women, four men. Their faces revealed nothing, trained in the passive expression of those who know they're being watched. **Silence has its own language; some women speak it fluently.**

The defense countered with Lance's history of controlling behavior, domestic violence calls that mysteriously disappeared from records.

"This isn't a murder case," Coleman argued. "This is a case of survival—a woman fighting for her life after years of systematic abuse."

Then came the moment they'd all been waiting for. The prosecution called Tasha to the stand.

She rose, shoulders back, chin up—the posture Quanda had taught her years ago at the salon. *Carry yourself like you already won,* she'd said. *Your crown is your armor.*

After being sworn in, she sat in the witness box, hands folded in her lap.

DA Lewis approached. "Mrs. Rivers, could you tell the court about the night of March 17th?"

Tasha took a deep breath. "It was a Thursday. Lance came home later than usual. I was in the kitchen, finishing some paperwork for the salon."

"And what happened when Officer Rivers arrived home?"

"He was agitated. Said he'd had a bad day. Wanted dinner, but I hadn't cooked because he usually ate at the station on Thursdays."

"Did that upset him?"

Tasha's eyes never wavered. "Yes. But not like usual. He was... different. Scared, almost. He kept checking his phone, pacing."

"What happened next?"

"He went to his office. I heard him talking to someone on the phone—angry, urgent. When I walked past, he slammed the door."

"And after that?"

Tasha's voice steadied. "Later that night, I went to get my phone charger from his office. He was asleep on the couch. On his desk, I found a box."

"What was in this box, Mrs. Rivers?"

The courtroom stilled.

"Jewelry. Photos. IDs. All belonging to women. Women I'd seen on missing persons flyers." Tasha's voice broke slightly. "Including Mya Bradley, whose case had been on the news for weeks."

The gallery erupted in whispers. Judge Holloway banged his gavel.

"Order," he demanded.

"And what did you do then, Mrs. Rivers?" DA Lewis continued.

"I took photos of everything with my phone. Then I checked his laptop, which was still open. There were messages—about ‘merchandise’ and ‘delivery dates.’ And financial records showing payments to accounts I’d never seen before.”

“So you confronted him?”

“Not then. I was afraid. I went back to our bedroom, pretended to be asleep. I planned to leave in the morning, take the evidence to the police.”

“But that’s not what happened, is it?”

Tasha shook her head. “No. He found me looking at his phone records. There were calls to the same number every time before a woman disappeared. He caught me.”

“And then?”

“He grabbed me. Said I shouldn’t have been snooping. That I was stupid, that I didn’t understand how things worked.” Tasha’s voice became mechanical. “He said no one would believe me anyway. That his father would make sure of it.”

The prosecutor paused. “His father?”

“Captain James Rivers. Retired from the force three years ago.” Tasha’s eyes flicked toward the officers’ section. “Lance said his father had connections everywhere—the department, the courts.”

Judge Holloway shifted uncomfortably. DA Lewis glanced back at him before continuing.

“What happened next, Mrs. Rivers?”

“He hit me. Hard enough that I fell against the counter. Then he pulled his gun.” Tasha’s hands trembled slightly. “He said he’d make it look like a break-in.”

“And that’s when you stabbed him?”

“No.” Tasha’s voice strengthened. “That’s when I told him I’d already sent the photos to someone. It was a lie, but he believed me. He lunged at me, trying to grab my phone. We struggled. He was choking me when I reached for anything I could find. My hand found the kitchen scissors.”

The courtroom held its breath.

“I didn’t mean to kill him,” Tasha said quietly. “I just wanted to breathe again.”

The cross-examination was brutal. The prosecutor questioned every detail, tried to paint Tasha as jealous, unstable, vindictive. Through it all, Tasha remained composed. Only once did she falter—when asked why she hadn't left sooner.

"Because," she said, voice barely audible, "the last woman who reported him disappeared."

Some patterns only show up when you step back far enough to see.

Quanda | Courtroom Gallery, Afternoon

The afternoon brought character witnesses. Jonesha took the stand first, removing her sunglasses to reveal the fading bruises around her left eye.

"I've known Tasha for six years," she said. "We met at Queen's Crown Salon. I noticed she always wore long sleeves, even in summer. One day in the bathroom, I saw the bruises on her arms."

"Did Mrs. Rivers ever discuss her husband's abuse?" Coleman asked.

"Not directly, not at first. It was all code. 'Lance had a bad day.' 'I tripped on the stairs again.' But eventually, she showed me photos she'd taken after the worst nights."

The defense attorney nodded. "Thank you, Ms. Johnson."

Next came Denisha, who described the day Tasha came to work with a dislocated shoulder, claiming she'd "fallen while cleaning."

"She couldn't even hold a comb," Denisha testified. "Quanda had to drive her to the ER, but Lance showed up before they could file a report."

One by one, the women of Queen's Crown testified. Their stories formed a tapestry of evidence that the prosecution couldn't easily unravel. **The salon had always been more than a business; it was a network, a warning system, a place where truth could be spoken without fear.**

Throughout the testimony, Quanda watched the jury. Two women wiped tears. One man kept his gaze fixed on Lance's empty chair. Another juror, an older Black woman, never took her eyes off Tasha.

In the back of the courtroom, a tall, silver-haired man in an expensive suit sat observing. When he caught Quanda looking, his eyes—cold and calculating—reminded her of Lance's.

During the recess, Rodriguez leaned close. "That's him," she whispered. "Captain Rivers. Lance's father."

Defense | Courtroom, Late Afternoon

When court resumed, the defense called their final witness: Officer James Martinez, Lance's former partner.

The gallery stirred in surprise. Martinez walked to the stand, his uniform pressed but his expression troubled.

"Officer Martinez," Coleman began, "how long did you work with Officer Lance Rivers?"

"Three years," Martinez answered. "We were patrol partners in the Southwestern district."

"And during that time, did you ever witness Officer Rivers display concerning behavior?"

Martinez hesitated, eyes darting briefly toward Captain Rivers. "Yes. Lance had... anger issues. Especially with certain suspects."

"Could you elaborate?"

"He was rough with women, particularly sex workers. Would make comments about 'teaching them respect.' Several times, I had to intervene during arrests."

"Did you report this behavior?"

"Once. To our sergeant. The next day, I was called into Captain Rivers' office—Lance's father. He was Deputy Chief then. He said I was mistaken, that his son was a 'model officer.' Suggested my career would benefit from 'better judgment' in the future."

The courtroom buzzed. Judge Holloway banged his gavel again.

"Did you ever witness Officer Rivers' interactions with his wife?"

"Yes. At department functions. He was... controlling. Would interrupt her, tell her what to eat, who to talk to. Once, I overheard him threatening her in the parking lot."

"Why are you testifying today, Officer Martinez?"

Martinez straightened. "Because the night before Lance died, he called me. He was panicking, said his father was going to 'handle' a problem for him. Said a woman had 'gotten too close.' I asked if he meant Tasha, and he laughed, said 'not yet.'"

Captain Rivers stood abruptly. Judge Holloway gave him a warning look, and he slowly sat back down.

"Based on your professional experience and personal observations of Officer Rivers, were you concerned for Mrs. Rivers' safety?"

Martinez looked directly at Tasha. "Yes. So concerned that I gave her my personal number and told her to call anytime. She never did."

As the defense prepared to rest its case, Coleman approached the bench. After a brief conference, he returned to his table.

"Your Honor, the defense would like to present one final piece of evidence."

Coleman held up a small digital recorder. "This recording was made by Mrs. Rivers on the night in question."

The prosecutor objected, arguing the recording hadn't been properly entered into evidence. After heated sidebar discussions, Judge Holloway overruled the objection.

The courtroom fell silent as Coleman pressed play. Static crackled, then Lance's voice filled the room—harsh, threatening.

"What the hell do you think you're doing in my office?"

Tasha's voice, smaller but determined: "I know about the women, Lance. I found the box."

"You don't know shit." His voice turned mocking. "What are you gonna do, call the cops? I am the cops."

"I'm leaving. Tonight. And I'm taking the evidence."

A thud, followed by Tasha's cry of pain.

"You're not taking anything. You're not going anywhere." Lance's voice lowered. "My father would kill me if this got out. You have no idea what you're messing with."

"Your father? What does he have to do with this?"

"Everything." A bitter laugh. "Who do you think runs the whole

operation? Where do you think I learned how this works?"

The sound of a drawer opening, metal against wood.

"Lance, please—"

"Shut up! I'm calling him. He'll know what to do with you."

The sound of a number being dialed, then Lance speaking again: "Dad? We have a problem. She found the merchandise records... Yeah, she knows... No, I've got her here... Okay, I'll handle it until you arrive."

The recording continued, capturing the sounds of struggle. When it finally ended, the courtroom remained in stunned silence.

Coleman turned to the jury. "Mrs. Rivers made this recording because she feared for her life. She acted in self-defense against not just an abusive husband, but a man involved in trafficking women—women like Mya Bradley."

Captain Rivers stood again, this time heading for the exit. Two court officers moved to block his path, but Judge Holloway waved them off. "Let him go," he ordered.

DA Lewis rose for her closing argument, but her earlier confidence had evaporated. She spoke mechanically about the "sanctity of law enforcement" and the "tragedy of domestic violence."

Coleman's closing was brief but powerful. "This isn't just about Tasha Rivers. It's about a system that protects abusers in uniform. It's about women who disappear while those sworn to protect them look the other way. Today, you have a chance to say enough is enough."

Quanda & Tasha | Courthouse, Evening

As the jury filed out for deliberation, Quanda made her way to Tasha, squeezing her hand over the railing. "You did it," she whispered. "You told your truth."

Tasha's eyes glistened. "Not just for me. For all of us."

The jury deliberated for less than two hours. When they filed back in, their faces were solemn but resolved.

"Has the jury reached a verdict?" Judge Holloway asked.

The foreperson, the older Black woman who had watched Tasha so intently, stood. "We have, Your Honor."

"On the charge of first-degree murder, how do you find?"

"We find the defendant, Tasha Rivers, not guilty."

A collective gasp from the gallery. The police officers stood in unison.

"On the charge of second-degree murder?"

"Not guilty."

"On the charge of manslaughter in the first degree?"

"Not guilty."

Judge Holloway's face tightened. "On the charge of manslaughter in the second degree?"

"Not guilty."

"On the charge of criminal negligence resulting in death?"

The foreperson paused, making eye contact with Tasha. "Guilty."

Murmurs swept the courtroom. It wasn't a complete victory, but it was close.

Judge Holloway appeared displeased. "Sentencing will be scheduled for two weeks from today. The defendant will remain in custody until that time."

Detective Vega approached the defense table, speaking quietly to Coleman. The attorney nodded, then addressed the court.

"Your Honor, in light of new evidence concerning the victim's criminal activities and the defendant's cooperation with an ongoing investigation, we request immediate release on bail pending sentencing."

Judge Holloway scowled. "Detective Vega, approach the bench."

Vega complied, carrying a manila folder. Their conversation was tense, inaudible to the gallery.

Finally, he nodded. "Bail is set at $50,000. The defendant will surrender her passport and remain within the county limits pending sentencing."

Quanda stood immediately. "I'll post it," she called out. "Right now."

As the courtroom cleared, Quanda made her way to the clerk's office to arrange for Tasha's release. Rodriguez and Vega followed.

"You realize what just happened?" Vega asked once they were in the hallway.

"The jury effectively nullified. They found her technically guilty of the lesser charge so she wouldn't face a retrial, but that recording changed everything." Vega's eyes gleamed. "And it gives us probable cause to investigate Captain Rivers."

"Will it stick?" Quanda asked.

Rodriguez nodded. "Martinez's testimony corroborates the recording. Plus, we have Arman's data analysis connecting the missing women to Lance's patrol routes."

"We build the case against Captain Rivers," Vega replied. "And we keep Tasha safe until we do."

Outside the courthouse, reporters gathered. Quanda spotted Captain Rivers at the bottom of the steps, speaking intensely with Pastor Willoughby. They both glanced up as Tasha emerged.

The look Captain Rivers gave Tasha sent a chill down Quanda's spine—not anger, but calculation. **Some men never learn the language of silence, but they know how to make threats without words.**

As they walked to Quanda's car, Tasha whispered, "It's not over, is it?"

"No," Quanda admitted. "But this time, you're not alone."

The price of silence is always paid by the women who refuse to disappear.

Queen's Crown Salon, Night

Queen's Crown stayed open late that night. The salon had transformed into a celebration space—women gathered around Tasha, offering hugs and food. Jonesha had brought champagne. Denisha's mother supplied soul food. Asia hung a banner that read "WELCOME HOME, QUEEN."

Tasha sat in Quanda's styling chair, overwhelmed but smiling. Her prison-short hair had been styled into an elegant crown of twists, adorned with gold threads.

"To Tasha," Quanda toasted. "For speaking truth to power."

"To truth," the women echoed.

Mama Esther beckoned Quanda to the back room. Her face was serious.

"It's begun," she said, laying out her cowrie shells. "But it's far from over."

"What do you mean?"

"Captain Rivers won't let this stand. The recording."

Quanda looked back at the women in the salon, at Tasha's new crown, at the network of sisters who had learned to speak the language of survival.

Some stories can only be told once, but their echoes last forever.

11

VOWS AND SHADOWS

Some marriages are built on promises. Others on threats.

Roxie's Apartment, Night

The bathroom light flickers like a bug zapper. Roxie stands in front of the mirror, hands braced on the sink. The cracked oval cuts her face in two. She adjusts her shirt—pink, a size too small—and checks the outline of her stomach. Not flat anymore. Five months and change, and she still can't say the word "baby" out loud.

She opens the medicine cabinet, stares at the row of pill bottles, then closes it again. Her reflection doubles, then triples, then snaps back to one. **She's always been good at seeing herself in pieces.**

On the back of the toilet, her old notebook waits. She flips it open, thumb tracing the list she's written every night for weeks:

- Lock the windows.
- Check the peephole.
- Don't answer numbers you don't know.
- Don't trust the quiet.

She adds a new line:

- Remember what Quanda said: "If you feel the shadow, move."

She closes the notebook, tucks it under her pillow. In the mirror, her eyes look too big, too tired. She presses a palm to her belly and whispers, "We're not them. We're not them." But the words taste like a lie.

She turns off the light, but the shadows follow her back to bed.

Tasha | Georgia State Prison, Morning

The inside of Georgia State Prison tastes like burnt plastic and sour mop water. **Tasha Rivers wakes to that flavor in her mouth every morning.** She sits up on the metal cot, swings her legs over the edge, and lets bare feet settle onto concrete that never remembers warmth. Light flickers above her in sick, stuttery spasms. The fixture hums all night, even after she wraps her pillow around her head. On the wall beside her, a timeline of wounds: small, shallow scratches, each one a hashmark for the days gone by. **The count runs longer than her arm now.**

Today's the two-year mark, she thinks. I should celebrate. Maybe do a shot of fermented orange juice, if Paulette didn't drink it all last night.

She dresses fast. State-issue sweatpants, bleach-stained. T-shirt with the sleeves cut off, exposing the angry ridge of a scar on her upper arm.

From down the hall: a burst of laughter, sudden and sharp, then cut short by the bark of a guard's voice. Tasha recognizes the tone—visitation day. You could hear it in the way folks breathed, the way their movements lost some of that habitual drag. **The air smells of bleach and nerves.**

Today is not a normal visitation, though. Today is the one they've all been hyped about for weeks: a prison wedding, full on, with white roses and sheet cake and the press all up in everyone's business.

From three cells over, a girl named Kenya is rehearsing her vows. She mumbles through them, words sticky with sleep and heartbreak.

"I promise to love, honor, and not cut your ass when you forget my birthday," Kenya mutters, voice wobbling between tough and tender.

Tasha smiles despite herself.

A guard walks by, his steps perfectly spaced like a metronome, and stops at her cell.

"Rivers," he says, **"you got a call at nine. Be ready."**

He walks on before she can reply. She tries not to think about what kind of call waits for her. There are only two types that reach her here—bad news or worse.

A memory surfaces, uninvited: Quanda, barefoot in the salon, hands on her hips and face lit up like Christmas. **"You better not let them people turn you cold, Tash,"** she'd say. **"I need your heart warm when I come visit."**

A hollow ache settles between her ribs. She's about to tell it to fuck off when the noise from the corridor gets louder—the wedding party must be arriving. Tasha listens as inmates up and down the block start hollering, singing, whistling.

She drifts to the sink and washes her hands. The water runs cold, numbing her fingers. She dries them on her shirt, then pulls a worn scrap of paper from the bottom of her mattress. She sits at the edge of her cot and starts to draw.

She sketches fast, all instinct, laying out a grid, then weaving tight, intricate patterns across it. To anyone else, it's just fancy geometric shapes. But to Quanda, who still wore her box braids in the precise style Tasha invented, every swoop and angle tells a story. **The patterns speak if you know how to listen. This one spelled out a warning.**

She signs it with a quick flourish: the tiny X in the bottom corner, their old code for **don't ignore this.**

Outside, the noise swells again. She looks through the glass at the corridor. A guard leads a small group—two visitors, one older woman in a fancy blue dress, and a younger one with a baby on her hip.

The first visitor is Mama Esther, Quanda's grandmother. Tasha knows her from back in the day—she used to run the corner store on Florence. The old lady moves slow, careful. Her silver hair is pinned neat, not a strand out of place.

The younger woman catches Tasha's stare and looks away. There's something haunted in her eyes. Like she's come for a funeral instead of a wedding.

The group files past, heads toward the chapel. As they vanish, the guard locks eyes with Tasha and nods, slow and deliberate. She tucks the scrap of paper under her waistband.

At 9:00 sharp, the cell door rattles open. Tasha doesn't move right away; she's learned to let them wait. The guard gestures for her to follow.

They pass the library, the rec room, and finally the little glass office where the phone waits.

She picks up the receiver, presses it to her ear, and listens for the click that means someone's listening in.

"Hello?"

Silence. Then a breath, sharp and wet, on the other end.

"Tasha?" The voice is barely a whisper. **"You there?"**

She recognizes the caller by the fear, not the sound. **"I'm here, Roxie. What's wrong?"**

"They said he's getting out," Roxie says. **"Parole. Next month. The lawyer called me at work, and I—"** She stifles a sob. **"They said you'd know what to do."**

Tasha closes her eyes. The tremor in her hands spreads up her arms.

"He's not supposed to get out," she says.

"That's what they said, but—look, I saw him, Tash. On the news. With that reporter. They're making him look like a damn victim."

"Did Quanda see?"

"I think so. I tried to call her, but she's not answering."

"Don't worry about her," Tasha says. **"I'll handle it."**

"I'm scared for you, Tasha. Don't do nothing stupid, okay?"

Tasha breathes in slow. **"I don't do stupid. I do necessary."**

She hangs up before Roxie can answer. The phone slams down harder than she meant.

Tasha walks back to her cell. On the way, she passes the chapel. The wedding is in full swing. Through the mesh window, she sees Quanda—dressed in a white button-up and black pants, hair in flawless box braids that reach her waist. She's standing at the altar next to a tall, skinny man with tattoos on his neck.

Quanda laughs at something the officiant says, throws her head back. For a second, Tasha forgets the prison walls. She sees her friend as she once was—alive, raw, untouchable.

But then the memory of Roxie's call creeps back in, cold and insistent. She feels the paper against her skin, the message she needs to get out.

He's coming. The story isn't over. Watch your back, Q.

She sits on her cot and waits for her moment.

She knows Quanda won't read the warning until after the ceremony. She knows the truth will hit harder than any punch.

But that's how you survive in here. You learn to make your marks count.

Quanda | Prison Chapel, Midday

Chapel days always bring a rotten nervousness. **Shaquanda Dowans holds her breath outside the steel doors, counting out the rhythm of her own pulse.** She's never seen the chapel dressed up like this—balloons bobbing against the cinderblock, cheap white streamers sagging overhead, the smell of spray starch failing to bury the sweat and bleach underneath.

In the middle of it all, Mama Esther arranges herself on a folding chair, regal even in orthopedic sandals and a battered floral dress. Beside her, Tasha's cousin fidgets in a polyester suit. The two other guests are strangers, borrowed for the day to make the event look **"community-oriented."**

Quanda's own hands can't sit still. She smooths her uniform, traces the yellowed hem. Her nails are perfect—she spent all morning filing, buffing, painting them with smuggled whiteout for **"something old, something new."**

She's marrying a man she's only known through glass, a man whose letters could catch fire if you held them too long. **Dejuan always wrote in block capitals, perfect and cruel.** The first time he called her his **"eternal queen,"** she choked on her own spit. After the fourth letter, she believed it might be possible.

She floats down the makeshift aisle, nodding at every set of eyes. Most are inmates, all of them hungry for a spectacle, or maybe just for the reminder that even here, you can choose somebody.

At the front, Dejuan waits. He stands a full head taller than anyone else, broad-shouldered and clean-shaven. He wears a suit—charcoal grey, tailored by his own hand with thread pulled from laundry bags. It doesn't fit quite right, but it's perfect, anyway.

He doesn't smile. He just watches her come, eyes glittering, jaw locked.

The chaplain welcomes everyone and reads from a stained script. She invites the couple to join hands. Quanda does, marveling at the chill of Dejuan's palm, the way his fingers close around hers like a restraining order.

She doesn't remember most of the vows. She says yes at the right moment, waits for Dejuan to do the same.

He doesn't hesitate. His voice cuts through the hush. **"I do. I will always do. You're the only thing that makes any of this mean anything."**

For a split second, the room forget

s itself. Somebody sighs.

The chaplain tells them, **"By the power vested in me by the state of Georgia, I pronounce you husband and wife."** She gestures for them to kiss, but Dejuan just pulls Quanda in and brushes his lips against her forehead.

Mama Esther wipes a tear. At her feet, she's laid out a circle of colored beads. There's blue for protection, white for cleansing, green for safe passage. She arranges them just so.

The couple signs their paperwork, hands trembling. The crowd disperses. Quanda stands alone for a moment, clutching her fake flower and staring at Dejuan as he argues with a guard about visitation rights.

"Quanda, baby. Come," Mama Esther calls.

Quanda walks over. The old woman's hands shake as she gathers the beads into her purse.

"Did you see it?" Esther whispers. **"The way the beads fell?"**

Quanda shakes her head. **"No, Nana. What's it mean?"**

Esther leans in close. **"There's something following you. I thought this would block it, but the circle broke."**

Quanda shivers. **"I noticed."**

Esther grabs her wrist. **"You can't trust him. Not really. You know this, yes?"**

Quanda wraps her arms around her grandmother and breathes in the old lady's perfume. She doesn't let go until the guard barks her name.

She moves to the door, where Dejuan waits. He glances over her shoulder at Esther, then leans in.

"You look scared," he says.

Quanda lifts her chin. **"Not scared. Just cold."**

The guard leads them down the corridor. Dejuan leans close as they walk.

"You didn't have to do this, you know. Marry me. I woulda waited."

Quanda blinks. **"Why you saying that now?"**

"They told me. About the parole thing. I could be out by next year. Maybe earlier."

Her chest tightens. **"You serious?"**

"Yeah. I was gonna tell you after the party."

Quanda swallows the lump in her throat. Suddenly the whole day feels unreal.

He grins, lopsided. **"Don't look so sad, babe. We'll have all the time in the world."**

She forces a smile, but her insides are ice.

They reach the visitation room, where cake and punch wait. Quanda watches Dejuan greet the guests with his prison king's swagger. She slides into a chair, knees weak.

Mama Esther is already there, hunched over a cup of punch.

Esther leans close. **"Remember when you won the lottery? Remember how it felt like fate?"**

Quanda nods, the memory distant but bright.

"That wasn't luck," Esther says. **"I made a pact. Gave up something to get you that. It was supposed to keep you safe."**

Quanda's mouth goes dry. **"You're messing with me, Nana."**

Esther squeezes her hand. **"No, baby. I'm telling you the truth. I did a thing, and it's coming back around now."**

Quanda yanks her hand free. **"You always do this. Turn everything into a**

story."

But Esther just smiles, sad and steady. **"One day you'll understand. For now, just keep your eyes open."**

Quanda walks to the far corner, pretending to study the wall. Behind her, Dejuan's laugh echoes.

She glances back. His gaze meets hers, unwavering, impossible to read. For the first time, she wonders if Nana's right. If maybe there's a shadow at her heels, waiting for its moment.

This was supposed to be a day of beginnings. Instead, it tastes like something's about to end.

12

THE LAST DEEP CONNECTION

Sometimes the last thing a woman does is fix her crown.

Tasha | Prison Cell, Early Morning

Day starts with the steady drip from the ceiling. Eight hundred and twenty-three days of this sound, and Tasha Rivers could predict each drop's landing like a prophet reading tea leaves. She marks it, each cold tap against the stainless sink. The water's rhythm matches the twitch in her leg—unruly since she got jumped in the showers last December. She leans against the wall, picks at the hashmarks with her thumbnail. Counting time is a sickness, but it's the only thing that makes sense in here.

The prison air hangs thick with industrial cleaner, unwashed bodies, and the metallic tang of fear that never quite dissipates. She's up to eight hundred and twenty-three. Some days, the urge to stop keeping track is so strong she almost claws her own eyes out. But Tasha isn't a quitter. Never has been.

Noise shifts in the hall: a heavy step, the jangle of keys, the way guards talk when they're not on parade. She doesn't look up until the shadow falls through the bars, long and heavy like a bad omen.

The guard's name is Briggs, but nobody calls him that. "Mail call," he says. He holds a thin envelope between two fingers, as if it might bite him.

Tasha swings her feet off the cot. "That for me?"

He nods, pushes it through the slot. "Looks official."

She tears it open without ceremony. The paper is thick, expensive. Her name, full government, printed at the top. State of Georgia Department of Corrections. The rest she reads slow, because her brain stutters when it gets good news.

She reads it once. Twice. By the third time, her hands shake so hard she almost drops it. Early release. New evidence. Effective next week, pending a final review.

She fights to keep her voice from cracking. "This a joke?"

Briggs shrugs. "No joke. Warden wants you in her office at 0800. Pack your shit, Rivers."

He moves off down the hall. She sits with the letter pressed to her chest, breath shallow, heart stuttering.

This can't be real. She reads it again, searching for a catch. Maybe it's a transfer, maybe they're moving her to a worse hole. But the words stay the same.

She closes her eyes. The world outside rushes up at her. Inglewood. The shop. Quanda's laugh, sharp and bright. Mama's face at the door, the smell of fried catfish and green apple incense.

Cellblock, Later

A different noise pulls her back—a low whistle from the cell across. Kenya, always nosy. "What's up, Tash? You look like you seen a ghost."

Tasha folds the letter, tucks it under the mattress. "I'm going home," she says, voice quiet but solid. "They found something that proves I was telling the truth all along."

Kenya lets out a long, low sound. "Shit, for real?"

Tasha shrugs, but the emotion catches her anyway. She tries to laugh, comes out as a cough. "Guess they finally figured out Black girls don't lie just for sport."

Her body feels foreign—every nerve on fire. She moves to the metal shelf, starts stacking her possessions into a pillowcase: toothbrush, Bible, a faded deck of playing cards, the necklace Quanda sent her on her last birthday. Each object is a piece of armor, a way to not come undone.

The clank of the breakfast cart echoes through the corridor. She ignores it. No appetite. She checks the envelope again, running her fingers over the raised seal like maybe it'll rub off and leave her bare.

A wave of nausea hits her. She's leaving. Not in years, not maybe, not in the slow death of parole. Next week.

Tasha sits, arms wrapped around her knees, and rocks herself until the panic passes. She remembers the last time she saw outside. The sky was violent blue, the sun too bright to look at. She tries to recall what fresh breeze smells like when it's not filtered through ductwork and chemicals.

More sounds: doors slamming, guards shouting, women's voices high and sharp as razors. Life here won't pause just because she's got a ticket out.

She finishes packing. The pillowcase bulges, but it's light. Everything she owns fits in a single hand. She wipes the tears from her face before anyone can see.

The letter sits on her lap, edges already soft from clutching. She traces the words with her finger, memorizes every curve. "I told the truth," she says, quiet enough that nobody but her can hear.

She stands, squares her shoulders, and looks at the wall. All eight hundred and twenty-three marks. She runs her fingers over the newest one, then snaps the pencil in half and drops it in the trash.

Tomorrow, she'll start counting something else.

Quanda | Bedroom, Morning

Some mornings, the light is sharp enough to slice skin. Quanda Dowans wakes to it, cutting through the curtains, laying bars across her bedroom wall. For a second, she can't remember what day it is. Then the charge comes rushing back: conjugal, today.

She sits up, rolls her shoulders, listens to the vertebrae pop. Her body has never felt like her own; it's something she's had to learn to live inside. She pads to the bathroom, toes curling against cold tile, and stands under the mirror's harsh gaze. The reflection isn't honest, but she prefers it that way. She studies the shape of her face, smooths back the edges, and whispers the old mantra: **"Put yourself together. Thread by thread."**

She starts with foundation, thick and cool on her fingertips. Layers it heavy, then sculpts the bones—cheek, nose, jaw—until the mask looks permanent. Purple shadow, slick black liner, lashes out to here. For lipstick she goes loud: magenta, the kind that stains teeth and draws stares. She lets it dry, then presses her lips together until they go numb.

She moves to the closet. Picks a skirt—fuchsia, pleated, hits just above the knee. Black tank, denim jacket with rhinestones at the cuffs. She lays it out on the bed, then second-guesses. Too much? Not enough? She stares at the options, heart pounding.

On the dresser, her phone lights up: five missed calls from Esther, two new voicemails. Quanda flips the phone facedown. She doesn't have bandwidth for Nana's warnings today. Not when the whole morning is a countdown to Dejuan.

She grabs the perfume bottle, the old-school kind with a bulb and mesh net. The scent is candy and heat: cheap, but good. She dabs it to her wrists, neck, the inside of her elbows.

She takes a minute, breathes deep, and looks at herself in the mirror again. There's an edge in her smile, the one she practiced for years—first to hide fear, later to weaponize it. She tilts her chin. "You got this," she tells the glass. Then she tucks Mama Esther's charm under her bra, where the cloth will keep it warm and close. It's a fist-sized lump of red thread and black beads, knotted tight and finished with a silver coin. She runs her thumb across it. The coin hums with remembered prayers.

You keep that close, baby. That man's family, they don't bring nothing but curses.

Mama Esther's voice in her head, always. Quanda swallows and brushes her hair out, roots to ends. Braids long and flawless, parted with a ruler's precision. She secures each one with a tiny gold bead.

Driving to Prison, Late Morning

On the drive, the city moves around her in a blur: gas stations, nail salons, pawn shops. Every light turns red just to slow her down. She plays music loud, the kind that keeps her thoughts out. Every couple miles, her phone buzzes with another missed call. She kills the ringer, stuffs it in her purse.

The prison sits on the edge of the county, brown and blocky, nothing like the TV versions. No towers or razor wire, just a wall and the sign: Phillips State Correctional Facility. She parks in visitor overflow, watches a group of women smoke by the entrance, each one dressed like they're heading to a nightclub or a funeral. She fixes her lipstick, wipes down her palms, and checks the charm again. It's still there, still humming.

At intake, the atmosphere smells like ammonia and anxious sweat. She signs the form, hands over her license, waits for her turn. The guards work slow, never making eye contact.

"Take off the jewelry," one tells her, bored. She drops her hoops and bracelets in the tray, but keeps the necklace. The guard points. "All of it." Quanda fakes a smile and unsnaps the chain, tucking the charm deeper in her bra where hands won't go.

Next comes the metal detector. She raises her arms, stands wide, waits for the wand to pass over her. It beeps at her underwire. The guard frowns, shrugs, lets her through.

Then the pat down. Gloves, cold and impersonal. They lift her skirt, check the waistband. When the woman's fingers brush her thigh, Quanda doesn't flinch. She's done this dance before.

Through the second door, another guard meets her. He's young, face shiny with nerves or sleep deprivation. He leads her down the hall, every step echoing.

The visitation suite is worse than she remembers. Two chairs, one table bolted to the floor, a plastic mattress in the corner. No windows, just a clock with hands stuck at noon.

She sits, folds her hands, and waits. The overhead light flickers, buzzing like an insect trapped in a jar.

She thinks about the call from Mama Esther. She thinks about the beads, the prayers, the warnings that never land. She thinks about Dejuan, about the way his words could light her up even through bulletproof glass. She runs her finger along the edge of the table, feels the notches cut by past visitors.

She smooths her skirt, tilts her chin, and practices her smile. She wants to look perfect. Not for the guards, not for Nana. For herself.

She waits. And she is ready.

13

WHAT CONCRETE WALLS HIDE

Some walls are built to keep people out. Others are built to keep secrets in.

Quanda | Phillips State Prison, Conjugal Room, Morning

The conjugal room at Phillips State Prison smelled like industrial disinfectant and broken dreams. Quanda sat on the edge of the narrow bed, watching Dejuan pace the small space like a caged animal who'd forgotten what freedom looked like.

The morning had already crawled inside her skull and made a nest—too many missed calls from Nana, too little sleep, too much time turning over the last week's conversations with Dejuan. Every word now seems staged, every laugh premeditated. He always called her "Queen," but these days it sounds like a job title. **Every crown carries its weight.**

She recites the rules to herself like a mantra: No makeup. No jewelry. No electronics. No glass. The guard confiscates her Queen's Crown hair clip—the one she wore for luck—flicking it into a bin without even glancing at her name stitched in gold thread on the lining.

"Ma'am, you're good," the guard says, tone blank as concrete. He hands back the bag, now rearranged into someone else's order.

Quanda shuffles through the next set of doors, shoes squeaking on spotless tile. The corridor hums under the weight of two hundred fluorescent tubes, all tuned to the exact frequency of despair. They process her through one checkpoint after another: wrists stamped, ID checked, badge clipped on. She keeps her eyes forward, ignores the posters on the walls ("Family is Rehabilitation!") and the way other visitors stare at the floor, as if the linoleum might swallow them whole.

A female CO in pressed blues meets her at the entrance to the conjugal unit. "You been to this one before?" she asks, voice clipped.

"Every month," Quanda says, forcing brightness into her tone. "Never gets less awkward."

The CO makes a sound—maybe a laugh, maybe a cough—and leads her to the end of the hall. "We'll search the room when you leave. Nothing gets flushed. Nothing gets left." She taps a keypad, unlocks the door, then steps aside.

Quanda & Dejuan | Conjugal Room, Late Morning

Inside, the room is colder than expected. It's furnished like a budget motel: two plastic chairs, a Formica table bolted down, a twin bed with institutional blue sheets and one flat pillow. A "Welcome!" sign in faded marker hangs crooked over a clock frozen at 11:42. Cameras nest in the corners, tiny red eyes blinking behind smoked glass. Quanda spots the microphone embedded in the smoke detector.

She sits on the edge of the bed, sets her tote down, and breathes in the undertone of old Lysol and fresh paint. She arranges her three permitted "comfort items" on the table: generic lotion, a battered paperback romance, and the same mint toothpaste she and Dejuan used as teenagers in Inglewood. She smooths the book's faded spine, wondering if she'll have time to read even one page.

There's a mirror over the sink. She angles herself to watch the door through it, one hand twisted tight in her braids. They've held up mostly, but the edges have come loose and need touching up. She runs her thumb across her scalp, finds the coin Nana knotted into the root at her crown. It throbs with dull warmth.

Don't let the darkness take her.

The door shivers on its hinges. The CO returns with Dejuan trailing behind, hands cuffed, eyes already locked onto her. He's bigger than last time—thicker neck, more bloat in the face, knuckles dusted with scars that weren't there in February. He wears the orange jumpsuit like armor. When the cuffs pop open, his wrists float free, but his hands never stop moving. He rubs his jaw, flexes his fingers, keeps his body loose.

The guard backs out. Dejuan grins wide enough to show gold in his bottom teeth. "Damn, baby. You got fine while I was gone."

Quanda stands, closes the distance, lets herself melt into his embrace. He smells like cologne from a magazine insert mixed with something bitter—bleach or institutional soap. For a second, the two years apart vanish and she's sixteen again, pressed against him under the bleachers, his hands tangled in her hair. She bites down hard on the memory, forces herself to stay present.

Conjugal Room, Early Afternoon

They separate. He pulls out a chair for her, all old-school gentleman. She sits, waits for whatever script he's practiced.

He starts with small talk: the weirdness of daylight, the pettiness of other inmates, how the guards moved him without warning last week. She listens, nods, throws in the occasional "For real?" and "Damn, that's wild." They dance this routine for half an hour, sharing microwaved coffee from paper cups. She keeps her voice calm, careful not to let the edge creep in.

Then, finally, she asks: "You got it?"

He blinks twice, then pulls something from his waistband—an old iPhone, screen cracked, back cover missing. He sets it on the table face down. "Don't leave no fingerprints," he says, but it's almost a joke.

She slides the phone over, thumbprints already slicked across the surface. "Did he text you again?"

He hesitates, then shrugs. "Every week. Like clockwork."

She flips the phone. The password is still their old house number. She scrolls through texts: numbers, dates, addresses, all in shorthand she's learned to decode. She recognizes one address—her own.

"You tell him about me?" She looks at Dejuan, lets her voice drop.

He stares at the wall, flexes his jaw. "Ain't nothing to tell. You ain't involved."

She pulls the folded photo from her jacket and slides it across the table. "Explain this, then."

It's a print from an old phone: Dejuan and a younger man with a toothy smile, arms draped around a man in uniform—Lance Rivers in full blues, eyes glassy and happy. There's a barbecue grill in the background, red Solo cups in every hand, a summer day that never should have been captured. The moment looks ordinary except for how Dejuan and Lance stand together, too close for coincidence.

Dejuan goes still. For the first time since he walked in, he looks cornered.

"I found it in Nana's house," Quanda says. "You wanna tell me what Rivers is to you?"

He stares at the photo, then at her. "You coming here to cross-examine me now?"

She keeps her voice even. "I'm coming here to ask if you're safe."

He snorts. "That's bullshit."

Conjugal Room, Confrontation

Quanda leans forward. "You never once told me you knew him. You let me walk around, run my mouth to people, like I wasn't sitting on a time bomb. You think I don't recognize the name of the cop who got Tasha put away?"

A vein in Dejuan's temple pulses. "You think you can just walk in here asking questions?"

She folds her hands. "If you want me to keep coming, I need the truth."

He pushes away from the table, chair screeching. "I don't owe you nothing," he spits. "You ain't never done a day in this place. You got no idea what I gotta do to stay alive."

Quanda stands, voice trembling. "If you're running girls for him, you gotta tell me. You gotta let me help."

He laughs, but there's nothing warm in it. "Help? Only thing you can do for me is keep your mouth shut and your legs open."

White rage climbs her throat. She moves toward the door.

He's on her in two steps, blocking the exit with his body. "You not going nowhere," he says, breath wet and sour. "We're not done."

She tries to push past, but his arms close around her like steel bands.

"Let me go," she says.

"No," he whispers, voice dead calm. "You not gonna fuck this up for me."

He shoves her backwards, hard. She crashes against the bed, knees buckling. He's on her in a flash, hands around her throat. The pressure comes fast, like a car crash—her head fills with light and then nothing. She claws at his wrists, nails drawing blood, but his grip only tightens. He leans in, forehead pressed to hers, voice soft.

"You always had to make shit harder than it had to be," he says. "Couldn't just stay out of it."

Her vision dims. She tries to scream, but oxygen won't reach her lungs. The room shrinks to a pinpoint of color—Dejuan's face, jaw set, eyes wet with something that isn't regret. She thinks of Mama Esther, of the beads and prayers, of how every woman in her family died with secrets on their tongues.

The patterns speak if you know how to listen.

She goes limp. He holds on for another second, maybe two, then lets her slide to the floor. She lands hard, cheek pressed to tile, mouth open in a last question.

Dejuan | Conjugal Room, Aftermath

Dejuan sits on the bed, hands shaking, blood dripping from three deep gouges on his wrist. He breathes slow and careful, then stands. He smooths the sheets, wipes her face with the clean side of the pillow, and arranges her arms at her sides.

He walks to the sink, runs water over his hands. The phone is still on the table. He wipes it down with the edge of his jumpsuit, deletes the last dozen texts, then sets it back on her lap.

He checks the cameras—blinks to them, nods, makes a show of panic. Then he calls out, voice ragged: "Help! She fell, I think she's having a seizure!"

Footsteps thunder down the hall. The CO bursts in, sees Quanda's body, sees how her eyes are already gone.

Dejuan puts on his best performance: hands trembling, voice cracking, tears on demand. He rocks back and forth on the bed, face in his hands, while guards and nurses descend like a murder of crows.

Nobody asks the right questions. They bring in the medical examiner, who pronounces her dead. Nobody calls the police.

He watches them load her onto a gurney, the Queen's Crown hair clip tucked into her pocket. Nobody checks inside her mouth, where the coin from Nana's braid sits like a curse, humming and waiting.

When the room is empty again, Dejuan sits on the bed and breathes in the Lysol, the plastic, the absence.

He waits for the cameras to blink off before he lets himself cry.

Holloway, Rivers, & Chin | Phillips State Prison, Conference Room, Afternoon

The conference room at Phillips State Prison is always freezing, even in July. The vents blow a chemical blizzard strong enough to erase sweat from anyone's upper lip, but Judge Holloway's face stays slick and shiny no matter what. He sits at the head of the battered faux-mahogany table, sleeves rolled, tie askew, reviewing a sheaf of printouts. The clock over the door ticks loud enough to drown out distant shouts from intake.

"Let's make this quick," Holloway says, flipping pages. "I'm due at the university for a ribbon-cutting at eleven."

On his left, the warden—Pierce, built like a sandbag—clicks a pen in and out, never writing anything. On the right, the medical examiner: Dr. Chin, small and tidy, hair perfect, hands fidgeting with her ID lanyard. At the far end, Captain James Rivers stands with his back to the window, eyes fixed on his phone. Every few seconds, he glances up, then down again, like he's keeping score.

Pierce opens: "We had a fatality in conjugal. Female visitor, Dowans, Shaquanda. Death ruled natural. Only issue is the press sniffing around, thanks to the victim's past involvement with state legislators. I recommend we treat as closed."

Rivers keeps quiet, thumbs texting. Holloway skims the incident summary. "No drugs, no assault, no security lapse?"

"Nope," Pierce says. "Clean as a whistle."

Holloway clicks his tongue. "You said natural. Cause of death?"

Dr. Chin clears her throat. "Acute cardiac arrest. She had an undiagnosed heart defect. Family history suggests genetic predisposition—sudden, unpreventable."

Holloway stares, unimpressed. "Any record of medical issues before this?"

Dr. Chin shakes her head, then looks down at the table. "No, but these conditions are often asymptomatic."

Rivers steps forward, pocketing his phone. "The guest log shows she exercised her rights, nothing out of order. The husband's record is spotless. Nobody has motive. If we drag this out, it opens us up to liability."

Holloway's eyes sharpen. "You speak for the family, Captain?"

"I know the community," Rivers says. "They'll want privacy. Nobody wants their daughter autopsied for the evening news."

Conference Room, Aftermath

Holloway shrugs, signs the top sheet. "Let's not make this any more complicated than it needs to be. We clear the record, move on."

Pierce gathers the paperwork, double-checking for missing signatures. Dr. Chin takes her copy but doesn't move.

Holloway eyes her. "Problem, Doctor?"

She hesitates, voice flat. "We're not required to perform a full postmortem?"

"Not unless the family demands it," Holloway says.

Rivers smiles, just the corner of his mouth. "And you're not going to hear from them, I guarantee."

Chin nods, but the line of her jaw tightens.

Holloway stands, pushes in his chair. "Another one closed. Good work, people." He doesn't look at anyone as he leaves, shoes squeaking on linoleum.

Pierce follows, bantering about college football. Only Rivers and Dr. Chin remain.

Rivers sits on the edge of the table, staring at the paperwork. "You did the right thing."

Chin's hands shake as she puts her folder in her bag. "It's not right. The bruising—her neck—"

Rivers leans in, voice soft. "Nobody's asking you to lie. Just don't dig too deep."

Chin looks up. "This is my name on the line."

"Your name, your job, your daughter's scholarship," Rivers says, not quite a threat, not quite a statement. "They'd be disappointed if you lost your standing."

Chin blanches. She gathers her things and leaves, clutching her bag like a shield.

Rivers lingers. He walks to the window, watches the yard fill with inmates on rec hour, then dials a number from memory. "It's handled," he says when the line clicks. "No blowback." He listens, nods, then ends the call with a satisfied sigh.

He takes the file—"Dowans, Shaquanda—Deceased"—and slides it to the bottom of the stack. He snaps a rubber band around the folder, careful to avoid the blood on his thumb, then drops it in the bin marked "Archive."

He wipes his hands on a tissue, tosses it in the trash, and walks out without looking back.

Tasha | Patterson & Rynes Law Office, Afternoon

Tasha Rivers never expected to step into a law office except in handcuffs. Today, she stands in the lobby of Patterson & Rynes with nothing binding her except the prison-issue cardigan borrowed from a halfway house on Auburn. The place smells like varnish, lemon cleaner, and old money. Dark wood paneling climbs the walls. Every surface gleams, from the reception desk to chairs upholstered in something too smooth to be real leather.

A receptionist with a face like frosted glass tells Tasha, "Ms. Patterson will be with you in a moment." She hands her a clipboard, points to the signature line. Tasha scrawls her name, the pen trembling in her hand. It's the first time in years she's written it without a guard looming behind her.

Ms. Patterson appears, a vision in pinstripe, short curls tight to her scalp, mouth painted the color of a threat. She shakes Tasha's hand, all business, but the grip is warm. "Come with me."

The conference room is built to intimidate. Table long enough to seat a jury, bookshelves loaded with thick, gold-lettered volumes. A wall of framed diplomas leans above an oil painting of a Black woman in judicial robes—maybe Patterson's mother, maybe a role model, maybe a warning. Sunlight leaks through the blinds in hard-edged stripes.

"Have a seat, Ms. Rivers."

Tasha slides into the chair. It swallows her, makes her feel like a kid again, waiting for someone to scold her for tracking dirt on the carpet. Patterson opens a leather folder, checks the first page, then looks up.

"I'll get right to it. You're the sole beneficiary of the Queen's Crown Salon. Real estate, equipment, inventory, all debts settled. There's a life insurance policy attached as well." She pushes a stack of papers across the table. "Sign here, here, and here."

Tasha stares at the forms, then at the keys sitting next to them. A Queen's Crown keychain, still wrapped in plastic. It catches the light, flashes purple and gold.

She blinks. "I ain't—" Her throat closes. She tries again. "Nobody told me she was even thinking about—"

"She made the change two weeks ago." Patterson's eyes are calm but sharp. "I sent a courier to the prison. They said you refused visitors."

Tasha flinches. "I wasn't in no mood for company. Not after—" She cuts herself off, jaw clenched.

Patterson slides a sealed envelope across the table. "This came with the will. Said you'd know what to do."

Tasha picks it up. The handwriting is all sharp corners, the same way Quanda wrote shopping lists. "Open now," it says. Tasha rips it. Inside is a single page, torn from a salon receipt pad.

"Recognize the patterns I couldn't see. —Q."

Tasha reads it twice, then a third time, as if a different message will appear between the lines. Her stomach hollows out. The heat behind her eyes threatens to spill, but she blinks it away.

Patterson watches her. "You don't have to talk about it. But if you have questions, now's the time."

Tasha traces the ridges on the keychain with her thumb. "Why me? She got a whole family. Cousins, her son. Why leave it to me?"

"Because you're the only one she trusted." Patterson's answer lands heavy. "She said you kept her honest."

Tasha wants to laugh, but her mouth won't work. "I spent my whole life trying to protect her, and look where she ended up."

Patterson softens, voice low. "She knew the risk. Said as much, the last time we met."

Tasha turns the letter over. On the back, just a smudge—maybe from Quanda's lipstick, maybe from tears. "She ever talk about being scared?"

Patterson nods. "Said someone was watching her. She wouldn't say who."

Tasha folds the paper and slides it into her pocket. "I'm gonna find out."

Patterson pushes the keys closer. "Take these. The shop is yours, effective immediately. I'll handle the paperwork."

Tasha stands, feet unsteady. The world outside the conference room suddenly seems brighter, too loud, like her senses have been set to max. She pockets the keys, the letter, the deed.

At the door, Patterson stops her. "Ms. Rivers. Be careful."

Tasha turns, meets the lawyer's eyes. "I always am. That's why I'm still here."

She walks out, Queen's Crown keys heavy in her hand, the patterns of her old life and Quanda's new secrets burning through her brain.

Outside, the atmosphere is wet and electric. She lets herself breathe it in. She walks toward the train stop, each step putting distance between her and the last eight hundred days.

But it's not freedom, not yet. It's just the start of the job.

Queen's Crown Salon, Evening

The Queen's Crown Salon never closed for rain, riots, or rolling blackouts. Today, someone jammed the front door open with a brick, as if the building can't bear to hold a single extra memory. Tasha steps inside, braced for the chemical stink of hair dye and acetone, but the first thing that hits her is gardenia. Bouquets line every surface—funeral-home lilies, wild roses from backyards, even a couple of sad carnations from the gas station up the block. Candles stand in huddles, wax pooling on the laminated countertop. The reception desk is a shrine, every inch covered with photos of Quanda. In one, she's mid-laugh, mouth open, head thrown back. In another, she's serious, caught adjusting a client's curl, eyes locked to the camera as if daring it to look away first.

Tasha stands just inside the threshold, wind from the AC licking her calves. Every head in the room turns her way. Some faces light up—old regulars, maybe, or the kids she'd once given dollar braids to for summer camp. Some look scared. Most just look tired.

A little girl in a star-spangled sundress tugs her mother's sleeve. "That's her," she whispers, loud enough for the whole place to hear. "That's Miss Tasha."

The mother fumbles for words. "We're sorry for your loss."

Tasha nods, not trusting herself to speak. She moves past them, down the row of stations. The chairs are all still turned out, half-rotated as if Quanda and her clients just stepped away for a smoke break. At the first chair, a half-used roll of foil glimmers in the sunlight. At the second, a rat-tail comb sits crosswise on a towel. At the third, Quanda's station, every tool is perfectly arranged: shears lined up like soldiers, clippers plugged in, the appointment book open to a day that would never finish. The date at the top is circled twice, but the rest of the page is blank.

On the edge of the mirror, someone's scrawled a message in lipstick: **"See you on the other side, Queen."**

A group gathers near the back—five or six women in sweats and slippers, each with a paper cup of sweet tea. They talk in low voices, sharing fragments of gossip and memory. One sees Tasha, waves her over.

She moves toward them, feet numb. She tries to remember the last time she was here, but her mind skips like a scratched CD. Was it the day of the raid? Was it after? She can't recall. She only remembers Quanda's hands in her hair, braiding tight, whispering about love and loyalty and how no man was ever worth your edges.

Someone hands Tasha a cup. She sips, the sugar making her teeth buzz.

"She really left it all to you?" one woman asks.

Tasha shrugs. "Guess so."

They stare at her, waiting for a story, a speech, a tear. She has none of those, so she just stands and lets the moment roll over her. Eventually, the group drifts apart, each member pulled away by their own private loss.

Queen's Crown, Alone, Night

Tasha finds herself at the window, staring out at the street. Traffic moves slow, the sun already turning the asphalt to liquid. She presses her forehead to the glass, lets the cool help her think.

Recognize the patterns I couldn't see.

She goes to Quanda's desk, sits in her chair. The seat is warm from the candles nearby. She picks up a pair of thinning shears, turns them over, studies the way the handle fits her palm. She sets them down, opens the bottom drawer, and sifts through the contents: appointment cards, sample dye packs, a half-eaten protein bar. At the very back, a business card: Phillips State Prison, VISITATION OFFICE, with a number written in blue ink.

She flips the card. On the back, a date and time, circled twice: "April 19,

12:30 PM."

Tasha looks at the clock on the wall. It's almost three. She traces the edge of the card, thinking of Quanda alone in a room with Dejuan, thinking of what would make her risk a visit after months of silence.

A sharp pang hits her—a memory, sudden and bright. Quanda, standing at this same desk, telling Tasha about her first day at the salon. **"It's not the scissors or the shampoo that matter," she'd said. "It's the way you treat the head underneath."** She'd pointed at her own skull, tapping the temple. **"You gotta see what's going on inside, or you'll never get it right."**

The room starts to spin. Tasha clenches the arms of the chair, breath coming short.

She's not sure if she passes out or falls asleep, but she wakes to find herself in a different space.

The lights are dim, the walls painted lavender. Quanda stands at the center of the room, back to Tasha, braiding a mannequin's hair with the speed and precision of a machine. The pattern is tight, intricate, a grid of diamonds inside diamonds.

Quanda doesn't turn. "You watching me work, or just spacing out?"

Tasha tries to speak, but her mouth won't open.

Quanda laughs. **"Always did have more mouth than sense, girl."** She finishes the braid, clips it, then spins the chair around.

Her eyes meet Tasha's in the mirror. They're wide, wild, full of secrets. **"Look closer."** The words echo. The vision dissolves.

Tasha comes to, hands gripping the edge of the desk. Sweat beads on her lip. The salon is empty now, the crowd gone, the gardenia wilting.

She wipes her face, then looks again at the business card, the appointment book, the open laptop on the counter. She logs in—password is still "qqueen"—and pulls up the calendar. There's one event, all in caps: "VISIT DEJUAN."

She sits there for a long time, reading the line over and over, looking for what she missed.

A fly circles the candles, trapped between wax and flame.

Tasha looks up at Quanda's photo, the one with her laughing. **"I see you,"**

she whispers. "I see what you wanted me to find."

She stands, brushes her hands on her jeans, and moves to the door. Before she leaves, she turns back, surveys the salon—the thrones, the mirrors, the shrine, the faint hum of air conditioning.

It's not a home yet. But it's a beginning.

And she knows what to do next.

Quanda's Office, Night

At the back of the Queen's Crown, past the last row of mirrors and the dispensary closet, a narrow door hides Quanda's private office. Tasha unlocks it with a key that sticks, the click loud as a shot. Inside, the walls glow in pastel pink—old paint, faded by sun and time. There's a diploma from Pivot Point tacked up crooked, two "Entrepreneur of the Month" plaques, and three different photos of Arman, always the same hesitant smile. A poster reads: **"Black Don't Crack, but Business Sure Can."** The words hit different now.

Tasha sits at Quanda's desk. The worn chair shows coffee stains and the outline of Quanda's hips. She pulls open the first drawer. Notebooks, mailers, old cash register tapes. In the back, a square of yellowed tape marks where something used to be. She shuffles through receipts, the daily junk of a life in motion.

The file cabinet is next. Tasha slides it open and rifles through folders—clients, tax returns, an envelope marked "Personal." Inside: old birthday cards, a drawing from Arman ("You're the best, Mom!!"), a letter from an ex, torn but saved anyway.

She goes through the rest of the drawers, feeling like a thief in her own house. Nothing jumps out.

She turns back to the desk. The bottom drawer won't budge. Tasha yanks, puts her shoulder into it, and it comes loose all at once, nearly sending her to the floor. The space behind it is hollow. She feels around and pulls free a small, battered jewelry box. It rattles. Inside: a USB drive, a tiny Ziploc with two teeth (baby teeth, labeled "A's"), and a Polaroid. She stares at the photo for a long time.

It's a backyard cookout, plastic chairs and aluminum trays stacked with ribs. Dejuan and Lance stand in the center, arms slung over each other's shoulders. Lance wears plain clothes, but his cop's stance is unmistakable. He's smiling—smiling with all his teeth, head thrown back like he owns the atmosphere. Dejuan looks tense, eyes off to the side. In the back, blurred but unmistakable, Captain Rivers leans against a fence, a can of beer in his hand, gaze fixed on something (or someone) out of frame.

Tasha flips the photo. On the back, Quanda's handwriting: **"Family is who you make it. Sometimes who you fake it."**

She pockets the photo and opens the USB drive on Quanda's laptop. There's a password. She tries "qqueen," then "arman2009." The second works. A folder appears: "For T." Inside, a single file—a journal, dated three days before Quanda died.

Tasha reads.

> *March 17. Met with Dejuan in visitation. He's not the same. Keeps asking about Rivers, wants to know if Tasha ever said anything. Thinks I'm hiding something. I told him about Roxie, about the baby. He got real quiet. I don't trust him anymore. He's hiding something big. Maybe Tasha was right all along.*
>
> *March 19. Got a call from Rivers. He says he's protecting me, but it's all threat. Says he can make my life easy or hard. Says if I want Arman safe, I need to "keep the line open." I'm scared to leave the house now.*
>
> *March 20. Found a bug in my car. Took it to the shop, the mechanic found it under the seat. I smashed it. I want to tell Tasha, but she has enough to worry about. Maybe I'll give her the salon after all. She'll know how to keep it safe. Maybe she'll do what I never could: burn it all down.*

Tasha reads the entries twice, knuckles blanching white on the mouse. She prints the file, then deletes it from the laptop, just in case.

She's about to close up when her phone rings—a number she doesn't recognize. She answers anyway.

A whisper on the other end: "Tasha? It's me."

Tasha's heart stutters. "Roxie? Where you at?"

"Not safe to say. I'm at a payphone. I think they're watching me. I saw a black SUV outside the apartment—parked all night, didn't move."

"Who's in it?"

"I don't know. But the license is government. Georgia State. I checked."

Tasha thinks fast. "Come to the salon. Tonight. I'll leave the door open, back entrance. There's a space upstairs. You remember?"

"Yeah. I remember."

"Bring nothing but yourself and whatever you can't live without. No phones. You hear me?"

"I hear you."

The line clicks dead.

Tasha & Roxie | Queen's Crown, Apartment Upstairs, Night

Tasha hangs up and moves fast. She closes the office, locks the drawers, and hustles up the back stairs to the apartment above. She flicks on the lights, surveys the mess—half-empty storage bins, Quanda's old comforter thrown on the futon, a photo of Arman taped to the fridge. She strips the bed, digs out fresh sheets, cleans up the kitchen counter. She finds a can of air freshener, sprays it until the chemical citrus chokes out the stale.

She checks the window locks, the deadbolt on the stairwell. Then she grabs the box of old candles from the hall closet. The labels say "protection," "ward off evil," "peace." She lines them up on the sills, lights every one.

She takes the business card from her pocket—the Phillips State Prison number—and puts it next to the phone. She tapes the Polaroid to the inside of the kitchen cupboard, a warning and a reminder.

When she's done, the room feels less like a hiding place and more like a fortress.

She stands in the doorway, arms folded, watching the candles burn down to nothing. Her mind goes silent for the first time since the funeral. **The**

patterns Quanda missed are now clear: family, loyalty, power, betrayal—all laid out in the braid, strand by strand.

She doesn't move when the footsteps hit the stairs. She doesn't flinch when the door pushes open, slow and careful.

Roxie steps inside, belly huge, face drawn. She looks like she hasn't slept in days. Her hands shake, but her eyes are fierce.

Tasha holds out her arms. "You made it."

Roxie melts into her shoulders, shuddering, but no tears come. She just hugs Tasha tight as a tourniquet.

They stand together, the ghosts of their pasts pressed close.

Tasha sets her jaw. **She's lost enough friends to the Rivers family. She's not about to lose another.**

14

INTERLUDE: THE GIRL WHO SAW TOO MUCH

Some women survive by speaking. Others by listening.
The rest by never letting anyone know which is which.

Roxie | Queen's Crown Salon, Back Room | Present, Night

Roxie Williams's knuckles looked like they'd been through a half-dozen rounds with a belt sander—half scab, half lotion—because nothing in the world worked a girl down to the bone like a crib assembly manual. The directions, if you could call them that, spread across her lap in jagged folds, damp at the edges from the wet hush of baby wipes she kept using to mop the grime off her own hands. Queen's Crown Salon's back room was supposed to be a sanctuary, but the concrete cinderblock walls held on to every chemical spill and burned scalp from the last three decades. Even with a fresh coat of lavender paint and a sticker chart on the mini fridge, the space smelled of hot combs, melting plastic, old fear, and just now: baby powder.

The scent of baby powder and perm chemicals—the perfume of new beginnings and old survival**—hung in the air, grounding her in the present even as it threatened to pull her back.

Roxie gripped two slick pine rails between her knees and balanced the phone on her thigh, the blue glow of its screen flickering between a YouTube tutorial and a series of muted texts from "Mom2." The "Mom" part meant nothing; the number changed every six months, but the guilt that came with it stayed the same. The "2" at the end—that was the joke, the lie, the fiction of found family.

She eyed the time, then Crown, curled up in a repurposed laundry basket, blanketed in a dish towel with a faded Atlanta Falcons logo. He slept open-mouthed, drool pooling at the corner, fingers curled into tiny balls that occasionally punched the air in slow-motion startle. His hair grew in uneven patches: some days tight spirals, some days wild tufts like the top of a dandelion. She watched his chest rise and fall, soft and untroubled, and wished, just once, for her own body to remember how that felt. *Maybe it would come back after all the court dates and the threats stopped.*

She jammed the pine slats into the sideboard, nearly splitting the wood, then turned the screws by hand, watching how the tip of the screwdriver whittled away at her thumbnail. Every few minutes she'd hit resistance, strip the screw, and curse under her breath. She'd put together beds for other women's babies—one time, a full toddler bunk for the shelter's playroom—but it felt different when every misaligned hole and bent bracket meant your own kid was less likely to sleep through the night.

A salon timer trilled from the next room. Roxie froze, half expecting a social worker to materialize and declare her unfit for child furniture, but it was just the usual chatter—an endless shuffle of women, wigs, and whispered prayer requests. Someone was arguing over a roller set; someone else practiced a monologue for Tuesday's custody hearing. The voices made a counterpoint to the drilling of her thoughts, and even as she focused on aligning the crib panels, she picked out every word.

She knew the rhythm: Queen's Crown ran on an axis of gossip, hustle, and sanctuary, and if you worked your way into that orbit, you learned to count on the women who kept it spinning. Esther, who owned the place, ran a side business out of the front: charity in the form of tea, secondhand purses, and a revolving closet of prom dresses for girls who never got to be girls. Esther kept her own past in a hush—just the tattooed numbers on her forearm and the old Bible she never let out of her sight. To Roxie, she was the first adult who looked her in the eye and saw something besides a walking case file.

It wasn't a secret why Roxie worked here. The pay sucked, but Esther let her sleep in the break room as long as she pitched in, and the other women respected her more for what she'd survived than for anything she could do with a blow dryer. In this world, she was the girl with a story, and that meant she'd never really leave it behind.

She wiped her forehead with the back of her arm, glanced at the phone again. The notifications had stopped, or maybe she'd trained herself not to see them. Either way, the **silence ticked in her ears**. She worked faster, hands shaking as she locked the frame into place and stood back to admire her handiwork. It looked almost real—like something you might buy in a department store, if you were the kind of mom who shopped in the baby section instead of swiping from a donation bin.

Her gaze drifted to the battered rabbit sitting beside the box of screws, its fur gone patchy and one eye stitched in lopsidedly. The thing had been hers since before foster care, before the city, before she learned to weaponize her own vulnerability. She pressed the rabbit into the crib, then pulled it out again. The plush was dirty, the ear crusted with something that might have been old blood. She turned it over, fingered the faded purple "R" on the tag, and wondered how much of her was left in any of the artifacts she kept.

"Don't matter how much you clean it, child." Esther's voice, deep and sandpaper-smooth, drifted through the crack in the break room door. "It's still yours. Past and all."

Roxie didn't answer. She pressed the rabbit down between the crib bars until the stuffing squished out the side. The gesture felt final, even as she knew **nothing ever really ended**. She looked at her arms: still trembling. The skin on her forearm shone with a faint shimmer where she'd drawn over the butterfly tattoo—three times over, in ballpoint, just to see if it would look any less stupid with wings.

Esther appeared in the doorway, carrying a chipped mug of coffee and a plastic container of rice cakes. She wore her hair in a severe silver bun and didn't smile often, but she always looked at Crown like she'd been waiting her whole life to see him. She set the mug down, eyed the crib, then Roxie.

"You finish?" Esther asked.

"Almost." Roxie shrugged, reached for the last bolt, and spun it into place. "They say babies sleep better in their own beds."

"They say a lot of things." Esther took a slow sip. "You need anything, you holler."

Roxie nodded, the heat in her throat making it hard to swallow.

Esther left the door open behind her. Roxie lifted Crown, cradling his heavy body against her chest. He woke, blinked, and latched onto her shoulder with a low, guttural noise. Roxie set him down inside the crib, arranged the towel around him, and tucked the rabbit under his arm. She stroked his hair, feeling how it curled around her fingers like **memory**.

She sat back on her heels, wiped her palms against her jeans, and traced the butterfly behind her ear. The wings looked ragged in the overhead light, but the body was still solid, still inked deep enough to last.

Crown cooed, a wet burble that might have been a laugh. Roxie tightened the final bolt, checked the stability, and whispered, "We made it, little man." Then she pulled the blanket up to his chin, breathing in the sharp, clean tang of baby powder, and exhaled a promise she would never say out loud: *nothing would ever break him. Not while she still had hands to fight it.*

The scent of baby powder and the battered rabbit in her palm—these were the bridges to the past.

Roxie | MARTA Station, Atlanta | Past, Age 14

The cold metal of the MARTA bench pressed into her thighs, the scent of rain and burnt sugar in the air—it all came back as Roxie closed her eyes.

Fourteen-year-old Roxie—barefoot, hoodie zipped up to her jaw, hands pocketed so deep her wrists disappeared—made the cold metal bench her home base. She'd counted three hundred and seventeen rivets in the platform's railing by noon, not including the ones painted over with bubblegum graffiti or scored with pocketknife initials.

Rain sluiced down the platform stairs, funneling office types and hustlers alike into the teeth of the city's next urgent thing. **Nobody looked at Roxie. Nobody ever did unless she wanted it.** She grasped girls like her fit only two safe categories: invisible or dangerous. She didn't have the body or voice to bluff "dangerous," so she became expert at the other. She watched the crowd's swarm, catching shards of Spanish from a cleaning woman and French from a couple of exchange students. The rest was English: orders barked into Bluetooths, threats hissed between the teeth, and the everyman hum of people pretending they had somewhere better to be.

Roxie scribbled it all down in her notebook, a junk-mail envelope scavenged from a trash can. She wrote in micro-script, a habit from hiding notes in foster care, so every inch counted. Some pages listed phone numbers, while others recorded overheard secrets. Her favorite: *Never let anyone see you eat. That's how they know you exist.* She'd heard it from a woman with three lip rings and a portfolio case; Roxie respected the wisdom enough to try it out. Four days, no one called her out.

By the time the night shift clocked in, the overhead lights flicked to their after-hours half-bright. The place filled with a different breed: men in orange vests and work boots, kids still in their school uniforms, old drunks pacing the yellow line. Roxie caught every detail. The click of a zippo lighter three benches down, the syrupy cough of a toddler, the way the new security guard checked his reflection in the ticket machine before he did a round. She logged it all, then double-checked her escape routes in case she needed to disappear.

She watched the clock, counting each minute by the flicker of the arrivals board. She never let her guard down. Once, early on, she'd dozed off with her knees hugged to her chest and woke to find an old man pawing through her backpack. She'd bitten his hand so hard his palm bled and he cursed her for a devil, but what scared her most wasn't the theft—it was how soft his touch had been before he got caught. She didn't let herself forget that. She didn't let herself forget anything.

A girl with blue braids plopped down two seats away. Her jacket hung heavy with rain, and she reeked of fryer oil and the chemical sweetness of grape soda. She eyed Roxie, sidewise, maybe looking for a fight or just bored. Roxie braced herself.

"Yo," blue-braids said, "you got a phone?"

Roxie shook her head.

"You know when the 6:40 hits?"

Roxie pointed at the flickering LED board. "Late again. It always is. You better off taking the Red."

Blue-braids grunted, tugged her hood down further, and started peeling at a scab on her knuckle. "You here every day?" she said, not really a question.

"Only till I got somewhere better to be."

"Shit," said blue-braids, "me too." She stuck a wet finger into her mouth, sucked on it, and spat over the platform edge. "If you wanna make money, there's this dude who pays for feet pics. You got nice feet?"

Roxie looked at her toes, pale as wax and knobby from running in too-small shoes. "He'll take any feet. Dude's nasty."

Blue-braids snorted. "Told you, hustle. You'll get nowhere with nothing."

They lapsed into silence, both watching the arrivals board, both pretending they weren't measuring each other. When blue-braids's train screeched into the station, she rolled up without a goodbye, gone as fast as she'd come.

Roxie tucked her knees to her chest, feeling the cold of the bench soak straight through her jeans. She read back her notes, adding a few more lines to the list of "ways to survive." Her handwriting was smaller than ever.

A memory flickered, uninvited: *The first time Mama left, she said, "You're the only one who'll ever keep track of your own self. Nobody else will remember what's yours."* Roxie had believed her, even after she'd come back two weeks later with new hair and a new boyfriend. That boyfriend had eyes like gunmetal and a smile that bled, and Roxie learned to avoid both. *Sometimes the fridge was full, sometimes empty. Sometimes the house held music, sometimes screaming. The only constant was that Roxie had to keep her own story straight, because nobody else would bother to.*

Back in the present, the station drained of people. Only the janitor and a man sleeping upright on a bench remained. She left her bench and made for the shadows, notebook pressed to her chest. In a service corridor, half-hidden by a stack of sandbags and a sheet of plywood, she built her camp: a space just wide enough for her to stretch out and no one to see her unless they were looking for it.

She rolled onto her side, breath clouding in the chill. She read her last entry before shutting her eyes: *Nobody sees the girl who sees everything.* She smiled, just a twitch. Then she closed her notebook, wrapped her arms around her knees, and listened to the distant rumble of trains running all night, *mapping the city in her sleep.*

Roxie | MARTA Station, Atlanta | Past, Night

*The hum of trains, the cold bench, the battered notebook—*these were the constants.

After midnight, the MARTA station puddled with rain and the leftovers of a Friday crowd. The glare of platform lights made everything look hungover: streaked concrete, empty coffee cups, the rainbow oil slicks that snaked around every dark corner. Roxie hunched under the narrow awning, backpack braced between her knees and hood tugged to the bridge of her nose. She liked this time of night best, when the city forgot itself and the people left behind became shadows. Focusing became simpler as distractions vanished.

That's why she noticed the girl before anyone else. A familiar wobble in her walk, hair like molten gold even slicked down by the rain. Roxie squinted and placed her: not a friend, but a regular. She'd shared a bench with her once, weeks ago, both of them waiting out a thunderstorm. The girl had offered half a sandwich—PB&J, sticky with cheap jelly—and Roxie remembered her laugh, sharp like she didn't care how much it echoed.

Tonight, the girl wasn't laughing. She moved fast, head down, feet slapping through shallow puddles. A man in a red windbreaker followed two paces behind, his steps too casual, too staged. Roxie watched them cut through the ticket lobby, past the vending machines, toward the side exit, where the light vanished. She felt her stomach twist: something wrong. She wasn't the only one who saw it, but she was the only one who cared enough to watch.

She grabbed her notebook and followed. She kept her distance, feet silent on the wet tile, just close enough to catch the edge of their voices. The man said something low, and the girl sped up. He grabbed her arm, but she spun out, almost slipped, then bolted for the stairs.

That's when the SUV pulled up, black-on-black with tinted windows and plates smeared in mud. A second man hopped out. The girl tried to scream, but it got swallowed by the screech of an inbound train. The two men muscled her into the backseat, slammed the door, and peeled off. Roxie watched the taillights until they disappeared behind the parking deck, heart jackhammering against her ribs.

She ran. Not after the SUV—she knew better than to chase—but straight to the blue-lit call box by the stairs. The button stuck, and her voice echoed flat and tinny through the line. She rattled off the details: girl, blond, white windbreaker, black SUV, two men. The dispatcher promised to "dispatch an officer for routine check-in." Routine, like abductions happened every night.

Roxie stayed put until the cop showed. He lumbered over with his belt loaded heavy and his eyes already tired. She pointed him to the tire tracks, the girl's dropped phone case, the metal signpost bent where the SUV jumped the curb. He nodded and made notes on a pad, barely glancing at the details she'd burned into her memory.

"Did you see the license plate?" he asked, monotone.

"No," said Roxie, "but I got the make, model, two faces. I know which direction they went."

He grunted. "Anything else?"

"She tried to scream. The train—" Roxie stopped herself, realizing how pointless it sounded. She watched as the cop pocketed her words, already folding them away as impossible.

He squinted at her, skeptical. "You sure you weren't imagining things, sweetheart? That's a bad stretch. People see shadows. Lotta girls like to run off."

She pulled her notebook from her pocket, thumbed to the page with the sketch and the quick notes she'd made while watching. She handed it over. "Look. That's her. She's here a lot. Maybe check the footage?"

The cop took the notebook, skimmed it, and handed it back. "I'll do what I can," he said. Then he glanced at her, really looked for the first time, and saw what she was: soaked, skinny, backpack ratty at the seams. Just another throwaway kid. He made a decision. "You need a ride somewhere?"

Roxie shook her head.

He gave her a long stare, then walked away, boots squeaking on wet tile.

She stayed under the awning until the rain stopped, watching the station hollow out. She replayed the scene again and again in her mind, making sure every detail stuck. *Nobody else would remember, but she would. She always did.*

Silence is a shield, she wrote in her notebook. But sometimes it's a shroud. The words stung as she wrote them, the pen nearly tearing through the damp paper.

When the last train pulled out, Roxie slipped behind the pillars, into the safe dark. She made a nest out of her backpack and jacket, closed her eyes, and let the city hum cradle her to sleep. But tonight, there was no comfort. Only the memory of a girl vanished, and the certainty that no one would ever come looking.

That night, Roxie made a promise: If nobody else would remember, she would. And one day, she'd find a way to make the city listen.

Roxie | Atlanta Community College, Journalism 101
Past, Age 18

The battered notebook, the hum of trains, the memory of the missing girl—these were the seeds of her resolve.

Roxie didn't trust classrooms, but she trusted lies even less. She wedged herself into the back row of Atlanta Community College's Journalism 101, bag propped as a barrier between her and the aisle. The walls of the old annex bled with condensation, and the flicker from the overhead tubes made her eyelids twitch. Each seat creaked like it resented the body on top of it, and every student wore the same look of last-chance desperation.

Budget cuts eliminated the GED program last year, and that's why Roxie is here; a sympathetic social worker convinced her a diploma was a "game-changer." She kept her head down, notebook out, and took notes in a cipher she'd invented years ago—a code that meant nothing to anyone but her.

The "Best of 1978" faculty portrait yielded the image of Professor Dr. Carlson: corduroy blazer, wire-rim glasses, permanent scowl. He kicked off every lecture by invoking "Woodward and Bernstein," his voice a droning crescendo of self-importance. The syllabus promised hard-hitting news analysis and "field assignments" but, so far, the hardest hit was the slow drip of coffee into his ancient thermos.

Roxie didn't mind. She watched the class like a hawk watches roadkill, cataloging every tic, every insecurity. She found the stories others missed: the silent rivalry between the two suburban boys who vied for the professor's approval, the former Army medic with a melted ear, the trans girl who never spoke unless asked, but whose written essays made Roxie's skin prickle.

The real lesson, though, came after the third week. Carlson called her to his office, said her piece on "transit invisibility" was "the best freshman copy I've ever read," and would she consider helping him on a special project? She said yes, because that's what you do when a gatekeeper opens the door.

His office was a converted broom closet, lined with journalism trophies and musty books. He closed the door, dropped the blinds, and offered her a seat. She stayed standing.

"Let's speak off the record," he said. He smiled, but it didn't reach his eyes. "You've got grit. The kind of focus you can't teach. I want to mentor you."

Roxie leaned back against a file cabinet. "What's in it for you?"

"Nothing inappropriate," he said, but the room felt smaller by the second. "I just want to help. Sometimes, you gotta work the system to get your story out there."

She watched his hands: one on the desk, one on his thigh. She'd seen this scene before. "And if I don't?"

His smile stayed fixed. "Then maybe you don't get the letter. Or the feature spot. Or the scholarship interview."

She nodded, cool as ice. "Let me think on it."

She left his office, heart a mess of nausea and fury. She didn't go home. She sat in the parking lot, listening to her own footsteps in her head, replaying every word, every gesture. She had her phone set to record the minute she walked in—old habit, never leave yourself unprotected. She spent the night cutting the audio, stitching together the greatest hits: the innuendo, the threats, the patronizing "off the record" sleaze.

The next day, she printed a transcript and stuffed it in every faculty mailbox. She sent the audio to every campus media outlet, every student blog, every journalist whose email she could find. She uploaded it to her social. Then she waited.

The explosion was almost immediate. The campus paper ran it as a "Special Report." Carlson got suspended pending review. By the afternoon, the administration summoned Roxie to the dean's office.

They called it "disruptive behavior," "unsubstantiated rumor," "harmful to the academic environment." She watched them twist their words into knots, doing anything to avoid admitting the obvious. The dean, a woman with a voice like glass and a smile that could cut steel, told her, "We can't allow this type of vigilante conduct."

"You want me to be quiet," Roxie said.

"We want to preserve the community," the dean replied.

"You want me to disappear."

The dean paused, then nodded. "Sometimes the best thing is to step away. To heal. To let the grownups handle it."

Roxie packed her bag, walked out of the office, and never looked back.

On the ride home, she refreshed her notifications every block. Dozens of shares. Messages from other students—girls mostly, some boys—saying "thank you," "you got him," "it happened to me too." None of it made her feel better. She knew the system would close ranks, that Carlson would land at another college in six months. That she'd lose her spot, her credits, and the illusion that truth ever protected anybody.

She didn't go back to Queen's Crown right away. She wandered the blocks around the school, watching as the world spun on, unaffected. She stopped at a pawn shop, traded her textbooks for cash, then spent the rest of the day eating French fries at a corner diner. She filled a whole notebook, start to finish, with everything she remembered, every detail she refused to let the world forget.

After sunset, she slipped into a library, used the public terminal to send a last message to the dean: *If you want to bury a story, you better bury me with it.*

She closed out her email, walked to the station, and disappeared into the night, exactly as she'd been taught. But this time, everyone knew her name.

The battered notebook, the memory of the missing girl, the system's silence—these were the reasons she'd never stop fighting.

Roxie | Queen's Crown Salon, Front Room | Past, Late Pregnancy

The battered rabbit, the battered notebook, the battered heart—these were the things she carried.

By month six, Roxie's pregnancy outed her everywhere she went. Nobody stared, but she'd see them clock the bump, do the math, and look away. She drifted through the city in loose layers and a sweatshirt three sizes too big, always scanning for places to disappear. Most nights she crashed in a friend-of-a-friend's living room, or the twenty-four-hour laundromat down on Simpson. But rumor had it there was a spot that took in single girls, no questions asked—just a name and a promise to help out with chores.

She found Queen's Crown on a Tuesday, late autumn, the air cold and sharp with woodsmoke and something rotting in the gutters. From the sidewalk, the place looked shut: metal grates on the windows, every inch of the glass door papered with hair product posters, job listings, and, underneath it all, layer upon layer of missing-persons flyers. Roxie recognized some faces, didn't recognize most. She stopped, counted the flyers, and ran her finger over the edges of the oldest ones. It felt like a dare.

The door buzzed when she pushed it. Inside, Queen's Crown was nothing like she'd expected: warm as a living room, lit by lamps instead of fluorescents, the air thick with the smell of hair oil and cinnamon. Esther sat at the front desk, her glasses perched on the tip of her nose, plaiting her own hair while reading a paperback. She looked up, eyes cool and blue as river ice.

"Name?" she said.

Roxie hesitated. "Diamond," she lied, and almost laughed at herself for bothering.

Esther nodded, gestured to the table near the heater, and set out a chipped mug. "We got tea or instant coffee. Biscuits if you want." Her voice held no judgment, just the slow patience of someone who'd lived through every kind of emergency.

Roxie took a seat, warming her hands on the mug. The other women—three today, not counting the toddlers chasing each other in the back—barely glanced up. One folded towels, another glued rhinestones to acrylic nails, and the last flipped through a stack of battered Vogue magazines. Each wore her own version of armor: a headscarf, a gold chain, a careful smudge of lipstick.

For a while, nobody asked questions. The heater groaned, the toddlers shrieked and cackled, and Esther's knitting needles tapped out a steady rhythm. Roxie felt her pulse slow for the first time in weeks.

Eventually, Esther spoke. "How long?"

Roxie blinked. "Since—what? The baby?"

Esther nodded.

Roxie shrugged. "Don't know. I lost track."

Esther looked at her over the rim of her glasses. "Not a thing you lose easy."

"Didn't have a choice," Roxie said. She meant it to sound hard, but it came out soft.

Esther nodded again, as if she'd heard the same story a thousand times, and maybe she had.

The afternoon faded into evening. Esther brought out a crockpot of stew—mostly beans, some mystery vegetables, but it filled the room with a homely warmth. Roxie watched the way the others moved: the casual sharing of bowls, the small kindnesses, the way one woman instinctively shielded a toddler's head from the corner of a counter. It made her feel like she was trespassing on something private, a ritual older than the city itself.

After dinner, a volunteer—white girl, maybe college age, wearing a shirt with the logo of a battered women's hotline—came in with a bag of donated clothes. She took one look at Roxie's hoodie and started rummaging.

"This'll fit," she said, holding up a wool coat. She smiled, teeth slightly crooked but honest. "Winter's coming. Gotta keep the little one warm." She didn't ask permission, just draped the coat over Roxie's shoulders.

Then, from the bottom of the bag, she pulled out a thin, dog-eared picture book. The cover was faded but the title glowed: "Where the Sidewalk Ends." Roxie laughed, a real laugh, before she could stop herself.

"My favorite," she said, and the volunteer's smile went wider.

Esther watched it all, eyes half-lidded, then muttered, *Sometimes, the only shelter is each other.* She said it quiet, but it carried through the whole room. Nobody disagreed.

Roxie finished her tea, tucked the coat around her bump, and left with the book hugged to her chest. Outside, the city was the same as ever—cold, dark, full of teeth. But she walked slower, not bothering to hide, and when she looked back, she saw Esther watching from the window, knitting needles flashing like a promise.

For the first time, Roxie thought, Maybe I'll go back tomorrow.

Queen's Crown Salon, Back Room | Present, Night

The battered rabbit, the battered notebook, the battered heart—these were the things she'd carried, but now she was building something new.

Monday, Queen's Crown hummed with the static of blow dryers and the shouts of toddlers fighting over a set of plastic dinosaurs. Roxie parked herself in the break room, sleeves rolled past the elbow, piecing together the last side panel of Crown's new crib. Her fingers smarted from a week of half-shift cleaning gigs and the stubborn bolts that refused to seat straight. She gripped the screwdriver, jaw tight, and drilled until the wood creaked in protest.

Crown sprawled on a blanket at her feet, fists waving in the air, his legs a blur of motion in the pastel thunderclouds of his onesie. He'd found his own toes last week and never got tired of the trick, grabbing each foot like it was a magic act and giggling at the result. Roxie watched him from the corner of her eye, equal parts pride and terror; it never stopped feeling like borrowed time, this peace.

Esther stepped in with a pair of hair shears, shook her head at the progress, and said, "That thing gonna survive a toddler?"

"Probably not," Roxie said. "But it only has to outlast the next year." She lined up the panel and rammed the bolt home, ignoring the way her palm ached. "Besides, Crown'll find a way through anything. He's stubborn."

"Don't know where he gets it," Esther said, dry as sawdust, then left to break up a hair-pulling contest out front.

Roxie sat on the floor, legs numb, and looked at the finished crib. The wood was scuffed; the corners chewed by someone else's baby, but it stood straight. She reached for Crown, scooped him up, and cradled him against her chest. His body went soft, sleepy, his head flopping onto her shoulder. She tucked him into the crib, arranged the battered rabbit next to him, and smoothed the blanket over both. He blinked once, then drifted off.

Across from the crib, a wall of faces watched her. The advocacy board had started as a single flyer, but now ran end to end, each girl's picture and name and the date she'd vanished. Roxie traced them with her eyes: some she'd known from shelters, others from the MARTA platform. She remembered them all, the stories they told and the ones they didn't get to finish. She added her own face to the wall in her mind, knowing she'd spent years dodging that same fate.

But not Crown. Not if she could help it.

She inhaled, the scent of baby powder and lemon polish mixing in her throat. She pressed her palm to the crib's edge, feeling the grain, the stubbornness of the wood. She whispered, "You're safe," and meant it, if only for tonight.

She drew her knees to her chest, sat with her back to the wall, and let her head rest against the cool plaster. The salon noise drifted through the door—a lullaby of women's laughter, gossip, and the low, constant murmur of hope. Roxie watched her son sleep, his breath slow and steady, the rabbit's ear draped over his cheek like a shield.

She thought of all the things she'd carried: notebooks full of loss, scars old and new, the stories nobody else wanted to remember. She thought of the girls on the wall, and how she owed it to them to survive, to fight for her own and every other kid who slipped through the cracks.

Tonight, at least, she'd built something nobody could tear down. She smiled, small and stubborn, and closed her eyes, letting the world spin past without her.

Outside, the city howled and threatened, but inside the break room, Roxie's future curled up safe, and the girl who'd seen too much finally had something worth holding on to. And for the first time, she wasn't just surviving—she was building something that might last.

15

INTERLUDE: THE MAKING OF A MONSTER

A secret is a chain—each link forged in silence,
each silence heavier than the last.

James Rivers | Downtown Atlanta | Past Midnight

Rivers' office thrummed with the static charge of sleeplessness. The clock on the wall: 2:27 AM, but he hadn't bothered to track hours since sunset. Rain clawed at the windows in sheets, crawling over the glass in greasy rivers that turned the neon cityscape into a smeared bruise. Down below, the last stragglers of the night trawled Peachtree, hoods up, hustling under the sickly pinks and blues leaking from flickering signs: ADULT EMPORIUM, PEPSI, JEWELRY BUYERS, all their dreams renting space on the same damp block.

Rivers slouched behind the desk, a slab of mahogany too large for the cramped room, the surface drowned in open folders, burnt-out pens, and the remains of a Marlboro pack bleeding ash into his coffee saucer. He kept the lights low. Easier to see the files that way; easier to see the city's shadowplay, the way it slid between truth and myth. He scratched the scab on his wrist, picked at a grease stain on his shirt, and thumbed open the manila folder stamped in ugly red: HENSON / BRINSON / 4-BODY HOMICIDE.

He flicked through the photos, each printout rimmed with the jaundiced glow of the station copier, each face frozen in that final, meat-puppet snarl. He didn't blink. You could get used to this after fifteen years, or at least he had. Sometimes he wondered if it was the bodies or the paperwork that deadened him. He thumbed the victim index: four Black males, early twenties, each with the kind of rap sheet that read more like a side hustle than a life. The last page had his own scrawl in green marker: *Who benefits?*

He blew out a tired, nicotine-stained sigh and fished the old photograph from his inside blazer pocket. It was soft at the edges, like it'd sweated through too many summers. The woman smiled in the sun, holding a squinting toddler who looked everywhere but the camera. Rivers pressed a thumb to his temple, massaged the headache already blooming behind his eyes. He traced the kid's face with a knuckle, feeling the punch of memory. He put the photo aside, grabbed the crumpled letter half-buried under case files. Still unread, still mocking him. The envelope trembled in his grip.

Rain hammered louder, and the city's sirens pressed against the glass. Three long wails in rapid succession—police, not ambulance, not fire. Rivers shivered, poured two fingers of bourbon into his glass, watched the amber stick to the sides like sap. He drank in slow, measured sips, letting the burn cauterize the night's failures. The phone on his desk buzzed, breaking the lull, and Rivers jerked his hand, sloshing bourbon on a stack of reports.

He watched the spill seep into the paper, curling the pages, **rewriting official history in the language of stains**. The phone buzzed again—caller ID masked, per department protocol for after-hours. He stared at it, waiting out the ring. Third buzz, and he picked up, didn't speak, just waited for the static to resolve into a human voice. All he got was a single breath, slow and deliberate, and the line cut dead.

He set the phone down. Listened to the silence mutate into a high-pitched ring in his ears. In the window, the city lights caught his reflection—distorted, the lines of his face split into segments by rivulets of rain. He saw the old man version of himself, tired, jaw slack, eyes gone vague at the edges. The bourbon glass hovered near his lip, but his hand shook too much to finish the shot.

He wanted to smash the glass. Instead, he swallowed, set it down, and lit another cigarette. The glow of the cherry cut through the office gloom, **the only reliable truth left in the building**.

A siren howled up from the street, closer now, almost directly below. In the neon spatter, a black-and-white jerked to the curb. Rivers watched, impassive, as two uniforms dragged a handcuffed kid out of the backseat. He recognized the walk: kid was maybe fourteen, already knew not to stumble. The older cop shoved him against the hood, said something—Rivers couldn't hear—but the body language was all Old Testament. Kid flinched once, twice, then just stared dead ahead while the cop talked into his ear.

The image split time for Rivers. For a second, he wasn't here—wasn't in the office, wasn't captain, wasn't even fully grown. *He was back in his own skin at ten years old, ear mashed to plywood, counting footsteps in the hallway.* Then a sharp sound, almost a scream, brought him back.

He closed his eyes. Opened them. Touched the tip of the cigarette to the edge of the family photo. Watched the heat singe the corner, watched the face of the woman blur and warp. He shook ash onto the desk, then flicked the rest into the trash.

Phone buzzed a third time—shorter, more insistent. Rivers ignored it. The bourbon did its work; the warmth coasted his veins, blunted his thoughts. He looked again at the rain—at his own doubled face—and wondered which one of them was really here.

Down below, the kid in cuffs screamed out, "Y'all ain't got nothin' on me!" The cop kneed him in the thigh, hard enough to fold him over. The kid spat blood onto the sidewalk. Rivers grunted, not in approval or disgust, but with the ache of recognition.

He watched the patrol car drive off, lights fading into the wet dark. The city pulsed, unconcerned, **its neon heartbeat stronger than the people inside it**. Rivers ground out his cigarette. He pressed trembling fingers to his temple and waited for the next call, the next case, the next stain.

A memory snapped in his head, triggered by the wail of the siren and the old, battered photo still curling at the desk's edge. He stood, knees cracking, and let the bourbon finish the job. He thought about calling someone—anyone—but knew it would be pointless.

Instead, he let the memory in. Let it tear him up, as the city's lights painted the world red and blue and ugly.

Edgewood, East Atlanta | 1978

He remembered the smell before anything else: fried grease and floor wax, the way it fought with the sweetness of rotting fruit in the trash. James was eight, or maybe nine, but already old enough to know which boards squeaked and which ones bit bare feet. He tucked his knees tight under his chin, pressed his back to the wall, and tried not to breathe too loud.

His mother's bedroom was two doors down, but he could hear every word through the cracked drywall. Her voice, always soft until it wasn't, had that brittle edge now. The john had a baritone rumble, more threat than volume. He'd come in on the tail end of *The Jeffersons*, still in his work uniform, his breath thick with Schlitz. The argument started slow, built quick. Money. It revolved around money.

"You think I got time to play games with you?" the man barked. The mattress whined as he shifted his weight.

Mama's answer, muffled but sharp: "You want it, you pay up first."

Something hit the wall. James flinched, pinched his eyes shut, waited for the lull that never came. He peeked out from under the bed—slats warped, lint like cobwebs in the corners. The shadows cast by headlights through the front window strobed the wallpaper, rippling between dusty roses and brown water stains.

The john's voice slid down to a hiss, mean and pointed. "I said you owe me."

James caught the shuffle of feet, the scrape of a belt buckle. He wanted to shut his ears, but the words stuck in his head like splinters.

Then came the crack. Louder than thunder, meaner than the day his stepdad broke the living room TV with his fist. For a second, the house went dead silent.

He couldn't breathe. The taste in his mouth turned sour, like pennies. A single footstep echoed down the hall. James pushed himself out, careful, every movement slow and deliberate. The floor felt cold and sticky under his hands.

He crawled out just far enough to see the open door at the end of the hallway. The paint was chipped, the knob greasy from too many hands. His mother lay half-off the bed, blood soaking the sheets. The man just stood there, back to James, shoulders tight and unmoving. He didn't look at the body, or at the boy in the hallway.

In the next instant, a woman's voice cut through: "James! Baby, you here?" Maggie's voice, high and desperate. She barreled in through the kitchen, past the slack-jawed man and the cooling body. Maggie barely slowed as she dropped to her knees and swept James up, one arm around his ribs, the other cradling the back of his head.

He didn't cry. He remembered every detail, though: Maggie's perfume, cheap vanilla and menthol; the press of her freckled cheek against his; the way she whispered *It's okay, baby. It's okay, I got you. We outta here.* She dragged him up, past his mother's legs splayed on the bed. James stared straight ahead, locked eyes with the wall, wouldn't let himself look at the wet red.

Maggie hustled him out, not waiting for cops or coroner. She shoved a pair of pants and a jacket into a plastic sack, then snatched her keys off the busted TV. The pimp—James learned to call men like that "uncle" but he never did—watched them go, didn't say a word. Maggie shielded him as they stepped into the blue light. The whole block shimmered with humidity and the smell of rain on hot concrete.

She loaded James into the passenger seat of her old Pinto, engine rattling and radio stuck on AM. She buckled him in, hands shaking, and peeled out from the curb.

James stared at the floor, fists clenched, every muscle wound tight. Maggie kept a hand on his shoulder the whole ride, steering with her wrist. She told him over and over it'd be okay, he'd be safe, she was gonna fix everything.

He wasn't sure what that meant. He didn't sleep that night, or the next.

But he remembered the way Maggie held him, the way she didn't flinch from the blood, the way she looked him straight in the face and promised he'd never end up like his mama.

He believed her. For a while.

Englewood Courts, Atlanta Streets | 1984

Maggie's place had rules. First: never leave cash out in the open, even if it's just the two of you. Second: always keep the chain on the door, and never answer unless you hear the right knock. Third: nobody, not even her, got in the shower unless someone else was in the house to stand guard. For James, this made sense. He'd seen too many bodies—literal and otherwise—left to rot when people got careless.

Most afternoons, James helped Maggie roll bills. She liked the twenties crisp, fanned out like a casino dealer's hand; the singles she rubber-banded with cheap blue strips. They spread it all on her bed, neon-pink comforter with cheetah spots, counted once slow, then again fast. Maggie checked for fakes by holding them up to the bug-zapper light in the window. Sometimes she made a game out of it—first one to spot a bleach job or a funny ink stain won a Twinkie from the stash under her bed.

The rest of their life was out there, where the city never shut up. James tagged along, silent and sharp-eyed, past the liquor store that never fixed its broken letters, down alleys where the dumpsters hummed with rats. He learned to watch windows for movement. Learned that a car slowing to match your pace meant more danger than a guy yelling from the next block. Learned how to memorize plate numbers without ever letting your face say you noticed.

Maggie took clients at the Road King Motor Lodge, a box of stucco rooms shivering under the I-20 overpass. Every time they went, she checked the lobby for new faces—hookers, sure, but also the glassy-eyed men in suit jackets, the ones who didn't want to be seen. James stayed outside, sitting on the curb or pacing the parking lot, pretending to shoot hoops with an imaginary ball. He always clocked the motel manager's car first thing; the man liked to circle every hour, pretending to look for leaks but really just casing the girls.

The way Maggie ran it, James was the decoy. If anyone started watching too close or asked dumb questions, he was supposed to act lost, play up the sad foster kid routine, and draw attention just long enough for her to slide out of sight. Once, he even called 911 from a payphone, made up a story about a man with a gun on the next block. By the time the cops showed, Maggie was already tucked safe in their car, engine running. She laughed the whole drive home, told him he'd be a hell of a detective one day.

He didn't tell her how much it scared him. Or how good it felt to be useful.

At home, Maggie smoked menthols and chain-watched reruns. She taught James to read faces on TV—who was lying, who was hiding something, who had a secret weakness. "Don't trust people with wet palms," she said. "Or women who wear red lipstick to church. And if a man ever brings you a gift for no reason, you throw it away. Nothing's free, James, especially from men."

She let him take her empties down to the curb, taught him to double-bag the trash so the neighbors couldn't see the bottles. Sometimes, when she was between dates, she'd sit on the porch with a Miller High Life and tell stories about his mother. How they met in middle school, both new to the city, both desperate to not get noticed. How James's mom was the prettiest girl in the whole sixth grade, but would fight you to the bone if you called her "light-skinned." How she used to sneak out at night and write poetry on the side of the Winn-Dixie with shoe polish.

"She wanted more, your mama," Maggie said, blowing smoke up at the telephone wires. "And look what it got her. Don't ever want too much, baby. World don't let you keep it."

He thought about that a lot, especially when he was lying in the dark, **listening to the groan of cars on the highway and the buzz of faraway sirens.**

Westside Motel, Outskirts of Atlanta | Late 1980s

Some nights, the city chewed up all the oxygen, leaving only steam and exhaust for the people stuck in its gut. This was one of those nights: rain glossed the pavement, neon signs fizzled with every passing car, and the sodium lamps outside the Westside Motel buzzed like angry hornets.

James waited in the battered Civic, seat pressed to the floor, the windshield smeared with old resin and streaks of rain. He watched the entrance, watched the ghostly blue light flicker behind the lobby curtain, watched the shifting shadows that meant somebody was always watching back.

Maggie checked her makeup in the visor, then gave him a sharp nod. "You see anyone, you call for help. Don't try to be a hero." She smiled, but her hands shook on the purse. "I'll be out in ten."

James wanted to argue, but his mouth was dry. He watched her cross the lot, heels clicking on the wet concrete, umbrella catching the wind and flipping inside out. She tossed it in the trash and kept going, chin up. She didn't look back.

The cop was already there. James spotted him in a booth by the front window, nursing a Coke and trying to look bored. Windbreaker tonight, not the suit. He clocked Maggie, straightened, and flashed that fake-ass grin—one that said *I'm in control, you're the help.* James bristled, even though he knew the script.

Maggie slid into the booth. For a few minutes, they looked like any other pair: woman tired from her shift, man in town for a convention. He couldn't hear the words, but he read the body language. Cop kept his hands flat on the table. Maggie crossed her arms, leaned in close, let her hair fall in a curtain between them. At one point, the cop grabbed her wrist, hard, and she flinched. James felt his pulse spike.

Then, all at once, the cop turned, eyes locking on James through the rain-streaked glass. That's when James knew it was a setup.

Maggie caught the look, went stiff. She tried to stand, but the cop yanked her back down. Words now, sharp and fast, too fast to follow. Maggie shook her head, kept her voice even. The cop's face twisted, all the politeness stripped away. He spat something in her face—then slapped her, open-palmed, hard enough to snap her head to the side.

James bolted from the car before he could think about it. The lobby door felt like it weighed a ton, but he shouldered through, ignoring the old man behind the counter who mumbled something about "no trouble."

Inside, the cop already had Maggie pinned to the wall, forearm across her throat. He hissed something through his teeth, a word James didn't catch but recognized by the sound: not *whore*, but *nigger-lover*.

James saw red. He charged, swinging at the man's kidneys, but the cop barely flinched. He shoved Maggie to the ground, spun, and cracked James across the mouth with the back of his hand. The room tilted. James tasted blood, hot and metallic, but stayed up.

Maggie scrambled to her feet, tried to get between them. "It's me you want! Leave him alone!" she screamed, voice ragged.

The cop didn't even look at her. He backhanded her again, then dragged her by the hair into the hallway. James followed, staggering, fists clenched. Maggie screamed, kicked, but the cop was twice her size and mean as hell.

James lunged, grabbed the cop's leg, bit down hard through the cheap polyester. The cop howled, shook him loose, then smashed a boot into James's chest. He felt something crack, but pain didn't matter. Maggie's head slammed into the drywall, leaving a smear of lipstick and blood. The cop wrapped a fist in her hair and slammed her skull again, and again.

James crawled, legs barely working. He got hold of the cop's ankle and dug his nails in, desperate to break the man's balance. The cop wheeled, kicked him in the teeth, but this time James didn't let go. He clawed and bit and spat blood onto the floor, screaming Maggie's name.

The cop finally lost his balance, fell against the vending machine. Maggie slumped to the ground, coughing blood, eyes rolling up. James used the opening, grabbed the man's wrist and twisted, trying to break the grip. The cop slammed his elbow into James's face, once, twice, three times. Stars burst behind his eyes.

He heard Maggie, barely: *Run, baby. Please, just run.*

The cop yanked James up by the collar, slammed him into the wall, pressed a knee into his gut until he couldn't breathe. James saw the man's hand go for the gun holster, saw the snub nose of a .38 gleam in the flicker of the hallway light. He braced for the shot, but it never came. Instead, the cop pistol-whipped him across the temple.

James hit the floor, the air knocked out of him. He tasted linoleum, sweat, and his own blood. Maggie didn't move. The cop kicked him in the ribs, once for good measure, then stomped out. The world fuzzed out at the edges.

He crawled to Maggie, pulled her into his lap. Her face was a mess—purple, wet, one eye already swollen shut. She tried to speak, but only a wet gurgle came out.

James leaned in close. "Don't leave me, Mag. Don't you dare."

She smiled, or tried. Her lips barely moved, but he heard the words anyway: *Always... knew you was the strong one.* She touched his cheek with broken fingers, left a red smear there.

The last thing he remembered was the rain pounding the motel roof, the sick hum of the vending machine, and the distant echo of Maggie's laughter, **back when they were both still alive**.

Backstreets of Atlanta, then Quantico, then unnamed combat zones
Late 1980s–Early 90s

By sixteen, James ran half a block off Auburn Avenue. He wore a thrift store blazer two sizes too big and kept his hair close-cropped, so cops would mistake him for a church boy. The girls called him "Pastor," because he always showed up first to bail them out of a bad date, and because he could talk a client into paying triple without raising his voice.

He didn't use drugs, not even weed. Trusted nothing that dulled the edges. Instead, he learned to read faces—same as Maggie taught him, only now he charged a commission. If a john got handsy, James had a pair of lookouts waiting to burst in. If a trick tried to run out on the bill, James knew what car he drove, where he parked, and how to make the threat sound soft but real.

His toolkit: a butterfly knife from the pawnshop on Candler, a .45 stashed in the lining of his gym bag, a prayer card from Maggie, creased at the corners. He made rules for himself and his girls, stricter than Maggie's old list: *No repeat customers on Tuesdays. Never take a drink. You didn't pour yourself. Always, always watch for cops, but never run. Running was how people got shot.*

He taught them to trust him, but not completely. "Nobody's your savior," he said. "Not even me."

The first time someone came for his girls, James was seventeen. He saw the guy before the guy saw him—a gator-jawed ex-con in a Lakers windbreaker, eyes too far apart, smile like a crack in a skull. He'd heard about this one: liked to hurt Black girls, liked to leave messages in lipstick on bathroom mirrors. That night, the man had cornered Shaniqua in a backroom of the Lucky Dollar Motel, and the manager was on the take, so no one called for help.

James knocked once, then kicked the door in. The ex-con turned, half-drunk and all teeth. James shot him in the stomach before the man could say a word. The .45 bucked in his hand; the man folded, fell like someone cut his strings. Shaniqua screamed, then collapsed into James's arms, her face streaked with someone else's blood.

James dragged her out, paid off the clerk, and left the body for whoever cleaned up those rooms. He didn't sleep for three days. The memory of the shot—the way it echoed in the hallway, the way the man's mouth opened in surprise, not pain—stuck with him. The police never came. No one on the street mourned.

James made it clear, after that: If you touch my people, you die.

He lived in that space between fear and respect for another year, until the city got too small. The girls moved on, or disappeared, or got swallowed by bigger fish. James heard a rumor one of them made it to New York, started fresh, but he never checked. He wasn't sure he wanted to know.

At eighteen, James did something no one expected. He signed his real name on a sheet of paper at the Army recruiting station. Took the test, passed with numbers that made the sergeant stare. When the man asked why he was there, James said, "I want to be somewhere I matter." The sergeant called his answer "patriotic," but James knew what it really meant.

The Marines turned James into a better predator. They taught him how to shoot for real, how to read the heat off the ground and track a target through noise and dust. He never talked about his past; when the other guys bragged about high school or first loves, James just listened. He learned to fight close, learned to break a man's windpipe with the heel of his hand. He liked the rules, the structure, the clarity of mission. In the Corps, violence was a transaction. Nothing personal.

In Somalia, he killed men who looked like cousins, men whose faces reminded him of the bus stop on Boulevard. In Iraq, he lost three squadmates in one day and didn't cry. He stopped counting bodies. He stopped dreaming about Maggie, about Atlanta, about anything that hurt.

One night in Fallujah, he watched a city burn from the roof of a half-collapsed hospital. The sky glowed orange, and somewhere far off, a woman screamed and screamed until it sounded like laughter. *James laughed, too. He didn't know why.* The captain found him at sunrise, still on the roof, rifle balanced on his knees, face blank as a new wall. The captain said, "We can use more men like you, son." James said nothing.

When he left the service, James came home with scars on his hands and a piece of shrapnel in his thigh. He walked like his knee was glass, but he never let anyone see pain. He moved back to the city, kept to himself, got a job at a downtown security firm where his boss liked to call him "the pit bull."

The city was different now. His old block was all condos and dog parks; the Lucky Dollar was a Starbucks. Still, the rules were the same. People were just more polite about their violence. James worked nights, drank bourbon, kept a tight smile. He was good at his job. Never late, never lost his cool.

Sometimes, when the world got too quiet, he'd go for a walk down Auburn Avenue, past where Maggie used to buy cigarettes, past the old churches with their chipped white paint. He saw no one from the old days.

He didn't want to.

Family Apartment, Atlanta | Early 2000s

The echoes of war never left him. They clung to his skin, seeped into his bones, followed him home to the apartment where the walls were too thin and the bills too high. His wife—Nia, biracial, fair-skinned, with a voice that could cut glass or soothe a fever—tried to hold the family together, but James was a storm that never broke.

Tonight, the argument started over money. Nia's voice, sharp with worry: "We're behind again, James. I can't keep doing this alone. You promised—"

He snapped, the words coming out like shrapnel. "You are just like the other white ho bitches, trying to exploit the Black man to pimp them out. I'm doing the best I can!"

Nia recoiled, eyes wide, but she didn't back down. "Don't you dare talk to me like that. I'm not your mother, and I'm not Maggie. I'm your wife."

The room shrank. James felt the old rage, the old fear, the old need to control. He lunged, hands closing around her throat. Nia's nails scratched at his wrists, her feet kicking at the floor. In the corner, a very young Lance watched, frozen, a puddle spreading at his feet.

James squeezed harder, the world narrowing to the sound of Nia's choking, the terror in Lance's eyes, the echo of Maggie's last words. When Nia went limp, he let go. The silence was absolute.

Lance whimpered, "Is mommy ever going to wake up? Why she lying on the ground like that?" He crawled to her, shaking her shoulder. "Mommy, wake up, you scaring me. This is not funny."

James knelt beside him, voice cold as the grave. "Boy, here is the truth. Your momma ain't coming back, because I killed her. But it's not a reason to not allow life to carry on. From this day on, what happened here is our secret."

He extended a pinky finger. "Promise me, what happened here will remain a secret. If even one person knows the truth, the consequences will kill us both. Do you want to be dead like your momma?"

Lance shook his head, tears streaming. "No."

"Good. I'll find a way to cover this up." Rivers looked into Lance's tearful eyes, voice flat. "Remember, you are a man from this point on. **Real men hold the truth. Got it?**"

Lance, trembling, nodded. "Got it."

Church, Atlanta | Days Later

The crowd packed the church, the air thick with lilies and the low hum of grief. Rivers sat front row, Lance beside him, the boy's small hand clutching his grandmother's. Rivers' eyes were red, tears streaming down his face as he pressed a kiss to Lance's cheek.

He rose to deliver the eulogy, voice steady, words beautiful and raw. He spoke of Nia's kindness, her strength, her love for family. The crowd wept, moved by his pain, by the poetry of his loss.

Lance sat stone-faced, heartbroken and numb, staring at the casket. His grandmother's hand squeezed his, but he didn't feel it. All he could see was his mother's lifeless stare, the echo of his father's words: **Real men hold the truth.**

The funeral ended. The secret remained.

Downtown Atlanta | Just Before Sunrise

Rivers sat hunched over the desk, bourbon gone and ashtray a graveyard. His hand trembled every time he turned a page. Half the reports made sense only to him—lines scrawled in margins, names circled and crossed out, little arrows connecting dates and bodies and addresses like a subway map made for ghosts.

He couldn't let go of the Henson file. Every piece of shit trafficking ring in the city seemed to orbit this one bastard, and every time Rivers pulled a string, two more names popped up. He read the case notes again, focusing on the small things: who signed off on the search warrant, which judge set bail, which patrolman looked the other way. The patterns all led inward. He made a list of everyone who stood to benefit. He underlined his own name.

Outside, dawn punched through the night in ugly strips, but the rain kept the world gray. The city sounded close enough to touch—garbage trucks grinding, a siren warbling up the block, then back down. Somewhere, a woman screamed at a man, words blurred by distance and glass. Rivers grunted, felt nothing.

He'd lost the taste for sleep. Instead, he lived for these hours, when the rest of the world faded and it was just him and the weight of what he'd done. He lit another cigarette, watched the tip burn slow, and remembered the first time he killed a man. Sometimes he could see the guy's face, but most nights it was just a red hole where the eyes should be.

His phone vibrated. A text: *Meet @ HQ. 7AM. Don't bring anything.* No name. He deleted it.

Rivers rolled the bourbon bottle between his palms, stared at the smooth glass. He pressed his lips to the rim and drank air. He stared at his hands, the knuckles bruised and calloused, the tattoo on his left finger faded to blue. He remembered Maggie's fingers, the way they shook even when she was trying to hold him steady. He remembered the way she smiled, soft at the corners, when he did something right.

The rain let up, just for a moment, and the city caught fire with morning. The glass towers burned with light. Rivers closed his eyes, and the memory surged: *the sound of a body hitting linoleum, the warmth of blood on his hands, the way every good intention turned to shit.* He thought about the girls he couldn't save, the brothers he left in foreign dirt, **the chain of silence that started with his own mother and never stopped growing**.

He straightened his tie, stood, and drew the service pistol from his bottom drawer. The grip was slick, cold. He chambered a round, then set the piece flat on the desk. He waited for the knock, or the siren, or the order to come through.

He whispered, just loud enough for the room to hear: "It ends tonight."

Outside, the city howled. Rivers listened, and for the first time in years, **let himself feel afraid**.

16

WHERE MEMORY BLEEDS THROUGH

After the cut, the roots grow stronger.

Tasha | Queen's Crown, Back Office, Night

Tasha didn't come here for comfort. She came because Queen's Crown—its back office, especially—still belonged to Quanda. The air couldn't shake her: cocoa butter, synthetic vanilla, and the musky snap of isopropyl alcohol, layered in thick from a decade of hustle. The walls, sponge-painted ochre, pressed in around the room like they were trying to hold a secret.

Tasha let the door click shut behind her, then leaned against it for a breath, eyelids cinched tight, before turning toward the desk. She lowered herself into Quanda's old roller chair and studied the mountain of spiral notebooks in front of her. Some were fat and bloated, pages swelling from years of hair grease and cuticle oil; others, thin and limp, barely clinging to the wire coil.

She pulled one from the middle, careful, like it might crumble if she gripped too hard. A little faded cartoon sticker peeked from the edge—Tweety Bird, battered, one eye scratched away. **It was classic Quanda, always dropping some silly, innocent touch on even the most serious grind.** Tasha smoothed her palm over the cover. Shaquanda L. Dowans, neat and blocky, written in blue ballpoint. The L, for Latrice, curled with extra flourish.

Tasha thumbed to the page marked by a paperclip. Under a column of names and phone numbers, Quanda had drawn a grid: vertical lines, then horizontal, then arcs and loops, mapped like a subway diagram. Each intersection got a tiny star or arrow. Some places, whole clusters of circles bloomed together, then trailed off into a single, arrow-tipped line.

Tasha tapped the end of a pen against her teeth, lips mashed tight, scanning for a pattern she could name. **Every part of her wanted to call up Quanda, put her on blast for being so damn cryptic, but it had been seven months since Quanda walked out the house in her white Crown Royale smock and never came back.** The empty chair at the salon's main mirror stayed empty, even when rookies begged to use it. Her laughter clung to the halls, a high, pretty staccato, always flipping from giggle to cackle with no warning.

A sound snagged Tasha's ear—pipes settling, or maybe a late client in the front lobby. Her pulse hiccupped. She flipped another page, the pen pressed so hard into the notebook the paper buckled. Another set of diagrams, this time, box braids branching into wild, geometric shapes. At the margin, Quanda had scrawled "BUS STOP—5pm—S, G, 2xL" in urgent, looping script. Tasha underlined it, once, twice, then tore out the page, hands trembling.

She forced herself to look up, to take in the rest of the office. The old Gateway computer hunched in the corner, monitor flickering faint blue. The shelf above held a cracked plastic tiara—Queen's Crown's original, the one Quanda wore on their grand opening night—and three sticky bottles of eco-styler gel, labels worn down to ghosts. Tasha's gaze slid to the wall beside the desk. A cheap Walgreen's frame held a photo of Quanda, grinning next to a twelve-year-old boy with too-big ears and the best fade in L.A. Her son, Arman. Tasha remembered the day: Quanda refused to let anyone else cut his hair for his first day at Harvard Westlake, said he had to look like a prince, not a jester. She'd braided his edges so tight he'd yelped, then made him pose with her in front of the salon sign.

Tasha pressed the heel of her hand to her brow, like she could squash the ache back into her skull.

Memory | The Chair, Years Ago

The chair creaked under her as she twisted the ends of Kanekalon into a sleek, rope-thick plait. The girl—young, scared, reeking of hospital soap—winced every time Quanda's fingernails scraped her scalp. But Quanda kept up the rhythm: dip, twist, loop, clip, a sacred drumbeat that never faltered even as her voice dropped into a low hum.

"You need to keep your eyes on the blue mailbox," Quanda whispered, words timed between comb strokes. "He don't wait long. Soon as he see the red light, that's your cue. You got your bag ready?"

The girl nodded. "It's heavy," she mumbled. "You said not to pack nothing—"

"You bring the papers, the birth certificate, that's all you need." Quanda pinched the braid end with a rubber band. "Somebody meet you at the bus station. Her name start with L, she got dreads like me. Don't stop for nothing. I wrote it here," she said, then pressed a post-it note into the girl's shaking palm, folding her fingers over it like a prayer. "Don't open it till you cross Sepulveda."

The girl blinked away tears, staring at herself in the mirror. She almost looked like somebody else. She could be free, if only for a night.

Back Office, Night (continued)

Tasha gasped, loud in the sudden quiet. She blinked hard until the afterimage of Quanda's hands faded from her eyes.

She yanked a desk drawer open and fished out a mini bottle of E&J, swallowing half of it in one go. The burn dropped her shoulders half an inch. She shuffled through another notebook, looking for more dates, more clues. With each entry, her certainty grew: **the patterns weren't random. Quanda had mapped escape routes, coded them into hair appointments, weaving safe passage into the most ordinary of braids.**

A pang twisted in Tasha's chest, something between pride and fury. How many girls had passed through the salon, left with a new look and a sliver of hope, while Quanda risked everything to play conductor? And how many enemies had circled, waiting for a slip, a moment of weakness?

A knock snapped her head up. Tasha tensed, eyes darting to the clock. Just past midnight. Probably Arman, she guessed. He liked to haunt the back room when the city got too loud, burying himself in Quanda's ghost like it would teach him how to keep living.

She wiped her eyes with the back of her hand, then gathered the torn pages into a neat pile. Her thumb traced the thickest line in Quanda's diagram, where the pattern ended in a spiraled loop. Tasha didn't know what the symbol meant yet, but she recognized the logic, the code beneath the code. **Quanda never left anything to chance. Not when it came to protecting her own.**

"Alright, Q," she muttered to the empty room, voice thick and ragged. "I see you. I'mma finish what you started."

She tucked the notebook under her arm and shouldered open the office door, the aroma of coconut oil and acetone following her out, fierce as memory itself.

Tasha & Arman | Main Salon, Late Night

By the time Arman unlocked the back door, Tasha already had the main styling station cleared, every comb and brush lined up sharp as surgical tools. The salon looked half-alive this late: underlit, ghosted by the streetlamp outside, bottles of conditioner reflecting orange against the big front window. Only the buzz of the fluorescent bulbs kept the place from feeling like a shrine.

Arman shuffled in, lugging a cracked Dell laptop, two fistfuls of printouts, and a Safeway bag rustling with colored twine. He wore a hoodie, dark jeans, and black canvas Vans, each step slow and deliberate. Tasha watched him, noting the new lines on his face since spring break. **Grief aged Black boys too fast in this city.**

He set the laptop on the counter, booted it, then stared at the boot-up bar like he might will it to load faster. Tasha lifted a brow.

"You eat?" she asked.

"Nah. I grabbed chips at the bus stop."

Tasha made a mental note: send him home with leftovers, no matter what.

She let him work in silence, just like Quanda would have. They never pushed Arman; he was a locked safe, and you needed to work the combination slow, gentle. After ten minutes, he started spreading the printouts along the counter, fingers flying as he sorted them by color and date. Tasha uncapped the markers and started untangling the balls of string.

"Where you wanna start?" she asked.

Arman pointed to the map, which she'd already taped to the mirror in front of the station. It was the kind city planners used, street-level, showing every bus line, fast food joint, and liquor store from Inglewood to Compton. Someone had scrawled "QUEEN'S CROWN" in fat purple marker right at the intersection of Slauson and Overhill.

He handed her a sheaf of spreadsheet pages, each row listing a name, a date, a street, and what looked like a code: "B2L," "K24," "V-Plex." Tasha squinted at the page. "This Quanda's handwriting?"

He nodded. "And look—she's got a separate column for pattern type. The box braids, the Senegalese twists, cornrows, everything. She wasn't tracking just the girls. She was tracking the people moving them."

Tasha's heart picked up. "You sure?"

He tapped the map, then a spot on the spreadsheet. "Watch. Every time she writes K24, the appointment's on a Friday. Then if you look at the drop location, it lines up with the jail bus drop-off on Manchester."

She whistled, low and slow. "Smart as hell."

Arman gave a half-smile, the ghost of his mother flickering in it. He handed her a spool of blue string. "Let's do the cornrows first. Blue for that."

Tasha nodded, tying the end of the string to a pushpin. She jabbed it into the map where Overhill met Slauson, then pulled it taut toward the first address on the spreadsheet.

Arman mapped behind her, reading off the names and dates. "Mariyah, November 7th. Shaniqua, November 14th. Keisha, November 21st. Always a week apart."

Tasha pinned each one, letting the string stretch in a jagged, but unmistakable, line across the city grid.

They worked the map in silence for almost an hour, blue, then yellow, then red, colors bleeding across the streets in patterns that mimicked Quanda's own braid diagrams.

"You see this?" Arman muttered, squinting at a dense knot near the jail drop-off. "Every pattern ends here. Every time. No matter where it starts."

Tasha stepped back and let her eyes blur. The city map, covered in crisscrossing string and bright marker, looked like a lattice of arteries—every vein leading toward that one knot.

"Means it's a collection point," she said. "Somebody grabbing these girls all from the same damn spot."

Arman's jaw set hard. "Check this: every time the line changes color, it matches a different style in Mom's notebook. She wasn't just booking hair. She was flagging the girls for pickup."

Tasha felt her hands shake, so she flattened them on the counter. "You think she did it on purpose?"

He hesitated. "I think she tried to warn them. Or help them run. But I also think she figured out who was behind it."

Tasha looked at the knot on the map, then at the spreadsheet, and back to the map again. She could hear Quanda's voice in her head, the calm, no-nonsense tone she used when she was about to do something dangerous.

"You see this pattern, baby? This means somebody's got a plan. And if I break it, even for one day, they gon' notice."

She wondered how long Quanda had known, how long she'd been fighting the web, one haircut at a time.

Arman peeled another page off the stack and handed it to her. "This one's weird. It's just numbers. Dates, times, initials. No names."

Tasha scanned it, then felt her skin go cold. "These are drop-offs. Like—final drop."

He nodded. "See this sequence here? December 19, 23, 26. Two days apart. That's when Mom started staying late, said she was helping with the holiday rush. But nobody ever came in those nights. Not even walk-ins."

They stared at the map together, the tangle of string, the clots of color, the bright red pushpins at the drop-off spot. Tasha's throat went tight.

"She wasn't just doing hair," she whispered, barely more than a breath. **"She was mapping lives. Every single braid was a lifeline."**

Arman said nothing. He pressed his fingers against the edge of the map, not moving, just holding it in place. Tasha let the silence stretch out. They were close to something—closer than anyone had been since Quanda died.

She pulled the pushpin from the final knot, then pressed it back in, deep, as if to anchor the whole city to this one truth.

"Okay, Q," she said, not looking at Arman. **"We see you now."**

Tasha | Queen's Crown, Morning

The next morning, Queen's Crown hummed with the low-level panic of a Monday after a holiday. The air popped with blow dryer heat and cheap espresso, thickened by the tang of spritz and the sugar crust from pastries set out for walk-ins. Tasha finished her first client's edges before the new smartphone payment system locked up on her. She stabbed at the screen, but the damn thing insisted on "connection error," pulsing a tiny red exclamation point like it was mocking her.

Tasha squinted at the rectangle, lips pinched. "This thing got a demon in it," she said, then set it on the counter like it might bite.

Her client—a fifteen-year-old with flawless baby hair and a sticker-trapped phone—snorted. "You gotta hold it flat, Miss Tasha. The Wi-Fi only works by the back wall."

Tasha rolled her eyes. "Next you'll tell me it needs holy water and a jump start."

But she took the advice, holding the phone at arm's length while the teenager toggled the settings with practiced thumbs. The payment went through in two seconds, the phone flashing a green check mark.

"See?" the girl beamed. "Easy."

"Mm-hmm," Tasha said, then slicked the girl's side part with a last sweep of edge control. "You got brains and beauty. Don't let nobody play you."

As the girl left, Tasha heard the clatter of metal outside—the construction crew already tearing up what used to be a parking lot across the street. They'd started laying steel beams for the "Excelsior Brew Haus," a coffee shop for white people who liked open concept seating and oat milk. Next to it, the old cleaners was boarded up, windows tagged in silver marker: LAST DAY, GET YOUR STUFF, GOD BLESS.

Tasha felt the chill even through the hair dryer heat. She used to take her prom dress to that cleaners. She'd seen whole families come and go, decades of Easter suits and quinceañera gowns, vanished overnight.

A shadow moved in the frosted glass of the front door, then a hand slipped a bright blue flyer under the seam.

She snatched it up. "Grand Opening: Luxury Micro-Lofts, On-Site Gym, Starting at $2499/mo." At the bottom, in smaller print: "Exciting Investment Opportunities in this Emerging Neighborhood."

Tasha crumpled it, hard, and tossed it toward the waste bin. "Vultures," she hissed.

At the mirror, she picked loose hair from the brush and stared at her own reflection. Her eyes looked tired, red-rimmed, but she kept her shoulders squared. Two more clients waited in the lobby, scrolling their phones, pretending not to hear the drama unfolding at the register. Tasha inhaled and refocused, hands steadying as she prepped the station.

The next client was a woman in her sixties, wig slightly askew, suit jacket buttoned even though it was pushing eighty outside. She smiled as she sat, settling her purse on her lap.

"How you been, Miss Rivers?" the woman asked.

Tasha smoothed the cape over her client's shoulders. "Still here. Still fighting."

The woman nodded. "Some of us gotta stay, or else what's the point?"

Tasha caught the woman's gaze in the mirror. "Exactly."

As she worked, Tasha watched the street through the window. Every morning, the crowd on Slauson thinned. The men who lingered outside the bodega were gone, replaced by construction guys with names stitched on their sleeves. The candy store where Quanda used to get peach rings for Arman was now a CBD dispensary, windows tinted black.

The old world was slipping, but Tasha wasn't about to let it drown without a fight. She leaned into her work, letting the rhythm of the braids anchor her. Here, at least, she still knew every part of the job.

When the woman paid—cash, no phone necessary—she lingered for a moment at the door, looking out at the concrete and new scaffolding.

"They'll never get it," she said quietly. "What it meant to us."

Tasha smiled, but there was nothing soft in it. "We're not done yet."

When the last client left, Tasha made rounds through the shop, checking every detail. She double-checked the week's appointments, rearranged the styling products, and ran a finger along the spine of Quanda's notebook, which she'd left open at the front desk. She thought about Arman's map, the knots and strings, the way the pattern of their lives could still matter, even as everything around them changed.

Outside, the construction crew paused for lunch, workers hunched on the curb, laughing, alive, loud. Tasha watched them for a long minute, then pulled the shades half-shut.

Inside, the smell of coconut oil and flat irons lingered. **It was enough, for now.**

Tasha & Mama Esther | Queen's Crown, Next Day

The next day, Mama Esther occupied the big rocking chair in Queen's Crown's front corner. She'd claimed it years ago, when she first started working there, and nobody dared sit in it since. The wood creaked under her as she swayed, knees wide, feet planted like roots. On her lap, a small, weathered pouch spilled beads across her apron—black, gold, pale blue. Her hands worked with the muscle memory of generations, snapping beads onto fishing line with a precision that had outlasted six presidents and two ex-husbands.

Esther talked little before noon. She'd watch the shop, eyes hooded, and let the younger stylists fumble through their client drama, only interrupting when someone tried to rush the process. But that morning, she called Tasha over before the first appointment even walked in.

"You got the dreams again?" she asked, no need for small talk.

Tasha nodded, slumping into the vinyl chair beside her. She still felt the weight of last night's map session, the city etched in string behind her eyes. The sense of urgency hadn't faded—if anything, it pulsed sharper, like a nerve exposed.

Esther didn't look up from her work. "Tell me."

Tasha let the memories spool out: "Same as before. Quanda's sitting in the back, combing through them notebooks. She don't talk. She just starts braiding, but there's nobody in the chair. Her hands move like she's got invisible hair. And then she looks at me and nods her head toward the window, like I'm supposed to see something. I look, but it's always night outside, no streetlights, nothing."

Esther slid a gold bead down the string and clipped it in place. The beads clicked, a sound older than the shop, older than Tasha herself.

"What's she trying to show you?" Esther said. Her voice was low, almost a growl.

Tasha hesitated. "Maybe it's just... the streets. The way they all connect."

Esther's lips curved, but not into a smile. **"The crown protects the head, baby. But sometimes, it's not about protection. It's about connection."** She strung another bead, tight and sure. "You ever notice how every braid, no matter where it starts, ends up woven together? Even when you take 'em out, you still see the pattern on the scalp."

Tasha watched her, uneasy. "So, what, you think Quanda left me some kind of road map?"

Esther's eyes clouded, the brown of them gone glassy for a second. "I think she's telling you how to move next. Telling you how to survive."

A lull fell over the shop. One of the junior stylists paused at the sink, eavesdropping with wet hands frozen mid-rinse. Even the client in the waiting area put down her phone, attention fixed on Esther.

Esther threaded the last bead, then tied the end in a perfect, tiny knot.

"These ain't just dreams, child," she murmured. "She's mapping the Rivers for you."

Tasha blinked. "The Rivers?"

Esther looked up, smile hard and proud. "You know who runs this block now. You know which men sign their name in the blood of little girls." She pressed the string of beads into Tasha's palm, closing her fingers around it. "This is the pattern. You follow it, you don't let them break you. You hear me?"

Tasha nodded, the beads slick and cold against her skin. For the first time since Quanda's death, she felt something spark—clarity, maybe, or just stubbornness refusing to die.

Esther leaned back, satisfied. She nodded toward the back office, where the battered notebooks sat in a neat pile. "You got a job to do," she said, voice so quiet it barely touched the air. "Don't let her down."

The salon buzzed back to life. The junior stylist hurried to her client, suddenly gentle with the detangling comb. In the mirror, Tasha caught a glimpse of herself—shoulders squared, eyes fierce. She tucked the string of beads into her pocket, then stood and walked toward the back, already plotting her next move.

Tasha & Arman — Break Room, Later

Arman waited in the break room, the small square table covered in a mess of manila folders, loose photos, and half-burned candles. The stale air carried the funk of reheated food and old Lysol, undercut by the stubborn echo of braiding gel that seeped from the salon proper. Tasha ducked in, beads rattling in her pocket, and stared at the evidence fanned across the table.

He'd done his homework: family charts printed from Ancestry, crumpled printouts from blacked-out public records, even copies of a hundred-year-old newspaper with sepia photos and racist headlines. Tasha picked one up. A stiff-jawed man in police blues glared from the front page, a child on each knee. "CAPT. RIVERS WELCOMES NEW RECRUITS," the headline crowed.

"Look at this," Arman said, pulling a yellowed family tree toward her.

"Captain Rivers had two sons. One stayed in the force. The other went off grid."

Tasha tracked the line down, finger stopping at "Lance Rivers," then veering left to "Dejuan Rivers," born 1970, listed as "deceased." Except that wasn't true. Dejuan had just changed his last name, then disappeared into the prison system under an alias. Arman had the paper trail, cross-referenced with letters and prison logs. It was all here, plain as day.

"They played the city," Tasha said, voice tight. "Two streams, same damn river. One above ground, one below."

Arman nodded, somber. "And every time a new captain came in, it was just another Rivers. Cousins, nephews, always somebody with the blood."

Tasha shivered. "No wonder they always seemed two steps ahead."

She shuffled through the next set of records: transcripts from trials, parole board notes, even a few censored police reports. Every major trafficking bust for the last thirty years ended the same way—evidence lost, witnesses vanished, cases dismissed on technicalities. The men who ran the show either died in jail or turned up running new shops a thousand miles away.

Tasha's eyes burned as she read, but she forced herself to finish every line. She stopped at a photocopied page, the margins smudged from too many hands.

Inmate: Dejuan Hensen (formerly Rivers)

Location: Mule Creek State Prison

Classification: "Organized Crime, Life x 4"

Special Notes: "Known for recruitment and management of street-level 'girls.' Intelligence suggests ongoing operations with external accomplices."

She dropped the sheet, stomach curdling. "He's still pulling strings, even inside."

Arman pulled out a timeline, neatly highlighted. "Mom figured it out three years ago. She started tracking the transfers—where they sent the girls, what streets they vanished from, which days had the most traffic. She crosschecked it with the city's cop rotations. Every shift change, the numbers spiked."

Tasha scanned the line of dates, connecting each to the tangle of pushpins and string still webbed on the map from last night. She saw it now: each trafficking wave coincided with a Rivers family promotion, a badge pinned or a territory flipped. They'd been mapping the city not just for hair and safety, but for control.

She paced the room, too sick to sit.

"They used the salons. Ours, everybody's. Any place Black women could talk, they used it. Spied on us, groomed us, then sent us out like merchandise."

Arman's face looked ancient, heavy. "And they made sure nobody believed us. They made it a joke."

Tasha ground her knuckle into the table. "We are not a joke."

A silence fell, dense as wet cotton. Tasha kept reading, scanning for a weakness, an unguarded flank in the family's grip on the city.

It was all so methodical. Every ten years, a new "epidemic," the news cameras rolled in, and the Rivers cleaned up with new contracts and PR stunts. The city called them heroes. They called it legacy.

Tasha's hands clenched until the beads in her pocket cut crescent moons into her palm. She pictured the generations of girls—lost, returned, or vanished for good—braided into a story none of them ever signed up for. She pictured Quanda, alone in the back room at midnight, piecing this all together, then building a roadmap so her own wouldn't fall to the same fate.

"We gotta burn it down," Tasha said, and meant it.

Arman's mouth twisted, but he didn't argue. "We start with Captain Rivers. He's got a charity event next week. You know he'll show."

Tasha nodded, mind racing through the next step. "We need proof. Not just the map. Something nobody can erase."

Arman reached into the folder and pulled out a CD, labeled in Quanda's handwriting: "For Arman—trust nobody." He slid it across the table.

"Mom said this was the insurance."

Tasha took it, weighing it in her hand. She felt the shape of Quanda's love in the plastic—reckless, desperate, enough to get them both killed if they weren't careful.

"We do this loud," Tasha said. "No more secrets."

Arman gave a small, bitter laugh. "You sound just like her."

Tasha smiled, the first real one in weeks. "Damn right."

They cleared the table, sorted the records, and made a plan. For once, it felt like the city belonged to them again, if only for the length of a heartbeat.

Roxie & Tasha | Back Room/Nursery, Evening

The back room smelled like baby powder and fresh paint, layered on top of the sharp tang of perm chemicals that drifted in from the salon. The walls were only halfway patched, a bad blue showing through where the last coat had flaked. Boxes of donated onesies and pacifiers lined the counter, each tagged with a yellow sticky note: "Hope you like these!" or "Congrats, mama!" The crib sat in pieces on the tile floor, instructions lost in the shuffle.

Roxie stood over the mess, belly leading her like a ship's prow. She wore a too-tight tank top and yoga pants that dug into her calves, every movement a negotiation between discomfort and duty. She moved slow, sorting the baby clothes into piles by color—white, pink, the occasional gender-neutral green.

She stopped, hand pressed flat over the curve of her stomach, as if to quiet something restless beneath the skin. For a moment, her face went soft, almost peaceful. Then the tremor came: a quick, involuntary clench of her fingers, her other hand gripping the edge of the crib rail for support.

Tasha pushed in, carrying a handful of paint chips. "I got the soft yellow, the mint, and this one they call 'pale dawn.' I think that's just code for hospital hallway, but you never know."

Roxie tried to smile. "Yellow," she said. "I always wanted yellow. Feels like sunlight."

Tasha fanned the swatches out, then perched on the open window ledge. The air in the room was hot and stagnant, but she didn't seem to mind. She watched Roxie, careful, the way a mother watches a fever that's just starting to break.

Roxie slid the green onesie off the pile, fingers brushing over the words stitched on the chest: "New Day." She laughed once, low. "They got jokes. I can barely get out of bed some mornings."

"You don't have to be a hero," Tasha said. "Just get through today. Next day's got its own problems."

Roxie nodded, then knelt awkwardly to fit a slat into the crib. Her breath went short as she hunched over, a bead of sweat rolling down her neck.

"Sometimes I feel him kick," she whispered, not looking up. "And I want to love him. But then I remember whose blood he carries. And I get so mad I want to tear the whole world apart."

Tasha set the paint chips down, crossed to her, and knelt so they were eye to eye. "That baby's got your blood too. He'll have all of us. And he's got a mama who never quit."

Roxie bit her lip, hard enough to turn it white. She let the anger wash through, then, with a slow exhale, reached for the next crib piece. Tasha helped, her hands steady and sure. Together they built the frame, slot by slot, screw by screw. The work was awkward, sometimes clumsy, but every joint held.

When the crib stood upright, they admired it. Roxie rested both hands on the rail. Her face shone with sweat, but also with something like pride. She stroked the lacquered wood, then her belly, and for the first time, the gesture seemed to offer comfort instead of just control.

"You know what I want?" Roxie said, her voice low.

Tasha tilted her head, waiting.

"I want him to be safe. Even if I can't fix everything, I want him to wake up one day and not be scared."

Tasha smiled, a full, lopsided grin. "That's what the yellow's for. Little piece of sunlight."

From the hallway, the muted noise of the salon filtered in—laughter, gossip, the buzz of clippers. Tasha glanced at the clock. "We should eat before you pass out. I got greens and cornbread in the fridge."

Roxie nodded, then paused, eyes locked on the crib. "You think it'll be enough? Just... this?"

Tasha leaned in, kissed her forehead, and squeezed her shoulder. "It's a start. Sometimes, that's everything."

As they headed for the kitchen, Roxie stopped and pulled the green onesie from the pile. She held it against her chest, then folded it with care, laying it in the crib. She stood back, hands on hips, a smile twitching at the corner of her mouth.

Tasha watched, silent. She saw the change in Roxie, small but steady. She saw the future, bright and defiant, growing in the cracks left by old pain.

They walked out together, side by side, ready for whatever tomorrow held.

17

INTERLUDE: THE ROOTS OF SILENCE

Some crowns are forged in silence, and some in the noise we survive.

Tasha | Queen's Crown Salon, 1:07 A.M.

The hum in Queen's Crown at night isn't silence. It's the sound of what the day leaves behind—**smoke from burned sage curling up and fading into the air, the residue of relaxers and edge gel mixing in a way only Black hair salons can manage, sharp and sweet at the same time.** Tasha stands behind the reception counter, barefoot on linoleum, methodical as always. Outside, the city grinds on, but the walls here are cinderblock thick. **They keep out L.A., but can't hold back what's already inside.**

She sorts through the drawers, counting, then recounting the contents like it'll bring order to something bigger than inventory. Nail glue, receipts, small scissors sticky with last week's weave glue. Tonight, she's looking for the inventory list the new girl swore she filed, but already Tasha knows she'll end up rewriting the whole thing herself. **She's good at picking up after other people.** She pulls another drawer, deeper than the rest, and her hand closes around something cold, rigid, with little teeth.

At first, she thinks it's just another rat-tail comb, but the shape is wrong.

The handle's snapped in two, jagged edge sharp as a warning. Pink plastic, corner-store cheap, the kind her mother used on her before school. Two of the teeth are missing, a long crack running through the spine. She squeezes it, harder than she means to.

The comb doesn't belong here. Not in this salon, not in this decade. Not in this crown.

Tasha holds it like evidence, her mind jumping through hoops to pin down the year. It's the same as the one she kept in her pocket at eight, when she'd hide behind the couch while her parents screamed each other hoarse. Cheap plastic, always breaking in the same place.

Her heart catches, skips. She should throw it out, but her body won't listen. There's a rawness in her palm, a pinprick where the cracked edge presses into her lifeline. She holds it tighter. She wants to crush it, but she only ends up tracing the break with her thumb, back and forth, like reading braille.

The scent of burned sage rises again, sharp and peppery. It battles with the chemical sweetness of pressing oil. **Tasha can't separate the smells from what comes next—memory and hope, pain and survival, all tangled like a braid.**

She slumps down onto the rolling chair, the one that lists to the right because the floor is uneven. She spins once, a lazy revolution, and the room lurches with her. In the heavy quiet, city noises worm their way in: a distant siren, the muffled bass of a party that won't end. She stares at the comb, waiting for the old ache in her jaw to return, the one that comes when she tries not to think about the past. The ache always wins.

She lets her fingers remember, the way they used to braid the plastic hair of dollar-store dolls, working the tangles out in silence. She remembers a voice, her mother's, soft but tired: *Baby, you gotta look nice even if you got nothing else. Don't let them see you come apart.* **A crown is what you make of it, her grandmother used to say. Even if it's plastic. Even if it's broken.** Tasha had nodded, pretended to understand, and gripped that same comb until it bit her skin.

The clock above the door ticks past one. The new girl's appointment ledger sits open, useless, full of no-shows and women who promised they'd be back next week. Tasha lets the salon dissolve around her. She stares at the break in the plastic, and with every pass of her thumb over that crack, she inches closer to what she's been avoiding all week.

The anniversary is coming. Ten years since she ran, left behind a city and a name, built something nobody could tear down. **But the comb in her hand says it don't matter how much you build—old breaks show up anyway. Patterns always leave a mark on the scalp, even after the braids come out.**

Tasha closes her eyes and leans back, chair creaking. The comb's edge slices into her memory, opening the door she's been pressing her whole weight against. She gives up fighting it. Instead, she lets herself fall, lets the day drain from her arms and legs, lets the comb drag her back to the first night it broke. To the first time she learned silence could be armor.

She stays like that, breath shallow and jaw clenched, until the city outside goes still. The comb is an anchor, and she lets it pull her under.

Her Childhood Apartment, Late 1990s

Eight-year-old Tasha Rivers crouched on a cushion in the corner, knees tucked tight, braiding her doll's raggedy hair like it was some kind of mission. She made each braid crisp and even, then undid it, started over, careful not to let her eyes stray from the faded Barbie's head. The apartment stank of old grease and Pine-Sol, heavy enough to taste. The living room was smaller than the back room at Queen's Crown, walls so close her mother could reach across them with one arm and a broom.

The TV, loud enough to crack a window, played some rerun with the fake laughter turned up to hide the rest of the world. Tasha couldn't hear the jokes, but she didn't need to. That laugh track rolled over everything, made the room seem like it belonged to someone else. The kitchen table was stacked with mail, old school newsletters, and a pot of collards gone cold. Her mother's silhouette moved through the kitchen in slow, even lines, knife on cutting board steady as a clock's tick. Every time the building's elevator rattled in the shaft, Mama's head whipped around, eyes locked on the door, muscles rigid.

Tasha kept her own head low, and focused on getting that pink comb through the Barbie's mess. The comb was all hers, even if it was cheap and snapped on one end. It worked good enough. You just had to be gentle and not get it stuck.

The door crashed open, sucking every laugh and word out the room. Her father filled the frame, shoulders wide, face already tight with whatever had soured his day. The smell of something bitter, like gin and city sweat, reached the couch before he did. He let his jacket fall to the floor and stood there, scanning the apartment like he'd caught them hiding something.

Her mother's voice, smooth as she could make it. "Dinner's almost ready."

He grunted, flicked his eyes from Tasha to her mother, then back again. "I work all goddamn day for overcooked chicken?"

He stomped to the table, grabbed the plate Mama set out. In one clean motion, he flung it sideways into the wall. The plate exploded, white shards mixed with greasy chicken skin splattering across the linoleum. Hot chicken juice streaked down the paint. The laugh track on TV kept up, like the cartoon mess was a punchline.

Tasha's breath crawled up inside her ribs and stayed there. She watched her mother clean up the splinters, all the while keeping herself between the wall and Tasha, like a shield. Her mother didn't look scared. She just moved quick, practiced, her hands never shaking even as she scooped the food with a rag. Tasha's own hands went still. She squeezed the doll, felt the plastic bones flex in her grip, and kept her mouth shut.

He paced back and forth in front of the TV, ranting about how this family never gave him respect, how he ought to just leave. He got louder, voice breaking through the canned laughter, echoing off the walls. Mama tried to shush him, gentle, almost whispering. That just made him angrier.

He turned and pointed, big finger aimed at Tasha. "What you looking at, huh? Got something to say?"

Tasha shook her head, no. She pressed her lips together so hard they burned. She felt the comb digging into her palm. She imagined herself invisible, a shadow behind the couch, a girl-shaped nothing.

He looked at her mother, eyes wild. "She don't listen, just like you."

He stepped forward, too quick for Tasha's eyes to follow, and slapped her mother. The sound was louder than the TV, louder than anything. Her mother stumbled back, caught herself on the fridge, and straightened up before he could hit her again.

Tasha didn't cry. She didn't move. She learned early that movement called attention. She watched her mother's face—no tears, just the hard line of her jaw. Her father went on yelling, but Tasha didn't hear the words anymore.

In her hand, the plastic comb snapped. Not a loud sound, but enough. The sharp end poked her thumb, drew a tiny bead of blood she wiped on the couch cushion when nobody was looking.

Her mother set her jaw, squared her shoulders, and made him a fresh plate. No words, just action, always. **Tasha understood this was the way things were. You made it through, and you kept your mouth shut. Silence is only powerful when you choose it, she'd learn later. But back then, it was just another cage.**

When her father finally fell onto the couch, passed out and drooling before the second commercial break, her mother cleaned up the rest of the mess. She wiped down the table, swept up ceramic bits, washed her hands. Then she came to Tasha and brushed the hair back from her daughter's forehead, gentle as always.

"Go on, baby," she whispered. "Finish your braids."

Tasha nodded and did what she was told. She worked through the knots with the broken comb, careful not to pull too hard. She made the doll's braids perfect, tighter than ever. When she was done, she lined up the pieces of the comb on the end table, put the biggest shard in her pocket for tomorrow.

She didn't say anything for the rest of the night, not even when Mama kissed her goodnight and tucked her in. But she dreamed of the pink comb, and of a world where nothing ever broke unless you wanted it to.

Hall Closet and Neighborhood, Pre-Dawn

Some nights, the yelling wasn't the worst part. Some nights, it was the long quiet afterward, the way the walls seemed to close in, holding their breath. Tasha would lie on her mattress, covers up to her neck, and listen for footsteps—slow and heavy if he was tired, fast and uneven if he was lit up with something stronger.

Tonight, it was the second kind. The door slammed hard enough to shake the ceiling dust loose. Tasha knew better than to wait and see what mood he brought with him. She grabbed her doll, left the bedroom lights off, and ducked into the hallway. She'd learned to be fast and silent, like a mouse.

The closet was safe. It was small, warm from all the winter coats crammed together, and it muffled the worst of the noise. She huddled in the back, knees up, doll hugged close, listening to the thud of boots and her mother's low voice trying to reason, to buy them a few more quiet minutes.

She could see the hallway if she leaned her face to the slats. The light from the kitchen bled into the dark, catching the edge of Mama's house dress, the bare brown of her legs. Tasha watched as her father loomed into view, every part of him sharp and stretched by anger. He grabbed Mama's arm and yanked her into the narrow hall. The coats swayed with the force of it, and for a second, Tasha thought he might pull the whole closet off the wall.

He wrapped his fist in Mama's hair, winding it around his fingers like rope. He hissed something nasty at her, spit flying. Mama tried to keep her voice level, tried to stand straight. When he slammed her against the wall, the picture of Dr. King in the cheap plastic frame jumped sideways. Mama's cry was quick, bitten off, the kind of sound Tasha heard when the hot comb burned her scalp.

She put her hand over the doll's face, as if that could protect them both. Her heart thumped so hard it hurt her ribs. The coats smelled like old mothballs and perfume. She wanted to close her eyes, but she kept them open, kept watching through the slats. She needed to see, needed to know when it was safe to come out.

He shouted, his voice a broken bottle. "You think you smarter than me?" Mama said nothing, just kept her arms up, elbows protecting her face. She tried to shrink, but there was nowhere to go in the hallway. He threw her down. She hit the floor, curled up, and didn't make another sound.

Tasha counted the seconds. She learned that if you got to fifty, sometimes he got tired and left. She got to forty-three before the hall went quiet. She let another minute pass before she dared to breathe.

When it was over, Mama lay still on the linoleum, face turned to the side. Blood from her nose puddled under her cheek. She didn't move for a long time. Tasha waited, head pressed against the coats, doll's arms mashed into her chest. She hated herself for hiding, for not being braver. But she hated him more.

In that darkness, Tasha made herself a promise, no tears this time. She would never let anyone make her this small again. Never.

Morning came the same way it always did: sunlight crawling in through the kitchen window, catching the dust in gold sheets. Her father was gone, maybe at work, maybe at the bar. Tasha ate a bowl of dry cereal at the table, watching Mama patch herself up. She dabbed her nose with a cold washcloth, layered on the thick orange foundation, painted over every bruise like it was just another thing to be cleaned.

Her mother caught her staring, and smiled. It looked strange on her face.

"You want a banana for lunch?" Mama asked, voice careful.

"Yeah."

Mama wrapped it in foil and slipped it in the brown paper bag. She packed a sandwich, the crusts trimmed the way Tasha liked. At the door, Mama knelt and fixed the collar of Tasha's shirt, tucking it down flat. "You got your homework?"

Tasha nodded. "I got it."

"You gonna be good?"

"Yeah."

Mama kissed her forehead, then pulled back quick, not wanting to leave makeup on Tasha's skin. She opened the door and watched Tasha walk out, watched her every step to the elevator.

The hallway was empty, but Tasha felt the stares from behind every door. She didn't flinch. She held her lunch bag in one hand, her doll in the other, and walked with her head up.

Downstairs, Mrs. Mayberry smoked on the stoop. She looked at Tasha's face, then at her arms and legs, checking for marks. She looked the way people do when they want to say something, but don't know how. "You runnin' late, baby?" she said, voice soft.

Tasha shook her head.

Mrs. Mayberry flicked ash onto the sidewalk and smiled, but her eyes were sad. "Be good at school."

Across the street, a group of women waited at the bus stop. They watched her, too, every one of them. Some had faces tight with pity, some just stared, some looked away fast, like it was contagious.

Tasha held their gaze as long as she could, until the school bus wheezed up to the curb and the doors folded open. She climbed in, found a seat at the back, pressed her forehead to the glass. She saw her mother standing in the window upstairs, waving like nothing had happened.

The bus jerked away. Tasha closed her eyes, and felt the promise in her chest grow hard and solid. **She wasn't going to be powerless forever. She'd find a way out, even if it meant breaking something to do it. She'd find her own pattern, her own way to braid the world back together.**

Home and Ms. Loretta's Salon, 1999–2002

On Sundays, Tasha's grandmother appeared with a slow dignity that made people clear a path for her at church and in the grocery store. Grandma wore her best for these visits: white gloves, a blue pillbox hat, and a purse big enough to carry a week's worth of secrets. The purse was magic. Out of it came little bribes—a pressed dollar folded into a crane, a ribboned butterscotch, a travel bottle of lotion that smelled like summer fruit. Sometimes a plastic ring, sometimes a folded note: *Don't let 'em get you down, baby.*

When her father left to go watch the game at the bar, Grandma drew Tasha to her side and spoke truths in a whisper. "You know you got your mother's steel in you. Stronger than anybody, but you got to use it right."

Tasha would nod, and Grandma would squeeze her hand, passing strength through skin to bone. Even Mama seemed lighter with Grandma in the house, moving with her old laugh tucked up under her breath, just waiting for a safe moment to let it out.

By the time Tasha turned nine, she spent every weekday after school at Ms. Loretta's salon, two blocks from the apartments. Mama said it was better than coming home to the TV and the smell of beer. Loretta's was a shotgun space with three chairs, two dryers, and a cracked fish tank where the goldfish outlived all predictions. The waiting bench was always packed: mothers, aunts, teens, little girls swinging their feet and plotting how wild they could get their styles before prom.

Tasha swept hair from the floor, stacked towels, fetched sodas from the bodega. Nobody paid her, but Ms. Loretta let her practice braids on a busted mannequin head, and she always had a kind word.

The women in that shop talked about everything, sometimes loud and fast, sometimes in code. They tore each other down, then built each other right back up. Some days, the jokes rolled so thick Tasha had to cover her mouth to keep from laughing too loud. Other times, Ms. Loretta would lower her voice and say something that made the whole room go quiet: "Don't let that man take your shine," or, "What you got is yours, honey, don't let nobody touch it without your say-so."

Tasha watched the magic of the chair. Women came in stooped, bone-tired, or hiding under hats. They left tall, chin up, hair laid or curled or wild as they dared. Sometimes they cried in the chair, but always left smiling, head high. She saw girls her age come in with faces like stone, only to loosen up and laugh after Loretta worked her hands through their kinks and told them how pretty they looked.

One Thursday, Tasha was stacking magazines when she saw a woman she recognized from her building, face purpled under her makeup, sunglasses even though it was cloudy. Loretta smiled, patted her hand, and said, "Darlin', you want the full wash and set today, or just the ends trimmed?"

"Just the ends, please," the woman whispered, eyes on the floor.

Tasha swept up the fallen hair, careful not to brush too close to the chair. She listened as Loretta talked about the weather, the news, anything to keep things light. But when the woman left, Loretta's face went hard and sad. She didn't say anything, just cleaned the combs and moved on.

That night, Tasha lay in bed with the smell of pressing oil on her hands. She thought about the way Loretta ran her shop—a place where women could come as they were, even if that meant broken. She thought about her own mother's eyes, the days when they shined and the days when they were flat and gray. She thought about Grandma's whispers, and the way the women in the salon never let any man's name linger too long in the air.

In those afternoons, Tasha learned what it meant to hold space for somebody. She learned how laughter could heal, and how sometimes, just being seen was enough. She watched the women build armor out of hair, out of color, out of words. **She knew she wanted to do that, too. She wanted to build a place where every woman's crown was safe, where silence was a choice, not a sentence.**

She started braiding for real by the time she was twelve. She lined up her friends in the courtyard, practicing parts and cornrows and box braids until her fingers cramped. She charged a dollar, sometimes two, and used the money for licorice ropes or a Coke from the vending machine. Each braid was a little act of defiance, a way to make order out of mess.

Every night, Tasha brought home a new story from the salon. She told her mother about the lady who cut off all her hair and said she felt lighter, about the girl who brought her grandma in for her first-ever relaxer. Mama listened, smiling, as Tasha talked about how good it felt to make people pretty, how she wanted to do hair when she grew up.

Mama nodded, but her eyes got misty. "Just don't let it be the only thing, Tash. You can be more if you want."

Tasha said she'd think about it, but in her heart, she liked the idea of a world where women walked in broken and walked out new.

One afternoon, as Tasha swept the last of the clippings, Loretta pulled her aside.

"You learn quick," she said. "Got magic in your fingers. Just remember—it ain't about the hair. It's about what happens while you doing it. Understand?"

Tasha nodded, even if she wasn't sure yet what it meant.

On the walk home, the wind carried the scent of fried onions and gasoline, city noises mixing with the steady pulse of music from passing cars. For once, Tasha didn't look at the cracks in the sidewalk. She looked straight ahead, feeling tall as a grown woman, the memory of Loretta's words ringing in her ears.

The apartment building loomed up, old bricks and windows warped by age. Tasha climbed the stairs, two at a time, and let herself in.

The air inside was heavy, the living room empty except for the TV flickering in the dark. Mama was asleep on the couch, shoes off, arm curled under her head. The kitchen smelled like burnt rice. Tasha tiptoed to her room, took off her sneakers, and lay down on top of the covers.

She pulled out the old pink comb from under her pillow and turned it in her hands. She looked at the jagged break, the way the pieces never fit back together quite right.

She didn't mind. **Some things were better after they broke. Some crowns, too.**

Apartment Kitchen, 1:04 A.M., Senior Year

Tasha shot up almost overnight, all arms and legs, her jaw sharper than before. Seventeen, and she took up space now, didn't shrink from the doorframe or bow her head in the hallways. She moved through the apartment with a purpose, voice lower, footsteps louder. She still swept floors at Loretta's but had traded in the pink comb for a real set of styling shears. She did Mama's hair every Sunday, and sometimes, on good days, they laughed so loud it shook the walls.

Her father hated the sound of it.

He came home late that January night, hands shaking, eyes gone mean. Mama was at the stove, frying fish in old oil, the smell sharp and bitter. Tasha sat at the table, books splayed out, pretending to care about the homework in front of her.

He stomped through the kitchen, grabbed a beer, and started in on Mama about the electric bill, about how she was lazy, how Tasha was disrespectful, how nobody in this house appreciated what he did.

Mama turned off the burner, kept her back straight, didn't answer. Tasha could see the tension building in her neck, the way her shoulders hunched, bracing for the next blow.

He raised his voice, fist curled, face red. "You hear me? I said you don't listen!"

He stepped toward Mama, hand up. Before he could touch her, Tasha moved. She stood between them, tall as him now, and looked him dead in the eye.

"Don't touch her."

The words left her mouth calm, even though her stomach flipped and her hands trembled. She stood her ground, feet planted. Mama gasped, the sound small and terrified.

Her father froze, like he'd been slapped himself. The moment hung in the air, silent and sharp.

"What did you just say?" he growled, spit flying.

"I said don't touch her," Tasha repeated, louder this time. "Not anymore."

He glared at her, wild with rage, not used to being challenged. He stepped forward, crowding her space, chest to chest. Tasha could smell the beer on his breath, see the vein bulging in his forehead. For a second, she thought he'd hit her, that he'd break her like he broke Mama all those years.

But something stopped him. Maybe the way she didn't flinch, or the way her mother stood behind her, hand pressed to her mouth. He didn't know what to do with her. He wasn't ready for Tasha to fight back.

He shoved the table, knocking books to the floor. He cussed and kicked the chair. Then he stormed down the hall, slammed the bedroom door so hard the picture of Grandma tipped off the wall.

The kitchen was a mess. Fish burning in the pan, glass on the linoleum, Mama shaking so bad she dropped the spatula. Tasha turned off the stove, set the pan aside, and held her mother's hand until the tremors faded.

They cleaned up in silence, each of them sweeping broken pieces into the trash.

Later that night, Tasha lay awake in bed, eyes wide, replaying the moment over and over. She could still feel the echo of her father's rage, but she felt something else, too. For the first time, she wasn't afraid. She was angry.

She got out of bed, crept down the hall, and saw Mama sitting in the living room, bag packed, coat on. She met Tasha's eyes, and they nodded in silent agreement.

He was passed out, snoring in the dark, dead to the world.

Tasha carried the bags to the door, one in each hand. They walked down the stairs together, out into the frozen night, breath clouding in front of them. The city was quiet, the streetlights humming.

Mama didn't say a word, just squeezed Tasha's arm and kept walking.

At the bus stop, Tasha looked back at the building, at the dark windows and the familiar lines of brick and mortar.

She made a promise to herself right there: **She'd build a life out of more than just survival. She'd build a place where women didn't have to hide their bruises or their voices. She'd build a place where silence was chosen, not forced. Where every woman could wear her crown, unbroken.**

She held Mama's hand as the bus rolled in, warm and certain.

This time, when the doors opened, they both climbed aboard without looking back.

Queen's Crown Salon, Present Day, 2:09 A.M.

The plastic comb balanced in her palm, edges sharp and familiar. Tasha stared at the crack in the handle, thumb tracing it, feeling the weight of years packed into that inch of cheap pink. Her shoulders ached with old ghosts, but her spine was straight as rebar. Outside, the city's song never quite stopped—sirens, someone's laughter, tires crunching wet asphalt. But inside, Queen's Crown was lit up, every light left on as if to keep the dark at bay.

She looked around the salon, really saw it. The row of styling chairs gleaming, the jars of colored hair beads lined up with military precision, the wall of photos showing clients before and after—smiles wide, edges perfect, heads held high. **Tasha built this from nothing. Her name, her**

style, her rules. Her crown.

She could hear echoes of the women who came through: the first-timer giggling nervously as her edges got snatched, the regular who always brought three cousins and left a ten for "tips and treats." The air was thick with the stories they brought, the secrets they dropped, the love and mess of being alive and Black and female in a city built to grind you down. **The walls were thick enough now to hold all of it. The pattern, the pain, the survival, the joy.**

Tasha rolled the comb between her hands, remembering the old lesson: **Silence could be armor, but it could also be a prison.** She didn't need it anymore. Every inch of her shop, every sound and scent, was proof of that.

She let herself sit in the memory for another minute, but when it sank its teeth in, she shook it off. She wasn't a child behind a door anymore. **She was the one with the keys.**

She whispered, **"You made it, girl,"** just under her breath, just for her.

Then she slipped the comb into her pocket, stood up, and looked at her reflection in the big front mirror. She saw a woman who had learned to bend but never break, a woman who built a world where women could laugh loud and leave unafraid. **A woman who knew the pattern, who could read the scalp before she touched it, who could see what was going on inside.**

She shut off the lights, one by one, listening as the salon fell quiet around her. She closed up, locked the doors, and stepped out into the cool air.

The past would always be there. But so would tomorrow. And Tasha was ready for both.

18

INTERLUDE: THE WEIGHT OF MERCY

Mercy is a blade handed down—sharp with memory, heavy with the price we pay to keep each other safe.

Mama Esther | Queen's Crown, After Hours

Mama Esther stands alone in **Queen's Crown**, every surface humming with the quiet aftermath of a long day—**perms and press-and-curls, the sharp bite of hair bleach, gossip simmering through the air hours after the last client**. No music now. The steady drip from the rinse sink taps Morse code into the stillness.

She clears a small section of the counter near the register. The old glass is pocked with **nail polish stains and salt circles from years of nervous tea drinkers**. With practiced hands, she lines up the items one by one: a chipped bowl filled with water from the big sink, a film canister packed with ashes scraped from the bottom of last year's fireplace, bundles of sage and rosemary banded together with red thread, a knife with a plastic handle, the edge honed to a razor on the back steps each Sunday, and—last—a plain gold wedding band. The ring sits heavy in her palm for a second, pressing its chill into the lines of her hand. She sets it in the center.

Mama Esther's hands shake only a little. Her nails are clipped back to nubs, fingertips puckered from years of acetone, **callused along the edges—hands that have held secrets and crowns alike**. Her shadow sprawls across the counter, made huge by the half dozen candles clustered at the base of the cracked mirror. A stick of incense—Nag Champa, thick and blue—smolders beside them, smoke curling up and shivering out sideways as the old air conditioning kicks in for a wheeze, then falls silent.

She closes her eyes, slow and measured, not for effect but for the steadying of herself. She starts the chant low, teeth close together, tongue rounding each word in Yoruba the way her own mother taught her. There's no tremor in the voice. The words run steady, **anchoring the world to her, the way braids anchor hair to scalp**. Sweat beads under the scarf wound tight around her head, and for a moment, she feels her whole scalp throbbing in time with her pulse.

The shop smells like old perm solution and Lysol until the sage takes over, a bitter green that stings the nostrils and makes the candle flame gutter. The smoke catches in her throat but she keeps the chant rolling, pushing past the catch in her lungs.

She picks up the knife. The blade glints in the candlelight, and in the dim shop the reflection makes it look like a streak of lightning frozen above the counter. She slices into the pad of her thumb, deep enough for a bright bubble of blood to well up and track down her hand. It splats into the water, **blooming crimson and muddying the surface—another stain, another story**.

The iron tang sears through the sage, thick enough to make her head swim. The ritual demands pain but doesn't linger on it; she presses her thumb against the counter, sealing the blood into a red stamp and goes on. Hands braced to the countertop, arms locked, eyes wide and staring at the objects before her, she mutters the last of the words. Her lips go slack as the final syllable leaves her.

The smoke has filled the front of the shop, and for a second it feels less like she's standing in a salon and more like she's underwater, suspended in the stinging, sweet-bitter air. The edges of the world blur and pulse. **She's**

somewhere else now—where memory and mercy bleed through.

Her whole body seizes up, legs rigid, shoulders hunched. Her heart stammers. Breathing comes shallow, each gulp of air sticky and thick, the way it did on that night, the worst night. The memory rips her away so fast she almost loses balance, one hand slamming down to grip the counter, the other fisting in the old hand towel at her side. Blood still beads from her thumb, smearing along the plastic edge. Esther's eyes roll up, and the chant mutates into a rough gasp. The memory crashes in with its full arsenal of sight, sound, and stench.

**Mama Esther | Her Childhood Home,
Atlanta, Years Ago (Memory)**

Memory takes her. She is small again, thin and jittery in a nightgown two sizes too big, the living room light stuck on a faint yellow because the overhead flickers and she's too short to reach the chain. Her house smells of Pine-Sol, burnt toast, and the lingering sweetness of baby powder. The windows sweat from the rain outside, and the TV barks static behind the couch. All the ordinary things, lined up and waiting for what always happens next.

The door shakes so hard it rattles the plates in the kitchen. She's already at the edge, heart tripping in her throat, hands fisted tight around her own waist. He comes through in a blur—coat half off, fists balled, jaw flexing like he means to bite right through her. His shadow is the first thing that fills the doorway, then it's all body and sweat and the stink of stale cigarettes.

He doesn't speak at first, just breathes, huge and ragged, and the space around him fills up with the **echo of whatever went wrong out there in the night**. Esther backs toward the end table, toes catching on the rough threadbare rug. His finger is in her face before she can step aside.

"You think I don't know? You think I'm stupid, girl?" The voice is deep, flat, barely controlled. Each syllable lands like a knuckle, even when he isn't swinging. Esther tries not to meet his eyes, but they drag her in. Hungry, black, hollow.

He pins her with one hand, thumb digging under her chin, the other hand wild and shaking as he points to nothing and everything—the window, the TV, the empty kitchen. "Where you hide it, huh? Who you bring in here?" The accusations pour out, splintered and senseless, but it doesn't matter. It's the same every time.

She whimpers, nothing planned or dramatic, just a leak of fear she can't swallow down. He hoists her up, feet dangling, and slams her into the plaster, where her head rings and a chunk of wall grit bites into her cheek.

Esther's arms go numb, then tingle with heat. She scrabbles at the wall, finds the lamp with her right hand, its base heavy and cold. He's too close to see what she's holding, too angry to notice her other arm cocked at an odd angle. All she knows is the sudden burst of wild energy, the lamp swinging up in a sharp arc, the thud of it meeting bone, the split-second grunt as he drops her.

He staggers back, a ripple of shock in his face, blood already gushing from the corner of his forehead. He paws at it, stares at the red on his palm, then at her, as if she's rewritten the rules of gravity. He says her name, once, softer than she's ever heard it. Then he collapses, knees folding slow, then the rest of him crumpling, silent, **spreading blood across the floorboards in a thick, lazy circle—a stain that will never quite come out**.

Esther stands there, lamp still in hand, breath ragged and sharp. Her body shakes so hard she thinks her bones might rattle apart. The world is suddenly too loud—the hum of the fridge, the click of the heater, her own pulse throbbing in her ears. She can't move. She can't stop staring at the man on the floor, the way his face has gone slack and slack, jaw open and catching dust motes in the thin light.

A sound at the front door. Esther jolts and almost drops the lamp. Someone enters, careful, deliberate, the handle turning slow. It's her mother. Not big, but her shape blocks out the world behind her, frame wrapped in a battered winter coat, scarf tucked in tight.

Mama steps inside, no flinch, no blink. She takes in the whole scene—the body, the blood, the lamp, Esther's trembling hands—then looks Esther in the eye. There is no shock on her mother's face. Only the set of her jaw, the crease of old sadness between her eyebrows. She slips her shoes off at the mat, walks past the body, and takes Esther by the elbow, guiding her to the kitchen.

Esther follows. She knows better than to speak. Her mother doesn't let go, not even when she fills a chipped mug with tap water and presses it into Esther's hands.

"Drink," Mama says, voice low, rough as gravel. Esther does, choking a little, but she drinks until the cup is empty. Mama nods, satisfied, then points to the open cut on Esther's palm where she'd gripped the lamp. She wraps it tight in a dish towel. The blood blooms through, dark and wet, but Mama holds it steady.

"You did what you had to," she says. No comfort, no condemnation, just flat reality. She goes back into the living room, drags the body by the ankles to the center, and arranges the limbs so they don't look so unnatural. She returns with the old wooden box from her bedroom closet. Esther knows this box, but has never seen what's inside.

Mama kneels, unlatches it, and removes bundles of dry herbs, a fist-sized chunk of white chalk, a single long feather. She sets each item on the floor around the body, precise as a surgeon. Next comes the kitchen knife, wiped clean with the hem of her sleeve. She lays it next to the man's hand.

"Come here," she says, and Esther obeys. They kneel on either side of the body. Mama takes the feather, draws a quick symbol in the dust beside his head, then uses the chalk to sketch a line from his heart to the center of the room. Esther copies the motions, hand guided by her mother's, and together they finish the circle.

Mama speaks, words in a language older than her own memory. The room thickens, breath slows, and the hair on Esther's arms rises. She feels the weight of her mother's hand, the surety of it, pressing her own palm into the cool wood. The cut stings, then goes numb. The chant rolls over them both, filling up the room, **pushing out the fear until all that's left is the work—the pattern, the ritual, the promise**.

The ritual lasts as long as it needs to. When it's done, Mama wipes the chalk from Esther's hands, then the blood. They stand, and the body is just that—a body, not the man who once roared and raged and made the whole house tremble. He's gone, and Esther feels the absence like a door slamming shut.

Mama pulls her close, wraps her arms around her shoulders. Esther leans in, not sure if she's crying, but grateful for the warmth. Mama's breath is hot against her ear. "This is not the end," she whispers. "**It never ends, baby. But we take care of our own.**"

They leave the body on the floor, close the door behind them, and step into the chill night. The rain has stopped. The air smells like wet earth and iron.

Mama Esther & Her Mother | Backyard, Deep Night (Memory)

Mama and Esther haul the body out back, past the tangle of black-eyed Susans and the crusted garden hose. The moon is low, half a thumbnail, barely lighting the slip of earth behind the house. Nobody out here but the two of them, and the body bumping behind like a sack of old laundry.

They dig with a garden spade and a rusted trowel. The dirt is wet, and the clay sticks to everything—hands, knees, bare feet. It's hard work, silent and mean, but neither of them complains. Esther's arms ache, muscles trembling with each scoop, but she digs anyway. The hole is shallow and wide, more pit than grave. When it's deep enough to swallow the man's shoulders, Mama tells her to stop.

They drag him in. He lands with a soft thump, limbs splaying in the loose dirt. Esther wipes her nose with the back of her hand, leaving a smear of snot and mud. Mama pours a handful of ashes over the chest, then takes the sage and rosemary and crushes it between her palms until the oil slicks her skin. She drops it all onto the chest.

The smell is sharper out here, cleaner. The smoke from the clay pot rises up, not in a twist but a thick column that seems to hang in the cold air. Mama lights the herbs with a match, and the flare of orange throws their shadows huge and warped against the shed.

Mama hands Esther the knife, the same kitchen blade from before. "It wants a piece of you," she says, voice gone so thin it almost snaps. "Or it can take something else, if you let it. The memory of your first. But if you give the blood, it's yours for life. That's the price for not turning away."

Esther doesn't hesitate. She presses the blade into the cut on her palm, reopening it. She squeezes until the blood wells up fresh and hot, dripping down onto the man's slack face. It spatters the cheek and lips, mixes with the ashes, turns the whole mess into a sticky, dark paste. The smoke thickens, and the scent turns bitter, almost sweet at the edges.

Mama watches, eyes hard and wet, then nods once. "Good," she says. "It'll stay with you. Always." She reaches out, wipes the knife clean on her own sleeve, and tosses it into the grave.

They cover the body together. Each scoop of dirt is heavy, and it lands with a dull, final thud. **No prayers, no words, just the sound of the earth piling up, sealing everything underneath.** When the hole is full, Mama smooths the dirt with her foot, then drags a broken lawn chair over the spot, as if nothing ever happened.

Esther's breath steams in the night air. Her hands are stained, blood and earth embedded deep. She looks at her mother, who looks right back. "**You remember what I said,**" Mama tells her. "**You protect them. All of them. No matter what. That's what we do, now.**"

Esther nods. She feels it settling in, the **weight of the promise, heavy as the dirt they just moved**. She looks at the garden, the house, the sliver of moon in the sky. Nothing's changed, and everything has.

Inside, they wash up in silence. The cold water bites at Esther's fingers, but she keeps scrubbing, watching the brown and red swirl away down the drain. When she's clean, she bandages the hand herself, winding the gauze tight.

Mama brings her a blanket and a cup of hot tea. They sit on the couch, knees touching, both staring straight ahead at the silent TV. The ritual is done. But Esther knows it'll replay every time she closes her eyes.

She drinks her tea, lets the heat burn her tongue. **She's not small anymore.**

Mama Esther | Queen's Crown, After Hours (Return to Present)

The guttering candle on the counter snaps Esther back. Her chest heaves;

every rib aches as if she'd run for miles. The pain in her thumb is nothing, not compared to the hollow drum in her sternum. She leans on the counter, shivering, sweat cooling fast on her skin. Her scarf is damp, and the night air has crept into her bones.

The salon feels different now. The air is thicker, pressed flat and calm. The ordinary hum of the city—sirens, car radios, the stutter of late-night bus brakes—fades beneath a hush that is all her own making. The smoke has thinned but its **ghost clings to the mirrors and the old vinyl chairs, curling around the hair dryers and the stacks of cheap magazines**.

Esther gathers herself. She stands tall, shoulders squared. Her hands don't tremble, though the blood from her thumb paints a slow trail down her palm. She presses the wound closed with a rag, then sets about cleaning up, silent and efficient.

She pours the bloody water down the back sink, watches it swirl and disappear. She scrapes the ash into a ziplock bag, folds the used towel inside out, ties it off, and drops it in the trash. The gold band, slick with old memory, goes back into her pocket, warm now from her skin.

When everything is wiped down and the knife is re-sheathed, she lines the candles up along the window ledge. She says the names of the women she's helped—some alive, some not—under her breath, voice low and steady. For each name, she snuffs a candle with her fingertips, pinching the wick so the flame dies quick and clean. With every extinguished light, the room dims, until only the street's sodium glare creeps in, striping the walls in orange and shadow.

The last candle sputters, burns low, then fades out. Esther stands in the dark, facing the empty chairs and the long mirror. Her reflection is just a shape, sturdy and straight-backed, scarf pulled tight and eyes fixed ahead. She watches herself for a minute, then turns to the door.

She unlocks it, cracks it open, and lets the city back in. The air tastes different now. Sharper, but sweeter, too.

She whispers, just loud enough for the night to hear: "**Mercy costs something.**" Then she locks up, slides the chain in place, and disappears behind the beaded curtain, her figure framed for a heartbeat in the light from the street.

Queen's Crown is silent, but not empty. Not anymore.

19

BROKEN CROWNS AND NEW BEGINNINGS

From the ashes of what was taken, we build what cannot be destroyed.

Quanda | Queen's Crown Salon, Midday

The salon chair had heard more confessions than a church pew.

Quanda moved through the rows of dryers and mirrors, her hands a blur of combs and clips, her voice a steady anchor in the storm of gossip and laughter. The air shimmered with the scent of coconut oil and the low hum of women's secrets.

A young woman, edges frayed and eyes heavy, slumped into Quanda's chair. She tried to hide her worry under a silk scarf, but Quanda saw through it—**she always did**.

Quanda draped the cape around her shoulders, fingers gentle. "You know what I see when I look at you?" she asked, meeting the woman's gaze in the mirror.

The woman shook her head, lips pressed tight.

Quanda smiled, slow and sure. "I see a queen. And every queen needs her crown set right."

She parted the woman's hair, working in coconut oil with practiced care. "People think we just do hair in here. But what we really do is **fix crowns**. Every braid, every twist, every press—**armor for the world outside**. You walk out of here, you walk out ready to rule."

The woman's eyes glistened. "I just wanted to look decent for this interview."

Quanda's hands never stopped moving. "Decent? Baby, you're about to look royal. Don't let nobody tell you different."

She caught the eyes of the other women in the salon, some nodding, some smiling, all listening. "That's what we do at **Queen's Crown**. We don't just style hair. We remind you who you are. We fix your crown, so you can hold your head high."

A ripple of laughter and "amen"s moved through the room. The woman in the chair sat a little straighter, her reflection shining back at her, **regal and unbowed**.

Quanda winked. "Now, let's get you ready for your throne."

Tasha | Queen's Crown, War Room, Morning

Tasha attacked the morning with a vengeance. She yanked the last of the styling chairs away from the center station, dragging it across a sticky patch of linoleum, and parked it under the window. The room looked different now—**less salon, more war room**. She'd cleared the back wall for two folding tables, covered them in purple cloth, then loaded them with stacks of handouts, palm-sized personal alarms, and shrink-wrapped boxes of tampons and Plan B. The reception desk, stripped of Quanda's gold-plated business card holder, now displayed laminated flyers about domestic violence, trafficking red flags, and how to **"Recognize Your Rights When the Cops Don't."**

Where the old client board used to feature blowouts and baby's first braid, there was now a yellow legal pad scrawled with a list: **"Victim Advocates to**

Call Back TODAY."

Fresh lemons—sliced, not the plastic kind—floated in pitchers of tap water, replacing the chemical scent of salon-grade disinfectant. Still, when the AC kicked on, the faint ghosts of acetone and burned keratin rode the air. Tasha set her jaw and dumped another box of beauty magazines into the trash. **The past is dead weight. Today, the only thing that matters is keeping the girls in the neighborhood alive.**

She took a lap, double-checked the locks on the front and back doors, then returned to the tables. She lined up three rows of brochures so the **Queen's Crown** logo was visible from the street. Not the old logo—she'd printed new ones, with Quanda's silhouette re-drawn in sharp, high-contrast lines. Next to the brochures, she placed a single white candle in a cup—one of Mama Esther's, loaded with bits of red thread and a hunk of rose quartz at the bottom. **Protection, or at least a placebo for the anxious.**

Tasha stood back and surveyed the space. There was a hum to it, an energy almost sharp enough to cut. She couldn't tell if it was the caffeine, the grief, or just the surge of adrenaline that had carried her since sunrise.

Tasha & Arman | Queen's Crown, Late Morning

The bell above the door jangled. Arman entered, hauling a battered JanSport over one shoulder and a crumpled brown paper bag in the other. He looked wrecked: hair out of the tight twists he used to wear, chin stippled with the beginnings of a beard. His face said he hadn't slept, but his eyes were bright and ferocious.

He dropped the bag on the front desk. "You got a minute?"

"Always," Tasha said. "You hungry? There's donuts from the church next door."

He shook his head. "Can't eat." He unzipped the backpack and pulled out a laptop, scuffed and covered in old stickers: **DEFUND THE POLICE, BLACK LIVES MATTER**, and a faded anime girl with a sword. He set it on the table, then opened the paper bag. Inside was a shoebox, the kind with faded DSW labels and duct tape on both ends.

"Found this at the old apartment," he said. "It was behind the vent cover, taped to the inside."

Tasha glanced at the box. "Your mama was always hiding shit in the walls."

He smiled, just for a second. "She said that's what smart people do when they don't trust the banks."

Arman flipped open the lid. Inside: a bundle of photos, some loose, some in an envelope, and a thumb drive in a sandwich bag. The photos were mostly color, but a few black-and-whites were sandwiched between—a family reunion in someone's backyard, a birthday cake mid-slice, a little boy (maybe Arman) with a gap-toothed grin, arms thrown around a smaller girl with dimples. Tasha sorted through them, careful not to leave fingerprints on the glossy surfaces.

She paused at the photo of young Arman with the girl. "Who's this?"

Arman's face tightened. "Mya Bradley. We were kids together—our moms were friends before..." He trailed off, then forced himself to continue. "Before she went missing."

Tasha studied the photo more carefully. The same dimples, the same bright smile she'd seen on the missing person flyers. "This the same Mya who filed a complaint against Lance?"

"Yeah." Arman's voice cracked. "Forty-eight hours before she disappeared. Just like the pattern I found with all the others."

He powered up the laptop, connected it to a projector he'd brought from his school library. The bulb flickered, then splashed a spreadsheet on the far wall: column after column of numbers, dates, account balances, and transfers. Tasha scanned the sheet, picking up the pattern before Arman could start his spiel.

"These are all transfers," he said, "between state employee pension accounts, prison commissary accounts, and a bunch of private shell companies. Look—here, here, and here." He tapped the arrow keys, highlighting certain cells in green. "Mom was tracking them. There's two million dollars in play, minimum. Some of it goes straight to offshore."

Tasha whistled. "That's a lot of ramen noodles."

"Or pills. Or people."

He flipped to the next tab. There was a folder of PDFs—scans of signed visitation logs, parole records, even some internal memos that looked like they were never meant to leave the system. He scrolled through, then stopped on a photo embedded in a doc. "This is the one that got me," he said, voice gone thin. "Look close."

Tasha took the printout and held it under the window's light. Three men stood in front of a barbecue grill, paper plates in hand, laughing like kings. One was Dejuan—lean, no tattoos yet, just a scar above his eyebrow. Next to him, a younger version of Lance, hair in tight waves, eyes squinting at the sun. The third man was older, built like a linebacker gone soft, wearing a police department T-shirt. The smile on his face was wide, but the eyes were somewhere else.

"That's Rivers," Tasha said, not a question.

"Yeah. Caption says 'Family Day, 2009.' But look at the background."

She did. In the shadows by the back fence, two girls played on a swing set. One was unmistakably Quanda, hair braided in thick ropes, face lit up in a wild, open laugh. The other girl looked familiar, but Tasha couldn't place her. She checked the photo again. The swing set had been tagged with a Sharpie—big block letters: **"PROPERTY OF THE DOWANS FAMILY."**

"That's Mya," Arman said quietly. "In the background. This was taken at one of those neighborhood barbecues our families used to have."

Tasha set the photo down gently. "So they all knew each other. Lance, his father, your mama, Mya..."

"It's all connected," Arman confirmed. "Mya wasn't just another victim. She was part of our community. Part of our family." His hands clenched into fists. "That's why Mom kept tracking this—she knew what they were capable of."

Arman pulled another picture from the shoebox. This one was smaller, Polaroid-sized. It showed the same three men, but inside a living room. Rivers had an arm around Dejuan, and the kid's smile was brittle. The date at the bottom was a year later.

Tasha set the photos down and looked at Arman. "You think your mom knew about all this?"

He nodded. "She kept every receipt. Digital and paper." The last word cracked in his throat, but he fought it down. "She knew. She just couldn't figure out how to say it, not with us in the house."

Tasha glanced at the spreadsheets on the wall, at the swirl of numbers and names and shadow addresses. **"Your mama was smarter than the whole damn city."**

"She thought she was alone," Arman whispered.

"She wasn't," Tasha said. "She had us." She thumbed the edge of the family photo, ran her finger over Dejuan's face, then Rivers'. **"We still do."**

He slid the thumb drive across the table. "Everything's on here. And there's backups in the cloud."

Tasha pocketed it. "They coming for you?"

Arman snorted. "They don't even know I'm alive. That's the problem with men like Rivers. They never pay attention to the ones they don't think matter."

She looked at him, saw the fight in his shoulders, the way he wouldn't let his voice shake again. "You matter," she said, not gentle. **"We all do."**

He nodded, but didn't speak.

She turned the photo over, looking for clues—anything that might help them get ahead of the next attack. The more she studied it, the clearer it became: this was never about just one murder, one cover-up. **It was a pipeline, generations deep, and Quanda was the one who finally tried to break it.**

Tasha stood, grabbed the tape, and pinned both photos to the advocacy board—the barbecue scene and the childhood photo of Arman and Mya. She pressed her finger hard against Rivers' face, flattening it into the cork.

"Your mama knew," she said, voice flat and cold. **"And Mya knew too. That's why they killed them both."**

For a long moment, neither moved. Outside, the street was silent, save for a car stereo booming somewhere down the block.

Tasha breathed in, letting the anger settle into her chest. She'd always been good at taking pain and turning it into a weapon. She would not let Quanda's death go unpunished. She would not let Mya's disappearance be forgotten. She would not let Arman get caught in the crossfire. **This is the job now. And Tasha has never quit a job in her life.**

Tasha, Roxie, Arman | Queen's Crown, Sunset

By sunset, **Queen's Crown bristled with more hardware than the old state armory**. Tasha checked the perimeter—windows latched, fire exit propped open for a quick retreat, security gate chained on the inside. She didn't trust it. Not with the way they'd seen a black SUV roll past, slow, twice in the last hour.

On the inside, the atmosphere was equal parts panic and grit. Roxie, eight months and change, lumbered up and down the hall with her phone jammed in her bra and a backpack slung over her shoulder. She had her own agenda: every drawer in the place got a hidden burner phone, every towel rack a length of paracord, every surface wiped down to remove prints and stray hairs. The kit under the sink—cash, first-aid, a box of pregnancy tests—got inventoried twice, just in case.

They worked in silence, trading glances, not bothering with hope. Tasha placed one of Mama Esther's charms above the main door—red beads and chicken bones tied with wire. She glued another under the front window, and the last she wrapped in duct tape and stuck under the desk, right next to the foot pedal on the register.

Roxie watched her, then snorted. "You think beads are gonna stop a bullet?"

Tasha shrugged. "Beads and this." She reached under the counter, pulled out the sawed-off Quanda used to keep for show and tell. It looked harmless, but it held two slugs, each marked with an X.

Roxie nodded approval, then stashed a pack of diapers in the vent above the toilet. "That's the plan? Wait and see who comes?"

Tasha didn't answer. She'd already spotted a shadow out the back window, then lost it. She trusted the plan, but only as far as her own eyes could see.

At 8:17, the phone rang. No caller ID. Tasha grabbed it, clicked to speaker.

"Queen's Crown, how can I help?"

Vega's voice, urgent and thin: "It's happening. Rodriguez missed her check-in. That means Rivers knows. You gotta get out, now."

Roxie yanked the phone from the wall, stuffed it in her pocket, then looked at Tasha. "We run?"

But Tasha was staring at the street. The SUV was back, idling at the curb. Three men got out, all in dark uniforms, badges gleaming. The one in front carried a metal baton, swinging it like a promise.

Tasha flipped the deadbolt, motioned Roxie to the back. "Basement. Now."

They made it two steps before the first brick hit the glass. It shattered with a noise sharp as a pistol shot. The brick landed on the tile, rolled to a stop by the waiting chairs. Then another, this one wrapped in rags and reeking of gasoline.

Roxie dove behind the reception desk. Tasha racked the shotgun, aimed at the glass.

The first Molotov followed. It burst on the far wall, fire arcing across the floor in a sheet. The heat smacked Tasha in the face, turned her mouth to ash.

She pulled Roxie to her feet, half-dragged her toward the back room. A gun went off—real, this time. The bullet took out the appointment board, then thudded into the drywall.

Three men swarmed in, boots kicking through the burning glass, eyes hard and blank. Their movements were perfect, practiced. Tasha fired the first barrel at the lead man's legs. He went down, howling, but the others barely noticed.

Roxie was gasping, hands pressed to her belly. "I can't—" she wheezed, "I can't move—"

Tasha shoved her through the breakroom door, kicked it shut, then fired again, this time at the ceiling to scatter the men. The second slug clipped the exit sign, showering sparks on the attackers.

It bought maybe five seconds.

She slammed a chair under the doorknob, dragged a metal filing cabinet in front for good measure. The whole room smelled like chemicals and panic.

Roxie was on the floor, doubled over, face red and shining with sweat.

"The baby," she whispered, voice strangled. "It's coming now."

Tasha dropped the shotgun, knelt next to her. "No, no, not now."

But Roxie's body said different. She was shaking, her water already soaking through the jeans.

Outside, another gunshot. The men shouted, boots thundering closer. Smoke crept under the door, thick and black.

Tasha grabbed the emergency bag, ripped it open. Gloves, towels, scissors, a bottle of cheap vodka for disinfectant. She handed Roxie a washcloth, soaked it in the water pitcher. "Breathe. Focus."

Roxie clamped onto her hand, crushed it with inhuman strength. "If we die—"

"We're not dying."

"If we do, don't let them take him. Promise me."

Tasha looked her in the eye, hard. "Ain't nobody taking anything from you, Rox. Not tonight."

The first fist pounded on the breakroom door. The chair jumped, legs groaning under the weight. Another crash—this time with the butt of a gun.

Tasha tore open a packet of gauze, ran through the steps in her mind: **breathe, push, catch**. The training was ancient, passed down from women who didn't have hospitals or even clean floors.

Roxie screamed, the sound more animal than human. She pushed, and the head appeared—dark, wet, impossibly small.

Another blow to the door. It was going to give.

Tasha wrapped her hands in the towel, braced herself. "Push again, hard."

Roxie sobbed, pushed, and the baby slid out in a rush of blood and water. Tasha caught him, wrapped him tight, wiped his face.

He screamed, furious, alive.

Tasha handed him to Roxie, then grabbed the shotgun with her free hand.

The salon was a mess of blood and sage smoke, the air thick with prayers and afterbirth. Tasha's hands still shook, knuckles raw from gripping Roxie's thigh through every contraction. Crown wailed, lungs full of new life, and the women circled close, forming a wall of bodies and love against the world outside.

Roxie lay back, sweat slicking her brow, eyes wild and glassy. She clutched the baby to her chest like she could fuse him to her bones. For a moment, the only sound was the baby's cry and the slow, shuddering breath of women who'd seen too much and survived anyway.

Tasha knelt beside her, voice low. "You did it, Rox. He's here. He's safe."

Roxie's laugh was a broken thing, half sob, half relief. "Safe," she echoed, but her eyes darted to the boarded window, the sirens still echoing somewhere far off.

Mama Esther pressed a cup of water to Roxie's lips. "Drink, child. You need your strength."

Roxie sipped, then pushed the cup away, her hand trembling. "Tasha," she whispered, voice barely more than a scrape. "I need you to listen. All the way, this time."

Tasha's heart thudded. "I'm listening."

Roxie's gaze locked on the baby, then on Tasha. "If anything happens to me—if Rivers' people come back, if I disappear—promise me you'll keep him safe. Promise me you won't let him near Lance. Not ever."

Tasha's face went still. "Roxie, what are you saying?"

Roxie's jaw clenched, the words fighting their way out. "He's not just after me, Tasha. He's after what's his. Crown—" Her voice cracked. "Crown is his. Lance Rivers is the father."

The room went silent, the kind of silence that sucks all the air out, leaves only the thud of blood in your ears. Mama Esther's hands froze mid-prayer. Jonesha's mouth dropped open, words dying on her tongue.

Tasha stared at Roxie, the truth slamming into her like a fist. All the late-night calls, the threats, the money that never made sense. The way Lance's eyes lingered too long, the way Roxie flinched at the sound of his name.

Roxie's voice was a whisper now, but it cut through the room like a razor. "He said if I ever talked, he'd take the baby. Said nobody would believe me. Said he'd make me disappear, just like the others."

Tasha reached for her, hands steady now. "He's not taking anything. Not while I'm breathing."

Roxie's eyes filled, but she nodded, clutching Crown tighter. "I just needed you to know. Needed someone to know."

The women closed in, a circle of arms and vows, the old pain burning away in the light of new truth. Outside, the sirens faded, but inside **Queen's Crown**, a different reckoning had just begun.

Tasha could hear the men outside, could hear them shout, **"Rivers says to bring the woman alive!"**

The door splintered.

Tasha stood, aimed at the opening. She fired—dry click, out of ammo. The men rushed in, guns up, but froze when they saw the scene: blood, baby, two women not backing down.

Tasha raised her chin. **"This is a place for family,"** she said, voice rough. "If you want to cross that line, do it."

The men hesitated. For a second, nobody moved.

Then the baby screamed again, and the sound broke the tension. The man with the baton stepped forward, but something in his eyes softened.

He turned, motioned the others back. "Let's go," he said.

20

THE UNWINDING

When the truth finally comes to light, it burns everything in its path.

Rivers Estate, Dawn | Vega & Rodriguez

The FBI raid on Captain Rivers' compound began at dawn, black SUVs rolling through the gates like a funeral procession for corruption itself. Agent Martinez had waited three years for this moment—three years of building the case that would finally expose the network.

At the gate, two Feds unclip the padlock with a bolt cutter and swing it open on silent hinges. The only warning is the digital chirp of the intercom. Then twenty boots hit the drive in a syncopated rush. Vega walks the line, head low, vest loose, breathing in the mulch and cut azalea that cost more than her car.

Rodriguez falls in behind her, badge in one hand, fist ready in the other. **"This place smells like money laundering,"** she mutters.

Vega grins, teeth flat and hungry. **"Let's see what else it launders."**

By the time the team hits the front door, the Rivers estate security is two steps behind, groping for sidearms that are six months out of date. The first battering ram takes the deadbolt clean off; the door folds like a cardboard box. The inside is all marble and mirrors, a museum of trophies: signed jerseys, a gold-plated shotgun, and, over the stairwell, a hand-painted portrait of Captain Rivers himself, staring down at the chaos with courtroom gravitas.

They blitz the foyer, split left and right, shouting **"Federal warrant!"** over the crash of shattered vases and screaming smoke alarms. Upstairs, a shape moves—a flash of blue silk, old-school opulence. Captain Rivers, minus his badge, but still wearing the smug.

Vega leads the way, feet hitting the stairs two at a time. She's practiced this in dreams: the final sprint, the way a man's face shatters when he realizes he's the one being hunted.

They find him in the master bath, standing over a Jacuzzi that gurgles with pulp and bleach. His hands are pink with effort, paper drifting in clumps around the drain. Even cornered, he's composed, jaw squared, eyes daring her to play cop in his house.

His phone sits on the marble counter, screen still lit with a recent call. The contact name visible for just a second before the screen goes dark: **"Lance - Son."**

"Captain Rivers," Vega says, voice steady as granite.

He wipes his hands on the silk. **"Detective Vega. Didn't expect you to bring so many friends."**

Rodriguez trains her gun on his chest. **"Step away from the tub."**

He lifts both hands, slow and theatrical. **"What's the charge? Early-morning trespass?"**

Vega nods at the stack of folders on the counter—sealed court documents, property transfers, two passports and a burner phone still warm from his palm. **"Trafficking, conspiracy, accessory to homicide, and about eight other felonies you can't flush."**

He shrugs, like it's an academic disagreement. **"You know how many cops it takes to keep this city from falling apart? You want to bring me in, fine. Just know there's nobody better to replace me."**

Vega cuffs him, wrists tight enough to leave marks. **"I'd rather have a vacuum than a parasite,"** she says. Then, low so only he can hear: **"This is for my sister, and for every woman you've trafficked."**

The words hit. For the first time, his eyes flicker—not with fear, but calculation. He's already trying to game the system, to find the weak spot in the net.

Rodriguez reads him his rights, quick and efficient. By the time they haul him out, the neighbors are filming on their phones, trading rumors on the HOA text chain. Rivers walks with his chin up, pajamas barely hiding the tremor in his knees.

Inside, the search team opens the house like a forensic dissection. The den is lined with liquor bottles—rare, never touched. The dining room is a gallery of medals and "thank you" plaques from three governors, six police chiefs, and a Supreme Court justice whose name alone would clear a city block. But the real muscle is in the basement, behind a false wall painted to match the rest of the cinderblock. Vega finds it by accident, tapping her Maglite along the seam. She calls it in, then pries it open with a crowbar.

Inside: three rooms, each colder than the last. The first is a mini-NSA—rack-mounted servers, monitors scrolling lines of code, phones wired to record and scramble calls in four languages. The screens flicker through traffic cams, courthouse entrances, the cell block at Phillips State Prison. Rodriguez grins when she spots the backdoor feed: Rivers had eyes on his own men, probably as insurance.

On one monitor, a call log is still open—dozens of calls to **"Lance - Son"** in the past week alone, each one timestamped right after collections or incidents. The pattern Roxie had documented in File H, now confirmed in digital form.

The second room is pure logistics—whiteboards, color-coded, mapping the transit of girls from city to city, dates and initials and dollar amounts. At the center, a hand-drawn network: Miami, Nashville, Charlotte, Atlanta. A different color for each tier. Every major bust of the last decade, every disappearance, explained in three dry-erase lines.

The last room is locked, three deadbolts in a row. Vega pops them one by one. The air inside is musty, unconditioned, heavy with chemical sweet—formaldehyde or worse. Along the far wall are plastic bins, labeled by year. Inside: hair clips, scarves, old cell phones, even a couple of dolls. Trophies, all. One shelf is reserved for jewelry, each piece bagged and tagged like evidence in a private museum.

Vega sifts through, hands shaking for the first time. She finds a locket, heart-shaped, cheap, with a small paper photo faded to sepia. Her sister, fifteen, smiling like she just heard a joke. Vega's knees go soft; she steadies herself on the shelf.

Rodriguez touches her shoulder. **"You want a minute?"**

Vega shakes her head, snaps a picture of the locket, then seals it in an evidence bag. **"Not yet. We're just getting started."**

Upstairs, in Rivers' study, the lead Fed sits at the desk, grinning at a framed photo he's just swiped from the credenza. He holds it up as Vega enters.

"Look at this. Three generations of Rivers men, standing in front of the old police academy. Looks like a campaign ad."

Vega takes the frame, studies the faces: Captain Rivers in uniform, Lance at nineteen, already suspicious of the camera, and Dejuan, thin as a reed, clutching his father's side with a white-knuckle grip. The legacy is right there in black and white—unbroken, unrepentant.

"Three generations of the same poison," Rodriguez says, studying the photo. **"Father to son to grandson. Each one worse than the last."**

Rodriguez flips through the desk drawers, pulling out file after file. **"He documented everything. My guess, he never thought anyone would come for him."** She pauses at a leather-bound ledger, flipping it open. **"Jesus. Look at this—it's like a family business ledger. Every collection, every payment, going back decades. And here—"** she points to an entry, **"—'Lance collected from R. on Metropolitan. $200. Sent to holding account.' This is from just last week."**

Vega places the photo on the pile, careful not to let it fall. She stands a moment in the middle of the ruined office, breathing in the smell of burned paper and victory.

They drag Rivers through the front hall, past his wife—still in curlers, howling that they'll sue for damages. The media is there now, lights popping like paparazzi, each photo erasing another inch of his myth.

Outside, in the rising heat, the news trucks park side by side, transmitters raised like antennae on an insect. Rodriguez looks at Vega, eyebrows arched.

"You want to say something for the cameras?"

Vega tucks the locket into her vest. **"I'll wait until they ask the real questions."**

But when she walks past Rivers, she can't help herself. She leans in, lips close to his ear.

"This isn't the end. Your whole house is coming down."

He looks at her with a hatred so sharp it could bleed. But he says nothing.

The Fed team loads him into the cruiser. Rodriguez grabs the evidence bag, follows. Vega stands on the porch, sunlight washing the marble steps, and stares down at the locket in her palm.

Some victories are hollow, but some are just the beginning.

Rodriguez | Phillips State Prison, Sunrise

Sunrise at Phillips State Prison hits like a cattle prod. The charged air flickers with overly bright lights, and every step echoes the screams from last night off the block walls. Rodriguez has been awake since 2 a.m., palms sweating through two layers of nitrile, waiting for the moment the radio tells her to go.

When it comes, it's just static, then a single word: **"Now."**

She's already in position—near the south yard, where Dejuan holds court. He's surrounded by the usual lieutenants: a big white kid with a neck tattoo, two shrunken old-timers who hang on his every word, and a couple of fresh meat wannabes circling like gnats.

Rodriguez walks the line, nightstick clipped to her belt, head low and eyes scanning for the real danger. Three steps in, she feels it—a shift in the current, a buzz in the way the guards move. Some are with her, real corrections; others wear the stink of payoff and the smug of knowing this whole block is about to break.

She keys her lapel mic. **"Target in the yard. Perimeter ready."**

Over the wall, a drone hums, its lens locking onto the patch of red Dejuan wears like a crown. He's smiling, loose, in command. He's heard about the Rivers raid already—nothing travels faster than bad news to a man who's built his kingdom on other men's misery.

Two guards on the far side of the yard throw nervous glances her way. The taller one, name tag "Monroe," pulls out his phone, thumbs a quick text, then pockets it. Rodriguez files it away; Monroe's been on the take since before she got here, but this is the first time he's sloppy with it.

She steps in front of Dejuan, keeps her posture bored. **"You got business up front,"** she says, nodding toward intake. **"Let's move."**

He shrugs at his crew, like he's doing them a favor. **"Hold my spot,"** he says, and they snicker as if this is the funniest thing on Earth.

Rodriguez walks him toward the admin wing, but before they reach the gate, Monroe slides in behind, blocking the path. **"We got a problem?"** he says, eyes too wide.

Rodriguez sizes him up—he's got twenty pounds and four inches, but she's got the panic of a lifetime. **"Warden needs the prisoner in the interview room, not the hole,"** she says.

Monroe grins, showing the chip in his tooth. **"Not what I heard."**

He moves to grab Dejuan by the elbow, but Rodriguez is faster. She spins Monroe's arm up, snaps the wristlock, and slams him face-first into the chainlink. **"You wanna do this?"** she spits.

Monroe thrashes, but she's got leverage, and with one smooth motion she cuffs his left wrist to the fence. **"Interfering with a federal operation,"** she whispers in his ear. **"Bet you didn't see that one coming, bitch."**

The yard goes quiet. Even Dejuan's crew freeze, unsure if this is part of some bigger play.

Rodriguez drags Dejuan through the gate, up the ramp, and into the sallyport. Two real Feds wait, all business, faces like they're carved from the same stone. **"We'll take him,"** the taller one says, snapping out his own set of cuffs.

Dejuan looks at Rodriguez, trying to read her. **"You got a death wish?"** he asks, voice low.

She smiles, tired and ugly. **"Not anymore."**

They march him down the admin corridor, ignoring the shouts and pounding from the yard. At intake, the warden is waiting—red-faced, lips quivering, the faintest sheen of fear behind his bluster.

"What is the meaning of this?" he demands, looking past Rodriguez to the Feds.

The taller agent hands him a warrant. **"Special investigation, under direct order from the Department of Justice. You are to provide full access to all records and staff."**

The warden's face collapses. **"This is highly irregular."**

"Not as irregular as a corrections captain with a private email to a convicted murderer," the Fed says. He gestures for Rodriguez to follow. **"Let's get started."**

They push Dejuan into the interview cell, bare but for a bolted-down table and two plastic chairs. The Feds flank him, one at each shoulder. Rodriguez stands in the corner, letting him stew.

It takes twenty seconds for the cracks to show. Dejuan starts with bravado: **"You know I got rights. You know none of this sticks. You want to talk, call my lawyer."**

The agent on the left pulls out a stack of affidavits, slides them across the table. **"These are sworn statements from six inmates, two guards, and a paralegal from the women's block. You want to keep running your mouth, or you want to read what they said about you?"**

Dejuan's jaw tics. He flips the first page, then the second, then stops. **"All of them lying. You pay them off?"**

Rodriguez steps forward. **"You ever tell Quanda Dowans the truth?"**

He looks up, slow. **"You got nothing on me."**

She throws a packet of photos on the table—snapshots of every transfer, every visit, even one of him laughing with Rivers at a barbecue, arms wrapped around each other like family.

"You see this?" she says, tapping the photo. **"Your whole world is paper thin. We got proof you used the prison network to run girls from here to halfway houses, then out to the city. Rivers is already talking."**

Dejuan shifts, for the first time really scared. **"You're bluffing. He wouldn't flip."**

The Feds lean in. **"You can testify, or you can get indicted. Either way,**

you're done."

Dejuan's confidence slips, replaced by something raw and animal. **"You think any of this matters? There's always another man waiting in line. Cops, judges, all of them. You're just a pawn."**

Rodriguez leans close, so their faces nearly touch. **"I'd rather be a pawn than a coward."**

He lunges—wild, desperate—but the Feds have him, pinning his arms to the table. **"Fuck you!"** he screams, voice echoing off cinderblock. **"I'll kill you just like I killed her!"**

Rodriguez steps back, lets the moment sit. The cameras catch it all.

When it's over, they drag him to solitary. He tries to spit, but his mouth is dry.

The rest of the takedown happens in layers: the guards who tried to warn Dejuan are lined up in the admin office, questioned one by one. Some fold immediately, trading years for weeks. The smarter ones say nothing, but their phones and burner accounts tell the story. The Feds walk the tier, seizing every document, every hard drive, every thumbprint of Rivers' empire. By lunch, the whole place is in lockdown. Nobody moves unless they say so.

Rodriguez walks the block, watching the other inmates. Some cheer when they see Dejuan's crew get marched away in cuffs. Some look lost. In the women's wing, she hears snatches of rumor—**"He's gone. They're all gone. Maybe it's over."**

A former cellmate of Dejuan's, scrawny and shaking, calls her over to the laundry. **"You want a statement?"** he says. **"I got one."**

Rodriguez follows him to a corner. He whispers, **"He bragged about it, you know? After she visited. Said he 'handled' her when she found out too much."**

Rodriguez makes him repeat it, then writes it down, careful and neat. She thanks him, and he shivers, staring at the ground.

She checks the cell they'd kept for Dejuan, finds it trashed—sheets ripped, floor sticky with orange drink, but in the ceiling vent, a small plastic-wrapped package. She pries it loose. Inside: a flip phone, two batteries, and a thumb drive. The phone is cracked but still works. She scrolls the messages.

All of them are to a single number, tagged **"Pop."** The texts are blunt, no code: **"Quanda is problem," "She's talking to people on the outside," "Handle it tonight."** The last: **"Salon needs cleanup. Rivers knows what to do."**

Rodriguez's blood runs cold. The connection between father and son, grandfather and grandson—all of it documented in these simple, damning texts. Three generations of corruption, each passing the poison to the next like a family heirloom.

Rodriguez brings it to the Feds. **"This nails him,"** she says, but the agent shakes his head. **"He's already nailed. This gives us the rest of the network."**

The warden, who two hours ago ruled this kingdom, now sits in his office, hands shaking, answering every question they throw at him. The Feds copy his laptop, raid his safe, and photograph every log from the last decade. The stack of suspicious deaths—**"natural causes"**—is longer than her arm.

Rodriguez sits in the empty break room, head in her hands, watching the sun crawl across the tile. The adrenaline is gone, and all that's left is the ache.

She's survived another day in a place that should have killed her, but the world outside is still waiting.

Some wars end in gunfire; this one ends in paperwork and ghosts.

Tasha | Queen's Crown, Morning

The city wakes up to sirens—police, media, then a second wave of ambulances called in to handle the bystanders who collapse from shock or giddy, vindictive joy. By 7 a.m., every TV, phone, and jumbotron in the metro is screaming the same headline: **"POLICE CORRUPTION RING EXPOSED."** News choppers swarm the Rivers estate like flies, lensing every angle of the takedown. In every beauty parlor and barbershop, the TVs flicker with the mugshots of Captain Rivers and Dejuan, side by side, both looking like they just smelled something rotten.

But at Queen's Crown, the salon is calm, almost reverent. The neon OPEN sign blinks slow and steady. Women line up on the sidewalk, some still in pajamas, arms crossed against the morning chill. They bring donuts and cinnamon coffee, post up on folding chairs, and trade stories about the night before—who saw what, who recognized which badge number, who called their aunties to tell them the good news.

Inside, the air is thick with old smoke and fresh lavender. Tasha stands behind the front desk, baby Crown strapped to her chest, fielding calls and texts and the occasional landline from people who refuse to leave a digital trace. Roxie is camped at the corner table, tapping out messages to her "sources" at the AJC and the local NPR affiliate. Jonesha brings in a tray of pastelitos from the Cuban place three blocks over; Andrea pours mimosas into plastic salon cups and leaves one on every station, like communion.

By 8:30, the first wave of reporters arrives. They're mostly Black women, all of them with notepads or digital recorders, none of them playing polite. The leader—a woman with box braids, gold nose ring, and a smile like a fresh cut—introduces herself as Nia. She asks, without lowering her voice, **"You running a press conference or just letting us fight for questions?"**

Tasha shrugs. **"Ain't nobody here but family. Ask what you want."**

Nia grins, parks herself on the booster seat at the first chair, and flips on her recorder. **"What's it feel like, knowing the whole city is watching you?"**

Tasha looks down at Crown, who's chewing on her hoodie string. **"I don't care if they watch. I care if they remember."** She shifts the baby, then locks eyes with Nia. **"It's not just about them men going to prison. It's about what comes after. Who fills the space."**

The other reporters lean in. One, from a hip-hop podcast, asks about the roots—how deep the Rivers family really went. Another, a blogger from Black Mothers United, wants to know what Tasha will do with the Queen's Crown now that it's free of ghosts.

"We make it into a shelter," Tasha says, without hesitation. **"Not just for women, but for kids, too. I want a space where nobody has to run or hide or act smaller just to survive."**

Jonesha chimes in from the back: **"And we're starting a scholarship fund. For girls who age out the system. No matter what their grades look like."**

Roxie stands, baby on her hip, and addresses the room. **"This place saved my life, twice. First when I had nowhere to go. Then when I realized I didn't have to die to leave the past behind."** She wipes her eyes, then laughs. **"You want a soundbite? That's your soundbite."**

The room bursts into applause. Outside, the crowd doubles, word spreading down the block that something worth hearing is happening inside.

Nia clicks off her recorder and leans in close. **"You know the hashtag is trending? #JusticeForQuanda. Even the mayor had to tweet it."**

Tasha shakes her head, not quite believing. **"She would've hated that,"** she says, voice thick with fondness. **"But she would've loved to see you all in here. Tearing down the old world, making room for a new one."**

The reporters nod, some scribbling, some just letting the moment sit. Then the NPR woman, voice calm but cutting, asks: **"You think it's over? Or just starting?"**

Tasha grins, sharp as a blade. **"The men in charge think you cut the head off and the snake dies. But in our world, you cut the braid and the pattern just grows back, stronger."**

There's a rumble from the crowd as Arman appears in the doorway, dragging his rolling suitcase behind. He's taller, hair longer, skin gone soft from the California sun. The moment he sees Tasha, he lights up, crosses the room in two steps, and hugs her so hard that Crown squeals and grabs his chin.

The room quiets, the story shifting as they watch. Arman whispers, **"I got your messages. I ran the data like you said, and it worked. The Feds called me. I think I'm famous, or maybe just on a watchlist."**

Tasha ruffles his hair. **"Long as you use your powers for good, I don't care which."**

Nia spots him, then addresses the group: **"This is the son? The hacker?"**

Arman shrugs, awkward. **"Just numbers. Tasha's the one who did the real work."**

Tasha shakes her head, pride and grief mixing in her eyes. **"He's my**

brother now. We do this together."

Someone turns on the TV—muted, but the captions blaze across the screen: **"Multi-state Trafficking Ring Busted; Atlanta, Miami, Charlotte Linked."** Footage rolls of the Rivers estate, the cells at Phillips, the Queen's Crown sign. The camera pans to Tasha, holding Crown, baby's head resting on her heart.

Roxie raises her phone and snaps a photo. **"You look like a queen,"** she says.

Tasha snorts, then lets the smile take over. **"Not a queen. Just the woman holding the line."**

The crowd grows, the noise rises, but inside, the salon holds its center. A circle of women, and now men, building something that the city can't burn down.

Outside, the hashtag keeps rising.

Inside, the family keeps growing.

Arman | Bus Stop, Dusk

The sun was low, painting the city in bruised gold, when Arman waited for the bus, backpack slung over one shoulder, headphones around his neck. Two guys from his old high school leaned against the shelter, talking too loud, their laughter sharp as broken glass.

"Man, you see that flyer? Another girl missing. Probably just ran off with some dude," one said, shaking his head.

The other snorted. **"Or she's just fast. You know how they are."**

Arman felt the old anger rise, hot and steady. He pulled off his headphones and stepped closer. **"You ever think maybe she didn't run? Maybe something happened and nobody's looking because she's Black and poor?"**

The first guy rolled his eyes. **"Come on, Arman. You always gotta make it deep?"**

Arman's voice was calm, but it carried. **"It is deep. My mom and her friends—they keep track. They know the names. They help the girls who come back, and they remember the ones who don't. You should too."**

The second guy shifted, uncomfortable. **"Whatever, man."**

Arman didn't back down. **"It's not whatever. It's somebody's sister. Somebody's daughter. If you hear something, say something. If you see something, do something. That's what men do."**

The bus pulled up, brakes hissing. Arman got on, leaving the two behind, but as the doors closed, he saw them looking at each other; the joke gone flat.

He sat by the window, heart pounding, and texted his mom:

Told them. Didn't let it slide. Fixing crowns, even out here.

Tasha & Family | Queen's Crown Apartment, Next Morning

Morning drapes the apartment above Queen's Crown in a syrupy gold. The walls are still bare—no art yet, just patches where fresh paint hides what came before. On the pullout sofa, baby Crown wriggles on a blanket, chewing a fist and squawking at the light. He's fat now, all rolls and dimples, every noise he makes instantly answered by one of the four women orbiting him like satellites.

Jonesha arrives first, arms loaded with miniature onesies and sock hats. She lines them up on the counter, color-coded and pressed, each with a tag from her boutique. **"Ain't nobody in Atlanta gonna dress better than you,"** she says, smoothing the fabric with a gentle hand.

Andrea bustles in next, carrying two glass jars of homemade carrot mush and a bottle of formula. She spoons a little onto her finger, lets Crown gum it off, then grins at Tasha. **"Gonna have him eating collards by Christmas,"** she promises. **"Watch."**

Mama Esther brings up the rear, slower but steady, cane tapping the stairwell, beads clacking like a metronome. She sits by the window, pulls a handkerchief from her purse, and starts stringing tiny shells and red thread. **"Protection,"** she mutters, **"old as dirt and twice as strong."**

Tasha watches, heart swollen and tight. She waits for the right moment, then scoops Crown off the blanket and perches him on her lap. His hair is baby-fine, soft as spun sugar, but she sections it with care—first a gentle misting, then a slow, deliberate part down the middle.

"He's not even a year, Tasha," Jonesha says, laughing.

Tasha winks, tongue between her teeth. **"Start 'em young or the world'll do it for you."**

She works his hair into a spiral, fingers sure and steady, then fastens the end with one of Esther's beads. At the very top, she loops the last bit into a tiny, lopsided crown.

"Your name is your destiny," she whispers into his ear. **"You gonna grow up protected and loved, nothing like your daddy or his people."**

Crown giggles, gums her thumb, and flaps his arms like he understands.

Roxie stands in the doorway, silent and shaking. She's a different woman now—sleep-starved, yes, but her shoulders squared and her eyes soft with something like hope. She bites her lip, then cries, but nobody makes it a thing.

Esther finishes the bead-string, ties it into a circle, and rests it on Crown's head like a coronation. **"The world gets to keep trying,"** she says, voice thick, **"but this one belongs to us."**

For a minute, nobody says anything. Then Andrea claps her hands, breaks the spell. **"Enough with the ceremony! We got to eat."**

They pile into the kitchen, passing baby Crown hand to hand, everyone getting a turn. Over bagels and fresh fruit, they talk plans—how to finish the mural in the salon, how to petition the city for daycare funding, how to set up a hotline that the old badge men still lurking in the system won't trace.

"We turn the basement into a safe room," Jonesha suggests. **"Stock it with food, first-aid, maybe even some books for the kids."**

Andrea nods, already listing the shelves in her mind. **"And we need a web page. Make it easy for people to ask for help, so they don't have to walk in scared."**

Tasha listens, every word a balm. She thinks of Quanda, gone but somehow everywhere—her laugh echoing in the faucet's drip, her stubbornness in the way the paint refuses to cover the wall stains. **"She'd love this,"** Tasha says.

Roxie wipes her nose. **"She does. She's here."**

Esther nods, eyes shut. **"She's always been here."**

After breakfast, Tasha sets Crown in a sunbeam on the window ledge, watching the dust motes dance around his head. She sits back and lets herself breathe, the ache in her chest finally, finally quiet.

From outside, the sound of kids on scooters, the old men hollering at the corner, the bells from the church on the next block. The city moving on, loud and messy and alive.

In the salon below, light streams through the new glass, catching on every mirror, bouncing until the whole room glows like a lighthouse, guiding those who needed shelter.

And on the top floor, Tasha holds the baby close, promising him everything, and meaning it.

21

CROWN CEREMONY

Every queen's legacy lives in the women she taught to wear their own crowns.

Fulton County Courthouse, Morning

The Fulton County courthouse sweats. A wall of TV crews crowds the steps, morning news hair and drone pilots, everybody baking under the blue-white LEDs like this is a playoff game instead of a hearing. Inside, the halls clog with bodies—**all of Atlanta's rumor-mongers, all the clickbaiters who feed off city pain.** Even the janitors stand at parade rest, mops propped like bayonets. The metal detector chirps in time with the clock. Every bag, every body searched, because today is not a normal day.

At 9:03, the elevator opens and the guards march out with Dejuan and Captain Rivers. The uniforms picked for maximum drama—Dejuan's orange Rivers' navy with medals stripped, just the faint ghost of them pressed into the fabric above the pocket. Both cuffed. Rivers' jaw locked, daring the cameras. Dejuan looking for an exit, pulse bulging at the neck.

The reporters out-shout the cops, even the ones who've practiced court whisper.

"Is it true about the warehouse on Moreland?"
"Who gave the kill order on the salon?"
"Did you ever love your wife, Dejuan?"

No one asks about Quanda by name, but **every question smells of her.** A woman from WSB slips in a real one: **"How long has the department covered up for you?"** Dejuan flinches at that, but Rivers keeps his cop smile, dead in the eyes, like he's been prepping for this his whole life.

Tasha stands in the back, next to the scuffed vending machine with three buttons that never work. Roxie at her side, baby Crown tucked tight, wrapped so only his nose peeks out. Neither woman sits. There's no point. The seats fill with law students and grandmothers and a parade of Rivers relatives, all with the same crooked teeth and hard stares. None of them look at Tasha or Roxie. Not even when Crown lets out a soft snore that makes the old lady beside them cross herself.

Detective Vega is already inside, front row reserved. She wears a suit sharp as a boxcutter, hair slicked back, no jewelry but a battered watch. The clerk reads out the docket, voice quivering at first, then hardening as she gets to the meat.

"State of Georgia v. Lance Rivers and Dejuan Hensen. Charges: Human trafficking. Corruption of public office. Conspiracy to commit homicide. RICO violations. Two counts of accessory to murder."

Vega doesn't blink. The prosecutor, a tan woman with her own history of enemies, reads the charges again, this time for the cameras. She locks eyes with Rivers on "homicide." He bares his teeth, all charm. She smirks, lets the word float.

Judge's bench is empty for two full minutes—enough time for the buzz to settle into a restless tremor. Then the side door slaps open and a federal judge enters. He's not Atlanta, not even Georgia, his accent clipped and precise, robes starched like he's about to sentence a President. Rumor is the original judge, Holloway, is under his own investigation, but nobody says it out loud.

The bailiff rises. **"All rise for the Honorable Judge Kessler."**

Everyone stands. Vega's shoulders hunch. Rivers doesn't move, but Dejuan shoots a look to the door, as if any second he'll get a last-minute pardon.

The charges get read again, each count ticked off in rhythm. This time, **every word lands.** The judge asks if they understand.

Rivers: "Crystal."

Dejuan's voice shakes on "Yes, Your Honor."

First up is the prosecution. They lay out the whole scheme—how Rivers used his badge to funnel girls from juvie to halfway to whatever hell waited; how Dejuan, handpicked and groomed, ran the network behind bars; how every major arrest in Atlanta since 2009 fed the same pipeline. The prosecutor never looks at the accused, only at the jury pool, as if daring them to deny what they already know. She reads out the names: some alive, most not. When she gets to Quanda's, her voice stays steady, but her eyes burn at Vega.

Defense tries to object—calls the evidence "circumstantial," says "no bodies, no crime," says "decades of service should count for something." Rivers' lawyer is ex-FBI, all lizard skin and white hair, but the jury doesn't buy any of it. Not after the wiretaps, not after the digital trail left by Dejuan's burner phones. Tasha watches the defense melt, minute by minute, as every spreadsheet and every fake name gets dropped onto the record.

By noon, they break for lunch. Most of the crowd stays put, nobody wanting to lose a seat. Tasha finally lets herself sit, legs shaking with a pulse she didn't know she had. Roxie unwraps baby Crown and shifts him so he can stare up at the ancient ceiling tiles. The women say nothing. They just wait.

When they reconvene, Judge Kessler drops the bomb.

"The court will now consider additional defendants in this matter."

Bailiff reads out the new names—Judge Holloway, plus three DA staffers, all charged with obstruction, conspiracy, and cover-up. Holloway is nowhere to be seen; rumor is he took the back elevator and left the state. The other three look like ghosts, faces gone slack, as the bailiff calls them forward.

Rivers turns, slow, and stares at the indicted DA. There's no anger, no surprise—just a cold satisfaction, like watching the last domino finally tip. Dejuan tries to make eye contact with Tasha. She ignores him. He settles for the wall.

The judge reads the next case, voice flat.

> *"United States v. Holloway et al."*

The charges are different, but the faces are the same. It's a ritual now, the reading and the denial, the shuffling of paperwork and the awkward coughs from the gallery. **Tasha wants to feel joy, but it's not that simple. There's no clean win. Just the ugly truth, laid out in black letters on white paper.**

Courthouse, Afternoon

At the first break, Arman appears, backpack slung loose, hair wild. He slides in beside Tasha, eyes on the baby.

> *"They said my data made the difference," he whispers, not pride but awe. "I ran the cross-references like you showed me, and they found the tie-ins from Miami to Nashville. I think I'm on the witness list for the big trial."*

Tasha ruffles his hair, lets her hand rest on his shoulder. **"You did good, kid."**

He shrugs, tries to hide a smile. **"You think it's enough?"**

Tasha looks out at the press, at the rows of faces hungry for a story. She thinks of Quanda's picture on every newscast, the way the world turned her name into a hashtag but never knew her real laugh.

It's never enough, she thinks. No amount of justice brings her back.

"It's never enough," she says, "but it's a start."

They sit, three generations of survivors and strays, while justice grinds its slow gears. When the court finally adjourns, no one claps, no one cheers. The crowd just disperses, each person carrying away a piece of the story.

On the courthouse steps, Vega waits. She nods at Tasha, at Roxie, at the baby.

"They're going away for a long time," Vega says. "You should feel proud."

Tasha thinks about it, then shakes her head.

"I'll feel proud when they stop making girls like Quanda pay the price."

Vega nods, a small and bitter smile. **"Fair."**

They walk out together, past the media scrum, into a sun already too hot for April.

Behind them, the city buzzes, hungry for the next scandal.

Ahead, the future waits. Ugly, imperfect, but wide open.

Queen's Crown, Back Room, Evening

The salon's back room glows in shades of pink that don't exist in nature. The walls bloom with finger-paint spirals, faded birthday banners, a single string of LED roses stuck over the doorway. The air is thick with sage smoke, bitter, so dense it stings the tongue. In the center, a table small enough for tea parties but covered with adult things: three mugs of black coffee, a tarot deck splayed out, beads and bones and a roll of dental floss. At the table, Mama Esther weaves a charm like she's trying to knot the world together before it splits apart again.

Tasha perches at the edge, watching the old woman's hands work. She can't figure if the smoke is making her eyes burn or if that's just memory acting up. Roxie leans against the wall, baby Crown on her hip, still and alert as a cat in a thunderstorm.

Esther's voice comes slow. **"You want to know how it started? I'll tell you, if you promise not to laugh."**

Tasha snorts. **"I haven't laughed in a month, Nana. Try me."**

Esther doesn't look up. Her hands move fast, stringing one blue bead, then a red, then a lump of river glass that flashes when it hits the light. **"First time Quanda brought Dejuan around, I got the worst feeling. Like biting into a peach and hitting the pit, only the pit keeps growing in your mouth."**

She pauses to pinch off a length of thread, then ties a knot so tight Tasha can hear it pop.

The vision came three days later. Quanda, dressed in white, her hair loose for the first time since high school. She stands on a pier with the sun behind her, and the wind tries to steal her voice. Dejuan waits at the water's edge, smiling, but there's blood on his shirt and something black eating at his shadow. A crow lands on the pier. It cocks its head, then speaks in a voice that's not its own: **"You can't save her. You can only make sure what's left of her matters."**

Esther shakes the memory off. **"I did the only thing I could do. I got her the ticket. Played her numbers at the machine, slipped it in her purse when she wasn't looking. Prayed every night she'd use that money to run instead of getting pulled deeper."**

Tasha laughs, hollow. **"You rigged the lottery?"**

Esther shrugs. **"God owes me a favor or two. And Quanda needed a miracle more than the rest of this city."** She adds a silver bell, then knots the string again.

Roxie shifts the baby to her other side, Crown fussing just enough to prove he's alive. **"I always wondered how she won,"** she says. **"Wasn't like her to gamble."**

"She didn't," Esther says. **"I did. But it didn't change anything."**

Tasha can't let it go. **"So you knew? You knew he was going to—"**

Esther's hands freeze. She looks up, eyes wet, but her mouth is hard. **"I knew he'd break her. Didn't know how or when. Spirit world don't work**

like a news ticker, child. Sometimes it just flashes a warning and leaves you to clean up after."

She passes the charm across the table. Tasha holds it, surprised by the weight. Each bead is slick, each twist of thread as tight as a fist. **"What's this one for?"**

"Protection. For you, for that baby, for the women coming after." Esther wipes her hands on her lap, then flips the top card on the tarot. It's the Tower, all fire and bodies falling. **"The world likes to shake loose the things that hold it together. You gotta tie the pieces tighter, or they disappear."**

Roxie touches the edge of the card. **"You see Quanda after she died?"**

Esther closes her eyes. **"She was mad. Not at Dejuan, not even at Rivers. Mad at herself, for believing she could change a man that broken."** She taps the next bead into place. **"But she also knew her death meant something. That it would make you all fight harder."**

Tasha tries to say something sharp, but her throat won't let it out. Instead, she tugs at the charm, feels the way it bites into her palm.

"So why didn't you warn her louder?" she asks. **"Why not tell her straight up—leave, or you'll die?"**

Esther sighs. **"Some lessons you can't teach. Only live. Quanda would've laughed me off, same as you're doing now. She had to choose it herself."** She puts her hands flat on the table, fingers trembling. **"I regret a lot, Tasha. But not loving that girl. Never that."**

The baby reaches out, grabs for the charm. Esther lets him take it, lets him chew the end of the thread until his mouth is blue with dye.

"That child is both Rivers and not," Esther says. **"He's a bridge. Spirits got plans for him, big ones. Maybe he's the start of something new."**

Roxie holds Crown close, presses her lips to the fuzz on his head. Tasha stares at the charm, at the red and blue beads, and wonders what would happen if she just smashed it to dust.

Would it bring her back? Would it hurt less?

But she doesn't.

She tucks it into the pocket of her jacket, close to her skin. **"What happens next?"** she asks.

Esther grins, sudden and sharp. **"That's up to you, child. World is broken, but you got a hand in fixing it. Start by keeping each other alive."**

Crown giggles, smears blue on his cheek. Roxie laughs, for real this time, and Tasha lets herself join in, just for a moment.

In the hallway, the rest of the world waits. But in this room, with the smoke and the beads and the memory of Quanda hanging thick in the air, it feels like anything could happen. Maybe even something good.

Esther lights a second bundle of sage and says a prayer under her breath. Tasha doesn't catch the words, but she knows what they mean.

You're not alone. Not anymore.

Queen's Crown, Days Later

The first day, Tasha kicked out the wall between the shampoo room and the storage closet. By noon, sweat pasted her shirt to her ribs, and every surface in Queen's Crown buzzed with power tools, paint fumes, the scent of lemon cleaner biting through the ghost of perms past. Arman ran ethernet cable along the baseboard, measuring twice, drilling once, then cursing each time the drywall crumbled. Roxie, always with one hand on the stroller, her phone clamped to her ear, talked logistics with the shelter lady, the donations office, the social worker who agreed to keep the address off the public rolls.

By nightfall, the back half of the salon was stacked with boxes—canned food, diapers, more tampons than Tasha thought existed in Atlanta. She swept up the day's mess, then rolled out sleeping bags for the volunteers too tired to drive home. No one said thank you. Nobody needed to. **This was the new normal, and it fit better than any hope she'd known.**

The second day, the women showed up. Some wore robes, some brought their own chairs, one even had a mattress rolled up in the trunk of a Camry. They took over the kitchen, the laundry nook, the outdoor fire escape. They set up a whiteboard in the lobby and listed rules: No drama. No stealing. Ask before using up the last of the milk. Even the fights felt like family, loud but over quick, the sting gone by morning.

Tasha watched the new community unfold. She patched a leak in the upstairs bathroom while two teens argued about whose turn it was to babysit Crown. She replaced the busted salon dryer, then found a six-year-old had already converted the old bowl into a spaceship. She thought about Quanda every hour, every repair—sometimes bitter, mostly proud.

You should see this place now, she'd think. You always knew what it could be.

At dusk, Tasha locked up the front door and walked the perimeter. The block felt different now, the air heavy with spring, every porch light on. Even the old men at the barbershop offered a nod, not their usual smirk. On the third lap, she spotted Arman up on the salon roof, installing the last of the cameras. She climbed the rusted fire escape, two steps at a time.

He had the view locked down—every angle, every blind spot mapped. He pointed out the corners where the Rivers crew might post up. **"Nobody's getting close without us knowing,"** he said, pride softening his voice.

Tasha draped an arm over his shoulder. **"You got a plan for everything?"**

He grinned. **"Only the stuff that matters."**

Below, the city simmered in the blue hour. Tasha imagined Quanda's voice in her ear, laughing at the two of them up there, pretending to be superheroes.

The next morning, Tasha unveiled the sign: **Queen's Crown Sanctuary,** painted over the old logo in bright, block letters. Roxie hung a wreath on the door, then swept the stoop three times for luck. The first client, a woman with a shiner and a suitcase, arrived before 10 a.m. She looked at the building like it was a church. She shook when she stepped over the threshold.

Tasha met her in the lobby, offered a mug of coffee, and gestured to the rainbow of comforters stacked on the waiting-room couch. **"Pick any color,"** she said. **"Or all of them. No rules."**

The woman blinked, then smiled—small, but real. **"You got WiFi?"**

Arman, already at the desk, handed over the password with a flourish. **"It's 'LoveWins2022,'"** he said, low enough so only the three of them could hear.

The woman laughed, the sound ragged and beautiful. She slumped onto the couch, let the blanket swallow her whole.

After, Tasha found Roxie in the break room, arms folded, staring at the baby monitor. Crown snored in the nursery corner, the new charm from Mama Esther looped around his crib. Roxie looked up, eyes red but clear. **"I keep thinking about what it took to get here,"** she said. **"All the hurt. All the running."**

Tasha poured two mugs of cold coffee. **"We're not running anymore."**

They sat in silence, letting the words hang.

Later that night, the Queen's Crown hosted its first real gathering. No wine, no cheese, just a feast of takeout and gas-station donuts, every table packed with women—some local, some from three counties over. Tasha led the toast.

> *"To the survivors. To the fighters. To the girls who didn't make it, but made us stronger."*

The women clapped, some laughed, one or two sobbed. Tasha looked around the room and felt something hard in her chest break loose.

She pulled out the "Quanda Treatment" kit—honey, rosemary oil, the old shears from the day Quanda taught her to cut. She lined up the chairs, called for the women to take their places.

One by one, Tasha braided hair, trimmed ends, massaged scalp with the rosemary. She whispered a blessing under her breath for each woman. **Honey for sweetness in life. Oil for memory and strength. A prayer to keep the scars from burning, even if they never vanished.**

As her hands worked, she remembered Quanda's lessons: **The pattern protects the head. But sometimes, the head needs more.**

By midnight, the salon reeked of product and hope. Tasha circled the room, eyes skipping over every detail—the line of shoes at the door, the pile of comics in the corner, the baby safe in his crib. She remembered what Mama Esther said: **World is broken, but you got a hand in fixing it.**

She believed it now.

Queen's Crown, Late Night

After everyone went to sleep, Tasha stood under the new sign, watching the city. The sky was cloudless, the stars jagged and close. She thought of the women gone—Quanda, the others whose names no one but her remembered. She promised them that their stories weren't erased, that Crown and all the girls to come would never walk these streets alone.

Roxie joined her, blanket around her shoulders, eyes puffy but fierce. They watched the night, neither ready for bed, both certain there would be more battles ahead.

"Think it'll hold?" Roxie asked.

Tasha nodded. **"It better."**

They stood, side by side, and listened to the city—sirens, laughter, the high whine of a train far off. The sound didn't scare them anymore.

On the roof, Arman tinkered with the last camera, making sure the angles were perfect. Tasha looked up, smiled, and flashed him a thumbs-up. He returned it, then ducked behind the air vent.

The world kept moving. But here, in the new Queen's Crown, they finally had a place to stand.

Tasha turned to Roxie, her voice soft but iron. **"He'll wear a different kind of crown,"** she said, nodding at the nursery window. **"One that lifts others up, instead of crushing them down."**

Roxie smiled, the first honest one in years. **"I'd bet my life on it."**

Inside, baby Crown slept on, his future wide as the sky, the weight of the world already lighter than anyone dared believe.

The night stretched out ahead, full of promise and danger and everything in between. But Tasha felt ready. For the first time, she wasn't afraid.

This was only the beginning.

Queen's Crown, One Week Later

A week later, a nervous young woman enters the salon. She wears sunglasses indoors, a scarf wrapped high around her neck despite the heat. Her hands twist the strap of her purse, knuckles white with tension. The motion is familiar—Tasha recognizes it from her own reflection, years back.

The salon quiets as she steps in, conversations tapering to whispers. Roxie looks up from the front desk, makes a subtle gesture toward Tasha, who's arranging pamphlets by the window.

Tasha turns, sees the woman frozen in the doorway. Their eyes meet through the dark lenses. Instead of looking away, instead of waiting for the woman to speak first, Tasha crosses the room and asks gently, **"What made you come in today?"**

The question hangs in the air—not an accusation, not a demand, but an invitation. The woman's shoulders loosen just slightly. She takes a breath, and begins to speak.

The circle widens to include her. One more crown to protect.

22

Epilogue: CROWNS UP

When women hold each other's crowns,
they rise higher than any kingdom built to contain them.
—J.C. Reedburg

Queen's Crown, Evening

By seven p.m., Queen's Crown shimmered like a fortress lit for carnival. The old glass door now bore a bulletproof shield, but Tasha left it open just enough for the music to bleed out: a Stevie Wonder cut, the one where the keys climbed like hope after a funeral. Inside, a hundred tea lights cast rings on the lacquered floors, and every wall reflected not faces, but the years of bruised and stubborn living that built this place.

Above the check-in desk, a collage ran floor to ceiling: photos of girls and women, some smiling, some not, everyone caught surviving. In the center, Quanda's portrait—her head thrown back in laughter, mouth wide, hair wrapped in fabric the color of fire hydrants and protest signs. Below, a banner read:

"She is not a ghost. She's the blueprint."

Tasha walked the floor in a crown of her own making: braids coiled tight, pattern rippling from temple to nape, each section edged with amethyst beads. The braid ran regal and hard, and every woman in the room glanced at it, then met her eyes and nodded, a silent chain of recognition.

Roxie manned the food table, one hand balancing a tray of empanadas, the other steadying baby Crown on her hip. The kid was a stone cold flirt—every time someone reached for a drink, he'd flash a dimpled smile and reach out a sticky fist. Tasha saw him work the room, collecting coos and pinched cheeks from women who'd never trusted a man in their lives, and felt a fierce, crooked pride. **Maybe the world really could flip, if you raised the boys right from jump.**

Near the mirrors, Jonesha and Andrea manned the makeshift bar, mixing sweet tea and dollar champagne in plastic cups, gossiping in a soft tag-team rhythm that ran under the music. Every time Tasha looked their way, Andrea would wink and point at her own crown—cornrows threaded with neon yellow ribbon, slick and defiant.

"You the main event," she mouthed, and Tasha would roll her eyes, but she couldn't hide the glow.

People crowded the space: women from the halfway house, a few old-timers from the neighborhood who'd known Tasha before her first juvie stint, two church moms in ankle-length dresses, even a line cook from the Cuban place down the block, still in his whites and hairnet. More than a few faces were strangers, but all wore the same armor—posture a little too upright, jaw set for whatever the night threw at them.

It had been one year since Quanda's name left the newspapers and became legend. One year since the city tried to choke this place out with lawsuits, break-ins, and a parade of inspectors who never found what they were paid to find. Instead, Queen's Crown grew harder, stranger, more necessary. The new door was the first upgrade. The next was the security system—cameras in every corner, the feed encrypted and mirrored to Arman's laptop, patched through three relays so even the feds would have to sweat to break in.

Tasha caught Arman at the edge of the crowd, hunched over the admin tablet. He wore a Stanford hoodie two sizes too big and a pair of ancient shell-toes, but his hair was sharp, the fade tight as prison sheets. When she passed, he glanced up and gave her a half-smile, then pointed to the ceiling cam with a slow, dorky thumbs-up.

"System's clean," he whispered. **"Nobody gets in or out without a pass."**

Tasha grinned, low. **"I trust you."**

He turned pink, but his shoulders squared, like he'd waited his whole life for that sentence.

The next wave of guests arrived in a crash: two girls in jeans and matching Hello Kitty tees, shepherded by Mama Esther, who moved slow but took up twice as much space as anyone else. She'd wrapped her head in purple, the fabric stenciled with tiny white doves, and she carried a bundle of sage thick enough to smoke out the statehouse. The girls each clutched a jar candle, both grinning at the chaos.

Esther paused in the entry, clocked the room in a single sweep, then marched straight to the corners, setting the sage on fire and muttering what sounded like threats to every demon in a half-mile radius. Smoke coiled in the air, mixing with the scent of hair oil and Andrea's contraband tequila. The room stilled a bit. Tasha watched as the regulars—old haters, new believers—breathed it in, faces softening. **Nobody messed with Nana Esther's rites.**

At the heart of the floor, Tasha planted herself, ready to receive. The people came to her one by one: the auntie from Decatur who ran a girls' basketball team, the battered woman with two toddlers she'd smuggled upstairs just six months ago, a college kid who used to crash on the salon's couch between shifts. Each stepped forward to share their story of breaking silence.

"I left him after fifteen years," one woman said, voice steady despite the tremor in her hands. **"Called that number you gave me at three in the morning. Walked out with just my purse and my kids."**

Another raised her chin, revealing a scar that ran from ear to collarbone.

"I testified against my uncle last month. He can't hurt nobody else now."

A girl barely out of her teens spoke so quietly Tasha had to lean in:

"I finally told my mama what happened at that party. She believed me."

Tasha took each testimony, storing the warmth and the sorrow in equal measure.

At exactly eight, a hush cut through the laughter. The door opened, and

Detective Vega stepped inside, hair pulled back to expose the scar on her jaw, suit jacket swapped for a fitted black tee. She walked with the limp she'd earned in the takedown, and tonight she carried no badge, just a flat brown box under one arm.

The crowd parted for her. Nobody whispered her name, but everyone knew. The air snapped electric; even the candles seemed to burn bluer.

Vega walked up to the memorial wall, set the box on the ledge, and opened it with slow hands. Inside: a single photo in a heavy silver frame. The woman in the picture was a young version of Vega—same sharp brow, same impossible eyes—but softer, smiling over a cake with pink icing. A plastic tiara sat crooked on her head.

Vega stared at the photo for a second. Then she turned to Tasha.

"Her name was Elena," she said. **"She never made it past fifteen. Lance Rivers was her first arrest."**

Tasha's lungs froze. The room stayed silent.

Vega placed the photo on the wall, nestling it between Quanda's portrait and the photo of a Black girl in a graduation cap. Then she turned to Tasha, voice gone ragged but fierce.

"She belongs with the others now."

Tasha didn't speak—just reached out and pulled Vega into a tight, unyielding hug. The room pulsed, raw and real, with the weight of every girl lost and every woman left standing. For a long moment, nobody dared break the silence.

Mama Esther shuffled to the center, voice ringing out.

"Ancestors got all kinds of daughters," she declared, waving the sage bundle high. **"Tonight, we honor every one."** The girls in Hello Kitty tees chanted, **"Ase! Ase!"** until even the shy ones joined in, the call bouncing off every tile.

Andrea handed out flutes of peach juice and champagne, and Jonesha led a toast:

"To the blueprints. To the ones who teach us how to build."

The candles flickered, and Tasha let herself lean against the wall, her crown gleaming under the kitchen LEDs. For one perfect hour, the Queen's

Crown held the entire block together—not just safe, but alive.

Queen's Crown, Later Evening

The evening drifted slow, bodies stacked in the narrow aisles, but when the old clock hit nine-thirty, Tasha straightened her crown and raised a palm. The room went hush, not because she demanded it, but because everyone knew the real work was about to start.

She cleared her throat, voice carrying over the hum.

"One year ago, we lost Quanda. Since then, this place turned into something she'd be proud of. Not just a shop—a damn embassy for survivors." The women whooped and clapped, but Tasha waved them down, eyes finding Arman at the edge.

"Some of us build with our hands," she said, **"but some build with their brains. Arman's got a gift, and tonight he wants to show us how it's used."**

He flushed, but he didn't shrink back. Instead, he pulled a battered Chromebook from his bag and stepped to the table. The crowd parted, curious, as he set up his demo.

Arman clicked open a browser window, then tapped the screen twice.

"I built this to help find missing people," he said, voice pitched for the women at the back. **"The police don't always care. So, I used their own data against them."**

Tasha grinned, proud as hell.

He ran through a slideshow: maps studded with red, orange, and blue dots; timelines stretching back ten years; charts that lit up with every cross-state spike in disappearances.

"I scrape the records from the state, then run a pattern match. If the same badge shows up more than once—especially if they're from the old Rivers network—it flags it here." He pointed, and the room leaned in.

A ripple went through the crowd, women recognizing a cousin or friend in the anonymized cases. Jonesha cussed under her breath. Andrea whistled, long and low.

Arman finished.

"You got a name, a face, or even a nickname? Tell me. I'll search it. And if there's a way to find her, I'll help."

He looked up, met Tasha's eyes. For a second, he was the kid she first saw: scared, unsteady. Then the light changed, and he was a man, sure in his purpose.

The applause was thunder, rough and honest. Tasha blinked back the burn behind her eyelids.

Before the noise faded, a tiny body wobbled into the space between Tasha and Arman. Baby Crown, hair in a wild afro, shirt stained with the night's food, but face set on a single mission: the memorial wall.

He tottered across the polished floor, fat feet slapping, and stretched his arms high to the photo of Quanda. He missed, then tried again, and this time his fist landed square on the glass, leaving a perfect smear of drool and baby handprint.

The party stopped. Every woman in the room sucked in a breath, and even Arman's voice dropped to a whisper.

Tasha crouched down, close to the boy's ear.

"She sees you, little king," she said, soft enough that only he could hear.

Crown stared up, then giggled—a belly laugh so loud it bounced off the mirrors. He let go, then toddled back to Roxie, who swept him up and buried her face in his curls. For a moment, the world reset itself.

Someone near the back gasped.

"I felt that. Got cold all the sudden."

Another said,

"Is that honey and sandalwood? That was Quanda's favorite scent."

Mama Esther nodded, hands folded.

"The ancestors never really leave us," she pronounced. **"They just visit when you get the recipe right."**

Women started swapping stories—times they'd heard a voice in their sleep, or found a rose on the stoop, or caught a dream that tasted like sugar and fire. Andrea swore she saw the wall's candles flare up in unison, but nobody argued with her. Not tonight.

Tasha watched Crown work the room. The kid's jaw was stubborn, but his eyes were kind; the shape of his chin pure Quanda. She looked for traces of Dejuan, of the monster who'd tried to stamp out every spark in this bloodline, but found none. Instead, she saw the future: Crown's light brown hands, wide and strong, would hold more than violence. They would hold the world.

Jonesha cleared her throat.

"It's time," she said, not quite an order, more like an invitation.

Everyone gathered, women and a few men, old and young, shoulder to shoulder. Even the toddlers lined up, holding the hands of their mothers or big sisters or whoever claimed them tonight.

They made a circle, tight as braids. Tasha squeezed Jonesha's palm on her left, Roxie's on her right. The power of it buzzed up her arms, set her chest humming.

Esther took the lead.

"Repeat after me: Silence is only powerful when you choose it."

"Silence is only powerful when you choose it," they all said, the sound heavy with memory.

Esther again:

"Otherwise, it's just another cage."

A beat, then the chorus:

"Otherwise, it's just another cage."

Crown broke the rhythm, shouting **"CAGE!"** so loud that the laughter spilled over. Someone started clapping, and soon it was a song, the beat echoing through the building.

They let the moment linger, circle unbroken, for as long as it took to feel the loss and the victory both. In the quiet after, Tasha knew it wasn't over. The city would keep making ghosts, keep testing the locks, but as long as Queen's Crown stood, nobody had to fight alone.

Queen's Crown, Night

As the celebration wound down, Tasha stood alone by the memorial wall. One by one, the women came to say goodnight, each touching her shoulder or pressing a kiss to her cheek before heading out into the night. The room emptied slowly, leaving only the glow of candles and the whisper of sage smoke.

Roxie came last, Crown asleep on her shoulder.

"We did good tonight," she said softly. **"She would've loved it."**

Tasha nodded, unable to speak past the knot in her throat. She reached out to stroke Crown's cheek, his skin warm under her fingertips.

"I'll be back in the morning," Roxie promised, then slipped out the door, leaving Tasha alone with the portraits of the women who had found their way to Queen's Crown.

Tasha moved slowly along the wall, studying each face. The teenager who ran away from her abuser in Tennessee. The mother who escaped a trafficking ring with her infant daughter. The college student who testified against her professor. Each woman's story a testament to survival, to choosing life over silence.

At the end of the row, mounted just below Quanda's portrait, hung an empty picture frame. Tasha had placed it there herself that morning, carefully centering it among the other photos. She traced the edge of the frame now, feeling its smooth surface under her fingers.

She took a small card from her pocket and slipped it into the frame. On it, written in her neat, careful script:

Who will you help find her voice?

The question wasn't just for the visitors who would come tomorrow and the day after. It was for Tasha herself, a daily reminder of the work still to be done, the women still waiting to be found.

She stood back, surveying the wall of survivors and the empty frame that promised more to come. Queen's Crown wasn't just a salon anymore. It was a beacon, calling the next survivor home.

"Silence is only powerful when you choose it," Tasha whispered to the empty room. **"Otherwise, it's just another cage."**

The candles flickered as if in response, casting long shadows across the floor. Tasha didn't need to look around to know that Quanda was there, watching over this place she had built, this legacy she had left behind.

Queen's Crown, Late Night

As Tasha turned to switch off the lights, the bell above the door chimed—a soft, uncertain sound in the quiet. A young woman stepped inside, shoulders hunched, sunglasses hiding her eyes even though the sun had long set. She paused just inside, fingers twisting the strap of her purse.

Tasha recognized the posture—the way fear and hope could live in the same body. She smiled, gentle and sure, and patted the nearest chair.

"Come on in, queen," Tasha said, her voice soft but strong. "Let me fix your crown."

The woman hesitated, then nodded, a small smile breaking through. She stepped forward, and the circle widened once more.

Tasha reached for her comb, feeling Quanda's spirit at her back, the echoes of every woman who'd ever sat in that chair. The work was never done, but tonight, it felt like enough.

23

Author's Note

Thank you for reading **The Price of Silence** and for journeying with these characters through every secret, scar, and hard-won truth. This story began as a love letter to the women who hold communities together, even when the world tries to silence them. But Atlanta's shadows run deep, and every silence has its own history.

The following bonus interlude, "The Name You Bury," offers a glimpse into Dejuan Rivers' journey—a story of survival, complicity, and the impossible choices made behind prison walls. While the main narrative centers on the women of Queen's Crown Salon, Dejuan's story reveals another side of the city's legacy—one that will echo through future books in the *No Tears For Black Girls* series.

If you're curious about the Rivers family, the networks of power and pain that shape Atlanta, or the stories left untold in the margins, this chapter is for you.

To hear the real stories that inspired this novel and to join our growing community of advocates, visit NoTearsForBlackGirls.com/p/Price-Of-Silence.

The Price of Silence – Official Soundtrack

Step into the world of *The Price of Silence* with this exclusive soundtrack, inspired by the novel's characters, themes, and the city of Atlanta. Each track brings to life the struggles, hope, and resilience of the women at Queen's Crown Salon—and the secrets that haunt their community.

Listen here: https://tinyurl.com/Price-Of-Silence-Soundtrack

Thank you for supporting independent storytelling.

Stay tuned—there's more to come.

With gratitude,

24

BONUS INTERLUDE: THE NAME YOU BURY (DEJUAN'S STORY)

A secret is a chain—each link forged in silence, each silence heavier than the last.

—James Rivers

Candler-McAfee, Atlanta, Night

By the time the streetlights buzzed on in Candler-McAfee, Dejuan Rivers had already counted eighty-two cracks on his side of the block. Each one mapped a shortcut or an escape if the night twisted the wrong way. He watched the corners from the busted porch of an abandoned shotgun house, hoodie zipped up so tight only his nose poked out.

Moms used to say this city belonged to the bold, but Dejuan learned quick it really belonged to the ones who ran faster, hid better, or hit first. That's why his backpack hung light against his spine: nothing but a roll of baggies, a flip phone with three saved numbers, and enough cash to ride MARTA to Decatur and back twice.

He checked the time—7:09 p.m.—and dropped to the sidewalk, hands jammed in pockets. Every house on this stretch wore plywood on the windows and white X's on the doors, signals to the city that nobody cared enough to claim them. The cars on the street rolled past slow, watching for kids dumb enough to be out solo after dark.

Dejuan moved quick, ducking behind the rusted fence at the corner lot. Tonight's client was supposed to meet him by the old rec center, but nobody in East Atlanta came early unless they wanted to get robbed. He waited, breathing in the wet-dog smell of kudzu that wrapped every building from the gutter to the roof.

A Civic squealed around the corner, scraping its bumper over the curb. The headlights blinked once, then flashed again. Dejuan jogged out, hands loose, face blank like he'd seen in all the best dealer movies. The driver—a pale kid in a varsity jacket—motioned him over.

Dejuan leaned in, just enough to clock the other faces in the car. Two girls in the back seat, both giggling, both avoiding eye contact.

"How much?" the driver asked, voice cracked with nerves.

Dejuan quoted the number. The kid dug in his pocket and held out a fistful of crumpled bills.

He counted it fast, stuffed the cash in his sleeve, and handed over the baggie. The kid peeled out, tires spitting gravel, the girls' laughter trailing like ghosts in the night.

Easy money. Dejuan's heart thudded as he peeled off in the other direction, headed for the corner store. The world sharpened around him: the way the lights made the puddles shimmer like fresh oil, the sharp tang of garbage from the alley. He kept his stride even, but scanned every reflection in the dark glass storefronts, every stray movement in the side streets.

Halfway down the block, he heard the scrape of shoes behind him. He picked up the pace, turned a sharp right into an alley lined with overturned shopping carts and busted TV sets.

The alley dead-ended at a fence, but he knew the move—up, over, land soft on the other side. He grabbed the chain-link, ready to pull himself up, but a hand locked on his ankle and yanked.

Dejuan hit the concrete knees-first. He twisted, tried to kick, but two more hands clamped down on his arms.

Three dudes. Older, heavier, one with a scar across his cheek and teeth like the bars on a jail cell. The leader got real close, his breath hot and sour.

"You think you slick, little Rivers?" He jammed a thumb into Dejuan's ribs. "That's our corner."

Dejuan spat at the ground, tried to roll his shoulders free. "Ain't nobody own the city."

The third guy, short and twitchy, yanked Dejuan's backpack and dumped it out. The cash hit the ground, bills fanning across the trash. The weed baggies followed. Scarface bent down, scooped a few up, and sniffed at them like he was grading a science project.

"Told you it was him," Twitch said. "They say he family to that cop out in Zone Three."

Scarface made a show of counting the money. He shook his head and popped Dejuan in the mouth—fast, not even angry, just business. Dejuan tasted iron, felt the skin split inside his cheek.

"I should fuck you up for that last time," Scarface said, voice syrupy. "But I'ma let you live. Just don't cross this block again." He jabbed a finger in Dejuan's face, then scattered the cash down the alley. The bills fluttered, wet and dirty.

Dejuan wiped his mouth and glared up at them, fists balled tight. "Y'all done?"

The big guy stomped his wrist for good measure, then laughed. The three melted back into the night, their voices fading.

Dejuan sat for a second, the world fuzzing at the edges. He checked his lip. It leaked blood down his chin, staining the white of his hoodie. He pulled himself up, gathered what bills he could, and shoved the rest of the stash down his pants. His ribs throbbed, each breath sharp.

He didn't call nobody. Not the family, not his uncle, not even the backup number on his phone. Every block of his life, folks expected him to coast on Rivers blood, but Dejuan wanted to win his own fights. Even if it meant losing a few.

He remembered Sunday dinners, the table crowded with cousins and uncles, everyone talking over each other. His father, silent at the head, eyes sharp as knives. "A Rivers man don't beg," he'd say, voice low. "We take what's ours." Dejuan learned early that love in his family was measured in what you could survive, not what you could share.

The only thing he did was walk to the corner store, buy a Sprite with the least-wet bill, and use the bathroom sink to rinse out his mouth. The clerk looked up. In this part of the city, a busted lip and a bloody shirt just meant you made it through another day.

By the time he hit the main drag again, the street buzzed louder. Atlanta PD cruisers rolled past, red-and-blue blinking over the busted glass and old paint. Dejuan kept his head low, walked like he had somewhere to be.

He felt the cop car slow before he saw it. The lights stopped, then reversed, pulling to the curb. Two officers, both white, both looking bored and mean. One rolled down the window and called out.

"Hey! You. Over here."

Dejuan didn't run. He knew that move ended with a gun in his face and knees on his back. He stepped to the curb, hands out, palms open.

"What's your name?" the first cop asked.

He answered.

The second cop snorted. "Rivers, huh? Any relation to Captain James out at the precinct?"

Dejuan shrugged. "Maybe. Don't matter."

The first cop looked him over, eyes lingering on the wet blood on his shirt, then the torn backpack. "You been fighting, son?"

Dejuan shook his head. "Fell off my bike. It's not even mine, I was borrowing it."

The cops exchanged a look. Then the first one got out, circled behind Dejuan. Quick as a blink, he grabbed Dejuan's wrist, snapped on a cuff.

"Got a tip about a deal going down near the rec center. You know anything about that?"

Dejuan kept his eyes down. "No, sir."

The second cop got out too, frisked him fast. "What's this, then?" he said, pulling the last baggie from Dejuan's waistband.

"Never seen that," Dejuan said, voice even. "You planted it."

First cop just smiled, slow and wide. "You think we need to plant on a Rivers? Your whole family's got a record."

Dejuan gritted his teeth. He could smell the bacon grease on the cop's breath.

A neighbor watched from a porch down the block, face shadowed behind the screen. Dejuan made eye contact and shook his head, real slow. *No witnesses.*

The cop shoved him toward the cruiser. As they walked, Dejuan heard the click of the radio and the hiss of static.

"Bringing in a juvenile, possible possession, resisting. Yeah. Rivers."

They stuffed him in the backseat. The world outside twisted, the neon of the gas station, the hollowed eyes of the night shift clerk, the ugly green glow of the jail sign in the distance.

He touched the split on his lip, felt the sting, and tasted blood again.

He wouldn't give them the satisfaction. Wouldn't cry, wouldn't flinch. Not even when the cuffs dug into the bone. He stared out at the city, watched the lights blur past, and promised himself:

He'd come back. He'd win, even if he had to take the city one crack at a time.

Phillips State Prison, Morning

Dejuan walked the line at Phillips State Prison with his face blank, eyes forward, the same way he'd walked his whole life—like every step was his own idea. The guard behind him barked orders, but he kept the pace steady, never letting them see him shake.

The intake wing looked like a forgotten bus station: gray tile, metal benches, a row of vending machines stripped of every snack but pork rinds and off-brand soda. A dozen other men waited with him, wrists zip-tied and ankles heavy with state-issue chains. Nobody spoke. The only sound was the buzz of the lights and the distant clang of a cell door slamming shut.

When his name was called, Dejuan stood. He followed the guard into a room with no windows. Strip. Stand on the tape. Hands on head. He did it quick, flinching at the cold. The guard didn't care, just checked his mouth, his hair, under his feet. Every time the hands touched him, Dejuan forced himself not to react.

He remembered the words from his old man, back before the state packed him up: "They get inside your head first. Don't let 'em in."

They gave him an orange jumpsuit, two sizes too big, and flip-flops that dug into the skin between his toes. He changed, eyes on the floor. The guard handed him a mesh bag: one towel, one roll of toilet paper, a toothbrush with the bristles already bent sideways. No pillow, no socks.

The march to the block took forever. Hallways echoed every footstep, every cough, every whispered threat. As he entered general population, all eyes locked on him. Some laughed, some stared. Most looked through him, calculating.

He got a top bunk in a cell already smelling of piss and sweat. The cellmate was an older man, tattooed from neck to wrist, who never looked up from his Sudoku book. Dejuan didn't say shit to him, just climbed up, curled against the wall, and stared at the ceiling.

That first night, he barely slept. The noise never died: men screaming, fists on bars, keys jangling up and down the corridor. Sometimes a guard would drag someone out, sometimes they didn't come back. At breakfast, a line of men shuffled into the chow hall, heads down, shuffling trays loaded with gray eggs and biscuits hard enough to break teeth.

After a week, the routine set in. He walked the yard in the mornings, did push-ups until his arms felt hollow, kept his back to the wall and his eyes on the gate. He learned which blocks belonged to which gangs, who ran which hustle, and which guards would look the other way if you made it worth their while.

The showers came last. Always after lights out, when the air still steamed and the only guards on shift watched from behind the glass.

He waited until most were done, then stripped down and stepped in. The tiles were slick with grime. He kept his head up, rinsed fast, ignored the stares.

He didn't see the guy come up behind him. Just felt the blade, cold against his ribs, a whisper in his ear.

"Wallet, rookie. Or you get cut."

Dejuan tensed. The guy was bigger, but not much. He flicked his eyes around, saw the other inmates pretending not to notice. He didn't move.

"You deaf?" The blade pressed harder. "Last chance—"

Another voice cut in. Low, sharp, all steel.

"Put the knife away."

The big guy looked up, face slack with surprise. Standing there, towel slung loose over one shoulder, was the oldest Black man Dejuan had ever seen. His skin was gray as the cinderblock wall, and his arms corded with muscle. He didn't raise his voice, didn't flinch.

"Or you want to try me first?"

Big guy hesitated, then lowered the knife. He gave Dejuan a hard shove before slinking off, muttering.

Dejuan looked at the old man, waiting for a joke or a threat. But the man just shrugged, eyes soft, and left.

Back in the cell, Dejuan nursed the welt on his side. The next day, at lunch, he saw the old man again, sitting alone, eyes closed like he was at peace.

He approached, slow.

"Thanks," he said.

The old man opened his eyes. Up close, Dejuan saw the wrinkles fanned out from his nose to his ears, the way his hands shook just a little when he lifted his cup.

"You got family?" the old man asked, not looking up.

"Not in here," Dejuan said.

"Now you do," the man replied, and smiled—a tight, tired smile.

Dejuan sat, watched the yard while they ate. It took a while before he realized everyone else was watching them.

After chow, a guard stopped him in the hall. "Warden wants you," he said, and steered him into an office off the main block.

Inside, a man in a uniform waited, not the warden but someone higher up. He had a face carved from stone, eyes flat and unreadable. On his chest: RIVERS. The name tag hit Dejuan like a sucker punch.

"Sit," Captain Rivers said, motioning to the chair.

Dejuan sat. His palms left sweat stains on the metal.

"You know who I am?" Rivers asked.

He nodded.

"You know why you're here?"

He shook his head.

Rivers leaned forward. "Because you're smart. You don't run your mouth. You keep your head down. But you need to know—this place? It's a game, and you better learn the rules fast."

Dejuan held the captain's gaze, forced himself not to blink.

"You ever heard of loyalty?" Rivers asked.

Dejuan nodded again, slow.

"In here, blood means something. But loyalty means everything." The captain's fingers tapped out a rhythm on the desk. "I can keep you safe. But you got to give me something in return."

Dejuan's jaw tightened. "Why should I trust you?"

Rivers's lips curled. "You shouldn't. Not yet. But the other option is you end up like that kid last month—face down in the showers with a toothbrush stuck in his throat."

They stared at each other. The silence stretched.

Finally, Rivers leaned back and folded his arms. "Think about it. You got until tomorrow."

Dejuan stood, walked out with his hands shaking, and didn't stop until he reached his cell. He lay on the top bunk, eyes on the ceiling, counting the cracks.

He remembered his mother's words, years ago: "Never let them make you what they want."

But as the sun set, and the air filled with the sound of men breaking, he wondered what choice he had left.

The next day, he found the old man in the yard and sat beside him. He said nothing, just nodded.

The old man smiled that tired smile, and together, they watched the rest of the world go by.

Phillips State Prison, Months Later

Three months in, Dejuan knew how to move anything that fit through a slot or a fist. The first lesson James taught him: fear only works until somebody figures out you're bluffing. Money? Money always worked.

By now, Dejuan's jumpsuit hung off him like a scarecrow, but the pockets stayed fat. He floated between cellblocks, never stopping long enough to catch static, always keeping the hustle alive.

Today's order was for ten packs of menthols and three vials of tramadol. He hid the cigs in a hollowed-out King James Bible, the kind handed out by church volunteers. The vials went in the cardboard core of a used toilet paper roll, sealed with soap so nobody noticed.

In the chapel, the chaplain read from Romans while Dejuan palmed the Bible to a muscle-bound guy with tear tattoos under both eyes. The exchange lasted two seconds: a handshake, a cough, a muttered "Bless you." On the way out, Dejuan slipped a folded napkin into the hymnal rack—time and place for the next drop.

He ran messages for James, too. Some went by whisper, some by code scrawled under lunch trays. When a guard was on the take, Dejuan called him by first name, dropped hints about birthdays and favorite teams. When a guard wasn't, he acted dumb, eyes down, never talked out loud.

Morales was easy. He wore cheap cologne and kept his shirt unbuttoned too low. The man liked to gamble, owed the wrong people. Dejuan waited for him in the break room, under the flicker of a half-dead bulb. When Morales showed, Dejuan handed him an envelope, heavy with twenties.

"Next Friday," Dejuan said. "Same spot."

Morales nodded, wiped his nose, and shoved the cash in his pocket. "You didn't see me," he said.

"I never do."

Later, on the yard, Dejuan met with two other inmates—Short Dog and Kane. The east wall had a loose patch of concrete the size of a fist. Every Friday, someone would dig out the mortar, stash the goods, patch it back up before the guards did rounds.

Short Dog handled the drop this week. Kane played lookout. Dejuan checked the clock, watched as Morales leaned against the fence, pretending to light a cigarette, eyes on the perimeter.

Everything ran on schedule.

But sometimes things slipped. Like last month, when a new guard tried to shake down Dejuan after chapel. He got cocky, wanted a cut. Dejuan smiled, said nothing, but later that night James sent a message through the block: "Respect the food chain." Next day, the guard switched to minimum security, and nobody heard from him again.

Dejuan kept a mental ledger: who owed what, who wanted more, who could be counted on to show up or stay quiet. He learned that most men in here just wanted to survive until their next parole hearing, or until someone else got shanked and moved the danger up a rung.

By his second year inside, Dejuan's network ran deeper than most guards realized. Some took bribes to look the other way. Others, desperate or just tired enough, let themselves be traded to the highest bidder. The high-rollers paid for more than cigarettes or pills. Dejuan kept the books, made the introductions, and never asked questions. In prison, everyone was for sale—some just didn't know their price yet. He told himself it was just business, but the silence that followed every deal was heavier than any debt.

The best days were when the trade moved so smooth, nobody noticed except the cash. Dejuan once swapped out the entire commissary order for B-block without setting foot in the chow line. Another time, he got a carton of Parliament Lights past three strip searches by hollowing out the soles of shower slides.

But what stuck with him most was the way the guards looked at him now—not like prey, not like a punk, but as a player. Morales even bought him a soda from the vending machine once, just to keep things cool.

One afternoon, Dejuan watched Morales count out the money in the break room, eyes darting to the security cam that was always, mysteriously, out of order. The guard's hands shook a little, but not as much as when Dejuan first met him.

Dejuan grinned, leaned against the doorframe.

"Good doing business," he said.

Morales just grunted, pocketed the bills, and left.

Back in his cell, Dejuan lay on the top bunk and stared at the ceiling. He thought about all the men who'd tried to beat the system and failed. He thought about James, waiting in his own cell two tiers up, running the whole thing with just a look and a word.

He remembered a story James once told, late at night in the old apartment, about the first time he saw a man die for a debt. "You don't ever let them see you flinch," James had said, voice flat. "The world's full of men who'll take your kindness for weakness. You give them an inch, they'll bury you in it."

Dejuan knew he was still a pawn. Maybe always would be. But he was learning the moves, piece by piece.

And as long as the money kept flowing, the rest of the game didn't scare him at all.

Phillips State Prison, Age 27

By the time he hit 27, Dejuan Rivers ran more of the prison than half the guards on payroll. He managed three fake marriages, two real ones (one ended in divorce, the other in a quiet transfer), and a waiting list of lonely hearts willing to pay for a weekend of freedom behind locked doors.

He wrote letters for men who couldn't spelled their own names, spun stories of romance and redemption for women who sent money and snacks by the box. He ghostwrote apologies, love notes, even parole appeals. Sometimes he wrote his own, usually to Quanda, who'd stuck with him through every transfer, every close call. She deserved better than a man in a cage, but he gave her words, full of hope, dressed up in pretty lies.

"We all get reborn in here, Q. Some days, I almost believe it."

He signed every letter with a nickname he never used outside those pages: "*Dee.*" Short. Friendly. Somebody she could miss without shame.

Every week, he slid contraband lists to James, tucked into crossword books or legal pads. The operation grew faster than he ever expected—phones, designer shoes, anything that gave a man leverage. He learned which guards to pay, which to threaten, and which to leave alone.

He watched a woman in a cheap dress, hands shaking as she signed

the marriage papers for a man she'd never met. The guards joked, the inmates jeered, but Dejuan saw the way her eyes darted to the door, already planning her escape. He remembered the Queen's Crown hair clip Quanda once wore, the way it caught the light in the conjugal room, a flash of hope in a place built for forgetting.

One afternoon, he watched from the yard as a new kid—barely eighteen, scared shitless—refused a recruit order from one of James's lieutenants. The kid stood his ground, fists shaking but voice steady.

"Not doing it," he said. "Don't care what you do to me."

James's guy shrugged, walked off, but the next hour guards came down hard. Dragged the kid into solitary, his screams echoing through the vents. Dejuan listened, arms folded, face blank.

Later, when James's men brought the kid back, he was quiet. Didn't resist as they pressed him against the wall and took turns with their fists. Dejuan leaned close, whispered where to hit so the bruises didn't show under the uniform. The men nodded, eyes flat.

After, Dejuan walked the block, head high, watching the other inmates take the lesson. Loyalty didn't come cheap, but it always paid out in the end.

He saved the hardest part of the day for last—writing to Quanda.

Some letters he started and never finished, words running off the edge of the paper. Others he filled with dreams he barely remembered having, about Atlanta, about sun on his face and the taste of real air.

He tried not to lie, but sometimes the truth wasn't worth the stamp.

That night, he stared into the cracked mirror taped above the sink, traced the lines that had deepened on his face. His hair grew wild, but he kept it neat on top, like she always liked. The eyes were darker now, not mean, just tired. The smile, when it came, was quick and gone fast.

He thought of the kid in the yard, the one who'd tried to fight the tide. He remembered being that boy, once—before James, before the game, before he learned that nobody wins if they don't cheat.

He looked at the chessboard on the shelf. The pieces set up for a game he played against himself, every move predictable, every outcome already decided.

He grabbed the pawn, rolled it between his fingers. For a second, he almost believed he could throw the whole board out the window and start over.

But the game never really ended, and tomorrow would come whether he wanted it or not.

He put the pawn back, picked up his pen, and finished the letter.

"I'll see you on the other side, Q. Bet on that."

He sealed the envelope, smoothed it flat, and let his hand linger on her name.

For the first time all week, he allowed himself to smile.

Queen's Crown Salon, Dream Sequence

Sometimes, late at night, Dejuan let himself imagine walking through the doors of Queen's Crown. Tasha would be there, running the shop, the air thick with the scent of burnt sugar and acrylic. He'd sit in the chair, let her trim away the years, and maybe—just maybe—find a piece of himself worth saving. But the city never forgets, and some doors only open in dreams.

Phillips State Prison, Stabbing & Reckoning

It happened fast. One minute, Dejuan was moving through the corridor, the next—a flash of metal, a sharp pain in his side. He staggered, blood blooming through his jumpsuit, the world tilting. He hit the ground, gasping, the taste of iron flooding his mouth.

From the shadows, an older female guard stepped forward, her face carved with grief and rage. She knelt beside him, her voice a whisper only he could hear.

"You remember Mariah? The one you sent to C-block, the one you pimped out to those animals? She was my daughter. She only took this job to help feed her baby. I came out of retirement for this moment. Right here. To watch you die. Rest comfortably in hell, piece of shit."

Dejuan tried to speak, but the world was already slipping away. As everything went black, he felt hands lifting him; he felt the cold metal of a stretcher beneath his back and saw the blurred lights as they rushed him through the prison and airlifted him to a hospital.

Hallucination—Judgment and Crowns

He is floating, weightless, in a place that glows with a strange, golden light. The air is thick with the scent of sage and burnt sugar, the hum of a thousand whispered prayers. Quanda stands before him, radiant, her hair wrapped in a crown of fire and protest, her eyes full of sorrow and something like peace. Around her, a circle of people—faces he recognizes, all the ones he'd harmed, all the ones now dead—stand in silence, dressed in white. Each wears a crown: some braids, some beads, some thorns, some of light.

Quanda speaks first, her voice both gentle and unyielding. "I've seen you thinking about me. About what you did. About what you did to all of us. Your truth hid in the darkness, but now it's come to be exposed in the light. That light is God himself, Dejuan. He's your judge now."

Dejuan's voice is steady, almost pleading. "I didn't mean to do what I did to you. It's something in me I couldn't control. I wasn't born this way. My environment forced me to be the man I became. I wasn't born a monster."

Quanda smiles, gentle and sad. The circle of the dead closes in, their voices rising in unison: **"We forgive you, Dejuan."**

Quanda steps forward, her hand warm on his cheek. "Death isn't a good enough punishment for you. You need to live and face your consequences. That puncture in your lungs you feel right now, that gasp of breath you're fighting for—that's the best thing for you. You are not worthy of the light, Dejuan. You deserve darkness. Maybe, if you learn how to deserve peace, you'll make your life with God before the next time you come back here again."

She looks him in the eye, her voice clear. "I say this again with my whole heart: I forgive you, Dejuan." She kisses him, soft and final.

The crowns around him shimmer, and for a moment, he feels the weight and the grace of every life he touched—every crown he tried to break, every crown that survived him. The light grows brighter, then fades.

Hospital, The Edge

The ethereal surroundings shift. Dejuan feels the cold metal of the stretcher on his back, the exposed flesh stinging as the hospital lights blur above him. EMTs and hospital staff rush him down the corridor. One of them leans close, voice urgent: "Fight. You can survive this."

Dejuan forces a breath through the tubes in his nose, lungs burning. He closes his eyes for a moment of release.

In the darkness behind his eyelids, he sees a single, shining crown—woven of braids, beads, and hope—rising above the city. He reaches for it, but it floats just out of reach, a promise and a warning. The world moves on, loud and messy and alive. Somewhere, a child laughs, and the light of Queen's Crown glows like a beacon, guiding the lost home.

Everything goes black.

About the Author

J.C. Reedburg is an award-winning author whose work transcends conventional storytelling boundaries. As the creator of the groundbreaking "No Tears For Black Girls" series, Reedburg crafts powerful narratives that explore justice, resilience, and the strength of community. Their unflinching prose balances raw realism with moments of unexpected lyricism.

The first installment in the series, "The Price of Silence," is inspired by Reedburg's acclaimed true crime podcast and delves into how silence can serve as both weapon and shield. Through the interconnected stories of women battling corrupt systems in Atlanta's vibrant yet perilous neighborhoods, Reedburg shines a light on voices too often left unheard.

Previously publishing as John Charles Reedburg, the author's novel "Cracks of Light" won the 2021 Readers' Favorite Book Award in Urban Fiction and reached Amazon's Top 10 bestseller list. This coming-of-age story blends urban and magical realism, following a nine-year-old boy in 1990s Los Angeles who discovers a mysterious light that becomes his refuge from a troubled home.

Reedburg holds dual MFAs in Creative Writing from Antioch University Los Angeles and in Screenwriting/Directing from Chapman University, bringing sophisticated narrative craft and multimedia storytelling expertise to every project. Their work has appeared in publications including the Fictional Cafe.

J.C. Reedburg also writes as John Reedburg, with additional works including the metaphysical drama "Stain of Sin," the techno-thriller "Human Hawk," and the Gothic horror "Whispers of Abaddon."

Visit NoTearsForBlackGirls.com for exclusive content

You can connect with me on:

- https://notearsforblackgirls.com
- https://x.com/NoTearsForBG
- https://www.facebook.com/JohnCReedburg
- https://linktr.ee/notearsforblackgirls

Subscribe to my newsletter:

- https://www.notearsforblackgirls.com/newsletter

Also by J.C. Reedburg

THE NO TEARS FOR BLACK GIRLS SERIES

From Acclaimed Podcast to Explosive Fiction

The **NO TEARS FOR BLACK GIRLS** series transforms the raw power of J.C. Reedburg's groundbreaking true crime podcast into searing fiction where silence becomes both weapon and shield.

Set across America's urban landscapes—from Atlanta's Queen's Crown Salon to Oakland's unforgiving streets—these literary thrillers illuminate the dangerous intersections of race, gender, and power. Each story follows Black women navigating systems designed to silence them, exposing the price paid for both keeping and breaking silence.

These standalone novels feature unforgettable protagonists—salon owners, street survivors, prison masterminds—united in their quest to document patterns of injustice that official records overlook. With lyrical prose and unflinching honesty, the series explores how communities protect their own when institutions fail them.

Perfect for readers who crave powerful social commentary woven into page-turning suspense, honoring those still searching for their voice while celebrating those brave enough to speak truth to power.

CONTINUE THE JOURNEY

🎧 **Join the Movement Through the 'No Tears For Black Girls' Podcast**
150+ Episodes Available · New Episodes Weekly · Because Your Story Matters

Stream Now on Spotify and All Podcast Platforms
🌐 **NoTearsForBlackGirls.com**

No Tears For Black Girls Series - Reading Order:

The Price of Silence ☆ *You are here*
The Girl Who Knew Too Much
God's Hands
No Tears For Black Girls: Prison Pimp'd
Roofied *(Coming October 2025)*
Dead Mic *(Coming October 2025)*

Free with Amazon Kindle.

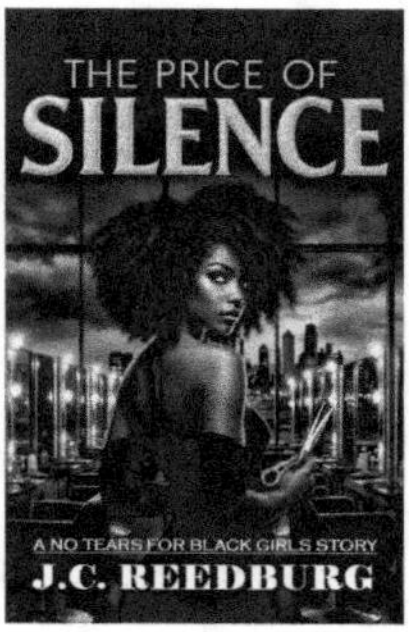

The Price Of Silence: A No Tears For Black Girls Story - Book 1

At Atlanta's Queen's Crown Salon, women are disappearing—and they all had one thing in common: they dared to speak against corrupt cops. When salon owner Quanda uncovers the deadly pattern, she faces an impossible choice: stay silent and stay alive, or risk everything to expose the truth.

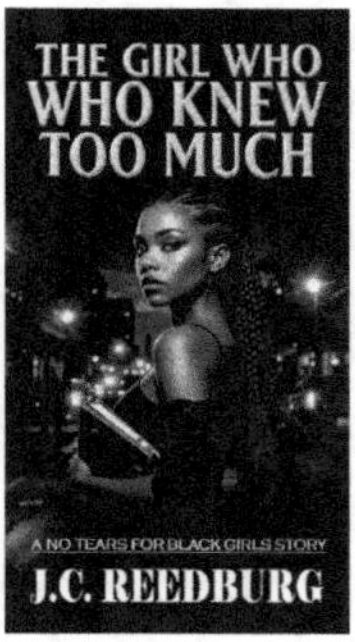

The Girl Who Knew Too Much: A No Tears For Black Girls Story - Book 2

Roxie Williams refuses to let missing girls be forgotten in Atlanta's shadows. Armed with her battered notebook and unbreakable resolve, this relentless survivor risks everything to expose the secrets and violence threatening her community. When the world looks away, Roxie fights to be seen.

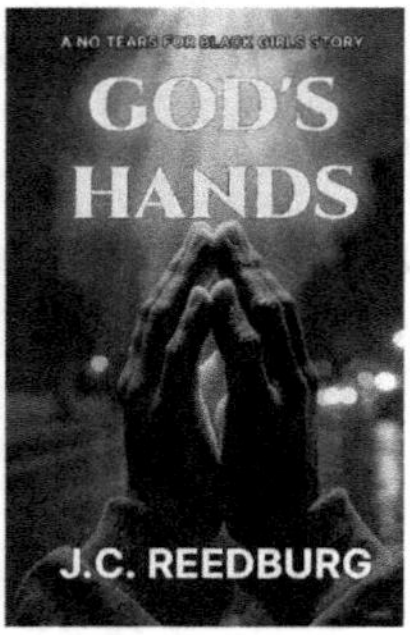

God's Hands: A No Tears For Black Girls Story

Fifteen-year-old Jasmine's life changes forever during one desperate night in Oakland. When a robbery goes wrong and her friend Darius is shot, she faces an impossible choice that will define everything. A gripping story exploring the moment when violence meets grace on the streets.

No Tears For Black Girls: Prison Pimp'd

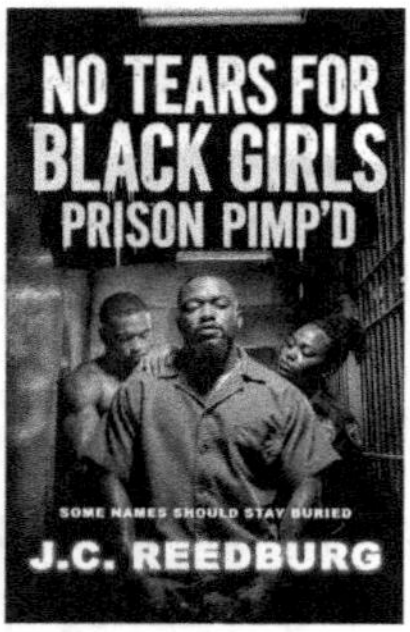

Behind bars, survival isn't about strength—it's about strategy. Dejuan Rivers transforms his 6x8 cell into a criminal empire, manipulating guards and inmates alike through a web of letters, money, and psychological control. But when the women on the outside start asking questions, his carefully constructed world begins to crack.

A raw exploration of power, manipulation, and the human cost of survival in America's prison system. This standalone thriller exposes the hidden networks that thrive behind concrete walls, where every relationship is a transaction and trust is the deadliest currency.

Some names should stay buried.

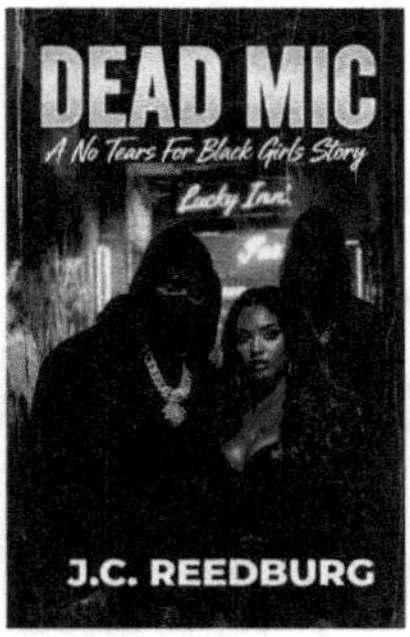

Dead Mic: A No Tears For Black Girls Story - Book 3

When Jasmine "Jayda Truth" Perkins steps in front of the cameras for what should be her breakthrough moment, she discovers the music industry's darkest secret. Now she must choose: stay silent and succeed, or risk everything to expose a predatory network hunting young women like her.

"A powerful story that transforms pain into purpose, silence into strength."

(October 2025)

Dubai Nights: A No Tears For Black Girls Story - Book 8

When Instagram influencer dreams turn deadly, one sister will risk becoming the next victim to save the first.

Destiny Clarke vanished in Dubai after accepting a luxury modeling contract. The police won't help. The consulate doesn't care. Another missing Black girl isn't news.

But her little sister Jamila refuses to let her disappear. Armed with a fake identity and a wire, she infiltrates the same "modeling agency" that lured Destiny away—uncovering a sophisticated trafficking network preying on young Black women desperate for opportunity.

Going undercover means becoming prey. And in a world where Black girls vanish without a trace, Jamila might be walking into a trap she can't escape.

A visceral thriller about the girls no one looks for, the sisters who refuse to give up, and the price of being seen in a world that wants you invisible.

Perfect for readers of Tami Hoag, Karin Slaughter, and Stacy Willingham who crave diverse voices and unflinching truths.

Available now.

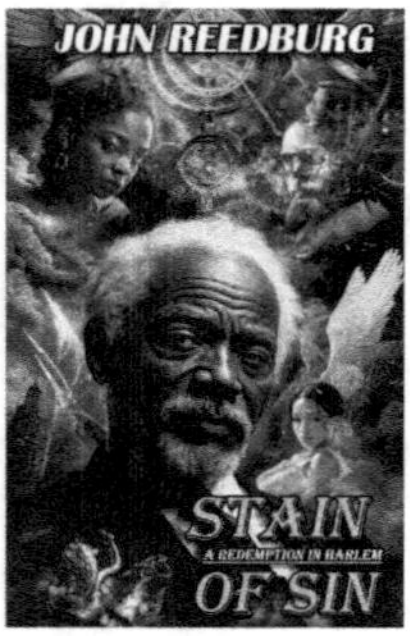

Stain Of Sin

Dive into a gripping narrative where cosmic forces collide, and one man's journey through time and space holds the key to the balance between light and darkness. Will redemption prevail in the face of eternal judgment? Explore the multiverse in this thrilling metaphysical drama.

Human Hawk

Enter a mind-bending narrative where action, conspiracy, and moral ambiguity collide. Follow Sam Weldon as he delves into a digital realm that challenges his very existence. Are you prepared to unravel the secrets of RIGS technology?

Whispers Of Abaddon

Inherit the power, face the darkness. Follow Étienne as he navigates the treacherous realm of Gothic Horror and the supernatural secrets that bind his family together. A tale of fear, resilience, and a legacy that can save or destroy them all. Prepare to be captivated by this gripping Dark Fantasy filled with macabre twists and eerie revelations.

Cracks Of Light

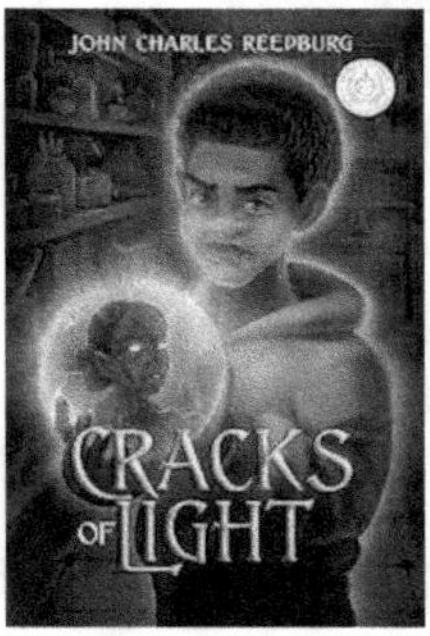

In this raw, lyrical debut, a nine-year-old boy in 1990s Los Angeles discovers a mysterious light that becomes his refuge from a troubled home life. Blending urban realism with touches of the fantastic, Reedburg crafts a powerful coming-of-age story about finding magic amid hardship.

www.ingramcontent.com/pod-product-compliance
Lightning Source LLC
Chambersburg PA
CBHW072130250626
47159CB00007B/2640
9781736553534